PRAISE FOR MARCIA CLARK

Snap Judgment

"Samantha Brinkman, Clark's flawed but sympathetic Los Angeles defense attorney protagonist, must deal with more than one explosive case in her highly suspenseful third outing . . . Clark keeps up the frenetic pace, but never allows the plot's tricky developments to overwhelm her characterizations."

—*Publishers Weekly*, Starred Review

"A twisting plot informed by Clark's legal know-how will keep readers turning pages."

—*Booklist*

"Fans of Clark's legal thriller series featuring defense attorney Samantha Brinkman will be pleased to learn that this third installment (after *Moral Defense*) continues to deliver fast-paced plotting and savvy style laced with a healthy dose of humor. Clark, once again, nimbly handles the warp and weft of her interwoven characters and story lines, knitting them into a satisfying conclusion that will leave readers eagerly anticipating another Brinkman episode."

—*Library Journal*

"Marcia Clark has a proven talent for storytelling that transcends novels . . . and *Snap Judgment*, like her other books, masterfully illustrates that prowess. Propulsive plotting, visceral action, dexterous dialogue, and a palpable sense of time and place all conspire to make for an undeniably exhilarating read. And just when you think you've got it all figured out, she flips the script. If you haven't yet become a convert for team Clark, you owe it to yourselves to do so. This is one pleasure that won't leave you feeling the least bit guilty."

—*Criminal Element*

"*Snap Judgment* sees the return of a terrific character in Samantha Brinkman. Marcia Clark renders the world of high-stakes law and flexible morals in perfect three-dimensional clarity."

—*Authorlink*

"Marcia Clark certainly knows the ins and outs of the litigation business, and fans will be thrilled with this new mystery."

—*Suspense Magazine*

Moral Defense

"*Moral Defense* by former Los Angeles prosecutor Marcia Clark has it all: a hard-charging lawyer heroine, tough-as-nails cops, realistic, yet somehow lovable 'bad guys,' as well as fly-by-the-seat-of-your-pants pacing and page-turning twists."

—Associated Press

"In Clark's outstanding sequel to *Blood Defense* . . . [she] deepens her already fascinating lead, while adeptly juggling several subplots."

—*Publishers Weekly*, Starred Review

"This second in the Brinkman series (after *Blood Defense*, 2016) is a nonstop ride marked by legal and moral gray areas, with a cliff-hanger epilogue. Another Clark legal thriller that's hard to put down."

—*Booklist*

"A murdered family leaves only one survivor in this second roller-coaster case for Los Angeles attorney Samantha Brinkman . . . [The case] builds to a rare intensity."

—*Kirkus Reviews*

Blood Defense

"Former LA prosecutor Clark kicks off a promising new series with this top-notch whodunit . . . Clark sprinkles jaw-dropping surprises throughout and impressively pulls off a shocker that lesser writers can only envy."

—*Publishers Weekly*, Starred Review

"On the heels of FX's blockbuster television series *American Crime Story: The People v. O. J. Simpson* . . . Simpson prosecutor–turned-author Clark . . . launches a new legal thriller series. Unlike in her well-received Rachel Knight books, which featured an LA prosecutor, Clark's latest calls on her earlier career as a criminal defense attorney to fashion protagonist Samantha Brinkman. VERDICT: Clark's deft handling of her characters through a multilevel maze of conflicts delivers an exhilarating read."

—*Library Journal*

"Clark, who served as a prosecutor for the trial of O. J. Simpson, clearly knows this world well. She has the most fun when she's showing readers the world of celebrity trials, from the media circus, the courthouse crowds, the crazies, and the police to the inner workings of the trial itself. You'll push yourself to finish the final pages just to keep pace with the defense team's discoveries."

—Associated Press

"Once again, Marcia Clark has reinvented herself—and the results are stellar. Her knowledge of the criminal justice system is unrivaled, as is her understanding of how the media influences public opinion of high-profile trials—and the actions of those involved. But the real magic of Clark's writing is her dynamic, richly textured characters and the visceral, often gritty settings they frequent."

—*Hartford Examiner*

FINAL
JUDGMENT

FINAL
JUDGMENT

A Samantha Brinkman Legal Thriller

MARCIA CLARK

THOMAS & MERCER

Published by Thomas & Mercer, Seattle

www.apub.com

Amazon, the Amazon logo, and Thomas & Mercer are trademarks of Amazon.com, Inc., or its affiliates.

ISBN-13: 9781542091176 (hardcover)
ISBN-10: 1542091179 (hardcover)
ISBN-13: 9781542091152 (paperback)
ISBN-10: 1542091152 (paperback)

Cover design by David Drummond

Printed in the United States of America

First edition

FINAL
JUDGMENT

ONE

The scene was idyllic. A clear sign that disaster was just around the corner.

For some reason, this time, I'd decided to ignore that universal truth.

I gazed at the horizon, where a persimmon sun glowed at the edge of an azure sky, and a soft, tropical breeze wafted across my body. I trailed my hand through the warm, gleaming white sand below my lounge chair and watched as Niko emerged from the water and moved toward me. His wet, muscled body sparkled in the dimming sunlight like a character in a Spanish telenovela. With a sigh, I closed my eyes and stretched my arms over my head.

Just your typical end of day at the most exclusive beach villa on Bora Bora. It was all so stunningly beautiful. So Hollywood perfect. So dream come true.

And so not me. I don't do "vacays." I'd never been on a vacation that took me any farther away than Santa Barbara—which is about an hour north of where I live in West Hollywood. And never for more than a weekend.

Then again, I'd never been in a relationship long enough to even consider spending that much alone time with anyone. I'm not sure how it happened.

True, Niko Ferrell checked a lot of boxes. Smart: check. Funny: check. Ambitious: check. Gorgeous: check. He'd achieved global fame—and banked a fortune in the process—by parlaying his skill as a martial artist (Krav Maga was a particular specialty) into an industry that included worldwide tours and master classes, videos, and inspirational speaking appearances. Right now he was in talks to put out a unisex clothing line and fragrance. Some people are just born with that combination of charisma, brains, good looks, and drive.

To put it mildly, this was definitely not my "type." Generally speaking, I'm drawn to the kind of guy your friends—in my case my bestie, Michelle—warn you about. The guy who seems like a great catch—until you find out he's either living *off* an ex-wife, living *with* an ex-wife, or living with the wife he just *claimed* was an ex. The kind of guy who gives your friends the golden opportunity to say, "I told you so."

I met Niko three years ago, after a long self-imposed dry spell. I'd decided that romance just wasn't my forte. At that point, he was still teaching locally, and his career was just starting to take off. I'd enrolled in—then immediately bailed on—his beginner's class in Krav Maga. I loved the idea of being able to defend myself in case I'd forgotten my trusty Smith .38, but I just couldn't commit to weekly classes. When I failed to show up for the next two sessions, Niko had called to find out why and then asked me to meet him for coffee to "discuss it further." We'd been dating ever since.

The truth is, it wasn't just my lack of commitment—I'd *had* to give up the Krav Maga classes. It's tough to run a solo criminal law practice and find time to do anything else. I'd love to hire some actual associates for my firm, Brinkman & Associates, but they cost money.

Michelle, my BFF since seventh grade, who's now my paralegal / bookkeeper / office manager—you get the picture—doesn't buy it. She says an associate or two would pay for themselves in the time they'd save me by doing the scut work like writing motions, letters, and briefs. Time I'd be better off spending in scoring more clients. The truth—according to Michelle—is that I'll never hire other lawyers because I'm a control freak who doesn't trust anyone. This is not an entirely unfair assessment.

The only other member of Brinkman & Associates is Alex Medrano, my investigator—and former client. Alex got busted for "liberating" a couple of top-of-the-line BMWs from the dealership where he was working as a salesman. He managed to hack into the dealership's database and "sell" the cars to two fictitious buyers, who conveniently asked that he deliver them himself. Alex's skill with computers is nothing less than magic. Seriously, the man's an artist. It was a sheer fluke that the cops caught him. I managed to get him a deal with straight probation on the condition he'd show the dealership how he'd done it. And then I'd hired him.

It was one of the smartest moves I'd ever made. After going through sixteen of your typical ex-cop, burnout case investigators, I'd landed someone who was a natural. And an amazing hacker. Doesn't get much handier than that.

We were a small but mighty trio. I'm not one to brag, but the truth is, among the three of us, we'd done okay. Actually, a lot more than okay. We'd scored some major wins in some very big cases.

And now, after just ten years of practice, I'd become kind of famous. Not Instagram or Twitter famous—not an *influencer* (a label that makes the bile rise in my throat; whoever created it should be locked in a cage for life). But I was a regular on the cable-show circuit, a favored panelist and guest at symposiums, and I'd even been asked to give a commencement speech at my old law school. Which was a damn riot, since I'd barely ever shown up for classes.

But as a result of all this, I had more work than I could reasonably handle alone. Even with my usual all-night-and-all-weekend routine, I was getting backed up and bagged out. So as much as I hated to admit it, Michy was right. It was time to get serious about hiring at least one hungry, young lawyer who'd take a minimal paycheck in return for the experience of working with the sort-of-renowned attorney Samantha Brinkman, i.e., me.

So although I'd tried to avoid this vacation and insisted that Niko cut it back to five days instead of ten, it was exactly what I'd needed.

I felt a shadow block the sun as cold flicks of water dripped onto my face. I held up a hand. "Hey! Knock it off." I opened my eyes to see Niko standing over me, shaking his wet head.

He laughed. "We need to get going. Dinner's in half an hour."

I took his outstretched hand, and we headed back to the villa.

Half an hour later, I was dressed in a gauzy white caftan, my hair wild and untamed on my shoulders. I decided I could really get used to this whole "going native" thing. As I joined Niko on the patio of our private pool, I mentioned the possibility of making it a ten-day trip after all.

He stared at me. "Wow." He paused. "Wait, now I get it. You packed your laptop, didn't you?"

"Nope." I didn't feel the need to tell him Michy had snatched it out of my suitcase when my back was turned. I smiled as I took in Niko, who looked particularly amazing in his flowing white cotton pants that were tied just below a perfect six-pack—which was visible because he'd left his shirt unbuttoned. I pointed. "They're going to throw money if you go out like that."

He gave a half smile. "There is no 'they.' It's just us."

"So we're staying in?"

Niko shook his head and put an arm around my waist. "Come on."

He led me out to the private beach, where a table surrounded by torches was set for two. A barefoot waiter stood at the ready and asked for our drink orders.

It was like something out of a fairy tale. A French Polynesian fairy tale. I ordered my new favorite drink: tequila with lime juice, shaken over ice and poured straight-up, like a martini.

"I'll have the same," Niko said. He ordered us bonito fish in coconut milk for appetizers.

When the waiter left, I stared out at the placid lagoon. It must've shown on my face that I was feeling a little sad coming to the end of this idyllic time, because Niko smiled and reached across the table for my hand. "If you really mean it, I can try and reschedule the jet to pick us up next week."

Yes. We took a private jet. It's disgusting. I know. I pondered the possibility of another five days. Five more gentle, languid days of sunning, snorkeling, and tequila-and-lime cocktails on the beach. I wasn't sure I could make it work. But I never like to run from a challenge. The waiter came back with our drinks. I raised my glass. "Okay, let's give it a shot."

Niko's smile was a little disbelieving, but he raised his glass, and we clinked. "Here's to words I never thought I'd hear you say."

I laughed with him. It was . . . so perfect.

Until we were in the middle of the main course—a delicious French Polynesian specialty, grilled tuna in Taha'a vanilla sauce—when the manager of the hotel hurried over to Niko. "I'm so sorry to interrupt, Monsieur Ferrell. But you have an urgent call from someone named Thomas Brewster. He asks that you call him as soon as possible."

Niko thanked him and said he'd make the call from his cell. His expression was worried as he brushed the napkin across his mouth and stood up. "I'm sorry, Sam. I'd better jump on this."

I nodded. Tom—one of Niko's longtime friends—wasn't the type to get worked up for no reason. If he was calling Niko during one of his rare vacations, it wasn't because he had a flat tire. "Want me to go with you?"

"No. Whatever this is, I'm sure it won't take long. Stay, finish your dinner."

Niko dropped his napkin on the table and headed to the room.

I wanted to finish eating, but I was too nervous. In situations like this, my mind always reaches for the very worst. Tom was in jail. His wife had been diagnosed with cancer. Their children had been killed in a school bus accident. Or, more likely, a school shooting.

Niko was back before I could get any further. His features were drawn, his voice tight. "My mother . . . all my friends . . . they've been wiped out."

I stared up at him. "What do you mean?"

"Gold Strike Enterprises. The company I invested in last year. The one I told everyone was a sure thing."

Then I remembered. It was a high-flying investment firm that promised—and, from what I'd seen, delivered—big dividends with a short turnaround. Niko had met one of the owners when he was in London teaching a master class. He'd persuaded Niko to invest in Gold Strike, and in the past six months, Niko had made more than half a million with them.

And now, suddenly, they'd gone belly-up. It was a shocker, to say the least. "Are you wiped out?"

Niko gripped the back of his chair. "No. I've probably lost a lot, but I sold off a bunch of my shares a few weeks ago. And I have other income streams. I'll be okay. But my mother . . . she invested everything she had, her whole life savings." He shook his head, his face a frozen mask of shock. "Tom just came from her house. He said she looked bad. Really bad." Niko swallowed. "She's had such a hard life. Her health has never been great. And now this. I don't know how she'll . . ." He stopped and pressed his lips together for a moment. "She refused to let me support her. That's why I told her to invest in Gold Strike. I thought she'd finally get enough money to live the good life she deserved." Niko looked at me with tears in his eyes. "Instead, I've ruined her."

I grabbed his arm. "Stop. You couldn't have known this would happen."

But Niko wasn't listening. He went on as though I hadn't spoken. "I'll take care of her, of course. Now she'll have to let me. But this was the last thing she wanted. She's got to be devastated." Niko finally looked at me. "I'm sorry, Sam."

I dropped my napkin on the table. "Don't be silly. Let's get going."

Like I said. I'd been living the dream for five whole days.

I should've known it had to end in disaster.

TWO

I'd never met her before, but Niko's mother barely glanced my way when he introduced us, as though even the effort to turn her head was too much for her.

And when I said, "It's nice to meet you, Mrs. Ferrell," a look of confusion briefly crossed her face before she reflexively responded with a faint, spidery whisper, "Sophia." Again, without meeting my eyes.

I have to admit, knowing the strong, passionate driving force that was Niko, Sophia wasn't what I'd expected. The loose-fitting beige, chiffon maxi skirt and ivory sweater emphasized the slenderness of her frame. Her large dark eyes, thick eyebrows, and eyelashes were her visible gifts to Niko, but where his jawline was strong and his lips generous, Sophia's chin was a bit recessive, her mouth smaller. The overall effect was soft, somewhat childlike. And the way she wore her hair—long and straight, an unadorned halo of silver and black—enhanced it.

I assumed the contrast in Niko's features came from the paternal side of the DNA strand. But I didn't know for sure because his father had left the family when Niko was only four years old. His mother had never remarried.

Now, seeing Sophia, I understood why Niko was so protective of her. Although I took into account the fact that she'd just suffered a terrible blow, I noticed an underlying timidity. Plus, Niko didn't seem at all surprised by the way she looked or behaved. I got the feeling Sophia had always been a little overwhelmed by the world and that she'd leaned on him for most of his life.

That not only explained why he was so protective of her—it also explained why he was so protective of everyone else. A child whose parent never grew up has one of two options: remain a child and suffer the consequences when the parent inevitably fails to show up or become the parent himself.

Sophia's gaze drifted over Niko's shoulder to the window behind him, where the clatter and squealing brakes of trash trucks filled the street. Her voice was barely audible over the noise. "I gave them everything I had." Her expression was numb as she stared out. Her lips barely moved as she said, "I'm lost." With every word, her body seemed to cave further and further in on itself.

I felt my throat tighten with sadness. I doubted she'd ever recover from this. She was retired, and at seventy-six, with no source of income other than the thirteen hundred dollars a month she got from social security, she'd barely be able to maintain the house and pay for groceries.

Luckily, she didn't have mortgage payments to worry about. Niko had bought the charming three-bedroom ranch house for her outright, so she owned it free and clear. But Niko said she'd prided herself on being able to pay for everything else on her own—had refused to even consider his offer to buy her a new car and put money in the bank for her to live on. That pride was her one show of strength. Now, she couldn't afford it.

Niko leaned forward, his elbows on his knees. His hands were clasped together, the knuckles white. "What happened, Mom? Do you know?"

Sophia shook her head. Finally, in a tiny voice, she said, "I-I'm not sure. Tom told me they made a mistake. Something they invested in didn't . . . go right."

Niko's frown was mixed with confusion. "That's what Tom said, but it makes no sense. Did you hear from Tanner or Bryan?"

Sophia shook her head. "Only Tom." She looked up at Niko with a painfully hopeful gaze. "Maybe he's wrong? Could he be wrong?"

Niko swallowed. I could see him struggle with the desire to believe it was a mistake. But he'd called Tom the moment we landed, and they'd spoken at length. "I doubt it, Mom."

Sophia's face crumbled. She dropped her head into her hands. "What will I do? I don't know what to do." Her shoulders shook with quiet sobs.

Niko reached out and put a gentle hand on her arm. "Don't cry, Mom. You know I'll take care of you. Always."

Sophia wrapped her arms around her body but kept her head down. "You always do, Niko. And you always have. But I wanted to pay my own way. To . . . to not have to worry about money or have to ask . . ." She shook her head. "I just never can get it right. Never can. No matter what I do." She looked up at Niko and put her hands on his face. "I'm so sorry. For . . . for everything."

I knew she was apologizing for a lot more than this financial crisis. And it confirmed my suspicion that Niko had been forced to take the lead in the household from too early an age. But it was odd to hear her apologize for this investment disaster. She may not have been the most effectual mother, had maybe screwed up a lot. But not this time.

Then again, hearing a mother apologize for anything was an odd, almost out-of-body experience for me. My so-called mother had subjected me to some of the most searing forms of abuse imaginable, and she'd never even considered saying so much as "Oops!" Far from it. She'd put the blame on me.

Maybe that was why, watching this wrenching, emotional scene between Niko and his mother, I felt tears prick my eyelids.

Niko took her hands between his. "You have nothing to be sorry for, Mom. None of this is your fault. It's all mine. I was the one who told you to invest in Gold Strike."

Sophia refused to go along. "But you never told me to put in everything I had. The opposite. You told me to take it slow." She shook her head. "No, this is all on me. I should've listened."

I knew it wasn't my place to chime in. We'd only just met. But her mea culpa was so heartbreakingly sincere—and misplaced—I couldn't stand it. I opened my mouth to tell her that something really bizarre and unforeseeable must've happened and that there was no way she could've known, but at that moment, Niko's phone rang—or rather, barked. His default ringtone is a dog barking. It might seem funny—he sure thinks it is—but let me tell you, it got damn annoying really fast.

Niko looked at the screen. His features tensed as he answered. "Tom, any word?" Niko listened for a few seconds, then said he was with his mother. "I'll get on it right now. But can you do me a favor?" He asked Tom to come stay with his mother, then ended the call. "Mom, I'm going to go see if I can get some answers. Tom will be here in ten minutes; he'll keep you company. Okay?"

Sophia sank even deeper into her chair as she nodded. "You don't have to babysit me, Niko. I'll be fine."

That obviously wasn't true, and I could see Niko wasn't buying it. "I know that, Mom. But he lost a lot, too. I think it'll make you both feel better."

Niko had said she wasn't the suicidal type. But there are many more ways to kill yourself than hanging, overdosing, or drowning. They may take a little longer and be less obvious—but they can get the job done just as effectively. It was a good idea to have someone else who was in the same boat stay with Sophia, to remind her that she wasn't the only one who'd crashed and burned.

Tom got there a half hour later, and as we left, I told Sophia I'd see her soon. She looked up at me with a vague expression, as though she wasn't quite sure who I was. It worried me.

And it worried Niko, too. As we got into his silver Maserati, his expression was tortured. "It's like she's . . . fading right before my eyes."

"Should we get her to a doctor? Might be a good idea to get her a short-term antidepressant, just to pull her through for now."

Niko snorted as he pulled away from the curb. "Yeah, good luck with that. She's about as antidrug as it gets. And antidoctor. She won't even take Tylenol."

I wasn't sure what to say. He couldn't spend the rest of his life monitoring her every move. But I could see that Niko had shifted gears, so I decided to let it go for the moment. "Where are we headed now?"

Niko gunned the engine as he turned left on Ventura Boulevard. "To get some answers."

I saw that we were headed into the city as he turned onto Beverly Glen Canyon. I assumed we were headed for the Gold Strike headquarters. Sure enough, Niko drove to Westwood Village and pulled into the parking garage under one of the nicer office buildings.

He punched the button for the elevator and cracked his knuckles as we rode up to the tenth floor. When the doors opened, he shot out into the corridor like he'd been fired from a cannon. I had to run to keep up with him as he barreled down the hall.

Niko stopped at the second to last door on the left. Etched into a classy-looking brass plate on the wall was **GOLD STRIKE, LLC**. There was no window in the door, just a peephole. Niko tried the doorknob. It was locked. He knocked on the door, and we waited for a couple of minutes. No answer. Then he banged on the door with his fist. No answer.

He'd just raised his fist to bang again when a door across the hall opened. An older man in a brown suede Members Only jacket—it looked worn enough to be an original—held up a hand. "Don't bother. They're not there. Or they're not answering."

Niko's expression darkened. I could see he was reining himself in with an effort. "So I take it others have been here?"

The man waved a hand. "Oof, felt like a hundred. Day and night they were coming. Banging and banging. And yelling. I couldn't hear myself think. Had to take my work home. Almost got into it with one of them. Didn't believe I was just an innocent bystander. Sounds like people lost their money, am I right?"

Niko nodded. "Have you ever seen the guys who work in that office?"

He glanced at the door. "From time to time."

"When was the last time you saw either of them?"

The man shrugged. "Last week? Yeah. I'm pretty sure that's when. And I'm sorry, but I don't know where else to find them."

Niko's eyes narrowed. "Yeah, well, I do. Thanks."

He turned and headed down the hall without even a backward look. I sighed and waved my thanks to the man, then trotted down the hall and just managed to catch up as the elevator dinged. "Look, I know you're upset, and you have every right to be. But could you please try and remember to be a human?"

Niko frowned and ran a hand through his hair. "Sorry. I'm just . . . a little distracted."

Ya think? But I said nothing. And as we flew out of the parking garage, I didn't ask where we were going.

I had a feeling I already knew.

Sure enough, fifteen minutes later, we pulled up to a Spanish-style duplex south of Wilshire Boulevard in Beverly Hills. It was one of the many beautiful—and beautifully kept—streets in this pricey neighborhood, and many of the houses and duplexes had preserved the original architecture, which ranged from Spanish style to Tudor. All the lawns were a manicured, vibrant green—no easy feat in drought-ridden Los Angeles. And very few of the cars parked on the street weren't BMWs, Mercedes, or Teslas.

I trailed behind Niko as he marched up the brick-paved walkway and stood back as he punched the doorbell. I thought it wise to give him plenty of room. It took no stretch of imagination whatsoever to envision Niko ripping the throat out of whoever answered the door.

But no one answered the door. Niko flexed his shoulders—a very bad sign for this resident—and pounded on the door with the heel of his hand. "Bryan! Bryan Posner! Open this door. Now!"

If that didn't scare the shit out of Bryan, he was either deaf or dead.

He was neither. Two seconds later, a tall, willowy, and very tanned man in his sixties with long white hair answered the door. "Niko?" He swept an arm back. "Come in, please. I'm so glad you're here. I was just about to call you."

What? Scared, I expected. Nervous, I expected. But glad?

No, this I did not expect.

THREE

We stepped into a spacious, high-ceilinged living room. The hardwood floors, crown molding, and finely cut baseboards looked original. Builders after the 1940s seldom bothered to do such detailed work, and the pristine condition of the place showed Bryan appreciated that. He also appreciated white.

The sectional couch was white, and it rested on a white rug that faced a white brick fireplace. In another house, all that white would make you feel like you were in an operating room. Or an asylum. But here, it provided the perfect canvas for the original artwork that lined the walls—the styles eclectic yet complementary—the multicolored hanging tapestry, the bronze sculptures that flanked the fireplace, and the well-tended potted palms.

I'd usually assume a decorator had made these sophisticated choices, but Bryan's wardrobe showed that same unique yet tasteful—and expensive—flair. He wore white linen pants that screamed "designer" and blue loafers that even I recognized as Stefano Ricci's. I knew those babies went for close to five thousand dollars.

As we moved toward the couch, a much younger man, who looked like he was in his thirties, entered from the hallway that ran to the back of the duplex. He wasn't as tall as Bryan, and he was a little more solid. But he was equally as handsome, with brown puppy-dog eyes and thick, dark hair cut in a fade. He was well dressed, in high-quality khakis, a Hugo Boss long-sleeve T-shirt, and Ferragamo loafers. Not cheap, but nowhere near in Bryan's league.

Though his expression was distraught, he managed to exude charm as he gave me a lopsided smile and extended his hand. "Pleasure to meet you. I assume you're Samantha. I'm Tanner Handel. I've heard wonderful things about you."

A good handshake is key to a good first impression, and Tanner had it knocked. Firm but not a knuckle crusher, just long enough to be warm, not so long you start to plan your escape. And although I'd heard the line about "wonderful things" a million times, no one had ever delivered it quite so convincingly. In short, Tanner was good. Very, very good.

Bryan was no slouch, either. He gave me a soft, fatherly smile as he gestured for me to take a seat on the couch. "Can I get you guys something to drink? Are you hungry? I can put something together. Or I can order in if you like."

That was hella hospitable for someone who was on the brink of total ruin. "No thanks, I'm good."

Niko shook his head and sat down across from Tanner and Bryan, his expression dark. His voice was low, but there was a palpable underlying menace. "What the hell happened? I thought we were diversified. How could all these accounts crash at once?"

Bryan's features sagged. His hands hung limply beside his legs. He suddenly looked ten years older. "About a month ago, we got an incredible tip on a slate of new cryptocurrencies."

Tanner leaned forward and spread his hands. His speech was rapid, and he exuded an intense energy that was both mesmerizing and a little unsettling. "It was a sure thing, Niko. Projected to triple our investment in less than six months. And all the indicators were solid gold."

His expression was earnest, pleading. "You've seen what's been going on with Bitcoin and Ethereum."

I didn't know much about cryptocurrencies, but I had heard of those two. What I'd never heard was a description characterizing those investments as "solid gold." But what did I know? I defended murderers, not stock traders.

Niko cracked his knuckles, his jaw set. His voice was low, but fury boiled under his words. "So you went all in—with everyone's money—without telling anyone. Not even me. What the fuck were you thinking?"

Bryan drew back, but he sounded more sad than fearful as he answered. "I was thinking that if word leaked out that we were buying big, there'd be a run on the market, and it'd drive up the price before we could move all the money."

Tanner chimed in. "Our source said he'd sell the tip to someone else if we didn't pony up with the whole amount within forty-eight hours."

"So how did this sure thing go bust so fast?" Niko demanded.

Tanner shook his head. "That's what we've been trying to figure out. I've got a call in to our source. There must've been something hinky with the currencies, but whatever it was, they hid it well. I vetted them upside down. It looked for real."

Bryan's voice broke as he said, "We'll get this straightened out, Niko. I swear we'll make it up to you."

Niko glared at him. "Forget about me. I'll survive. How do you plan to make it up to everyone else? Especially all the people I brought in—like my mother? My friends?"

Tanner held up his hands, his voice calm, reassuring. "Come on, Niko. Think about how much money we've made for all of you." He looked into Niko's eyes. "We've doubled your investment, haven't we? We'll find a way to get everyone's money back . . . and then some. You can trust us."

Niko wouldn't be mollified. "You did well by my mother and me. And most of my friends, as far as I know. But this disaster wiped it all out—not just the profits but their initial investments, too. They're completely broke." Niko leaned forward, his eyes hot. "So tell me, how do you plan to fix that?"

Bryan looked stricken. "I . . . don't quite know. Yet. But . . . we will." He glanced at Tanner, then down at his lap, where his hands were clasped together in a solid ball. "I feel terrible, Niko. Believe me."

Niko ignored his plea and turned to Tanner. "How about you? Any bright ideas?"

Someone else would've broken a sweat under the intensity of Niko's gaze, but Tanner met his gaze with nothing more than calm concern. "It only just happened, Niko. So no, I don't know how I'll get the money right at this moment. I can only promise you that I will. Somehow." He put his hands on his knees and blew out a breath. "Well, I don't know about you, but I could use a drink. What can I get you?"

Niko set his jaw. "Nothing." I shook my head. As Tanner stood up, an oval-shaped bronze coin fell out of his pocket onto the rug next to my feet.

Tanner was headed toward the wet bar and didn't seem to notice. I picked it up. Engraved around the edge were the words *From Shame to Grace*. When Tanner came back with his glass of what looked like three fingers of scotch, neat, I held it out to him. "You dropped this."

He stared at it for a moment as though he didn't recognize it, then took it from me and absently said, "Thanks," as he put it back in his pocket.

I wanted to ask him what it was, but Niko stood up. "I want a full accounting. Give me all the data on the company you invested in, how much each investor lost, and most of all, I want to hear how you plan to recoup the loss."

Tanner took Niko's elbow. "Of course, Niko. Of course. We'll get you everything."

As we all headed toward the door, Bryan said, "You know, Sam, I'd very much appreciate it if we could get your expert opinion about this company."

Tanner nodded. "Good point. We can't tell whether we've been had or this was just an unforeseeable catastrophe. But if it looks like this was a scam, then maybe you can advise us on what to do next."

I could. But he wasn't going to like it. "If you can find proof that the stock was negligently misrepresented, you can sue. But civil cases can take years. And good luck enforcing the judgment to get your money."

Tanner said, "But what if it's fraud? Can't they get arrested for that?"

"Sure, and I can put you in touch with the LAPD division that handles white-collar crime—"

Bryan's expression lightened. "That'd be great—"

I shook my head. "No, it wouldn't be great. Because assuming you did get scammed, the best you could hope for is that the heads of the company get convicted and the judge orders restitution. That'll move faster than a civil case, but you'll still have to chase them down to get your money. And again, good luck with that. Especially if they wind up in prison. Making license plates just doesn't pay the way it used to."

Bryan looked like he might cry. Tanner's features had hardened, but he maintained his composure. "Then it's up to us. We'll have to find a way to get everyone compensated for their loss." He looked at Niko. "And you have my word, we will."

Niko opened the door as he bit off the words, "I'll be in touch."

We headed for the car and rode in silence. I considered the partnership of Tanner and Bryan. They weren't exactly an obvious match. To put it mildly, they were a study in contrasts.

Bryan had a soft, gentle, paternal air, and his home reflected the tastes of a Renaissance man who enjoyed good living and appreciated the finer aspects of creature comfort.

Tanner, on the other hand, was a "sleep when I'm dead," charismatic speeding bullet, in perpetual forward motion.

When Niko stopped at a red light, I asked, "Was Bryan born into money?"

He paused for a moment. "I think so. I know his parents live close by in Beverly Hills. His mother's always stopping over to see him on her way to Saks Fifth and Neiman Marcus."

"His mother? Seriously?" It struck me as odd that someone Bryan's age had that kind of regular contact with his mother.

Niko glanced at me. "Why? What's wrong with that? They're close."

Whoops. Should've known better than to step on that land mine. Niko was super close to his mother, too. And really, what *was* wrong with that?

If I hadn't had an insanely dysfunctional, torturous relationship with my egg donor, I'd probably want to hang out with her, too.

I guess.

But it's hard to imagine. Every time I hear someone say they miss their mother or wish they could spend more time together, I can't help feeling shocked. And incredulous.

I have to remind myself that those people are the normal ones. That I'm the aberration. But at least I'd found my father—and even liked hanging out with him. Sometimes. Though to be honest, even that relationship was its own very strange can of worms.

I guess normal had never really been in the cards for me.

My thoughts drifted back to Tanner and Bryan. "How did those guys meet?" If ever two people seemed to run in different circles, it was those two.

Niko shrugged. "I'm not a hundred percent sure. But Bryan has a lot of younger friends, and I think one of them introduced him to Tanner."

But that still begged the question: What made these two—seemingly alpha and omega—become partners?

FOUR

Niko decided to stay with his mother that night, which was for the best. I needed to get to the office in the morning anyway. I'd been gone for almost a week, and I knew a pile of work would be waiting for me. May as well confront the teeming in-box and get it over with. It makes me anxious—I mean sweaty-palms anxious—when work is piling up.

But as I headed to the office the next morning, it didn't make me feel any better to know I was fending off an anxiety attack. All I could think of was how I was supposed to be floating in the warm waters off a French Polynesian island, having drinks with Niko on a private beach.

And the weather was doing its best to make matters worse. The sky was a gloomy gray haze. No sun in sight. It was the kind of in-between—not sunny but not rainy—weather that annoys the hell out of me.

At least Beulah couldn't die and completely ruin my day. My old jalopy, a creaking, rusty mess of an ancient Mercedes, had finally crapped out on me for the last time six months ago. Beulah used to break down so often, she'd even begun to piss off my mechanic, and he'd made a fortune fixing her—so imagine. He actually cheered when I finally called it quits and bought myself a new BMW 335i.

Although my apartment was just ten minutes from the office as the crow flies, crows don't have to deal with bumper-to-bumper traffic, and rush hour lasted twenty-four hours a day in West Hollywood. I crawled along at five miles per hour from the time I pulled out of the carport of my apartment building to the time I pulled into the parking garage below my office.

By the time I got in, I was in a truly foul mood.

Michy—who never misses a damn thing—picked up on it immediately. She pointed to a pink cardboard box on the coffee bar. "I brought doughnuts. I figured you'd need a little sweetening."

I huffed and dropped my purse and briefcase as I opened the box and inhaled the warm, mouth-watering aroma of sugar and yeasty goodness. I picked out a glazed doughnut and poured myself a cup of coffee.

The coffee bar was a spiffy new addition Michy had badgered me into buying for our otherwise plain-wrap office. She says—with obnoxious backing from Alex—that high-dollar clients won't go for a lawyer whose office looks like a half-empty storage locker. I tell them that clients—high-dollar or otherwise—don't care if my office looks like the home of the Pizza Rat, as long as I keep them out of jail. But the coffee bar had a practical side. We all drank the stuff by the gallon. So I'd caved.

I took a bite and let it melt in my mouth for a moment. "Any emergencies? Say no. I don't care if it's true."

"No." Michy folded her arms and waited.

I sighed. "Okay, tell me."

She pushed back her Scünci—a blue that coordinated nicely with her crewneck sweater—and punched a key on her computer. "The D.A. filed an amended sentencing memo on the Walters case asking the judge to impose a strike sentence. Apparently our client had an armed robbery conviction out of Texas we didn't know about." She raised an eyebrow. "Right?"

Oh, "we" knew about it, all right. We'd just hoped the D.A. wouldn't find out about it. Which is why I'd asked for early sentencing when we made our plea deal. Now I'd have to either find a way to get the judge to toss out that prior or tell the D.A. we'd force him to trial unless he dismissed it. The latter was probably my better option—assuming I could figure out how to convince him he'd lose if we went to trial. "Got it. Next?"

Michy ran down the list of cases that needed immediate attention. It was depressingly lengthy. When she finished, she rubbed the scar on her right temple—her tell that something was bugging her. That scar was her "souvenir" from a stalker who'd attacked and almost killed her. He'd been a client of mine, busted for burglary. I got him out on bail, so he'd been able to come to the office for meetings—which is how he'd met, and become obsessed with, Michy. When the stalking case got thrown out for no good reason by a moronic judge, I'd found a way to make sure he'd never be able to hurt Michy—or anyone else—ever again.

Michy gave me a stern look. I knew what was coming. "Whether you admit it or not, this is getting to be a little too crazy. You need to take on an associate."

She was right, of course. But I couldn't deal with it right now. I deflected with the latest news on Niko's situation. I'd given her a quick rundown before we got on the plane back to LA, but I hadn't had a chance to tell her about my meeting with Bryan and Tanner.

When I finished, she asked, "How long have these guys been in the business? 'Cause this seems like a rookie mistake, putting all their eggs in one basket."

I nodded. I'd thought the same thing. "Awhile, I think. At least, I'm pretty sure Bryan has been. Niko said it might've been a short-term move, because those stocks can really skyrocket." I made a face. "Before they fall."

Michy raised an eyebrow. "So they planned to do a hit-and-run. And then didn't run in time."

I shrugged. "Or couldn't, I guess. Niko's going to get into it with Bryan again tonight. Assuming his mother is in good enough shape to be left alone."

Michy gave a sad sigh. "That poor woman. To be wiped out like that at her age. I wonder how many others are in the same boat."

I'd been thinking the same thing. "I have a feeling we'll find out pretty soon." Losing your life savings was no picnic at any age, but it was certainly much worse for someone who had retired and had little hope of finding a decent-paying job. "I'm going to ask Niko if he wants me to sit in and hear what Bryan has to say."

"Say about what?" Alex came in, carrying what looked like a new laptop under his arm.

I stared at it. "I must be paying you too much. Didn't you just get a new laptop last month?"

He rolled his eyes. "It was on Craigslist. The owner thought it was toast, so he practically gave it away. Took me about five minutes to fix it." He put the laptop in his office, then came back out and poured himself a cup of coffee. "I heard about Niko and his mom. I'm so sorry. Especially about his mom. What a friggin' nightmare."

There isn't much Alex, my investigator / genius hacker, doesn't know, and I thought maybe I should talk to Niko about bringing him to the meeting with Bryan. It'd be good to get his opinion on this stock crash. And on Bryan. Alex knows how to read people. Plus, I'd gotten the sense that Bryan was gay. If I were right, he'd flip for Alex—who's a knockout, with toffee-colored skin, big brown eyes, a perfect body, and who just happens to be gay. A fact female clients and witnesses never seem to realize, and which comes in very handy when I need some cooperation.

I gave Alex the rundown I'd just given Michy, then asked what he thought of what she'd called their "rookie mistake."

Alex was a little more on the fence. "It's dicey as hell, that's for sure. But a fast move like that can work with volatile stocks—which cryptocurrency stocks totally are. And when it does, it's a huge win. So bottom line: it might not be as dumb as it sounds."

I asked Alex if he'd be available to come hear what Bryan had to say about it, but he and Paul, his boyfriend for the past year, who was equally as OCD as Alex—which is *really* saying something—had Lakers tickets.

As it happened, it wouldn't have worked out anyway.

I buried myself in my in-box and plowed straight through until about six o'clock—and only stopped then because Niko called.

His voice sounded worn. "Hey. Want to have dinner?"

I looked at the stack of file folders that were still waiting for me to plow through. I knew I should stay and get some more work done. And I had a feeling we'd be dining at his mother's place. Ordinarily, that'd be fine, but I really wanted to talk to him alone. The selfish thought made me feel like a jerk. I immediately tried to atone for it. "Sure. Your mom's place? Want me to pick something up?"

"No, my place. My mom's got some friends over. And I'll order in. Deli sound good? I'll call Greenblatt's."

I love Greenblatt's. Best deli ever. "I can leave now if you want."

He did want.

It was a damp, chilly March night, and Niko had lit a fire in the massive living room fireplace. The moon cast a pale light through the floor-to-ceiling windows as a soft mix of Miles Davis tunes played in the background. It was a soothing atmosphere that might've been a perfect lead-up to a romantic night. But Niko was in no mood. From the moment I walked in the door, I could feel the tension and anger swirling inside him.

I did my best to make calming conversation as we ate our dinner on the couch in front of the fire. The chicken noodle soup was fabulous, as always. I finished the whole bowl and got too full to eat my turkey sandwich—as always.

Niko smiled—the first time I'd seen him do that since Tom had called us in Bora Bora. "You always have such big eyes. I knew you'd never get through all that."

I do have a tendency to overorder from that damn deli. "I'm an addict. What can I say?"

We'd just cleaned up and opened a bottle of pinot noir when the doorbell chimed.

We stared at each other. It was late, definitely too late for a UPS or FedEx delivery. I asked, "Are you expecting anyone?"

Niko shook his head. He picked up the remote for his surveillance camera and clicked on the monitor. It was Bryan. I studied Niko's face. "Are you in the mood for this?"

He rolled back his shoulders. "The question is: Is he?"

Niko stalked toward the door. I didn't envy Bryan.

Bryan looked agitated as he entered the foyer. "How's your mother doing?"

Niko's voice was harsh, accusatory. "She hasn't eaten or slept for two days."

He shook his head, his expression mournful. "I can't find the words to express how profoundly sorry I am for this catastrophe."

Niko gave him a steely look. "I really don't give a shit how sorry you are. If that's all you came to say, then get out."

Bryan held up his hands. "It's not. I came here tonight because I think you deserve to hear what really happened."

Niko stood back and gestured for him to come in. Bryan gave Niko a nervous look as he moved past him and walked into the living room.

FIVE

Niko didn't offer Bryan a drink, a glass of water, or even a seat. But he took one anyway and sat down a few feet to my left on the sectional couch. Niko sat down on my right and leaned back, arms folded.

Niko has the ability to convey a range of feelings without uttering a word. With the tilt of his head, the lift of an eyebrow, the barest of smiles, he can bathe someone in a warm glow that makes them feel like the center of the universe—or make them want to put the barrel of a gun in their mouth.

Right now, I could tell Bryan was getting the latter cue. He rubbed his thighs and had to clear his throat twice before he managed to speak. The benign, fatherly gaze and rich, aged-whiskey voice were gone. Now his face sagged as though weights were attached to his jaw, and when he spoke, his voice was thin and strained. "The whole cryptocurrency idea was Tanner's, not mine. In fact, I only found out about it because I happened to pick up his phone when he was gone. It was the middle-man who gave him the tip; he was calling with an update."

Niko's eyes narrowed. "So you're telling me that Tanner went off on his own and put several hundred million dollars on the line without telling you?" His tone made it clear he wasn't buying it.

Bryan's expression was bleak and somewhat forlorn. "I know you think very highly of Tanner. A lot of people do. That's his gift. He makes it look like he knows everything, like he's in total control." His voice was bitter as he said, "But it's all bullshit. He's wild, impulsive, flies by the seat of his pants most of the time. And he doesn't know nearly as much about the market as he claims."

I wasn't supposed to be a part of this, but I couldn't help myself. "Then why'd you stay in business with him?" I voiced my most immediate suspicion. "What'd he have on you?"

Bryan gave a deep sigh. "He doesn't have anything on me. It's just that I needed a . . . a bit of a face-lift. Before I met him, I'd been on a losing streak for a while. My client list was down. Way down. I needed to"—he paused and made air quotes—"'refresh my brand.'" He spread his hands. "To put it bluntly, I needed a younger face."

A younger face. In the investment game. Got it. Screw wisdom, to hell with experience. Give me a guy who hasn't had his first shave. I wished I could say I didn't believe Bryan. But I did. It was eminently believable. And so LA. Where there's no bigger sin than aging.

But Niko wasn't interested in Bryan's woes. "So how do you plan to pay everyone back?"

Bryan spread his empty hands. "My only hope is to find someone else to stake me so I can take another shot at the market."

I didn't know much about the investment game, but that seemed like an impossible fantasy. "How? I mean, who'd take a flier on you now?"

Bryan sat up a little straighter, a note of defiant pride in his voice. "My past investors. I've had a long career in this business, and I've made good money for a lot of people." He nodded at Niko. "Present company included."

Niko looked at him coldly. "If this is your bid to get me to throw more money down the drain with you . . ."

Niko's response sapped what little confidence Bryan'd regained by reminding us of his glory days. His body sagged again. "No, I certainly wouldn't expect you to reinvest with me after this . . . disaster." He stared down at the floor. "I just came here tonight because I wanted you to know what happened. And to promise you that I'm going to do everything I can to make it up to all of our clients. Especially you, since you put your word and reputation on the line for us. I can't begin to express how deeply and profoundly sorry I am."

Bryan grimaced as he stood up, a painful-looking leverage of legs and back, like the unfolding of a rusty accordion. Niko glanced up at him but didn't move.

Bryan moved toward the door. "Okay. I'll leave you be. Thank you for listening."

He shuffled out, looking twenty years older than when he'd come in. I actually felt badly for him. I looked at Niko. "What do you think? Do you believe him?"

Niko poured us each a glass of the pinot noir we'd opened before Bryan showed up. "I guess it's possible Tanner went rogue. He's always been more willing to take risks than Bryan. But that's partly what made them so successful." He took a sip of wine. "On the other hand, I've never seen him go out on a limb to this degree before. So I don't know."

I wondered what Tanner's side of the story would be.

As it turned out, I didn't have long to wait.

I stayed the night to keep Niko company, but he spent most of it pacing around the house. I dozed off and on, but by the time I finally managed to drift off, it was after five a.m. I didn't wake up until eight thirty—when I was already supposed to be at the office. My eyes burned and my body ached. I wanted a long, hot shower but had to settle for a quick rinse and then a fast makeup job—just enough to avoid scaring small children. When I walked into the kitchen, I found Niko sitting at the table, hunched over a cup of steaming coffee. The half-empty coffeepot told me it wasn't his first.

I poured myself a cup and sat down across from him. "Did you get any sleep at all?"

His eyes were red and his facial stubble was longer than his usual short coating. He shook his head. "You?"

"A little more than you did." I took a long sip of coffee. "What's on the docket for today?"

His voice was weary. "I've got a meeting with my agent to talk about that cameo in *First and For Most* and supposedly a meeting with the rep from Jockey to do a line of action wear. But he's Tanner's guy, so . . ."

I took another sip of coffee and felt the caffeine kick in. Thank God. "Don't throw the baby out with the bathwater. I get it. You're not in the mood to do more business with Tanner. But didn't you say your manager checked out that Jockey rep?"

"Yeah. He did say the rep seemed legit." Niko stared down at his cup. "You're right, I guess." He rubbed his face. "I'm not thinking all that clearly right now."

The doorbell rang. Two seconds later, there were three sharp raps on the door. Someone was in a big hurry. I stood up. "Probably breakfast. I'll get it." Niko likes to have all his food delivered. I wouldn't mind, but a) I'm almost never home, and b) it costs a fortune.

But it wasn't food. It was Tanner. A very anxious Tanner, and he was in hyperdrive. His hands were on his hips, and he was pacing back and forth across the doormat. The moment I opened the door, he lunged at me as he said, "Can I come in?"

I barely had the chance to nod before he moved past me into the house. I pointed to the kitchen. "He's in there." I followed him in. I wanted to hear this.

Tanner crossed the foyer in three long, fast strides and dragged out a chair across from Niko. He plopped down, ran a shaky hand through his hair, and talked at warp speed. "Bryan went fucking crazy. The old man just had to show everyone that he still had it. So he goes whole hog for this crazy crypto thing." His tone was both desperate and incredulous. "Who does that? Everyone knows those stocks are volatile as hell."

Niko frowned. "So you're saying this was all Bryan's idea?"

Tanner looked shocked. "Are you kidding? Of course it was! I'd never have sunk all that money into this scheme without a test run." He spread his hands. "Come on, Niko. You know me better than that."

Niko, worn out from a sleepless night and days of emotional stress, spoke with a harsh bitterness. "I don't feel like I know much of anything right now."

Tanner sat back, his expression wounded. "Look, I know I move fast. But I never jump blindfolded."

Being a half step away from the situation, I could be a little more objective. And now that the caffeine had kicked in, so had my natural instinct to cross-examine. "How is it possible for Bryan to have moved all that money without you knowing?"

Tanner faced me, his expression earnest. "We set it up so we'd both have the power to sign on all accounts, in case one of us was traveling and something needed to get done quickly. But we were never supposed to make a move like this unless we'd both agreed ahead of time." He turned toward Niko. "And it's never happened before. Honestly, I'm wondering whether Bryan's kind of . . . losing it." He tapped two fingers to his head. "You know? He is getting up there."

I raised an eyebrow. "He's fifty-seven."

Tanner sat back and blew out a breath. "You're right. I mean, there is such a thing as early onset. But . . . yeah. Probably not. And I get that he wants to show he's still"—Tanner used air quotes—"'The Man,' but this . . . this was way over the top."

I didn't know what to make of it all. One of these guys had to be lying. But which one? Both seemed equally sure that the other had made the catastrophic investment. Both were equally angry about it. Could there be a third party in this mix? One neither of them knew about? A hacker, maybe?

But it only took me a moment to see the flaw in that theory. If it'd been a hacker, they wouldn't be finger-pointing at each other. They'd be saying that neither of them had made the trade.

Tanner heaved a deep sigh. "Anyway, the most important thing now is to get everyone paid back. The only way to get my hands on that much money is to—"

"Reinvest?" Niko shot back. "That's what you were going to say, right?"

Tanner blinked for a second but recovered quickly. "Yes. Of course. How else?"

Niko's gaze was steady and deceptively calm. "And you want me to give you, what? A hundred thousand? Five hundred?"

Tanner, completely missing the note of sarcasm in Niko's voice, said, "Probably five hundred thousand. You know what Warren Buffett says, 'Be fearful when others are greedy and greedy when others are fearful.' Everyone's scared right now, so it's time to be greedy."

Niko pushed away his coffee cup. "Yeah, you know what else Warren Buffett said? 'Risk comes from not knowing what you're doing.' Seems to me that pretty much sums up you and Bryan. I don't believe for one second that Bryan did this without you knowing. You both fucked up big-time. And now you expect me to trust you with another half a million? Are you insane?"

Tanner's face turned red, but he set his jaw and pressed on. "You can afford to support your mother. And maybe you'll be able to bail Tom out—or at least keep him from going bankrupt. But what about all the others? What are they going to do? You can't carry everyone."

I could see Niko struggling with the truth of what Tanner said. Niko had recommended Gold Strike to quite a few people—me included. But I have a deep and abiding aversion to financial investments of any kind. It's not based on anything as intelligent as research or experience. It's just that I don't trust anyone. To me, giving someone else money to invest is just an invitation to rip me off. Not a particularly sophisticated attitude, but I am who I am.

Niko shook his head. "You're not going to persuade me to throw that much money at you, so stop with the guilt trip. Find some other investors to go in with me and show me an investment plan that isn't based on the fever dream of some millennial with a Ouija board. Then I'll decide."

Tanner took a deep breath, then nodded. "Okay. It'd be faster if I could just work with you—and it'd be more money in your pocket, but if that's what you want to do . . ." He put his hands on the table and stood up.

Niko gave him a hard look. "It is."

I waited for the door to close behind him, then said, "You've gotta hand it to him. He's got brass balls."

Niko slouched down in his chair and folded his arms across his chest. "The problem is, he's right. The only way to bail out everyone is to find a hot new investment."

"Yeah, but who's going to want to invest with them? One—or both—of these guys has to be lying." It seemed entirely possible to me that both Bryan and Tanner were in on the crypto stock buy—and that both of them were lying about who'd made the deal now that it'd gone belly-up.

Niko nodded, his features haggard. "You're right. But I don't know any other brokers." He stared into his coffee cup. "They've made a lot of good calls up until now. If I could figure out who's telling the truth, I'd probably go ahead and put in the money, just to give everyone a shot at recouping some of the loss." Niko sighed. "But which one . . ."

Was really up for grabs. At first, Bryan—with his kind, fatherly expression—had persuaded me that Tanner, the reckless young Turk, had gone off the rails. But Tanner's sharp, angry denials, his assessment that Bryan had wanted to make the big move and prove himself to their clients, were persuasive, too. Then I remembered the chip that'd fallen out of his pocket when I met him at Bryan's place. I'd done some checking on it. "Did you know Tanner's in Sex Addicts Anonymous?" The words embossed on the chip, *From Shame to Grace*, made up the SAA tenet.

Niko had been staring out the window, lost in thought. He looked at me now with a confused expression. "What?" When I repeated what I'd said, he rolled his eyes. "Yeah, he said he got it so he could go to meetings and score."

I shook my head. "Seriously?"

He gave a small shrug. "I'm not sure it's true. Sometimes he just bullshits to get a rise out of people."

But what someone jokes—or bullshits—about can be telling. The question right now is, telling of what? A true sex addiction that he was embarrassed to admit? Or was he not bullshitting at all? Was he really just preying on vulnerable women who were trying to get their act together? If so, he was as bad as the pusher who goes to Nar-Anon meetings to sell dope.

But if he was a sex addict, would that mean he was more likely to act impulsively, as Bryan claimed? Or if he wasn't, if he was just a disgusting predator, would that mean he was a more deliberate strategist who—even though a pig—was not the type to jump off the cliff without looking?

I thought of one way to get closer to the answer. "Why don't I get Dale to check these guys out?"

Dale Pearson is a senior homicide detective with the elite Robbery Homicide Division in LAPD. One who also happens to be my father. A fact I didn't discover until he hired me to defend him in a double murder case.

Until then, I hadn't known that my father was even an identifiable person, because Celeste, my piss-poor excuse for a mother, had always told me that my father was just a one-night stand and that she'd never known his name. The truth was, she and Dale had been dating for months. But shortly after she'd found out she was pregnant, she'd also learned he had no money—so she dumped him and never told him about me. Why? Because a pesky ex-boyfriend who wanted to share custody would've gotten in the way of her quest to snag a billionaire. So she'd lied to me about Dale all my life. For Celeste, the truth is never a must. It's just one alternative.

Anyhow, I won the murder case against Dale. Actually managed to prove that someone else did it and got it dismissed. Now, we have an . . . interesting relationship, with some unpredictable traits in common. Some might call them quirks. Most would call them . . . something else. And we do lean on each other for help now and then. So we have a relationship. But I'll never be able to do the whole "my heart belongs to Daddy" thing. I don't know whether that's because I never knew him growing up or whether I've lost the ability to make that kind of connection. Or whether he's a little too much like me. Whatever the reason, ours is far from the traditional father-daughter dynamic.

Which is why, to me, he is, and always will be, Dale Pearson.

I'd brought up the possibility of bringing Dale in to help Niko because he'd have access to Bryan's and Tanner's background information. That might give us some clues as to which one was lying.

But Niko didn't like the idea. "The last thing I want to do right now is get law enforcement involved. Later, sure. But right now, I don't want to risk getting those guys busted. Not before they've had a chance to pay everyone back."

The hope that Bryan or Tanner could make back all that money struck me as the Hail Mary pass of all time. But I didn't blame Niko for hanging on to that thread.

Because he was right: if Dale got into it and found dirt on them, no one would get paid.

SIX

With no answers and no clear idea what to do next, neither one of us was exactly a ray of sunshine to be around.

And Niko was doubly stressed because he was worried about his mother but couldn't spend much time with her because he had to go meet with producers to start prepping his next video. "I don't think she's eating. It seems like she's shrinking by the second."

I hesitated a moment before making the suggestion I had in mind. But this was a real worry. Sophia was already on the skinny side of slender. She really didn't have any weight to lose. "Maybe you should get someone to stay with her? Make sure she gets some food in her?"

Niko shook his head. Anxiety tightened his features. "She'd never stand for that. She doesn't like the idea of strangers in her house. Friends would be okay, but I can't expect them to be with her all day." He finished his coffee and took the cup over to the sink. "I guess I'll just have to tell her friends to try and get her to eat."

I put our cups in the dishwasher. "You stopping by there now?" Niko said he was. "Want me to go with you?"

His eyes said yes, but he hesitated. "Don't you have a mountain of work to get to?"

I nodded. Unfortunately, I did. Those damn piles of motions, letters, and briefs wouldn't write themselves. "But I can come back tonight if you want."

He said he did, and the look of relief on his face told me just how heavily this was all weighing on him. It was unusual for us to spend this much time together. We ordinarily hung out on weekends—and not even then if one or the other of us was tied up. Which happened a lot.

As we exchanged a brief, distracted kiss and headed out to tackle the day, I wondered if we'd be able to deal with this much togetherness.

When I got into the office, I posed the question to Michy.

She laughed, then gave me an incredulous look. "Am I supposed to take that question seriously? Like *he's* the one who can't handle a real relationship?"

That was not unfair. Whenever she points out how little time Niko and I spend together because of our crazy schedules, I always say it's probably the only thing that keeps us together. "Okay, whatever. But you've gotta admit, this is a lot more 'us' time than we've ever had."

Michy held up her hands. "No argument there. But I'm not hearing that it's a problem for Niko." She raised an eyebrow. "You getting antsy?"

I thought about that. "Not so far, but . . ."

She gave me a steady look. "Then don't second-guess yourself. It's good that he wants you there. Believe it or not, that's what couples do when they're going through hard times—they're there for each other. You can always take a break if it makes you crazy."

Michy wasn't being patronizing. Or sarcastic. She knew that the weirdly shredded tapestry of what passed for my love life was the product of a pretty fucked-up childhood.

Because Celeste, AKA Mommie Dearest, eventually did wind up finding her Daddy Warbucks. Proof that some men don't really care whether a woman is a narcissistic pathological liar, as long as she's pretty.

And my mother was very pretty. Pretty enough to make most men stutter, and she ate it up. It always nauseated me.

But desk jobs—or any job that required extended focus—weren't her thing. So I guess it made sense that she settled on a gig that allowed her to move around a lot and became a real estate agent. The job suited her well, and by the time I was twelve and in seventh grade, she was one of the top sellers at her agency. But the money wasn't coming in big enough or fast enough for her. And working for a living had never been a part of Celeste's life plan. So when the CEO of the company, Sebastian Cromer—a billionaire who owned commercial properties both here and abroad—stopped by the office, she made a point of cozying up to him.

Et voilà, Celeste scored her billionaire. What was even better? He fell for her so hard and fast, he asked her to move into his mansion in Bel Air after dating for just one month. Celeste—no fool she—didn't give him a chance to change his mind. We began packing that same night. Within a week, we were ensconced in the luxe life she'd always dreamed of.

Except there was one little flaw. Celeste wasn't the one Sebastian "fell for." That lucky lady was me. Twelve-year-old me. While Celeste enjoyed her vision of heaven, I lived in an unending hell. Sebastian didn't waste any time on the preliminaries. Within a week of our moving in, he started coming to my room to "tuck me in."

Translation: tongue kiss, then fondle, then . . . rape. I'd thought I was so lucky when I saw that I was getting a big bedroom at the back of the manse with my own en suite bathroom. But it didn't take long for me to figure out that it wasn't meant to please me. It was just a strategic move so no one could hear me scream.

When I tried to tell Celeste what was going on, she refused to believe me. Called me a liar who just couldn't stand the fact that she was finally happy. Even when the housekeeper caught Sebastian with his hand up my shirt, Celeste refused to accept it. And when the housekeeper caught him a second time and called the police, Sebastian charmed the officer. That asshole cop wound up shaking Sebastian's hand and apologizing for the inconvenience. The housekeeper got fired.

I ran away a few times, but Sebastian had the means to hire some of the very best to find me and drag me back. And let's face it, how hard is it to track down a twelve-year-old?

That's when I started drinking. Southern Comfort and Jack Daniel's were my faves, but really, anything that numbed the pain would do. I thought I was being slick about it, that no one could tell. But Michy—who I'd just met in school that year (and who had quickly become my best friend)—could.

She told me I was heading for either a brick wall or a concrete cell. She wanted to know what was up with me. I was too scared to tell her what was going on with Sebastian. I was afraid of what he'd do if he found out I'd told anyone. And honestly, I didn't want to tell anyone because on some level, I thought it was my fault that he was doing this to me.

But I knew Michy was right. I couldn't keep living like this. I came up with a plan. It was a simple little plan, but if I pulled it off, I'd be out of that hell house.

Back then, cell phones weren't so ubiquitous. Not all kids had them. But Michy had gotten one for Christmas. I borrowed it from her and managed to secretly take photos of Sebastian with me—one of them as he was leaving my bed, in the nude.

Incredibly, even after I showed the photos to Celeste, she still didn't want to believe me. She called me a "little slut" and accused me of "setting him up." But I told her I'd made copies of the photos (I actually hadn't; I was too scared) and that if she didn't get us out of there, I'd take the photos to the police. That finally did it. Whatever fiction she'd been telling herself, even she had to admit they were damning. She had no choice. She had to move us out. I never knew whether she told Sebastian about the photos. My guess is she didn't. Probably because she hoped she'd be able to get back with him after I was out of her hair.

I got rid of the photos after we moved. There was no way I'd ever go to the police and let the world know what he'd done to me—not even Michy.

I'd love to be able to say that everything was groovy and copacetic after we moved out. But I was, in fact, an ungodly mess. It took years for me to pull my act together. And even then, it was just dumb luck. My mother accidentally married a good guy—who was, of course, a billionaire—when I was a junior in high school. He'd been able to see what Celeste had chosen to ignore: that I was sinking fast. Booze, pills, cocaine, even heroin. You name it, I was on it. He'd gotten me some real help—a drug counselor and a tutor—and I'd cleaned up my act. Did well enough to get into a decent college.

But none of that was thanks to Celeste—living proof that not every woman is meant to be a mother. Or, in her case, even a human being.

So, not surprisingly, my forays into the world of romance have been . . . sketchy. Niko is as close as I've ever gotten to what Michy calls a "real" relationship. It did say something that my usual instinct to cut and run hadn't kicked in. Yet. But I was seriously worried that it was only a matter of time. Still, Michy had a point. It wasn't as though Niko was threatening to chain me to the water heater. "Right. I guess I'll tough it out and see what happens."

Michy snorted. "Oh please. You'd think we were talking about running a 10K. For God's sake, all you have to do is tell him you have to go home to take care of some chores or something."

"Yeah, but then I'd have to go back, right?" I brightened. "Unless he has to travel. That could happen. That could totally happen."

Michy rolled her eyes. "Enough. Go get some work done. We need to bill some hours so I can buy those Manolos I saw at the outlet."

"Manolos. Wow." We were so uptown now. She used to tell me to get more work done so she could "pay the office rent" or "pay the electricity bill." Now . . . Manolo Blahniks. "I really am overpaying you guys."

Michy made a dismissive grunt. "You wouldn't be paying me what I'm worth if you tripled my salary." She waved a hand at me. "Now shoo. Go make some money."

I saluted and went to do the bidding of She Who Must Be Obeyed. Because Michy was right: I'd probably never be able to pay her what she was worth. I put my head down for the next three hours and managed to knock out all the motions—mostly continuance requests, but I also put together a sentencing memo and a pretrial motion to dismiss. Pretty good progress.

So when Alex stopped by to check in, I decided I deserved to take a break. He was going *très* casual today, in black Levi's and a dove-gray pullover sweater, but he managed to make the outfit look like Tom Ford haute couture. Some people just have it. That thing that makes whatever they throw on look like it was made for them—by Hugo Boss. Me, I don't rock anything. I wear the basics—jeans, sweaters, and suits—and I'm happy if I manage to leave the house with everything buttoned and zipped.

I pushed back from my computer and gestured for him to come in. "Nice workup on Blake Ettinger's background." I'd negotiated a deal that let Blake plead to just one of the five counts he was facing for breaking into an animal hospital to steal food and meds for his three dogs, one of whom had a bad case of worms. He was facing a maximum of three years, but I was shooting for straight probation—which would've been a lot easier if Blake hadn't been busted for cocaine possession a few years ago. So I'd asked Alex to dig into his personal history and find something I could milk for sympathy. It turned out that the dogs Blake had been trying to help actually belonged to his girlfriend—who had just been diagnosed with lung cancer.

I folded my arms. "If that doesn't bring a tear to the judge's eye, he's a damn robot."

Alex flopped down on the couch and stretched out his legs. "Here's hoping. What's going on with Niko and those genius brokers?"

I filled him in on my encounters with the geniuses. "I can usually suss out a liar, but this one has me stumped."

Alex opened his iPad. "What's the name of the stock bundle they jumped into?"

That would've been a good thing to know. "I have a feeling someone mentioned it at some point, but I can't remember."

He closed it and sighed. "Get me the name. I'd like to know what made one of those two decide it was too hot to miss."

I promised I would. Alex went back to his office to do one last computer run on Ettinger to make sure he hadn't missed anything. I've been accused of being Type A to the point of OCD, but Alex is Type A+++. It can be a little annoying at times, but it makes for a crack investigator.

I got back to work on the motion to dismiss and managed to finish by the unusually normal hour of six thirty. I'd agreed to go to Niko's after work, but I wasn't sure he'd still want company. When I called to check out his mood, he was still at his mother's house but said he'd be heading home in a few minutes. I asked if he still wanted me to come over.

"I really would." There was a vulnerable note in his voice that told me he wasn't the least bit worried about us spending too much time together.

Oh, right. That was me.

I left my briefcase in the office. No way I'd get any work done at Niko's. I stopped at Michy's desk and told her where I was heading. "And believe it or not, I'm picking up steaks."

Michy stopped typing and stared at me. "Why would you do this to him, especially at a time like this?" She shook her head. "Talk about kicking a man when he's down."

I gave her a mock glare. "I'm not that bad a cook." Actually, I am. I have zero moves when it comes to the kitchen. Michy's deadpan gaze said she was not persuaded. "I'm just throwing the steaks on the broiler.

He's making the salad. And the dressing." Niko actually likes to cook. As they say, all that and pretty, too.

Michy shrugged. "That might be safe enough. I guess we'll find out. But just in case . . ." She quickly typed, then printed out a page and handed it to me.

I read the page. It was the phone number and address for the urgent care clinic near Niko's house. "You're a real laugh riot."

But I tucked it into my purse as I headed out. Better safe than sorry, right?

I expected it to be another night of sadness and anger—and it was both—but as we sat in front of the fire and polished off the bottle of an excellent Adastra Proximus pinot noir after dinner (which I did manage to pull off without poisoning anyone), Niko's mood mellowed.

He put an arm around me. "I can't tell you how much it helps that you're here." He leaned his head against mine. "I know I'm not the most fun right now."

I leaned into him. "You never need to put on a clown face for me. I want you to be how you feel."

We sat in silence, and the wine and the warmth of the fire unwound the spring that always lives in my chest. I was about to ask if he wanted me to open another bottle when I heard a soft rumble. It took me a second to realize it was coming from Niko. He was snoring.

I gently woke him up, and we stumbled into bed. We both drifted off the moment our heads hit the pillows.

I usually hate to sleep with anyone else. I have this awful recurring nightmare of being swallowed alive by Sebastian that always makes me wake up in a feverish sweat—and frequently screaming. It hadn't happened when I was with Niko yet, but I always worried it might. Tonight, though, I was so tired, I was sure I'd make it through the night in peace.

And I probably would have—if it hadn't been for someone banging on the door at two o'clock in the morning. The sound of that hammering fist jerked us both awake, hearts pounding.

Niko sprang out of bed like a cat. I, much less gracefully, crawled out and grabbed one of his sweatshirts. He motioned for me to stay back. I thought, *The hell I will.* I waited for him to clear the bedroom, then grabbed the heavy bronze sculpture of Buddha's head that Niko kept on the nightstand and tiptoed out behind him.

He peered through the peephole, then sighed and opened the door. "What the hell—"

Tanner, his face pale, hair standing on end, could barely eke out the words. "He ripped us all off!"

SEVEN

Niko pulled him inside and headed for the kitchen, where he started a pot of coffee. "I assume you're talking about Bryan."

I put the Buddha sculpture back on the nightstand and joined them in the kitchen. Tanner was pacing in a circle and wringing his hands. "He's gone! Doesn't answer his cell or his landline. Doesn't answer the door. This is bullshit! I should've known he'd screw me the minute he got the chance!"

As we sat over steaming cups of coffee and tried to wake up enough to make sense of what Tanner was saying, it gradually became clear that he'd jumped to a conclusion. He didn't really know what had happened to Bryan—or whether Bryan had really ripped anyone off.

The night was chilly and damp, and I wrapped my hands around the mug for warmth. "Was his car in the driveway?"

Tanner stared at the table, his expression numb. "Yeah. And he always takes that Rolls-Royce wherever he goes."

I'd seen the flashy thing—which, of course, was *white*—when I'd gone to his house with Niko. I remembered thinking it was ridiculous and wondering whether he used it to impress his clients—and whether that worked. But the fact that Bryan's car was there and he didn't answer the door led me to a very different conclusion. "How do you know something didn't happen to him? Did you get inside his house?"

Tanner blinked. "N-no. But I didn't see any signs of a break-in."

"Do you have a key to his house?" I asked. He said he didn't. That killed one idea. And we couldn't break in. The houses on Bryan's street were close together. His neighbors would have the cops there in a heartbeat.

Niko studied Tanner's face for a moment. "I assume you checked the office."

Tanner nodded. "He wasn't there. And I didn't see any sign of a break-in there, either."

"How much checking did you do? Did you look in Bryan's office?" There might be notes or information on his computer that gave some clue as to where he'd gone.

Tanner shook his head. "I was just looking to see if he was there."

I suggested we all go and do a more thorough search. Everyone agreed that was a good idea. I had another one. "Mind if I bring my investigator?" Another pair of eyes couldn't hurt. Especially when they belonged to Alex, who misses nothing. Seriously. Nothing.

Tanner seemed a little unsure about the idea. "Is he, like, a cop?"

"No. He's, like, an investigator. As in someone who looks for things—and people. And usually finds them."

Niko sealed the deal. "That's a great idea, Sam."

It was a hell of a thing to do to Alex. It was two thirty in the morning. But I'd find a way to make it up to him.

When I called, he was so deeply asleep, I had to explain the situation to him twice before he understood that a) I wasn't in jail (though that was always a reasonable possibility), and b) I wasn't in the hospital (again, see above). But once he got it, he was on board. I told him to meet us at the office building in half an hour.

An hour later, Tanner unlocked the office door and turned on the lights. We entered slowly and took in the reception area. I saw nothing out of place. Tanner led the way into the main office space. We passed a glassed-in conference room that appeared to be untouched, then followed him into a large office that could only have been Bryan's.

Original mixed-media artwork hung on the walls, a floor-to-ceiling window offered a view that stretched to downtown, a thick Persian rug covered most of the floor, and the furniture was all glass and steel and clearly of designer quality. The desk was so clean, it sparkled. Not so much as a Post-it to mar the pristine effect.

There were two doors on my right. I opened the one closest to the window. It was a bathroom—with a walk-in shower and a bidet. The other door opened to a decent-size closet. Three suits—I spotted an Armani and a Tom Ford—three shirts, five pairs of shoes, and a leather trench coat. This man *really* lived the life. But again, nothing looked out of place, and Tanner confirmed it.

While I'd been scoping out the place, Alex had made a beeline for the desktop computer. His fingers were flying over the keyboard. I stared at him in awe. How had he managed to break into it that fast? "I knew you were good, but that's ridiculous. How'd you figure out his password already?"

Alex smirked. "I'd love to let you think I am that amazing—because I am. But . . ." He pointed to the monitor stand and a small piece of paper that was taped to it.

Aha. Bryan's password. That told me something else. "Then his security is probably a joke."

The smirk grew into a smile. "Totally. Took me five seconds to hack into his email account."

I should've known. Bryan didn't seem like the tech-savvy type.

I asked Tanner to show us his own office. It took him a second to unglue his eyes from what Alex was doing at Bryan's computer. His voice shook a little as he said, "Uh, sure." Was he worried about something? If so, was it about what Alex might find—or what he might not be able to find?

Tanner's office was next door to Bryan's, and it was a study in contrast. No rug adorned the plain beige carpeting, a whiteboard covered the wall opposite the standard-issue office desk, and while his office had a bathroom, it was just a toilet and a sink. No shower. And no closet.

I looked around at the spare room, the cluttered desk, and the computer monitor that looked like it had feathers there were so many Post-it notes stuck to the edges. "You really got the ass end of the office space deal."

Tanner replied, "Actually, when we signed the lease, the only difference was his office was a little bigger."

I almost laughed. "So he remodeled?"

"Yeah." His tone was disdainful. "Typical Bryan."

Niko left the room and wandered down the hallway. I was about to follow him when Alex called out. "Hey, Sam. Come check this out."

Tanner and I went back to Bryan's office. Niko joined us. Alex motioned us over to the computer and pointed to the screen. "This file that's marked 'T Rex.'" Alex double-clicked on it and then clicked on the document by the same name. A list of names—I thought they might be company names—popped up. "Do you recognize these, Tanner?"

"Yeah. 'T Rex' is the title we gave my investment recommendations."

Tanner's Recs—as in recommendations. Clever. Sort of. Alex clicked to the next page, which showed the same names with a number after each one. There was a number at the bottom that seemed to be the total: $100,000.

Tanner gave a startled cry. "What? No!" He practically shoved Alex aside as he turned the monitor to get a closer look.

Alex leaned back to give him room. "I assume those numbers show the amounts he invested in each company?"

Tanner was breathing hard. "Yeah. And it's about one percent of what we agreed on."

If what Tanner said was true, then Bryan had made nominal invest-ments just for show. In which case . . . "What happened to the other ninety-nine percent of the money?"

Alex looked up at Tanner, whose face had turned a bright red. "Mind if I get back in here?" Tanner stepped away, and Alex hit the keys in a flurry of motion. "It looks like he funneled a big chunk into some-thing called BYO." He spoke to Tanner over his shoulder. "Recognize the name?"

Tanner shook his head. "Is it a company? What is it?"

Alex resumed typing. "Hold on." He flew through the windows too fast for me to follow what he was doing, but five minutes later, he leaned back and blew out a breath.

Tanner had been pacing and rubbing the back of his neck. Now he stopped and stared at Alex. "What? What?"

Alex pressed his lips together. "That entity called BYO? Where ninety-nine percent of the money went? It's a private holding company."

Tanner groaned and shook his head. "I can't believe this." He turned to Niko. "That's got to be what he did with the cryptocurrency trade money, too! See? I told you he ripped us all off!"

Alex took in his reaction, then turned back to the screen and resumed typing. After a few seconds, he stopped and stared at the screen. "Seems so. As far as I can tell, there's no money in the BYO holding company account—now."

I was trying to process it all. If this was where all the investors' money had gone, and Bryan had stolen it, then what had they used to buy the cryptocurrency stock? I posed the question to Tanner.

He waved his arms. "How the hell should I know? I had nothing to do with that buy!"

Niko gave him a warning look. "You have every right to be upset, but watch your mouth when you talk to Sam."

Something else about this didn't feel right, but I couldn't put my finger on it.

Alex frowned at the monitor. "There's got to be some trace of the cryptocurrency buy." He resumed typing, but his frown deepened. He muttered, "It shouldn't be this tough to find. Bryan's not that good."

Tanner swallowed hard as he watched Alex for a moment, then went back to pacing.

I was starting to wonder whether there had ever really been a trade at all. Whether Bryan had set it up to look like he'd invested in the cryptocurrency stock and lost when in fact, he'd never made any kind of trade; he'd simply stolen all the investors' money. I made a mental note to ask Alex what he thought when we had a private moment.

But as I considered what Bryan would do if he'd wanted to hide the information on his cryptocurrency buy—or whatever he'd done with the money he'd pretended to invest—it occurred to me that he might not have wanted to do it on a computer. "Hey, Tanner. Does Bryan have a safe here?"

He gave me a bitter look. "Not that he ever told me. Which doesn't mean shit."

I agreed. I knelt down and lifted a corner of the Persian rug to look for seams in the carpet. I didn't see any. Niko went to the other side of the rug and lifted a corner. He shook his head.

We moved to the other corners of the rug. Nothing. I scanned my side of the perimeter of the room, looking for a gap between the wall and the carpet. Niko did the same on his side. Nothing.

I pointed to the bathroom. We searched the floor for loose tiles, the shower for any cutouts, and all the drawers in the vanity. I let Niko check the toilet tank. Nothing.

I glanced at Tanner. He'd stopped pacing. Now he was hovering over Alex and chewing on a cuticle. I would've felt bad that Alex had to deal with someone breathing down his neck, except he was so enrapt, he didn't seem to notice.

Niko had opened the closet and was shining the beam of his cell phone flashlight around the floor. I joined him there and studied the carpet. Nothing unusual. I shined my cell phone flashlight on the shelf above the clothing rod.

And finally saw something. I tapped Niko's arm and pointed the beam at the lines I'd noticed in the wall. He nodded as he reached up and pushed on the left side. It didn't move. Then he pushed on the right side.

A square-shaped piece of wall swung open. And there it was. A safe. It wasn't particularly fancy—which, given Bryan's other choices, surprised me. It was just an ordinary metal box that opened with a key. I called out, "Hey, we found a safe. Can you guys look for any smallish keys in his desk?"

Alex and Tanner pulled out all the drawers and rummaged around. It didn't take long. Bryan didn't keep much in it. Alex shook his head. "No luck."

Of course not. That'd be too easy. "Damn. Now what?"

Niko was unfazed. "Now we do it the old-fashioned way. This thing is junk. I can drill right through that lock."

Alex always carries everything in the trunk of his car—and this is why. He—of course—had a drill. He brought it, and several drill bits, from his car, and within fifteen minutes, the door to the safe was open.

I'd expected money. What I found was worse. Much worse.

Driver's licenses and social security cards in four different names. But all the photos were variations on just one face: Bryan's.

EIGHT

I handed the driver's licenses to Alex. "Maybe one of these . . ."

He took them. "Right. I'll know pretty quick."

Bryan wasn't slick enough to hide information on his computer from someone as good as Alex. Unless he hid it under a fake name.

Sure enough, it took just seven minutes for Alex to find the secret account. It'd been hidden under the name Stuart Mohler. Alex waved us over and pointed to the monitor. "Looks like Bryan / Stuart saved up a real fat stack."

Five point six million to be exact. I searched the screen but didn't see any clue as to where the money was stashed. "Can you find out where it is?"

Alex stared at the monitor. "I don't think he kept that information on this computer. At least, there's no indication of any bank account or money market account or anything. What I found here is just his kind of financial diary." He clicked backward to previous pages and pointed to the screen. "See this? It goes by date, and he logs in every week with a running tally."

Tanner had been silent as Alex showed us what he'd found. Now, he spoke in a whisper. "That's all the money from our investors. So he's been siphoning it off all along." He dropped his head into his hands and spoke in a strangled voice. "I'm ruined."

Niko's face looked like thunder. "Where would he go?"

Tanner ran a hand through his hair. "I don't know. Anywhere."

Alex looked up. "I take it you didn't find any passports in the safe." I shook my head. "Then we don't even know if he's in this country."

"But if he left the country, he'd have to use his passport." Meaning the police—or, rather, Dale—could find out where he'd gone. Then another stumbling block occurred to me. "Unless he also had a fake one."

Niko frowned. "He's tight with his mother. She must know where he is."

Tanner waved a hand. "Forget it. She won't tell you diddly-squat."

We were getting nowhere fast. "I can't believe I'm about to say this, but maybe it's time to call the cops."

Tanner held up his hands. "No! Absolutely not. We'll never get our money back if they grab him."

I gave an exasperated sigh. "Yeah, I know that. Because I'm the one who told you to begin with. But you have zero chance of getting any money back if you don't find him. At least if the cops bust him, you have a shot at getting some money back. Eventually." It wasn't what anyone wanted to hear.

Niko didn't look happy. "You're right, Sam. But let's give it a few more days. I'll talk to Bryan's mother and see if I can get any hints. If we keep hitting dead ends, we'll do it. We'll bring in the cops."

Alex shut down the computer, and I looked at the safe—which was now hanging open. "There's no way to hide that we broke into this thing, so I'm going to hang on to all his fake IDs. If these are the only ones he's got and he hasn't run yet, he'll be coming back for them."

"Which means we may have a chance to catch him," Niko said. "Tanner, you'll need to keep a close eye on the office. If you spot him, call me immediately."

Tanner gave him a dark look. "Don't worry."

I asked Tanner what he used to clean his monitor. His tone was puzzled. "Those soft cloths—like the kind you use for glasses."

"I need all of them." He opened his mouth, but I held up a hand. "Don't ask." He shrugged, went to his office, and came back with a handful of them. "Thanks." I gestured to Niko and Tanner. "You guys can go wait in the reception area. We'll just be a minute." They exchanged a look but wisely didn't press me for answers. When they were out of the room, I tossed half of the cloths to Alex. "We need to wipe this place down—everything we've touched." If Bryan didn't show up soon, the cops would be all over this place. It'd be okay if they found Niko's fingerprints or DNA or whatever. He had a legit reason to be here. But it'd be hard to explain what Alex and I were doing here—and frankly, I didn't want to have to try. That's why I'd needed to wipe the place down with something Tanner owned. His DNA belonged here. Mine and Alex's didn't.

We left the building with no better plan than to hope Bryan would come back for his IDs. In other words, with no plan at all.

It was four thirty in the morning when we got back to Niko's place. Exhausted and depressed, we went straight to bed.

The ringing phone woke me up, and I was sure I'd only been asleep for ten minutes. But as Niko answered, I saw that it was already ten thirty in the morning. I was still exhausted, so I started to burrow back in, but then I heard a frantic voice practically screaming into the phone.

It was Sophia's housekeeper. Niko's mother was in the hospital. She'd had a stroke. Niko and I both shot out of bed as he tried to calm the housekeeper down long enough to tell him which hospital his mother was in. It was Cedars-Sinai on Beverly Boulevard.

We jumped into clothes and broke all speed limits to get there. It'd normally take fifteen minutes to get from Niko's house in Beverly Glen Canyon to Cedars, which was in West Hollywood. We made it in seven.

Niko paced as I racked my brain to come up with something to say that would be supportive and calming. But every phrase I thought of either sounded counterproductive ("People make full recoveries all the time"—which only highlighted the fact that others don't) or ridiculous ("I'm sure she'll be fine"—because how the hell could I know?).

By the time the neurosurgeon, Dr. Hoffman, came out to see us, Niko's endless circular pacing had made us both dizzy. Hoffman was a short, wiry man with thick white Brillo Pad hair, heavy white eyebrows, and piercing blue eyes. He strode into the waiting room at a brisk clip, sat down, and gestured for Niko to do the same.

The doctor gave him a direct look. "I take it you're the son." Niko nodded. He opened his mouth, but before he could speak, the doctor continued. "Your mother has had an ischemic stroke. We've done a CT scan, and we're preparing to do an MRI. Just based on the CT scan, it appears the damage is extensive."

Niko's face paled, his breathing fast and shallow. "Is she going to . . . make it?"

Dr. Hoffman looked into Niko's eyes. "I don't know. Has your mother ever had a stroke before?"

Niko looked dazed. "N-no. I don't think so."

It was a measure of just how shaken up he was that he didn't remember. I tried to say it gently. "Niko, you told me she had a minor stroke five years ago."

He closed his eyes briefly. "Yes. That's right. But she didn't lose motor function or anything. Her right arm was just a little weak."

The doctor's heavy brows pulled together. "That explains why this stroke was so much worse. And it does make the prognosis for survival and recovery less . . . optimistic."

I tried to inject a positive note. "But she's alive so far."

The doctor nodded. "She is. But she's totally paralyzed, and she's completely lost the power of speech."

Niko dropped his head into his hands. "Oh my God!"

A flash of sorrow crossed the doctor's face. "I'm sorry. But I don't want to give you false hope. Even if she does survive, it's very unlikely that she'll regain any significant degree of motor function or speech."

Niko's eyes filled. He didn't seem to notice as tears rolled down his cheeks. "Can I see her?"

Dr. Hoffman stood up. "If they haven't taken her in for the MRI already." He pulled out his cell phone and stepped away.

I rubbed Niko's back, feeling ineffectual and overwhelmed. "I'm so sorry."

He dropped his head into his hands and began to sob. I wrapped my arms around him as tears sprang to my eyes. She wasn't my mother. I barely knew her. But Niko's pain pierced my heart like a glass shard.

The doctor finished his call and came back. "I can take you to her room if you'd like to see her, but I doubt she'll be awake."

He turned and set a rapid pace through the swinging doors, down the hall that led to the ICU and Niko's mother's room. I stood behind Niko as he went to her bedside. Sophia was asleep. She looked like a little bird, her body barely visible under the sheet and blanket.

Niko smoothed her hair back from her forehead and kissed it as he covered the frail hand that lay on top of the blanket. He spoke softly to her, saying he was there, not to be afraid, that everything would be okay. It was a heartbreaking sight, and I had to bite my lip to keep from crying.

After a few minutes, a young intern came in and said that it was time for the MRI. We followed Sophia's gurney until it reached the next set of swinging doors.

Dr. Hoffman stopped. "The nurses in ICU will keep you posted. Just know we're doing all we can."

We couldn't ask for more than that, but it wasn't enough. I supposed it never was for anyone in a situation like this.

I drove us back to Niko's place. He was in no shape to do anything more than move his body to and from the car and into the house. I put him to bed, then went to the living room and called Michy at the office. I filled her in on the day's tragic events. "I think I'd better stay with him for now."

Michy was her usual empathetic, supportive self. "Of course you should. God, I'm so sorry! What can I do? Do you want me to bring dinner over?"

I told her not to bother. There was plenty of food in the house. "I'll check in later—"

She cut me off. "You absolutely will not. There are no emergencies here. Luckily, all your clients are in custody right now. They're as fine as they're ever going to be. Just go hold Niko's hand. And please keep me updated on his mom."

I promised I would, then ended the call and made Niko some chamomile tea. It was all I could think of to do.

He cried off and on throughout the day and night. I did my best to soothe him, but I had no great, insightful words of wisdom that would make him feel better. The truth was, the picture for Sophia's future was bleak.

The following day, we got the news that I'd feared was coming: Sophia was on life support.

Though it was no surprise, it hit Niko hard. He sank even further. I held Niko as he wept, listened as he spoke of how he loved her, and sympathized as he railed at the universe—and more specifically, at Bryan.

He paced and punched the air with his fist. "That fucking monster! It's all his fault. I'm sick of waiting for that piece of shit to show up. We're going to the cops. I don't give a good goddamn about the money. I want that fucking asshole to die in prison!"

I agreed. I wanted to nail Bryan to the wall. Screw the money. But I had the wherewithal to admit that neither of us was in any shape to make a rational decision right now. I needed to buy us some time to think, so I used a stalling tactic. "I'm with you. I'll talk to Dale, see what's the best way to move on this."

That seemed to work. Niko calmed down a little, and I distracted him with some revenge therapy: the classic *Kill Bill*, with Uma Thurman.

For the next three days, we only left the house to go to the hospital and see Sophia. On the fourth day, I had a court appearance. I'd been considering asking one of my old public defender buddies to stand in for me. But Niko said he needed some fresh air and exercise. It was a good sign, though he was still far from himself. I asked, "You planning on going to the gym?"

Niko took his empty coffee cup and cereal bowl (he's a big fan of oatmeal) to the sink. "Yeah. I was thinking it might help." He rinsed out the dishes and put them in the dishwasher, then turned back to me. "I just realized, you've missed, like, days of work."

"And happy to do it. But since you're up and out, I should probably hit the salt mines."

He came over and put his arms around me. "I don't know how to thank you for all you've done. I can't imagine how I would've made it without you."

I kissed him. "All I did was sit here and hold your hand." I gave a little smile. "And heat up some soup."

He returned my smile. "It *was* the safest culinary choice." He walked me to the door. "I love you." I told him I loved him, too. As I turned to go, he said, "And damn, I'm going to miss you."

I stepped out and blew him a kiss. "Yeah, I'll miss you, too."

But as I got into my car, I knew I'd be relieved to go home tonight.

Would there ever come a time when I was sad to be alone? When I didn't need to reassure myself that every night and every weekend had an expiration date?

I didn't know. But it sure hadn't happened so far.

NINE

My afternoon appearance turned into the usual kind of bureaucratic night-mare. My client, who was in custody, wound up being a "miss out," i.e., he hadn't made it onto the court-bound bus for whatever reason, but the judge wouldn't allow me to waive time and set the case for another day, so I had to hang around the courthouse all day until my client got there. Which didn't happen until four o'clock.

Which meant that by the time I got to head for home, it was the peak of rush hour. Which meant that a drive that should've taken half an hour took me an hour and a half. When I finally got home, it was dark.

I dragged myself up the stairs to my little aerie of an apartment above Sunset Boulevard, dropped my briefcase inside the door, and poured myself three fingers of Patrón Silver. I took it out to my balcony and breathed in the night air. My one bedroom, one bath wouldn't make the cover of *Better Homes & Gardens*, but it did offer a sweeping view of the city that stretched from West Hollywood to downtown Los Angeles.

It was a cloudless night, with just a crescent moon. The red tail-lights of the cars streaming up and down La Cienega, Sunset, and, in the distance, the freeway looked like a moving collage. As I sipped my tequila, the tension in my body slowly began to ebb. I called Niko to check in but got his voice mail. He hadn't mentioned any plans to go out. I figured he must've gone to the hospital. Probably didn't have good reception there.

Worry about Sophia, Niko, and all the investors who'd been ruined had been eating away at me. I hadn't talked to Dale yet—the precursor to bringing in the police. And so far, Niko hadn't mentioned it again. It now seemed obvious that whatever had happened with the investors' cryptocurrency buy-in, Bryan was behind it, and that he'd been lying all along.

I briefly wondered whether Bryan would have the know-how to fake a paper trail well enough to fool Tanner. But then I realized that he already had. And besides, how much know-how did it take to dummy up some paperwork and invent a fictitious seller? Especially for someone who'd been in the investment business as long as Bryan had. No, the more I thought about it, the more likely it seemed that the trade had been a bullshit deal all along. But I hadn't discussed any of this with Niko. He had enough on his mind, and I didn't want to get him fired up about going to the police again. At least, not yet.

I considered talking to Tanner about my theory that the cryptocurrency trade was a scam but decided to wait and see if Alex came up with any proof one way or another. We hadn't heard from Tanner since the night we'd broken into Bryan's safe. I assumed he was lying low, hoping to find Bryan—and trying to figure out what to do if he didn't.

I'd picked up a hamburger and fries on the way home, knowing that I had nothing edible in the fridge. I headed back inside, sat down on the couch, and turned on the television. Finally, I had a chance to scarf junk food. Niko "your body is a temple" Ferrell never touched the stuff. After four days of total abstinence, it tasted especially good.

When I'd finished, I took a shower, poured myself another three-finger shot of Patrón Silver, and took it to bed with me. Another habit

I couldn't indulge in with Niko around. True, I fell asleep after one sip. But it's the fact that I had the choice that mattered.

I was so tired and distracted by all that'd been going on, I completely forgot to worry about having the nightmare. Which is why it was bound to happen.

It's always the same. I'm lying in bed in a dark room I don't recognize. The thud of heavy footsteps grows louder and louder. I'm terrified, and I want to get up and run, but I can't seem to get untangled from the blankets and sheets. Trapped, my heart pounds so hard I can barely breathe. And then Sebastian stands over my bed.

Somehow, I manage to break free from my bedding. I jump up and stab him, over and over again. But he doesn't die. He doesn't even bleed. He gets bigger and bigger until he turns into a twenty-foot monster who pins me to the wall. As he opens a gaping maw of a mouth, I realize he's going to devour me. My knife disappears as I kick and scream and try in vain to twist out of his grasp.

That's when I wake up, gasping for breath, the sheets damp and wrapped around my body, my throat scraped raw from screaming out loud in my sleep.

The kicker is, when I have the nightmare, I never get to wake up at a normal hour. It's almost always three or four o'clock in the morning, when it's still dark and the rest of the world is asleep. And even though I'm awake and fully aware that it was just a dream, I feel the same isolation and loneliness that marked my childhood.

I never want to try and go back to sleep or linger in bed after one of these sessions. I'm too afraid the dream will pick up where it left off, and between the damp sheets and my sweaty body, I'm usually freezing anyway. I looked at the bedside clock. It was almost five a.m. Not bad for me. But that was probably because I'd been so damn tired when I went to bed.

I dragged myself into the shower and made the water hot enough to sting as I did my best to wash off the memories that dream evoked.

I got dressed, made a pot of coffee, and had breakfast. My usual two fried eggs and half an onion bagel. I waited until six thirty, then put in a call to Niko. I got his voice mail and left a message. I hoped he was sleeping—but I doubted it.

I was pouring my third cup of coffee when the strains of Oliver Nelson's "Stolen Moments" played on my cell phone. It was Niko.

He sounded a lot better. Definitely not upbeat but pretty steady. His mother was still on life support, but there was room for hope. And he had some news—sort of. "I got ahold of Bryan's mother. She swears she doesn't know where he is."

Which didn't necessarily mean it was true. "What do you think?"

Niko sighed. "It seemed to me like she was telling the truth." He paused. "But who knows? If anyone would cover for him, it'd be her."

So interesting, this man in his fifties who was still that close to his mother. Niko was close to his mother, too, but he didn't hang out with Sophia on a regular basis—or call her every day. "I guess that leaves us at square one."

Niko agreed. "Unless she's actually telling the truth."

I said I'd put that possibility at the bottom of the list.

But I was wrong.

The next morning, as I was getting ready to leave for the office, I got another call from Niko.

His voice was tense. "I just heard from Gwen."

Distracted—I'd been checking my calendar to see if I had a court appearance tomorrow—I couldn't place the name. "Who's Gwen?"

"Bryan's mother. Seems she really meant it when she said she didn't know where he is. She's freaking out. She wants to get into his place, but she's afraid to go alone."

I assumed she had a key to his place. "So she asked you to go with her?" Niko said she had. "Why you? Why not Tanner?"

His tone was flat. "She hates him."

Gwen was either a good judge of character or, given how tight she and Bryan were, she was the jealous type. Maybe both. "I'm going with you." Niko started to protest. "Don't even go there. Another pair of eyes could only help. Remember, I was the one who found that safe in his office."

Niko gave an *ahem*. "Technically, I did—"

Uh-uh. Not having it. "Whose idea was it to—"

He interrupted. "Fine. You can come. I'll pick you up."

An hour later, we found Gwen—a zaftig, perfectly coiffed woman dressed in St. John's slacks and sweater, holding a black Gucci bag—standing in Bryan's driveway. I approached her. "Nice to meet you, Mrs. Posner."

But as I got closer, I saw that she was in no shape for politesse. Her eyes were wild, and she swallowed convulsively as she spoke. "He's never gone so long without calling me. Never!" With that, she turned and headed up the walkway.

When we reached the door, her hand was shaking so badly, she couldn't get the key in the lock. Niko reached out. "Here, let me do that for you." As he opened the door, I studied the lock and doorframe for signs of disturbance. I didn't see any.

We stepped inside, and I scanned the living room and kitchen. Everything seemed to be in its place. Gwen began to wring her hands. "I'm afraid. It doesn't . . . feel right."

I gestured to the couch. "Do you want to wait here?"

She looked up at me, her expression painfully anxious. "Yes. Yes, I think so." She sank down and clutched her purse in her lap.

Niko and I moved through the living room and down the hallway. There was a bedroom on the right that looked like a guest room. The bed was neatly made. An abstract painting hung above the headboard and a lavender diffuser on one of the nightstands. No sign of trouble. Nothing was even slightly askew. Farther down the hall on the left, we found what I assumed was the master bedroom—because it was all white. A big, fluffy white duvet covered the California king bed, and the nightstands on either side of it were bleached wood. But again, everything—from the vase on the dresser to the framed photographs on the wall—was pristine.

I pointed to a closed door on the left side of the room. "The master bath?"

Niko shrugged. We moved to the door and opened it. I heard the scream almost before I could process what I was seeing. Bryan's body—naked and bloated—was floating under the water in the large jetted bathtub. Judging by the condition of his body, he'd been there for hours. A nearly empty bottle of wine stood on the floor next to it. Gwen must've followed behind us. She'd screamed at the sight of her son—who was clearly dead. And now, tears streaming down her face, she couldn't stop screaming. "My son! Oh my God! No!" She sagged to the floor as she sobbed.

I leaned down and put an arm around her as I stared at Bryan's half-closed eyes. Was this an accident? Or—given all that'd happened—was it a suicide? Or . . . murder?

I couldn't really say I mourned his loss. Not after what he'd done. But it was a sad, strange feeling, seeing him lying there, dead, when I'd just sat next to him on the couch in Niko's living room.

I looked up at Niko. He was staring at Bryan, his expression frozen. I tapped his leg with my left hand—Gwen was gripping my right—and said, "You need to call the cops."

He nodded slowly, then pulled out his phone.

TEN

We gave the responding officers from the Beverly Hills Police Department the most minimal statement we could—leaving out what we knew about Bryan's investment scam. They could figure that out on their own. I had a feeling the BHPD wouldn't be handling this case for long.

The death of a wealthy white man from Beverly Hills—even if he was a con artist—was a fairly big deal. It was possible that the elite Robbery Homicide Division—also known as RHD, where Dale worked—would take it over. I told Niko I'd give Dale a call later tonight and find out what he knew. Niko headed to the hospital to see Sophia, and I went back to work.

Michy left me a message saying she'd gone out to buy office supplies (and put the phone on automatic answer), and Alex was tracking down a witness on my carjacking case. So the office was quiet. Usually it'd be a great time to get things done. But it was almost impossible to concentrate. I deal with homicide cases every day, but it's not every day I actually find the dead body myself.

After a couple of frustrating hours trying to put the sight of Bryan's blue-tinged face out of my mind, I put in the call to Dale. I made my voice as pleasant and nonchalant as I could. "Hey, how've you been?"

Dale's voice was flat. "About the same as I was when you asked me to run that witness's license plate last week."

I definitely did ask him for information now and then. Okay, maybe a little more often than that. But that road stretched both ways. He'd picked a bad time to play the "you only call when you need something" game with me. "So I guess that'd be about the same time you asked me to look over your search warrant for that yakuza gang house in Koreatown?"

Dale sighed. "Don't tell me—let me guess. You want to know what we've got on the Bryan Posner death."

The fact that he already knew who I was calling about was good news. It meant RHD was looking into the case. "That'd be nice."

Papers shuffled in the background. "Preliminary blood testing showed a BA of 0.12 percent."

It was a pretty high blood alcohol level. But I'd seen higher. "He wasn't blasted, then."

Dale grunted. "But if he hadn't eaten in a while, it was probably enough to let him fall asleep and drown."

That did seem possible. And yet . . . "You think they'll say it's accidental?"

"As opposed to suicide? BHPD didn't find a note—not that that rules it out. But according to the mother, he'd never off himself. Of course . . ."

That's what the parents always say. "Yeah." I noticed Dale hadn't mentioned anything about the recent investment debacle. For a change, I might be out ahead of him on this one. "Anyone fill you in on his cryptocurrency trade? It tanked, and he wiped out a lot of people."

"Hadn't heard about that trade specifically. But BHPD said they'd been getting calls from some investors involved in Gold Strike about a week ago, demanding an investigation. Hang on." He clicked off, then came back. "Gotta go. It's the BHPD captain. Call you back."

"Wait, tell me—" But he was gone. Damn. I'd been about to ask if RHD was taking over the case.

I hate when he does that.

A few minutes later, Michy came back. I went out to her desk. "I've got news, but let's wait for Alex." I didn't want to tell the story twice.

Half an hour later, Alex appeared, looking irritated. He didn't take even the smallest failure well. "No luck with the witness?"

He gave a disgusted snort. "I know where he hangs. I think his homies are just keeping a look out. But don't worry, I'll get him."

I waved him off. "I know you will."

Michy pulled a bag of Doritos out of her purse and held it up. "You mind? I didn't have time for lunch, and I'm starving."

I hadn't eaten, either, and I happen to love Doritos. I lived on them when I was in undergrad. "Hell no, I don't mind. If you don't mind sharing."

She took a few chips and held out the bag. "So what's the big news you couldn't tell me until Alex got here?"

I reached into the bag and grabbed a few. "Bryan's gone to that great big Ponzi scheme in the sky." I told them about how we'd found his body.

Michy shuddered. "I can't even imagine what that must've been like."

Alex, who'd grown up in a rough neighborhood, said nothing. I had a feeling he didn't have any trouble imagining what that was like. I posed the question that'd been on an endless loop in my head all day. "What do you think? Accident? Suicide? Or a homicide dressed up to look like one of the above?"

Michy wiped some chip crumbs off her chin. "I think it could be any of the above."

"Same." Alex paused with a chip in hand. "And I actually made some headway on that trade. Your hunch was right. There was no trade.

Bryan just straight-up stole the money. Dummied up some paperwork and diverted it all into a private account."

That definitely tilted my view on Bryan's death. "Any chance the other investors figured that out?" Getting bilked out of life savings was as good a motive for murder as any.

Alex shrugged. "Like you always say, anything's possible. But I got the impression no one except Tanner even knew about the cryptocurrency trade."

Michy plucked another chip from the bag. "Do you think Tanner figured out that there was no trade?"

He certainly had a better chance of getting that information than the investors. But I wasn't sure it mattered. "If we're thinking Tanner might've killed Bryan, he didn't need to know that the cryptocurrency trade was bullshit to have a motive. Finding out that Bryan had been stealing investors' money and all the Gold Strike profits would do the trick." The more I thought about it, the more sense it made. "Alex, could you—"

He stood up. "Yes, I can definitely look into Tanner."

Alex headed to his office, and I went back to mine and called Dale. Now that Bryan was dead, there was no reason to avoid the cops.

I told him what'd happened the night we went to the Gold Strike offices and what we'd learned about Bryan's financial scam.

He was less than thrilled to hear that we'd broken into Bryan's safe. "Burglary, malicious mischief, theft. Let's see, have I left anything out?"

"Trespassing and hacking. Technically speaking. You're complaining? It would've taken you guys a week just to get into his office, let alone his safe—"

He interrupted, "One day, tops."

"You wish the cops moved that fast. And where's the gratitude? We just gave you a prime suspect. Assuming the coroner says this was a homicide."

"Yes, assuming that minor detail. So you think Tanner did it, right? Because he found out Bryan ripped him off."

He had that semibored "I know you think you're smart" tone that always pisses me off. "Yeah. And was planning to disappear with the money."

His tone was sarcastic. "Awesome. That does it. Case closed."

He can be so annoying. "It's damn good evidence of motive. And there's more." I told him about the fake cryptocurrency trade. "I think Tanner was the only one who even knew about that trade. Which turned out to be fake. And which he could've found out before anyone else. So there's even more motive."

"Just one problem, Columbo: time of death. None of that spells motive unless the coroner puts the time of death at some point after Tanner found all that out." He paused. "Again, assuming the coroner even says it's a homicide."

I replayed Tanner's behavior the night he'd pounded on Niko's door. He'd already seemed pretty sure that Bryan had ripped him off. But he'd been so frantic, so crazed about finding Bryan. Could that have been an act? If so, it was a pretty good one. And a slick move to kill Bryan, then pretend he didn't know where Bryan was. "That's what we need to find out, isn't it?"

"Not 'we.' Me. Unless you plan to file a wrongful death lawsuit for Bryan's next of kin."

"An excellent idea. I hadn't thought of it. Thanks. Even more reason why you should look into Tanner. It'd help me out." Dale sighed. "Listen, I just think it's a little too convenient that Bryan happened to check out after pulling off a multimillion-dollar scam. And Tanner knew Bryan best, knew where he lived, knew his habits and probably how to get into his duplex. Might even have had a key." Of course he'd claimed he didn't have one. But I saw no reason to take his word for that—or anything else.

I heard computer keys clicking in the background. "Fine," Dale said. "I'll have him checked out. Now tell me you wore gloves when you broke into that office."

Ordinarily I would have. But I hadn't expected to do a full-on search of the damn place. "Uh, no."

"Shit, you've got to be kid—"

I interrupted. "Give me some credit. I wiped everything down. They won't find me anywhere."

He swore under his breath. "They'd better not."

This time I saw it coming. I pressed end—just in time to hear the three beeps telling me that he'd beaten me to it. Again.

I was on my way to go talk to Alex about the question Dale had raised, but just as I stood up, Alex appeared in the doorway, iPad in hand. "I've got some interesting background on Tanner."

I waved him in. "Perfect timing." He flopped down on the couch and opened his iPad. "Could Tanner have figured out that Bryan had scammed him before you hacked into his computer—I mean, for sure?"

"And pretend he didn't know so he'd have a cover for killing Bryan?" I nodded. Alex glanced at his iPad. "Not that I've seen so far. But he does have kind of a murky past."

Interesting. "How so?"

He scrolled upward on the screen. "If I have the right guy, he used to go by the name Tanner Gormansky. No legal name change, so I'm not a hundred percent sure. But the photos match up pretty well. And when he was still Tanner Gormansky, he worked at a stock brokerage house in Delaware for about a year and a half."

The name change was a little odd, but otherwise it didn't seem all that murky to me. "Anything else?"

Alex peered at the screen. "I think he might've gotten fired. I called the human resources department—"

I smiled. "Who'd you pretend to be?" No one could social engineer his way into confidential files like Alex.

He looked up with a little smirk. "A very bored managerial assistant at Coldwell Banker, doing a security clearance check on our boy Tanner, who'd applied for the position of commercial accounts manager."

Not too much. Just elaborate enough to sound legit. "Nice. How much did you squeeze out of them?"

He gave a slight shake of the head. "Not as much as I'd hoped for. When I asked whether she'd recommend him for the job, she just said all she could do was confirm he'd worked there. I said a year and a half wasn't that long—that it seemed to me like something must've gone wrong. She said, 'Let's just say no one sweated his departure.'"

Vague, but clearly something *had* gone wrong. "So he might've gotten fired."

Alex shrugged. "Or he might've quit."

"Hopefully Dale will come through." I told him about the conversation we'd just had.

Alex stood up. "Good. I'll keep at it, but let me know when you hear back."

I said I would, and Alex went back to his office. In deference to Michy's desire for Manolos, I dived into my billing sheets. There was no part of my gig I hated more, so this truly was an act of love. And—I had to admit—necessity.

At four o'clock, I'd just finished and was thinking I might just pack it in for the day when Michy buzzed me and said Dale was on the line.

"Thanks, Michy." I picked up, thinking he must have information on Tanner. "What've you got?"

I didn't hear the usual hum of activity in the background on Dale's end. Either he'd gone home to make the call or everyone else had left for the day. Still, he kept his voice low. "I shouldn't be telling you this. So whatever you decide to do after you hear it, you've got to cover me."

What the . . . ? Whatever it was, it wasn't good. I didn't want to hear it, but I had to. "I'll cover you. Tell me."

He spoke rapidly. "The coroner just filled me in on cause of death. It's a homicide all right, but I've never heard anything like it. He said Bryan Posner died of internal decapitation—"

I jerked up in my seat. "What the hell is that?"

Dale lowered his voice even more. "It's a super-rare injury. Happens when there's a blow to the head or neck that's heavy enough to sever the ligaments that attach the skull to the spine. Coroner said he's only seen it once before, when a six-year-old boy died in a car crash. I guess those ligaments are softer in a young kid."

But Bryan wasn't a child, and he clearly hadn't been in a car accident. "So how could he have gotten an injury like that?"

Dale took a deep breath. "The coroner didn't know. He had to look that up. Apparently, it's a kill method known to some martial artists. Takes strength and skill. According to the coroner, more skill than strength." He paused. "I'm not officially assigned to the case, but I know the detective who is. Doug Kingsford. He's good. Really good. It'll take him about ten seconds to put it together—if he hasn't already."

My heart was pounding so hard, I could barely catch my breath. A skilled martial artist. Like Niko. No doubt he had the skill. And he definitely had the motive. Because of Bryan, Niko's mother was on life support. One ray of hope dawned. "Did the coroner say when Bryan was killed?" Niko and I had been together almost continuously for days.

"On the sixteenth. Based on stomach contents, sometime between five p.m. and midnight."

The ray of hope died. The sixteenth was one of the only days Niko and I hadn't been together.

I couldn't believe it. Didn't want to believe it.

But it all fit so well.

ELEVEN

I knew Dale assumed I'd head straight to Niko's place to warn him that the cops were coming.

And he was right. I told Michy I had to go see Niko (though I didn't tell her why) and flew out the door. As I headed for my car, I thought about whether I should let him talk to the cops.

As a general rule, I tell my clients to keep their mouths shut. I warn them that no matter how "nice" they are, those cops are not their friends. You wouldn't think I'd need to tell them something this obvious, but you'd be wrong. For some reason, even a few of my repeat customers think if they just "explain" what really happened, the cops will say, "Thanks for clearing that up!" and let them go.

Niko was smarter than most of my clients—probably smart enough not to screw himself. Still, even smart people can say pretty dumb things. Especially if they're amateurs. Which, as far as I knew, Niko was. But I'd be sitting right next to him the whole time, and if he had a solid alibi for Bryan's murder, it'd be good to get him cleared as soon as possible. On the other hand, if he didn't . . .

I'd just gotten into my car when my cell phone rang. It was Niko.

He spoke evenly, but there was an underlying tension in his voice. "Sam, the housekeeper just called and said that a couple of detectives are at the door. What's going on? Did something happen?"

Shit! I tried to sound calm. "Where are you?"

His agitation was building. "In the car, almost home."

I didn't know whether they'd posted unis in the area to intercept Niko. But if they had, it wouldn't look good if they saw him make a sudden U-turn. And I was afraid to tell Niko what I'd just learned about Bryan's murder. I didn't know how he'd react, and I had no time to coach him. Right now, I just needed to keep him from talking until I got there. "Okay, then go home. Be nice, but do not let them pressure you into saying one fucking word. Tell them you'd like to wait for your lawyer. Got it?"

Niko's voice was tight. "Got it."

"I'm on my way." As I pulled out of the garage, I wondered whether Niko had killed Bryan. True, he'd sounded genuinely confused, but I wasn't sure whether that was real or whether he was just a much better actor than I knew.

I made it to Niko's house in just twelve minutes, but when I walked in, I saw it was already too late. Niko was seated on the couch across from two detectives, and they were deep in conversation. A mini recorder was on the coffee table. The red light showed it was turned on. He'd completely ignored my advice. Damn. After all the stories I'd told Niko about the clients who'd sunk themselves by talking to the cops, you'd think he'd have listened to me. And to make matters worse, I saw that there was a small plastic vial with a long Q-tip inside it on the coffee table. The detectives had already managed to get Niko to give them a buccal swab for his DNA.

As I walked into the living room, the bigger of the two detectives stood and put out his hand. "I assume you're the lawyer, Samantha Brinkman?"

He had short, sandy-colored hair and brown eyes, and he was tall, over six feet. His body was a solid—but not fat—rectangle. His hand engulfed mine as we shook. "I am. And you are?"

He fixed me with a direct look. "Doug Kingsford." He nodded to the other detective, who was bald and seemed to be a lot shorter and thinner. I couldn't tell how much shorter or thinner because he didn't stand. "My partner, Dan O'Malley."

Dan briefly looked up and gave me a curt nod as I joined them on the couch. I wasn't happy, and I didn't mind letting it be known. "Before you go any further, I'd like to have a private word with my client."

Niko held up a hand. "It's okay, Sam. They told me about Bryan, and I have nothing to hide. I already told them everything I know."

I turned to Kingsford. "What about Bryan?" I had to pretend I didn't already know the cause of death.

O'Malley threw an openly suspicious glance at Niko as he answered. "Internal decapitation—a pretty rare martial arts move."

This was not good. The last thing Niko should be doing was letting them question him about it. But I had no choice. Now I had to go along with the program. "And what exactly did you tell them?"

His expression was earnest, open. "That I had nothing to do with Bryan's murder."

Kingsford looked from Niko to me. "He said Tanner and some of the investors took martial arts classes from him."

Niko nodded. "That's how they found out about Gold Strike. They were my students."

I tried to act blasé, though I was anything but. "So you taught the technique? Internal decapitation?" If he said yes, it would probably hurt as much as it helped. But there was no avoiding the subject. If the cops hadn't already asked, they would in the next few seconds.

Niko either didn't realize how damning his answer might be or knew better than to show he did. He answered calmly. "No. I've heard of it, but I don't know it, and I don't teach it." He added, "But I'm obviously not the only martial arts teacher in town . . ."

So Tanner or one of the investors could've learned it from someone else. But now, Kingsford and O'Malley would question all the investors who'd studied with Niko. If anyone said Niko had shown or taught that move, it'd be a serious nail in Niko's legal coffin.

Kingsford sat back and crossed his legs guy-style, his right foot resting on his left knee. A deliberately casual pose intended to get Niko to drop his guard. "But wouldn't someone have to be a pretty advanced student to kill Bryan that way?"

Niko started to open his mouth to answer. I wanted to clap my hand over it, but I opted for the more subtle approach and just cut him off. "Not necessarily. I mean, how much of a master would a person have to be to get the jump on Bryan?"

Niko nodded. "That's true. Bryan wasn't in great shape."

I added, "And he'd been drinking. Besides, how complicated is this move?"

Niko paused a moment. "From what I remember, not very."

Dan—definitely the less polished member of the team—leaned forward. "You mind going over your timeline for that evening with us again? I just want to make sure we've got it straight."

Bullshit. He was looking for inconsistencies. I gave good old Dan an insincere smile. "He's obviously already gone over it with you, so you guys can just run with what you've got."

Dan was visibly irritated, but Kingsford returned my insincere smile with one of his own. He was smart—and smooth. This was not what I liked to see in a detective. I like my cops ham-fisted, slow-witted, and short-tempered. Kind of like Dan—at least from what I could tell so far.

But I got stymied again, as Niko came to their rescue. Damn him. He put his hands on his knees and stared at the mantel above the fireplace as he recounted his movements on the night of the murder. "I went to see Tanner around seven thirty that night. We brainstormed about what kinds of investments might help people recoup at least some of their money within the next year or so. I left his house around nine thirty, then checked in on my mother. Got home around ten thirty or eleven."

According to Dale, the coroner had put Bryan's time of death between five p.m. and midnight. But I knew Bryan's mother had said she'd called him at nine thirty and that he hadn't answered, which was well within that window. So Niko's timeline put him in the clear. Assuming it was true.

Kingsford stretched an arm across the back of the couch—just a chill bro talking to his homie. "Hey, maybe we should get ahold of Tanner. See if he'll back you up."

Niko gave a brief nod. "He will."

"Why don't you try him now?" Kingsford—the ever-helpful cop—suggested.

What an asshole. But a very friggin' smart asshole. This put Niko on the spot. He couldn't refuse to make the call without looking guilty. Time to give him some cover. I held up a hand. "He doesn't need to do this right now."

But of course, the ever-helpful Niko thwarted me again. "I don't mind." I wanted to throttle him as he pulled his cell phone out of his pocket.

He touched a key, and Tanner's name popped up on the screen. After a few seconds, he frowned. Then, in an impatient tone, he said, "Hey, man, it's Niko. Hit me up when you get this. Thanks." Niko slid his phone back into his pocket. "I'll tell him to get in touch with you guys when he calls. I know he'll back me up."

My heart—which had been beating so fast I could hardly breathe—slowed to a livable pace. Not that I doubted Niko's innocence. Well, I guess I kind of did. But it was nothing personal. I'm suspicious of everyone. Regardless, I definitely didn't share Niko's faith in Tanner. Who knew what might come out of that little punk's mouth?

It was time to put an end to this tea party. I stood and held out my hand to Kingsford. "It's been a pleasure, Detective." My tight smile said I was lying—and I could tell he knew it.

Not that he cared. He stood and shook my hand with pressed lips. "Actually, I was thinking maybe Niko wouldn't mind taking us to Tanner's office. See if he's hiding out there. We all know Tanner's got some pretty pissed-off investors on his tail."

I knew Kingsford was just trying to make sure he was on the scene when Niko asked him to confirm his alibi, so he could see for himself how Tanner reacted before Niko had a chance to try and program his response.

I was about to tell Kingsford he could go by himself. But if Tanner was there, that would leave him alone with the detectives. I didn't want to risk that. And now that I thought about it, I realized I could make this work to my advantage. "I'm good with that. In fact, I'll join you."

Dan gave me an icy glare and started to shake his head. But Niko—finally—got with the program. "I'll only go if Sam can come."

Kingsford shrugged. "Okay by me. You can ride with us."

I wanted to talk to Niko alone on the way there, maybe strategize how to handle it if Tanner didn't back up his alibi—and Kingsford knew it. He was heading me off at the pass. His constant one-upmanship moves were getting on my nerves. "That's okay. I've got my car—"

But Niko was already heading for the door. "Thanks. Probably safer to go with you guys, what with all those angry investors floating around."

Damn it. Niko was turning out to be one of the biggest pain-in-the-ass clients ever.

But before I could say another word, he was out the door, with the detectives right behind him. I slung my purse on my shoulder and vowed to have a serious talk with Niko about who calls the shots when cops come knocking.

TWELVE

When we got to the swanky building that housed the Gold Strike offices, I pretended to be seeing it for the first time and prayed Niko would know better than to let on that he'd been there recently. The cops would be coming to search this place any minute, and when they did, they'd find out someone had broken into Bryan's safe. I didn't need to give Kingsford any ideas that that someone might've been Niko—or me.

The building manager let us in. No lights were on, so the reception area was relatively dark. Niko pointed out Tanner's office. The door was locked. I didn't remember seeing Tanner lock it when we'd left, but I supposed he must have. Kingsford asked the manager to open the door. I folded my arms. "Excuse me? Aren't we forgetting a little something called a search warrant?"

Without a second's hesitation, he responded, "Exigent circumstances. We're concerned for his safety. For all we know, he could be lying there in a pool of blood."

I wasn't sure that'd fly with a judge, but truth be told, I didn't really care. Tanner wasn't my client, and I was sure there wouldn't be anything that incriminated Niko in his office. I shrugged. "Whatever. Your funeral."

Kingsford nodded to the manager, who sifted through his ring of keys and unlocked the door. It was a sunny day, and the floor-to-ceiling windows let in plenty of light. Nothing looked out of place. If anything, Tanner's formerly messy desk looked a little neater, like he'd cleared off some of the Post-its and notepads.

Kingsford and O'Malley took a long look around the office, then peered under the desk and checked out the bathroom. I had no doubt they'd have gone through the desk and maybe even tried to get into Tanner's computer if I hadn't been there. But I was, and now that it was clear there were no dead or dying bodies, there was no legitimate reason to search without a warrant. Kingsford thanked the building manager, told him to lock up, and we headed out.

But Kingsford wasn't giving up. When we got back in the car, he said, "I have a bad feeling about this. I think we should head over to Tanner's place."

I was stuck. If I objected, they'd just go by themselves, and if Tanner was home, I wanted to be there. I snapped on my seat belt. "Sounds like a plan."

Niko gave the directions to Tanner's condo, which was in one of those high-end forty-story buildings on Wilshire Boulevard, just five minutes from the office. Kingsford badged the doorman, who nodded at Niko and gave me a curious glance. He called the supervisor, a fluttery woman with wild red hair, and she accompanied us up to the thirty-fifth floor.

The hallway was wide with high ceilings, and the thick carpeting muffled our footsteps as we approached his door. Tanner's condo was the last one on the left. I scanned the doorway but saw no evidence of forced entry. Kingsford gestured for Niko to do the honors. "I think he'll be more likely to open up if he hears a friendly voice on the other side."

Niko gave a brief nod and pushed the doorbell that was on the wall to the right. We heard the *ding-dong* loud and clear. But then, nothing. I leaned in as Niko rang it again, listening for any rustling or footsteps—any sound that someone was there. Silence.

I'd been skeptical when Kingsford theorized that Tanner might be lying in a pool of blood. But now, I was starting to think there might be something to it. This time, when he asked the supervisor to open the door, I didn't object.

The foyer led into a living room with a 180-degree view of the city. It was an open-concept layout. The dining area was to the right of the living room, and it flowed into a gleaming white kitchen with the latest high-end appliances. But strangely, there was almost no furniture, and what few pieces there were—a sofa, a coffee table, two club chairs—looked like third-hand IKEA cast-offs that were way too small for the spacious, high-ceilinged condo.

O'Malley told us to wait in the foyer while they did a quick sweep. From where I stood, I couldn't see any signs of a struggle or ransacking. A few minutes later, he came out and waved Niko over. "We need you to take a look around with us and see if anything seems . . . off."

I wasn't specifically invited, but I didn't care. I followed closely behind Niko and ignored O'Malley's glowering look. We headed down a short hallway, looked into a large—and completely unfurnished—guest bedroom, an adjoining en suite bathroom, and then entered the master bedroom.

Niko stopped and stared at the king-size bed. He pointed to the blue blanket on the bed. "That's wrong. He had a gray comforter. I've never seen that blanket before." He moved into the room and headed for a set of double doors. "Maybe it's in here—"

Kingsford grabbed him by the arm. "Don't touch anything." He reached into his back pocket and pulled out a set of latex gloves. After he snapped them on, he gingerly grasped one of the doorknobs between his thumb and index finger and turned it.

I peered over his shoulder and saw that it was a walk-in closet. The hanging rod and shelves on the right were full, but the left side was empty. Niko scanned the space. Kingsford pointed to the empty spot. "Did he have clothes there before?"

Niko shrugged. "I don't know. I didn't hang out in his bedroom. I only noticed that the comforter was missing because we passed by this room to get to the den."

Kingsford and O'Malley shined their flashlights around the closet. There was no sign of the gray comforter.

O'Malley asked Niko to show them the den. He led us to a room at the end of the hallway. It wasn't as big as the master bedroom, but it was the only one that seemed to have been furnished well enough to be comfortable.

A large burgundy sectional couch, with navy and burgundy pillows, and a matching ottoman and recliner faced a huge ninety-inch flat-screen. I didn't know they made flat-screens that big. Game controllers in a shallow silver bowl on the square mahogany coffee table showed that this was where Tanner did most of his living, and probably entertaining.

But as I looked closer, I noticed a table lamp had been knocked to the floor, along with one of the couch pillows. On the side table between the ottoman and the couch, I saw a half-consumed bottle of beer and an empty wineglass. Tanner had had company. Possibly angry company. But I didn't see any bloodstains. If the lamp and pillow were signs of a struggle, it didn't seem to be a very violent one. I saw Kingsford and O'Malley exchange a look.

O'Malley put his hands on his hips. "You and Tanner get into a fight?"

Niko had been staring at the table lamp on the floor. It took a second for the question to register. "No. I mean, we argued. But it didn't get physical."

Kingsford homed in. "When was that? Before or after Bryan got killed?"

Niko seemed frozen for a moment. "A day or two after, I think."

I saw O'Malley write that down. If that turned out to be the last time anyone saw Tanner, Niko had just managed to screw himself again. I tried to give him some cover. I asked, "Do you know whether Tanner planned to have someone come over after you saw him?"

He shook his head. "But he must have. 'Cause neither of us was drinking beer or wine."

O'Malley gave Niko a sharp look. "Are you sure?"

Niko glanced at the glass. "Yeah. I'm sure."

Bad move. It's always better to give a wishy-washy "I don't remember" than a definitive "yes" or "no." I couldn't expect Niko to know that. And even if he had, with his mother hovering near death, he was in no shape to think clearly. But I got the feeling he had no idea how messed up he was.

I thought it was entirely possible he *had* drunk from that wineglass and just didn't remember. Or that he had knocked over that table lamp during their argument and didn't realize it. But the cops wouldn't see it that way. If Niko turned out to be wrong, if they found his prints on the lamp or the wineglass, they'd see it as a deliberate lie—and evidence that he'd been the one who'd fought with Tanner. And possibly killed him.

O'Malley had pulled his cell phone out and was taking photos of the room—and particularly the beer bottle and wineglass. He asked Kingsford, "Do we take them with us? Or wait for a warrant?"

Kingsford studied the bottle and glass for a few seconds. I knew what he was thinking. If someone had kidnapped or killed Tanner, and his—or her—prints or DNA were on the items, the evidence would be admissible. The only person who had the right to object to the cops seizing evidence from Tanner's condo without a warrant was Tanner. And he was unlikely to object if he was dead. On the other hand, if it turned out Tanner was okay, it wouldn't matter whose prints or DNA were on the bottle and glass. Kingsford made his decision. "Take them."

O'Malley nodded as he pulled a pair of latex gloves out of his pocket and snapped them on. "We need paper bags, right? Not plastic." Kingsford nodded, and O'Malley left the room.

Kingsford took another look around the room, then asked Niko, "Do you happen to know where Tanner keeps his passport—or his valuables?"

"No," Niko said. "The thing is, Tanner didn't really own pricey stuff, as you can see." He swept a hand behind him to indicate the whole condo. "He put on a good front in public, dressed well and all that, but for him, making money was an end to itself. He didn't care that much about what it could buy."

O'Malley came back with two brown paper grocery bags, and Kingsford carefully put the bottle and glass inside. He looked around the room. "Not much more we can do here for the moment." He gestured for us to head out and started to pull off his gloves, then thought better of it. "Make sure not to touch anything. I'll open the door."

As we made our way out to the elevator, I considered what I'd seen in Tanner's condo. It didn't look like a killing scene. I leaned more toward the theory that he'd just gone into hiding. With the long list of irate investors on his tail, it'd be the safest thing for him to do. And if he'd been the one who stole all the investor money, he'd definitely be able to afford to buy a high-quality fake ID and disappear. Maybe buy a small island. Hire people to build him a villa, make him delicious feasts, serve him all kinds of exotic drinks . . .

I'd veered into my own fantasy. But the more I thought about it, the more it made sense that Tanner was on the run. As we headed for the elevator, I floated that theory to Kingsford. "We haven't seen anything that even remotely looks like a crime scene, let alone a murder scene. Isn't it just as likely that he's hiding out?"

Kingsford didn't respond until we were in the elevator and the doors had closed. "Can't say it's just as likely. Too many people had motive to off him, and I'm not sure he's got the connects to get a fake ID good enough to get him out of the country. But obviously, I can't rule that out." He paused, then added, "Yet."

THIRTEEN

Niko was silent as we rode back to his house. I could see he was in turmoil as he stared out the window, his expression a mix of sadness and anxiety. Was it just because of his mother's condition? Or was he hiding something from me? Maybe something about Bryan's death—or Tanner's disappearance?

Niko had never given me the feeling that he was keeping anything from me before. But I was getting that feeling now. I knew Michy would say it was just my usual "issue." She says my suspicious nature borders on paranoia, that I could find an ulterior motive for a late mail delivery. Fair enough. But as they say, even a clock that's broken is right twice a day. I may be overly suspicious, but that doesn't mean I'm wrong.

When the cops dropped us back at Niko's house, he said he wanted to go see his mother. I put a hand on his shoulder. "It's been a pretty stressful day. Don't you want to chill out for a bit before you go?"

He seemed agitated. "Thanks, but I don't need to rest; I need to see her."

I knew better than to argue. "Call me later if you feel like talking. Or if you want me to come over, okay?"

He put his arms around me. "I'm so lucky to have you. I don't tell you that enough, but I want you to know that I'm aware of it." He leaned back and looked me in the eye. "And I think about it every single day."

This kind of loving sentiment—especially gratitude—always makes me uncomfortable. Like an impostor. I don't deserve it. I smiled. "I think you must've been with some real witches in the past if you think I'm all that."

Niko returned my smile and sighed. "I hope someday you'll be able to see the truth about who you really are."

And now we were in territory I liked even less. "You're not so bad yourself." I kissed him and pulled away. "Keep me posted about your mom."

Niko's expression showed he knew this was making me uncomfortable. "Will do."

I checked the time when I got into my car. It was six p.m. Early enough to put a dent in my in-box. I headed to the office and found Alex sitting on his blue exercise ball—one of those oversize, inflatable things that're supposed to make you use your core—next to Michy's desk. Michy was reading something to him that was on her monitor. Apparently it was hilarious because they were both laughing. I was in no mood for hilarity. "Nice to see everyone's hard at work."

Michy looked up and raised an eyebrow. "Nice to see you, too, Cruella. Actually, if you'd gotten here ten minutes ago, you'd have seen we were both slaving away."

Alex swiveled to face me. "Did Niko have any idea where Tanner might be?"

I'd forgotten to ask him, but the answer was clear. "No." I told them about Niko talking to Kingsford and O'Malley and our visits to Tanner's office and condo.

Michy asked, "So you don't think someone got to Tanner? You think he just took off?"

I shrugged. I couldn't be sure of that, and I was annoyed at my own indecision. "I *think* so." I asked Alex, "Did you dig up any more information on Tanner?"

"Not yet. But I will. I found his ex-girlfriend." I opened my mouth to ask how he'd managed to do that. I didn't think even Niko knew anything about Tanner's love life. But Alex held up a hand. "Don't ask. Just be thankful for the genius that is me."

Michy folded her arms and glared at him. "Who never would've figured out how to find her without the help of yours truly."

In spite of my foul mood, I couldn't help but smile. Somehow, these two always managed to pull me out of a funk. "Well, however you did it, thanks, guys." An ex-girlfriend can be a font of information. Especially if the relationship ended badly.

Alex's cell phone rang in his office, and he went to answer it. Michy ran through the list of calls we'd received. Mostly just routine stuff, clients and their families asking for updates on their cases. But one was encouraging. Michy's lips twitched as she read the message. "That D.A. on the Angelo Lopez case wants to meet."

Angelo Lopez got busted with two AK-47s in his trunk. Not only are those guns illegal in California, but Angelo also had a felony conviction for second-degree burglary. So he wasn't allowed to have any kind of gun. He insisted someone had put the guns in the trunk without his knowing. The problem with that story was that a passerby had reported seeing those guns when Angelo opened the trunk and showed them to the shot caller of a notoriously dangerous gang. The cops—rightly—deduced that Angelo was making a sale.

Angelo didn't admit it to me—my clients almost never did—but this case had "loser" written all over it. If I didn't get the D.A. to make a deal, Angelo was going to spend some serious time in jail. His wife and two little girls would most certainly wind up on the street.

I had just one ace in the hole. Angelo himself wasn't a gang member. He was an entrepreneur. Albeit one who didn't worry much about which side of the law his deals landed on. That meant he got around. A *lot*. I'd thought that might mean he was dialed in to some really high-level shot callers. I told Angelo that if he was willing to talk, I might be able to get the D.A. to give him a sweet deal. He didn't like the idea. Not because he had any loyalty issues, but because snitching might very well land him in a coffin. It'd taken some pounding . . . uh, persuading, but when I pointed out what would happen to his family if he got convicted, Angelo had eventually agreed.

Then I'd had Alex pay a visit to the shot caller and ask, i.e., suggest, that the passerby who'd supposedly spotted the guns in Angelo's trunk was actually a member of a rival gang who was out to get him and that there were no guns in the trunk, only car parts. The shot caller was happy to provide a written statement to that effect—in exchange for the promise of my free services the next time he got busted. I expected to have to deliver on that promise in the *very* near future. But in the meantime, I had ammunition to use with the D.A., and use it I did.

The fact that he wanted to meet with me now showed he was ready to deal. "So it worked. I love when that happens."

Michy asked, "When do you want to go see Angelo?"

I needed to find out what information he could give to the D.A. But I'd have no trouble finding him. He hadn't been able to make bail. "ASAP. Check my calendar for the earliest available date. I don't want the D.A. to change his mind."

I went to my office, sank down on the couch, and closed my eyes. A few seconds later, I heard footsteps and looked up to see Michy in the doorway. "What's up?"

She sat down at the other end of the couch and gave me a knowing look. "You've been wondering whether Niko killed Bryan, haven't you?"

I nodded. "And maybe Tanner, too." After all the sweet things he'd said to me, it made me feel like a shithead to suspect him. But the possibility existed, and I couldn't ignore it.

Michy sighed. "And you feel guilty for even thinking that." I gave her a wan smile. "You know I'm usually the first to say that you're so insanely suspicious, you'd think the dry cleaners were up to no good if they lost a napkin. But not this time. You think you'd be fooling yourself if you weren't considering the possibility that he might've killed at least one of them."

I leaned back and closed my eyes again. "You know, I always thought I'd be glad to finally hear you say you didn't think I was pathologically suspicious."

Michy shook her head. "Sorry."

Alex knocked on the doorframe. "I've got news." He walked in, turned the chair in front of my desk around so he could face me, and sat down. "Tanner's an asshole."

I rubbed my throbbing temples as I glanced at him through half-open eyes. "Really? The guy who trolls for women at Sex Addicts Anonymous is an asshole? No way."

Alex opened his iPad. "That's nothing. I just heard back from his ex, Amber Simmons. She's kind of a piece of work herself. But she told one hell of a breakup story. They met when she was working as a cocktail waitress at a pricey gentlemen's club."

I stared at him. "Really? You can't just say strip club?"

Alex gave me a flat look. "Why on earth you'd think that is beyond me. I say what I mean." He tapped a few keys on his iPad, then handed it to me. "Not a pole or a stage in sight from what I could tell."

I scrolled through the photos. He was right. It actually looked like one of those old-school "men only" clubs where the waiters wore white coats and black pants and carried a white linen towel over one arm. Persian rugs, potted palms, expensive-looking leather and cherry-wood furniture, and lots of brass accents. I handed the iPad back to him. "When did they get together?"

Alex paused, then said, "About ten years ago."

That meant Tanner had been in his twenties at the time. "How did he score a ticket to a place like that?"

"The manager. Amber wasn't clear on the details, but she remembered Tanner bragging about how he'd talked the guy into investing in some commodity stocks and made him a bunch of money."

I'd expected to hear he'd framed the manager or had some dirt on him. "Was that for real? Or did he scam the manager?"

Alex shook his head. "No, it was for real."

Not exactly Tanner's style, but now that I thought about it, that made sense. "Even if he didn't really have some great tip on commodities and just paid the guy out of his own pocket, it would've been worth it to get access to all those rich old guys. So what happened with the girlfriend?"

He crossed his legs and set the iPad on the chair next to him. "You were right. Tanner worked the club members hard and got a few to invest with him. Things went well at first. But he got greedy and jumped into riskier and riskier deals. He kept weaving them stories about all the money they were making, but he was losing money hand over fist."

Tanner was consistent. I'd give him that. "How does all that tie in with Amber?"

A look of disgust crossed his face. "Some of the investors wanted to take their profits and run. But of course there were no profits, so Tanner needed to come up with some cash fast."

I had a bad feeling about where this was going. "Don't tell me he—"

Alex nodded. "Yeah, he pimped Amber out."

I felt my gut clench. "How?"

Alex folded his arms across his chest. "When he was in London a few years back, he managed to get tight with some Saudi prince who was a kinkster."

Ugh. "And was willing to pay megabucks for his fun."

Alex nodded. "Tens of thousands per night for him and his friends to do . . . whatever."

Sometimes—like now—I wished I didn't have to know about all this ugly shit. "And Amber went along with it?"

"Yeah," Alex said. "Tanner said if she could find a friend to join her, he'd give her a cut. Amber needed the money, and she had a couple of friends who fit the bill, so . . ."

Michy frowned. "But even if that prince paid fifty thousand for the night, how would that be enough to bail Tanner out? It sounds like he was in bigger trouble than that."

Alex pointed at her. "Exactly. That's why he intended to make it a regular thing. But he didn't tell Amber that, and it turned out the Saudi prince was into some pretty painful kink. After the first night, Amber said she was out."

What a horrifying scenario. "So she refused to do . . . whatever? Did she tell you what it was?"

Alex held up a hand. "No, and I didn't ask. There's only so much despicable behavior I can take in one sitting."

I was puzzled. "You said their breakup was pretty gnarly. Doesn't seem that gnarly to me."

"Because that's not what happened. When Amber said she was out of the kinky prince business, Tanner said he understood, that he was sorry it turned out to be so awful. He invited Amber and her friend to have dinner at his house to make it up to them. And then he roofied them."

Oh God. An awful story had managed to get even worse. "And turned them over to the prince and his buddies."

Alex gave a grim nod. "Amber and her friend woke up on the floor of her apartment, naked and bruised from head to toe. They were afraid they'd get busted for prostitution if they reported it to the police. But Amber quit her job at the club and never spoke to Tanner again."

I'd thought trolling for women at Sex Addicts Anonymous was pretty low.

But that was probably the nicest thing that asshole had done.

FOURTEEN

Dale tore off a piece of pita bread and dipped it in the hummus. "You think her story's legit?"

I'd invited him over for dinner to tell him about Amber and my now-crystallized theory about Tanner. For the sake of convenience—and safety—I'd decided to order in from our favorite Middle Eastern place rather than cook. Shawarma with rice and tabbouleh—and the best tahini I've ever had.

I took a sip of my pinot noir—one of my favorites from Ancien, a great winery in Napa. "I can't see what's in it for her to lie. She swore Alex to secrecy, so it's not like she's looking to get revenge." The statute of limitations had probably run out anyway.

Dale refilled his glass of wine. "Agree. I buy her story. So you think Tanner killed Bryan?"

I nodded. "And then tried to fake his own death and took off."

He picked up his wineglass and leaned back against the wingback chair. "It's not a bad theory. Except that it makes me wonder why he didn't do a better job of it. Mess his place up more, leave a few drops of blood. He just threw a couple of things on the floor and hit the road."

It was a good point. "I don't think he had any time for big, elaborate plans. And he's not exactly a forensic expert."

Dale swirled the wine in his glass. "But what about that comforter? Why would he take that with him?"

I hadn't come up with an answer to that one yet. "Who knows? Maybe he rented a car and plans to sleep in it for a while."

Dale sighed. "I guess. But you're a long way from proving any of that."

I didn't disagree, but in my mind I added *yet*—and tossed the ball into his court. "Any news on your end?"

"So far it seems like Niko might've been one of the last people to see Tanner." He gave me a warning look. "There's no indication he used his cell phone or any credit cards after Bryan's death. And none of the contacts we have for Tanner heard from him after that point."

That didn't punch any holes in my theory. "So what? Isn't that exactly what Tanner would do if he wanted to disappear? I'd bet he's got a burner phone." Because . . . doesn't everyone? I do. "Anything else?"

Dale only looked semiconvinced. "Just that Kingsford sent the glass and bottle in for testing. Put a rush on it."

A wave of anxiety washed over me. "Which means we'll get results when?"

Dale looked me in the eye. "Could be as soon as tomorrow night. You're sure Niko's being straight with you?"

I'm never sure anyone's being straight with me. Ever. "I . . . Yeah. I think so."

His expression was understanding. "Listen, whatever happens, I'm on his side. If my mother was on life support, I'd probably have killed both those shitbirds."

I returned Dale's gaze with a hint of a smile. "Yeah." I would, too. If my mother had been anything like Niko's—instead of the narcissistic, heartless, sociopathic robot I'd had for an egg donor.

We moved on to other topics: Dale's current girlfriend, the CSI tech at the LA Sheriff's Department he'd been seeing for the past year—a major-league hottie who was surprisingly funny—and stories about my clients and his perps.

It was a nice distraction from my worries about the test results, but when he left, the anxiety came rushing back. I took a hot shower, which usually soothes me, but this time it didn't work. I got into bed, but I couldn't relax. Finally, I caved and took a half milligram of Xanax. I'm not a big fan of drugs, but I'm a very big fan of sleep. I don't function well—or, quite frankly, at all—if I don't get at least five hours. If I spent the whole night angsting about what might happen with Niko, I'd be useless for the whole day.

The Xanax finally hit at about one thirty, and I slept until my cell phone alarm rang at seven the next morning. I was still tired, but a megadose of caffeine would take care of that. I showered, dressed, put my face on, and downed three mugs of coffee, then headed to the office.

I didn't realize I was hungry until I saw the bag of bagels and tub of cream cheese on the table behind Michy's desk. "Whoever thought of this gets to drink free on me tonight."

Michy raised her hand. "And I get to pick the place."

I pulled out an onion bagel. "Sold."

I slathered on a thick layer of cream cheese and took the life-affirming deliciousness to my office. I savored the bagel as I scrolled through my emails, then dived into the usual mix of business for the day: phone calls, letters to the clients who were in prison, and a scan of the latest case decisions.

I was finishing up my last prisoner letter when Michy buzzed me to say Dale was on the line. I put the call on speaker and kept typing. "Hey. What's up?"

His voice was low. "Take me off speaker."

I'd been so focused on work, it took me a second to realize what Dale's call—and his urgent tone—might mean. My throat tightened as I picked up the receiver. "Okay, tell me."

"They got the test results back. Niko's prints and DNA are on the wineglass."

I dropped my head into my hand. "Shit!" I'd been afraid Niko's denial would be trouble. But still . . . "They can't bust him. They don't even know whether Tanner's dead."

Dale whispered, "Maybe so. But that's not their only option. Okay, I've gotta go."

The three beeps said Dale was gone. Damn it! What did that mean? "Not their only option"? Then it hit me. I grabbed my cell and called Niko. The call went straight to voice mail. I gathered my purse and briefcase and flew out to the reception area. I spoke over my shoulder to Michy as I headed for the door. "I'm going to Niko's."

She stood up. "What's wrong?"

"The cops are about to serve a search warrant on his place." If they hadn't already. "I'll call you later."

I ran out and hoped I could beat them there.

But when I turned onto Niko's street, that hope died. His driveway was filled with detectives' cars, and patrol cars lined the street in front of his house. I pounded the steering wheel. None of this would be happening if he'd just taken my advice and told Kingsford and O'Malley to go piss up a rope.

That wouldn't have stopped them from identifying his prints on the wineglass. The feds already had his prints. He had a passport and Global Entry. But now it looked like he'd lied. Not good. Very, very not good.

I got out and headed for the door, where a uni stood holding a logbook. He held up a hand. "I'm sorry, ma'am. No civilians allowed."

I was in a truly ugly mood, and I was A-OK with taking it out on a cop. "Yeah, well, I am allowed. I'm his lawyer." I handed him my card and pointed to his logbook. "So log me in and get out of my way."

He shook his head. "I'll have to check with the—"

O'Malley came up behind him. "It's okay, Van. Let her in."

I moved past the uni and said, "I want to see the warrant."

O'Malley gave me a sharp look. "You ever heard of the saying 'you get more flies with honey than vinegar'? A little civility might make things easier for everyone—especially you."

I glared at him. "If you want civility, then try showing some. Like by calling to let me know you were serving the warrant."

He wasn't required to tell me. But some detectives are decent that way. They don't give me enough time to let my client dump evidence, but they do wait for me to get there and give me a chance to check out the search warrant. The fact that Kingsford and O'Malley hadn't bothered to do that was a giant "fuck you." And I planned to pay them back for it every chance I got.

O'Malley was unmoved. "Your client's in the backyard."

He turned and led me through the house. A videographer was filming in the kitchen. It was as much a method of gathering evidence as it was an ass-covering move in case Niko complained they'd damaged his property. As we walked through the living room, I spotted two crime scene techs examining the couch and the surrounding area. The pillows had all been pulled off and thrown to the floor.

As I stepped through the sliding glass doors to the backyard, I saw that the weather had shifted. The day had started out sunny, but a dark bank of clouds had moved in, and the air was cold and damp with the promise of rain. Niko was huddled on the stone bench surrounding the firepit. The zipper of his down jacket was pulled all the way up. He held some papers in his hand—probably a copy of the search warrant—and stared at the swarm of activity with a numb expression.

O'Malley peeled off, and I went and sat next to him. "How're you doing?"

He shook his head. "I . . . don't know." He held out the papers. "It says I lied about drinking the wine." He swallowed. "But I didn't. I just forgot."

I took the papers and quickly scanned them. I'd been right. It was a copy of the search warrant. "What have they said to you?"

He continued to stare at the search team. "Nothing. Just that they had a search warrant."

Good. No one was talking about arresting him. Not that they had any right to. I skimmed through the affidavit, where the detective lays out his probable cause. There were no surprises. Bryan's cause of death, Niko's expertise in martial arts, his access to Tanner, his motive to kill Bryan and Tanner—though it was noted that Tanner might not be dead. And—of course—the fact that Niko had "lied" about drinking the wine with Tanner.

It wasn't the strongest showing of probable cause I'd ever seen, but probable cause is a pretty low standard. If they managed to build a case against Niko, I probably wouldn't get a judge to find the warrant invalid.

All I could do was hope the cops didn't find anything. But they'd put together a pretty sizable search team, and it was poring over every inch of the house. If there was anything here, they'd find it.

I sat next to Niko and watched as the techs and cops worked—and tried not to imagine what might happen next.

FIFTEEN

It took them hours to finish—in part because Niko's house is more than four thousand square feet. I hadn't seen anything in the bags they carried out that looked incriminating. But I knew Niko was smart enough to get rid of anything obvious, and so did the cops. What worried me was what I couldn't see, the small trace evidence that would only show up in the testing.

And that's clearly what they were focused on. One of the crime scene techs carried out two plastic bags with Niko's clothes. Most likely the clothes they'd found in the laundry hamper. And after everyone had cleared out, I saw that the techs had swabbed the hell out of all the showers and sinks. That figured. Dirty clothes and bathrooms were the most likely places to find traces of blood or hair that didn't belong to Niko.

When the last car had pulled away, I poured us both a stiff shot of Patrón Silver on the rocks. "Let's go sit on the couch." Niko, who still looked shell-shocked, followed me into the living room. I turned on the gas fireplace and threw a warm mohair blanket over our laps. "Did Tanner or Bryan hang out here a lot?" If so, that'd help explain away any stray hairs or even small traces of blood the techs might've found.

Niko shook his head. "In fact, I think the only time other than when you saw them here was months ago, when I first started investing with them."

Not what I wanted to hear. Neither of them had used the bathroom when I saw them at the house, and any trace they might've left when they visited months ago would be long gone. But that might not matter. "Did Kingsford or O'Malley ask you about that?" I held my breath and prayed for the answer I wanted.

He stared into the fire for a moment. "Yeah. I'm pretty sure they did."

Again, not what I wanted to hear. I had to bite my lip so I wouldn't swear out loud. That meant if the techs found Tanner's hair in the house—or worse, his or Bryan's blood—the cops would have a decent basis for claiming it'd gotten there because Niko had washed it off after he killed them. I didn't think Niko was putting all that together, and there was no benefit in my doing it for him. He was stressed out enough for one day—or for the next fifteen years. Right now, it'd be best to focus on something positive. Like the theory I'd been working on to get the heat off Niko. "Would you put it past Tanner to kill Bryan?"

Niko thought for a moment. "No. Not if Bryan really did steal all the money."

"It'd be a great reason for him to fake his own death—or kidnapping."

He sighed. "I guess so."

Niko still looked numb. This probably wasn't a great time to push for information, but I wanted to get things moving. May as well start now. "Do you have any idea where he might've gone?"

Niko took a sip of his drink. "I first met him in London, and I know he traveled a lot." He paused for a moment. "I remember listening to him talk about trips to Shanghai and Sydney. And I think the Gold Coast. But he never said what he was doing there. I didn't think to question it at the time, but now . . . for all I know, he made it all up and just went to Palm Springs for a weekend." He faced me, his expression sad. "I'm sorry I'm so useless."

I put a hand on his cheek. "You've never been anything of the kind."

He covered my hand, then kissed it. "I don't know what I'd do without you."

A smart-ass remark came to mind—involving the way he'd ignored my advice not to talk to the cops—but I just smiled and said, "Likewise."

We snuggled under the blanket and gazed at the fire in silence for a few moments. Niko finished his drink and held up his glass. "I'm getting a refresher. How about you?"

I gave him my glass. "I'll take a splash." While Niko made our drinks, I thought about his remark that if Tanner thought Bryan had stolen all the money, he might've killed Bryan. When he returned with our drinks, I said, "Have you considered the possibility that Tanner wasn't duped by Bryan? That he was in on the fraud the whole time?"

Niko settled in next to me. "Yeah, I have. And I've also been thinking that even if he wasn't in on it to begin with, when he figured out what Bryan had done, he might've found a way to get his hands on the money."

I nodded. "And just pretended that he'd been ruined by Bryan, like everyone else." It was a distinct possibility. "Either way, he had a great reason to want to disappear." And assuming we did find Tanner, I couldn't count on him to tell the truth and back Niko's alibi. Still, we had to try. If we found him, we'd at least have a shot. If we didn't, we had no shot. "Too bad he's your only real alibi."

Niko shook his head. "Yeah, I sure know how to pick 'em."

All at once, the stress of the day's events landed on me. It was as though someone had hit me over the head with a club. I sagged against Niko as I felt my eyelids drooping. At some point—I couldn't tell how long because I'd fallen asleep—we got up and stumbled into bed.

We both woke up at seven a.m. I jumped out of bed and hurried to the shower. I was nervous about what the search of Niko's house would turn up. The only way to make sure the cops couldn't arrest Niko was to find Tanner and hope he backed Niko's alibi. The only other option was for me to come up with another suspect—one who'd look good for Bryan's murder and possibly Tanner's. I knew myself well enough to know that the only antidote for my anxiety was action. I wanted to get started. I had no patience for breakfast.

But Niko wouldn't hear of it. He opened the refrigerator. "It won't kill you to at least have a smoothie. I'll put it in a travel cup."

I hate fucking smoothies. And kale and arugula and all that green junk. "No thanks. Do you have any bagels?"

Niko put his hands on his hips. "Do you know how bad those wheat products are for you?"

I rolled my eyes. "Yes, because you've told me a hundred times. You need to cut me some slack. We love what we love." I took a travel mug out of the cupboard and filled it with coffee.

Niko shook his head. "You're impossible. Here, at least have an apple."

I took the apple from him. "Thanks."

I kissed him and said I'd check in on him later. It was almost eight a.m. when I left. Plenty of time to make a stop on the way and get to the office by eight thirty. I headed straight to the East Coast Bagel Co. and picked up a half dozen of those circles of goodness—three egg, three onion, and a tub of cream cheese.

I thought I'd be the first to get in, but when I arrived, I found Alex hard at work at his desk and Michy busily typing away on her computer. I held up the bag of treasures. "Unhealthy wheat and dairy products, anyone?"

Michy smiled. "Another Niko lecture, I see. I'm surprised you didn't stop for Egg McMuffins, too."

I'm a little . . . oppositional. That's what my teachers wrote on all my report cards when I was a kid. And I still am. If you want to make sure I do something, just tell me not to do it.

Alex came out of his office. "What's sick is, I already had breakfast, but I still can't resist the siren song of those yeasty little wonders."

Michy chose an egg bagel. "I assume the cops didn't find anything at Niko's."

Because I'd have been a mess. "Waiting for test results. And for them to go through all the video footage and photos. They must've covered every millimeter of the place."

Alex cut an onion bagel in half. "The cops sure seem focused on Niko."

They really did. Not that I blamed them. "That's why we need to find them someone else to play with."

He spread a thin layer of cream cheese on his half bagel. "Not to mention find Tanner."

I nodded. "And that, of course. Even if he won't alibi Niko, we can at least take one dead body off the list." I tore a piece off my onion bagel as I told them about my conversation with Niko the night before and about my theory that Tanner might've stolen the investor money before he disappeared. "So if we find Tanner, we might just find the money." Which might help prove he was the one who killed Bryan.

"God, it'd be so nice to bail out those poor people who got screwed," Michy said.

I swallowed my bite of bagel and wiped my mouth. "But we need to move fast."

Alex dusted the crumbs off his slacks. "I'll dig into the Gold Strike records. Maybe they'll have some clues about where Tanner might've gone."

"Or whether he might've stolen the money," I said. "And while you're at it, see if you can figure out whether Tanner was in on the scam from the start." If we could prove that, it'd make it more likely he'd just gone into hiding. But there was a downside, too. I added, "If you do come up with proof that Tanner was in on it, try and see if anyone else knew."

Alex gave me a long look, then nodded. He knew what I was thinking. If it turned out that Niko knew Tanner was in on the fraudulent transaction, it'd add to his already strong motive to kill Tanner.

I told Alex and Michy what Niko had said about Tanner's travels. "I don't know if he really was such a world traveler."

"Maybe not," Alex said, his expression grim. "But he might be now."

True. With enough money, Tanner could buy a great fake passport. In which case, he could be anywhere.

SIXTEEN

It felt good to be on the move and proactive about Niko's defense. *Niko's defense.* Damn. He was the last person I wanted to have as a client. But I might as well face it. From the moment Bryan was found dead, that's how I'd been thinking of him.

And I was glad to be doing something about it.

That feeling lasted all day—until I got the phone call from Kingsford. His low, whispery voice chilled me to the core. "My partner tells me you two had words about civility, so I'm giving you a heads-up to try and keep things friendly."

Friendly? With me? When pigs fly. I knew he couldn't be calling me with good news, but I tried to keep my tone light. "I appreciate that."

He cleared his throat. "We found prints matching Niko Ferrell's in Bryan's duplex. A few hairs that might be his, too."

I could feel the phone receiver getting damp in my suddenly sweating hand. "So what? You probably found mine, too. We found his body, remember? And we were there a few days before the murder. Tanner was there, too. Matter of fact, Tanner was still there when we left." *Take that, asshole.*

Kingsford was unfazed. "I agree. That's neither here nor there. But we also got the footage from the building's surveillance camera. It shows someone at the back door who looks a lot like Niko Ferrell. And he was wearing a jacket we found in his closet during the search. This heads-up is to let you know that we're on our way to seize that jacket now."

Shit! This time it was impossible to hide the tension in my voice. "What exactly did that surveillance video show? Can you see his face?"

Kingsford paused. "No. His back was to the camera. But the height and weight look right. And like I said, that jacket—"

"Looks similar. Got it. I'll meet you at his house."

"Better hurry. We just turned onto his street."

I wanted to tell him what I thought of his so-called act of civility, but I didn't have time. I had to get ahold of Niko and keep him from getting chatty again. But at this point, there was no way I'd make it. I pressed Niko's number on my cell and prayed he'd answer. He did. I talk fast as a general rule, but I really rip when I'm stressed. I barreled through my report on Kingsford's call like a bullet train. I concluded, "And this time, listen to me. Do not talk to them. Don't even say hello."

Niko didn't sound nearly as concerned as I'd expected—or thought he should. "Not to worry. I'm not even home yet. I'm on my way back from the hospital."

Perfect. For a change. I asked how his mother was doing. He said she was the same. Not the best news but not the worst, either. "Don't go home. Wherever you are, just pull over and wait. I'll call you when I get to your house."

"Okay. But how can they say it was me on that video if—"

I grabbed my purse and ran out of my office. "We can talk later. Let me get going." I ended the call, and as I headed for the door, I told Michy I was on my way to Niko's place. "I'll call you from the car and explain."

And I did, as I broke all speed limits and practically ran a stop sign. I didn't think Kingsford and O'Malley would break down the door, but

I wasn't going to take any chances. I called Niko when I was one minute away from his house. "Okay, you're good to go; I'm almost there."

He pulled into the driveway and entered the garage seconds after I arrived. Kingsford and O'Malley were standing on the front porch. O'Malley held a brown grocery-size bag. Probably to transport Niko's jacket. Both of them looked irritated. I loved seeing that. It made me so happy, I actually smiled as I said, "Thanks for the heads-up, guys." I held out my hand. "Let's see the warrant."

Niko had gone into the house from the garage. He opened the door just as O'Malley brandished the search warrant. Niko had learned a few things since his chat with those two. He glanced at the warrant—which O'Malley was still holding. "I'd like to give my lawyer a chance to check that out before you come in."

I held out my hand to O'Malley. "No one's going anywhere or taking anything until I read it." He gave me the warrant. It was pretty straightforward, but I took my time anyway. Just to rub it in a little. When I finished, I said, "This is my copy, I take it?"

O'Malley nodded. I moved past them and entered the house as I motioned for Niko to lead the way. I hung back and followed behind to make sure everyone stayed on the path to the closet.

I could feel my heart thumping hard against my rib cage as we moved toward the master bedroom. If that jacket was distinctive, it might be enough to justify Niko's arrest. As we approached the closet, I took a look at Niko. He seemed pretty calm and collected. But he had one of the best poker faces I'd ever seen. For all I knew, he was ready to jump out of his skin.

The closet was a massive walk-in. As Niko opened the double doors, Kingsford took out a photo. He consulted it as he moved down the racks on the left, then turned a corner and scanned the clothes on the racks on the right side. Midway down, he stopped and pulled out a black waist-length jacket.

I'd hoped the jacket would turn out to be a standard-issue bomber or blazer style, the kind of thing you'd find in stores everywhere. But it wasn't. The sleeves were wool, but the body of the jacket was leather, and the front zipper was set on a diagonal.

This was not good. I pointed to the photo in Kingsford's hand. "Is that a still shot from the surveillance footage?" Kingsford nodded. "I'd like to see it."

He gave it to me. "I'll send you a link for the surveillance footage."

I tried to keep my hand from shaking as I studied the photo. It was a shot from behind, so all it showed was the back of the jacket. It was waist length, and the shape was similar. But the quality of the photo wasn't good enough to tell whether the sleeves were wool or leather. And the photo was black and white, so although the jacket looked dark, that didn't necessarily mean it was black—as opposed to navy blue or brown. My breathing slowed. This was no smoking gun. Hardly the "gotcha" Kingsford had implied. I handed the photo back to him. "Unless you have some jacket expert who can say the stitching is one of a kind, this won't do diddly-squat."

Kingsford slid the photo into his jacket pocket. "In the eye of the beholder. Anyway, I think the footage is a little clearer than this still."

I sure hoped not. "I'd like to get that link by the end of business today."

O'Malley put Niko's jacket into the paper bag, and Niko ushered them out of the house. I went to the living room and flopped down on the couch.

Although the jacket wasn't exactly a slam dunk, I didn't like the way these little details were adding up. The wineglass, the jacket, the person in the footage who was supposedly Niko's size. And I worried more was coming. No single thing proved Niko had killed Bryan—or Tanner. But if more details like these kept adding up, the cops might be able to build a strong circumstantial case against him. People say a case is weak when it's "only circumstantial." In reality, circumstantial cases are usually a lot stronger than cases based on direct evidence.

A case based on an eyewitness is a classic example of direct evidence. But there's nothing more unreliable—or easier to shred in court—than an eyewitness. Don't believe me? Just watch what happens to them on cross-examination. How far away were you from the robber? Do you wear glasses or contacts? Were you wearing them at the time? How dark was it? You were leaving a restaurant; what were you drinking? Can you describe the gun the robber was holding? They usually can't. Can you describe what he was wearing? Not usually.

And then, whatever is left of the eyewitness's credibility will be trashed by an eyewitness identification expert's testimony. So unless the prosecution has a bunch of eyewitnesses who all give the same descriptions—which never happens, because no two people see the same thing the same way—my chances of beating the case are pretty good.

But with a circumstantial case, I'm usually hosed. Because a circumstantial case doesn't depend on an eyewitness or on any one piece of evidence. It's a combination of a variety of sources, and it's usually a web I can't break through. I was worried now that Kingsford and O'Malley were weaving one for Niko.

I hid that fear behind a smile when Niko joined me on the couch. "Thanks for taking my advice—for a change."

Niko nodded, his expression solemn. "Yeah, I guess I've learned my lesson. I just thought before that if I told them everything, they'd see I was innocent and move on."

Just like so many of my clients. "Does this mean you'll start listening to me about the virtues of french fries and Taco Bell?"

Niko gave me an incredulous look. "Why on earth would I do that?"

I shrugged. "It was worth a try." I shifted gears and went back to the matter at hand. "Did you go to Bryan's house that night?" I'd worded the question carefully to give him a chance to come up with an innocent explanation if he was the man in the surveillance footage.

He shook his head. "No. I didn't. The jacket in that photo can't be mine, and I don't see how anyone can say it is."

I didn't, either. At least, not now.

SEVENTEEN

I had to get back to work, and Niko had meetings scheduled. He walked me to the door. "Thanks, Sam, for . . . everything."

His gratitude made me a little uncomfortable. "Of course."

He gave me a long hug, then opened the door. As I turned to go, he said, "Hey, when you get the link to that surveillance footage, will you forward it to me?"

I promised I would and told him to call me when he got done with his meetings.

The day was mild, with just a few thin clouds, and the palm trees swayed under a very blue sky. I rolled down my windows as I drove back to the office and tried to relax. But thoughts about that footage and what it might show kept my shoulders hunched around my neck. I couldn't stop thinking, *What if . . . ?* What if the guy in the footage really looked like Niko? What if the cops came up with more evidence tying him to Bryan's murder—and maybe Tanner's? What if Niko had been lying to me all along?

How would I feel about it if I found out he had killed one—or both—of them? I knew I wouldn't blame him. I knew I'd have probably done the same.

Because I had done the same—several times. Starting ten years ago, when Michy's attacker got out of jail after his case got thrown out. He hadn't been out for two days before he went back to terrorizing her. Banging on her window in the middle of the night. Leaving dead rats, snakes, and lastly a dead cat at her door. But Michy had no proof that it was him. She never caught him in the act and neither did any of her neighbors. The cops were sympathetic. They'd have loved to lock the asshole up. They just didn't have the evidence.

Michy was losing weight—and her sanity. This couldn't go on. I had to do something. I began to spend every spare moment tracking him, hoping I could catch him in the act. But after a week with no success, I began to consider a different plan. Over the next two weeks, I took note of his pattern of movements and where he'd be at certain times of night until finally, I was ready.

I remember sitting in my car, waiting for him to make his usual run to the local liquor store. I remember how my heart pounded, how a rush of adrenaline coursed through me as I watched him turn into the alley—the route he always took home. I remember how I lifted my foot and stomped on the gas pedal, how I barreled down that alley. How he turned to look back at the very last moment. How my headlights lit up his face, his look of disbelief and horror. But best of all, I remember the soaring feeling of smashing into him at full speed. The solid *whomp* of his body as it hit the grille of my car. It felt so good, I backed up and ran over him again. The case remains unsolved.

The next day—and for months afterward—I'd wondered whether the joy of that night would give way to depression and guilt. But as the days, weeks, and months passed, I realized that not only did I *not* feel any guilt, I felt at peace. There was something supremely fulfilling about lending justice a helping hand. So much so, I wound up doing it again and again—and again.

Bottom line: I had no moral qualms about it if Niko turned out to have given justice a little nudge. In fact, I'd love him even more. It only bugged me that he might be lying to me.

So I was apprehensive about what I might find when I opened the link. Michy—who, by the way, doesn't know about any of my extracurricular activities, and neither does Alex—could see something was up the moment I walked in the door. She gave me a worried look. "What happened?"

"Nothing really."

Alex came out of his office and echoed her question. I told them about the jacket and the link Kingsford had said he'd send.

"Michy, could you check and see if we've got it?"

She opened the screen for the office email on her computer. "Nope, not yet."

I looked at my watch. It felt like I'd been at Niko's house all day, but it was only two thirty. Kingsford hadn't even had time to get back downtown yet. "Guess I'll go try and be productive." I glanced at Alex. "Unless you have some news for me."

Alex shook his head. "Working on it, though. Gold Strike didn't have the most sophisticated security system. I'd expect that of Bryan. He was basically computer illiterate. But I thought Tanner was a little savvier."

I was confused. "Then how come you haven't broken through?"

He gave me a mildly exasperated look. "Who says I haven't? It's just that there're a million files to go through."

That made sense. With no new development to distract me, I was forced to get to work on some boring motions. I headed into my office.

I didn't get the link to the surveillance footage until five thirty. I'd said I wanted it by the end of the day, and Kingsford had made sure it wasn't a minute earlier. I went to my doorway and told Michy and Alex the link had come in. We gathered behind my desk and watched the monitor as I clicked on it.

A black-and-white shot of the area behind Bryan's building filled the screen. Within seconds, I saw a figure approach. But—as Kingsford had said—it was only a rear view. The figure headed toward the spot where I assumed the back door was, but then it moved out of view. The footage ended there.

I sat back, puzzled. "Why doesn't Bryan's security camera pick up his back door?"

Michy said, "I thought that, too. But maybe it wasn't his camera. Maybe it was a neighbor's, and it just happened to cover some of his property."

Alex agreed. "I was thinking the angle was wrong, too. If he had a camera, it should've been mounted on the wall of his building, so it would capture the guy's face, not just his back."

I played the footage another three times to give us a chance to study the size of the person. When I'd finished, I said, "What do you guys think? Could it be Niko?" I knew what I thought.

Michy sighed. "I mean, it does look like a man. And he is about Niko's height."

"I hate to say it, but I agree," Alex said.

Exactly what I'd thought. Another link in the chain—that'd be wrapped around Niko's neck if I didn't get a break. And then something occurred to me. I opened a search window on my computer and began typing. After a few minutes, I found what I was looking for. I magnified the picture and leaned back to give Michy and Alex a clear view. "Do you see what I see?"

Alex smacked his forehead. "How'd I miss that? I spent practically the whole night with the dude. Yeah, you're right, Sam."

Michy peered at the photo. "That's Tanner?"

I nodded. "What do you think?"

She cocked her head to the side. "I think he looks about the same size as Niko."

I let out the breath I didn't know I'd been holding. Then it wasn't just me, hoping to prove Niko was innocent. They saw it, too. I pulled out my cell phone and showed them the photo I'd taken of Niko's jacket earlier that day. "Do you think it looks like the one the guy was wearing in the video footage?"

Alex shrugged. "It looks similar. But you can't see much detail in that footage. There's no way to know whether it's Niko's jacket. At least, in my opinion." He turned toward Michy. "You?"

She frowned at the photo. "If I were on a jury and the D.A. tried to get me to believe that was the jacket in the video, I'd think they were desperate. And incompetent."

I was feeling pretty good about my theory that Tanner might be the man in the video. But I wanted confirmation. "Alex, can you get your hands on Tanner's DMV records?"

"You want height and weight, right?" I nodded. "I'll poke around. Niko's about six feet tall, isn't he?"

"Six one. And he weighs a hundred and seventy-five."

Alex nodded. "Sounds right."

He headed back to his office. Michy moved toward the door, then stopped. "It bugs me that the cops didn't notice the guy in the video might be Tanner."

It bugged me, too. "Maybe they did and just aren't telling me."

She looked skeptical. "Or they're stuck on the theory that Niko killed Bryan."

They sure seemed to be. Confirmation bias. It's what happens when cops decide the killer "has to be" the husband, or the boyfriend, or the gangbanger next door, then only pay attention to the evidence that confirms their theory instead of following the evidence where it leads them. It screws up more investigations than anyone knows.

But I wasn't convinced that was in play here. Kingsford was sharp. And he was under no obligation to share all his evidence with me. Not yet anyway. Not until Niko was actually charged. "My bet is they do know it could be Tanner, and they're just playing it close to the vest."

Michy sighed as she rolled her eyes. "Cops." She went back to her desk.

I smiled. She was actually pretty pro-cop for someone who worked on the defense side. But every now and then, the cat and mouse game that was the perpetual dance between the boys in blue and me got to her.

I made myself dive into the motion—a hopeless argument asking the judge not to let the prosecution use my client's prior conviction for burglary at trial—and was only three pages in when Alex showed up in my doorway holding his iPad. "You already managed to hack into the DMV? That was fast."

He gave me a quizzical look. "It's been two hours. And I'm sure I could've hacked the DMV in that time, but I didn't have to."

Two hours, and I only had three pages to show for it. I was definitely not myself. "What'd you get?"

Alex looked very pleased with himself as he sat down in front of my desk and opened his iPad. "Tanner's gym membership. He was way into the body beautiful." He smirked. "I think it had something to do with the trainer who worked there. She was, as they say, 'smokin'.' And she very helpfully kept records." He handed me the iPad.

There it was. Tanner's height: six feet and point five inches. And his weight: a hundred and seventy-two. "Does it show the date of his last weigh-in?"

Alex pointed to the top of the screen. "In the right corner."

I saw it and looked at Alex with a smile. "That's just a week before he disappeared."

He leaned back and folded his arms. "Honestly, I'm so good I sometimes scare myself."

I rolled my eyes as I handed back his iPad. "I've always said you scare easy."

Alex sniffed and decamped for his office. It was a small victory. But we hadn't had any in a while. I'd take it. For now.

EIGHTEEN

When I left the office that Friday, I'd hoped our little victory meant we were on a roll. And we were. The problem was the direction: straight downhill.

I'd spent most of the weekend catching up on errands and boring chores, like cleaning and laundry. Niko was busy taping his next video, and when he wasn't, he was sitting at his mother's bedside. I managed to join him there Sunday evening. Sophia still couldn't move or speak, but she was able to open her eyes and make a weird croaking sound.

Niko pointed out these small improvements to Dr. Hoffman. "She's getting better, isn't she? So maybe she'll recover." The naked hope on his face was almost painful in its vulnerability.

Dr. Hoffman grasped his shoulder and looked him in the eye. "It's important to hang on to hope. But it's just as important to be realistic about her prognosis. This is very likely as good as she's going to get. And it's quite possible this progress is only temporary. I'm sorry."

Niko's expression hardened. "But people have recovered from strokes before."

The doctor let go of his shoulder and looked away. "Yes, but from a stroke this severe?" He sighed. "I've never seen it happen. I'm not saying it's impossible. Nothing's impossible. But it's important that you accept the truth of the situation. For your own sake."

The stubborn look on Niko's face told me that was unlikely to happen. It broke my heart to imagine how devastated he would be if—and most likely when—the doctor's bleak prediction proved to be true.

It made me even more determined to prove he was innocent and get the cops off his back. So it was doubly upsetting when I got to the office Monday morning and found Dale sitting in the reception area, chatting with Michy.

The fact that he was here in person couldn't be a good omen. It meant he had something to tell me that a) he couldn't risk saying on the phone and b) required some discussion. Good news could be delivered in code on a cell phone.

And then, of course, there was Dale's grim expression. I gave him a curt nod and gestured toward my office. "Let's get it over with."

He raised an eyebrow. "Good morning to you, too."

I gave him a flat look. "Obviously, it isn't."

I sat at my desk, and Dale took a seat across from me. He didn't mince words. "Did you know Kingsford asked the crime lab to compare the fibers from Niko's jacket to the fibers found in Bryan's duplex?" I shook my head. "The report came in early this morning. They're a match."

Oh hell. But I reminded Dale, "No, they're not a match—they're consistent."

Dale waved me off. "Yeah, whatever."

But it mattered. Fingerprints match. DNA samples match. But fibers don't have that kind of individuality. The most that can legitimately be said is that their characteristics are consistent. Still, "consistent" was bad enough.

Dale offered, "I'm sure Kingsford and O'Malley realize Niko could've worn that jacket at Bryan's house on plenty of other occasions."

I'm sure they did. Or at least, I was sure Kingsford did. He was no dummy. The jury was out on O'Malley. "But it doesn't look good."

I didn't know whether the cops would be able to enhance the surveillance video footage enough to prove that the jacket the man was wearing in the video matched Niko's. Even if they couldn't, the fact that it looked similar to Niko's jacket and that the fibers from his jacket were consistent with those in Bryan's duplex was problematic. Again, it was no smoking gun, but it added to the evidence that was steadily stacking up against Niko.

Dale frowned. "He's still saying he didn't do it?"

I folded my arms. "You know that's privileged."

He gave me an incredulous look. "Really? You're playing the lawyer card? After I've leaked like a rusty colander for you?"

That was fair. Besides, I knew he'd keep anything I told him between us. He was squarely on Niko's side. And, like me, he secretly had a few dead bodies of his own under his belt. "Okay." I sighed. "Well, he could be telling the truth." I told Dale about how similar in size Tanner and Niko were and pointed out that meant Tanner could've killed Bryan.

Dale nodded. "Assuming the guy in the video is the killer."

We all know what they say about assuming things, but this assumption seemed pretty safe to me. "The neighbor who owns the video camera helped narrow down the timing. According to the time stamp on the footage, the guy showed up at Bryan's back door at eight twenty-five p.m. The coroner said Bryan died between five p.m. and midnight, and his mother said he wasn't answering his phone as of nine thirty. It fits. The guy in that video has to be the killer."

"Okay. Then have you worked out a motive?"

That was the question. "I've got Alex working on that."

"Keep me posted." Dale grasped the arms of his chair and stood up. "Better get going. Those bad guys won't catch themselves." He headed out, saying he needed to grab some breakfast.

My stomach rumbled at the mention of food. I hadn't had time to eat. Fond memories of the Scrumptious Café Bakery on Hayworth floated before my eyes. They had build-your-own omelets, and their parmesan scrambled eggs and croissants were a heavenly experience.

I walked out to the reception area and told Michy I was going to pick up breakfast to go. "Want me to get something for you?"

Michy winced. "I already ate. But those croissants . . ."

They really were irresistible. "You got it." I glanced at Alex's office. The door was closed. "Is he in?"

Michy blew out a breath. "Is he ever. I got in at eight, and he was already here. Said he got in at six thirty. He's hot on the trail of something."

Maybe he'd come up with some good news. I could use a little of that right now. I went to his office and knocked on the door. "Hey, NASA called. They want their satellite back."

A few seconds later, an exasperated Alex opened the door. "Seriously? You promised you'd stop with those dumb knock-knock jokes."

I gave him a mock glare. "I did no such thing." He glared right back at me. "Okay, fine, maybe I did." I told him I was picking up breakfast at Scrumptious. "Want anything?"

The glare gave way to a hungry look. "I'd love a ham and cheddar cheese omelet."

I looked over his shoulder. "What are you working on?"

Alex half smiled. "What on earth do you expect to see?"

True. He did all his work on the computer. It was just a reflexive move. "Treasure maps. Come on, tell me."

"Tanner. And if you stop screwing around with me, I may have some answers for you when you get back."

"So why are you letting me? Go hit those keys."

Alex rolled his eyes and shut the door, and I headed out to get some delicious breakfast things.

I—of course—ordered the scrambled eggs with parmesan and asparagus and some extra croissants because . . . I wanted them.

When I got back, I gave Michy her croissant and showed her there were extras. She shook her head. "You're the devil."

"That's Miss Devil to you." I saw that Alex's door was still closed. I knocked. "Get decent, the Girl Scouts are here to sell Thin Mints."

Alex opened the door with a world-class eye roll. "You just never stop, do you?"

I held up the to-go bag from Scrumptious. "Okay, cough up what you've got. No info, no breakfast."

Alex folded his arms across his chest. "Holding food hostage is about as low as it gets."

"Not true. I can go so much lower." I entered his office, which was so Spartan, it reminded me of a cement bunker. That cliché about gay men being great with decor? Yeah, not so much. I sat down on the only chair—a wooden ladder-back that he'd probably found at a garage sale.

Alex opened the Styrofoam box and dug into his eggs. I didn't object to waiting. He was a fast eater. And sure enough, he powered through the whole plate in two minutes. After a long drink of water, he hit a key on his computer. The screen lit up with what looked like an in-box. "I found a way into Tanner's email. It took a while because he was a lot more sophisticated about his security than I'd expected. And he had multiple accounts with different passwords."

I was out of patience. "For God's sake, spit it out. What did you find?"

Alex shot me a narrow-eyed look, then turned back to his screen. "You were right, Sam. Tanner was in on the cryptocurrency scam all along. In fact, it seems it was his idea."

I thought about what that meant. If Tanner knew the cryptocurrency trade was a total scam, then he had to have figured out that Bryan had stolen the money—and not long before the murder. The plan was so simple. Just pretend to do a big cryptocurrency trade, then claim the trade went south and split the money. All they'd had to do was create a realistic-looking paper trail. But what Tanner didn't realize was that Bryan wasn't into sharing. And he'd been stealing money for quite some time with his private holding company, BYO. So Tanner's frantic visit to Niko's house in the middle of the night was just an act. He was covering his ass, pretending he'd been duped so no one would catch on to the fact that he'd actually been the architect of the fraud. He was probably also hoping we could help him find Bryan so he could get his share of the loot.

Bottom line: Tanner had the best motive to kill Bryan. Not only because Bryan had ripped him off and he wanted to get his money back, but also because he needed to make sure Bryan could never bust him for setting up the scam.

Then another thought—a very ugly one—occurred to me. "He used that internal decapitation move in order to frame Niko."

Alex nodded. "That was my thinking. And he knew about Niko's mother, didn't he?"

I nodded. "Definitely. Which made Niko a perfect fall guy."

"Then doesn't it make even more sense that Tanner's not dead, that he's alive and just hiding out somewhere?"

The logic was sound, but that didn't make it true. And now I had a problem. "How am I going to get this news to Kingsford and O'Malley without getting you busted for hacking?"

Alex shook his head. "Good question."

But it was a step in the right direction. A big one.

NINETEEN

We kicked some ideas around for an hour, but ultimately, I decided the only way to make sure Kingsford found out that Tanner had set up the scam was to just tell him and make it sound like my personal opinion, based on who Tanner is. Or maybe was.

Not exactly genius, I know. But sometimes, the simplest solution is the only solution. "We'll see how long it takes for the cops to catch up with you, Alex."

He smirked. "You mean how long—if ever."

I laughed. "But speaking of cops, I should tell Dale about all this." And I had a few thoughts I didn't want to share with Alex or Michy. I went to my office and called Dale on his cell. "Are you anywhere close? I need to run something by you."

"As a matter of fact, I am. Just had breakfast at Blu Jam. But I don't have a lot of time."

I reassured him this wouldn't take long. I went back to Alex's office and told him to finish compiling the background on the Gold Strike investors. I wanted to broaden the list of suspects, and the investors seemed like a good place to start. Ten minutes later, Dale arrived, and I led him into my office. He sat down on the couch, and I closed the door. "So far, the cops are focusing on Niko for Bryan's murder. But I'm sure they're looking at him for Tanner's possible murder, too. Right?"

Dale nodded. "But it's tough. The only solid evidence they've got so far is that wineglass. It proves he was with Tanner that night—"

"Which he freely admitted—"

"And which would've been just fine if he hadn't lied about having wine with the guy." He shook his head. "Rookie move, by the way."

I shook my head. "Tell me about it. He told me he just forgot they'd had drinks."

Dale lifted his palms. "It's possible. But don't forget, he's got just as much motive to kill Tanner as he does Bryan."

I frowned. "But why kill Tanner? Tanner's his alibi for Bryan's murder. Unless . . ."

Dale raised his eyebrows. "Unless?"

I didn't like where my mind had gone, but I'd come this far. I may as well share it all. "Unless Tanner wasn't really his alibi."

"Meaning, Niko didn't have an alibi because he did kill Bryan."

I hated to say it. "Yeah. Which means he might well have killed Tanner, too."

Dale sighed. "So he used Tanner as his alibi, because he knew it was safe."

I shrugged. "Dead men don't talk."

Dale frowned. "Somehow I can't see Niko being that kind of calculating. That's pretty cold. Killing Tanner just so he could use him as an alibi?" He shook his head. "Doesn't seem like him."

I didn't want to believe it, either. "Well, not *just* for that reason. Tanner did basically kill Niko's mother. Niko didn't have proof at the time, but I think he was pretty sure Tanner had planned to steal the money all along. And as it turns out, he was right."

He sighed. "True." He fell silent for a moment, then said, "We'll have to see how it plays out. We about done here? I actually have a day job, believe it or not."

I shooed him out. "By all means, get back to work. I could use some new clients."

I told Dale to close the door behind him. I needed to think about the possibility that Niko had killed both Bryan and Tanner. I wished it'd never occurred to me, but now that it had, I knew it'd be stuck in my brain until I found evidence to disprove it.

I agreed with Dale. Niko didn't seem the type to plot a murder just so he could use the victim as an alibi. But he wouldn't have killed Tanner *just* to set up his alibi. He had a pretty solid reason to want to kill Tanner regardless. I wasn't sure what to think. Ordinarily, I trust my gut in situations like this. But that wouldn't work now. I was too invested in believing—and proving—Niko's innocence.

I rubbed my face. All this ruminating on possibilities was driving me nuts. And getting me nowhere. Until Alex dug up some dirt we could use to identify another suspect, there was no point in these mental gymnastics. The intercom on my phone buzzed.

It was Michy. "You know you have a two o'clock in Department 118, right?"

I did? Oh wait. "Yeah, the Stuart case. I'm all packed up." I wasn't.

"And you have to go talk to Angelo afterward. Remember?"

No. I didn't. "Of course I remember. I should get out of court in time to make visiting hours."

Michy sighed. "You're not packed, and you didn't remember shit."

It was my turn to sigh. "True and true." Honestly, I don't know why I even try to fool her. It never works.

She gave a mild snort. "Someday you'll learn."

I fished through my briefcase. "Unlikely."

I pulled out my iPad, made sure it was up to date with all the files on the Stuart case, and headed out. As I drove downtown, it worried me that I'd been so preoccupied with Niko that I'd forgotten my entire calendar for the day. I needed to get a grip.

I got stuck in traffic and wound up running all the way to the courthouse from the parking structure. I was still out of breath when I flew into court. And I was ten minutes late. Ordinarily, ten minutes is an acceptable grace period. But Judge Rafter doesn't do late. Not even one minute. I slid into a seat in the back row and prayed he wouldn't notice.

He was busy imposing a truly impressive sentence on a forties-ish female defendant who was bursting out of her orange jumpsuit. The judge was on the twelfth count of identity theft and still going strong. But he paused and zeroed in on me. "Just so you know, Ms. Brinkman, I saw you sneak in. You were ten minutes late. So make yourself comfortable. You're going to be here awhile."

Shit, shit, shit! I was doomed. Now I'd never make it to Twin Towers in time to see Angelo. I was due to meet with the D.A. and his investigating officer—the primary detective on the case—tomorrow, and I needed to be able to tell them what kind of information Angelo had for them. But I knew better than to let on that this was really screwing me. I gave the judge a weak smile. "No problem. Always a pleasure to spend time with you, Your Honor."

The judge dismissed me with a look and went back to the sentencing. When he got to count twenty, he asked his clerk, "How many years is that so far?"

The clerk peered at his computer. "Seventeen years and four months."

Judge Rafter nodded and continued. By the time he got to the last count, the total tally was thirty-five years and eight months. The defendant swayed against her lawyer—a young guy I didn't recognize. I saw him whisper something to her. Probably telling her to look on the bright side—she'd be eligible for Medicare by the time she got out.

Judge Rafter apparently took these financial missteps seriously. This did not bode well for my client, Jamie Stuart—who happened to be charged with ten counts of credit card fraud. I'd been hoping to make a deal for straight probation. Now I figured I'd be lucky to keep him off death row.

As they took her away, Judge Rafter called the next case. The clerk spoke in a nervous voice. "Counsel called to say she's been held up in another court and can't get here for another hour."

The judge huffed and called the next case. No one responded. He glared at his clerk. "I thought counsel had checked in."

The clerk's voice actually shook this time. "He did. I d-don't know what happened to him."

Judge Rafter, a look of utter disgust on his face, motioned for me to step up to counsel table. "I hate to reward you for tardy behavior, but it seems I have no choice." He turned to the bailiff. "Bring out Mr. Stuart."

As the bailiff went into lockup, I moved toward the prosecutor. "You don't want to take this thing to trial. Neither do I. How about time served, community service, and three years' probation?"

He gave a menacing chuckle. "Sounds okay to me. I hate paper cases. But I'm not your problem." He glanced up at the judge. "He is. Good luck with Judge Raptor. You saw that sentencing?" I nodded. "I offered to let her plead to three counts and do a total of seven years. Still not exactly a walk in the park. Our buddy up there on the bench called me a dump truck and threatened to report me to my head deputy if I didn't rescind the offer. I wound up having to take the case to trial just to save my neck."

That meant Jamie Stuart and I were in some very deep manure. The last time we'd talked, he'd said he wouldn't take any deal that involved more jail time. That goal now seemed—to put it mildly—unrealistic. And it wasn't as though I had some great defense. The case was pretty close to a slam dunk for the prosecution—as paper cases often are. The evidence is all there in black and white. But judges are usually willing to go a little easier on these cases simply because no one got maimed or killed. Clearly, this judge didn't subscribe to that philosophy.

I sighed. "Okay, give me a month to come up with something creative." And give Alex a chance to find something in Jamie's life story that'd soften up "Judge Raptor."

The prosecutor agreed to give me a month. "But if we don't have a deal by then, we'll have to go to trial." He tilted his head toward the judge. "Our fearless leader doesn't like continuances."

I nodded. "Sounds about right." The bailiff brought Jamie out of lockup. I leaned toward him and hissed, "We're going to continue your case—"

Jamie was irritated. "What? Why? You said you'd have me out by today."

I never said any such thing. To any client. Ever. For exactly this reason. But this was neither the time nor the place to argue. I whispered, "I'll explain later. For now, just waive time and act respectful."

Jamie wasn't the brightest bulb in the chandelier, but he couldn't miss the dire note of warning in my voice. He reluctantly nodded, and we set the next pretrial date a month out. I left court thinking Alex would have to dig deeper than usual for something that'd persuade Judge Raptor to let Jamie out before the Rapture.

I hurried out of court and walked the two blocks to the Twin Towers jail, where Angelo Lopez was housed. But when I gave my name and said I was there to see him, the deputy shook his head. "Lopez doesn't want to see you."

What the . . . ? "Did he say why?"

The deputy shook his head. "Just said he wasn't coming out."

I didn't like what I was hearing—and not just because it meant I'd have nothing to barter with to get him a deal. When I got back to my car, I pulled out my phone and called Alex. I told him that Angelo wouldn't talk to me. "Someone's threatening him, I'm sure of it. But can you take a run at him and find out?" Angelo didn't know Alex. Maybe when he saw the name Alex Medrano on his visitor list, he'd be curious enough to come out. Or be too afraid to refuse, because the name

Medrano might sound like someone who was in league with the guys who'd been threatening him.

Alex agreed. "Want me to come down now?"

"No. I don't want to tip off that you might be part of my operation. Wait until tomorrow." My phone beeped, signaling that I was getting another call. I told Alex I was on my way back to the office, then looked at my phone screen. It was Dale.

His voice was low. "Michelle said you were in court downtown. Are you still there?" I told him I was in the parking lot on Temple. "Meet me at Ocho."

Ocho—the restaurant, not the number—was a casual little Mexican grill joint near the Disney Concert Hall on Grand Avenue, just a few blocks away. Something was up—and by the sound of his voice, it was big. "Am I going to love or hate what you're going to tell me?"

He dodged the question. "I'll see you in ten."

I sighed and ended the call. As much as I respected his paranoia about phones, it really got on my nerves when he refused to even give me a hint about what was coming. But I knew it must have something to do with Niko, and my anxiety immediately kicked into overdrive.

Ordinarily, I would've made the uphill hike on foot, but I was wearing heels, and I didn't want to waste the time. I drove to the Disney Center and valeted my car—an expense I don't usually allow myself. When I got to the restaurant, I found Dale seated at one of the two-top high tables near the wall. I climbed onto the chair across from him. "I don't blame you for being, uh . . . overly careful about talking on the phone, but is this really necessary?"

He glanced around the restaurant, then looked me in the eye. "I'm sorry. I feel like this is all my fault. I should've checked him out when you first started dating."

I stared at him as my heart started to pound. "What on earth are you talking about?"

"Kingsford dug up Niko's history. Ten years ago, when he was staying in Chicago, he got into a bar fight. Almost killed the guy."

No. That couldn't be. I dropped my hands into my lap and felt my fingernails dig into my palms. "Are they sure it was Niko?"

Dale nodded, his expression grim. "He never told you."

I closed my eyes for a moment. "No." Why hadn't he? I stared out the window and tried to calm down enough to think. "Did he do any time?"

"That's the good news. The case never got filed. The cops and the D.A. said it was self-defense."

Actually, that was *very* good news. But I knew there was more. "What's the bad news?"

Dale took another glance around the restaurant, then met my gaze. "The blow that almost killed the guy? Was a chop to the neck."

I took a moment to absorb the shock. "Like the one that killed Bryan."

Dale gave a short nod. "Internal decapitation."

I felt like an anchor was attached to my heart. It wasn't just that the MO was the same; it was that Niko had said he'd never used the move.

He'd lied. Again.

TWENTY

I was upset on so many levels. As I snaked my way back to the office through rush-hour traffic, I couldn't stop thinking about what this meant. The cops didn't have enough to make an arrest . . . yet. But it was one thing for Niko to forget that he'd had a glass of wine with Tanner the night he disappeared. It was quite another to "forget" that he'd almost killed a man—by using the same move that'd killed Bryan. This time, Niko had really tightened the noose around his own neck.

And what got to me even more was the fact that he'd lied to *me*. I thought about how I'd approach this with him. As I rejected one idea after another, I realized there was no elegant way to do this. And honestly, I wasn't sure I cared. I was hurt and pissed off. If he didn't tell me about that bar fight in Chicago, then he obviously didn't trust me. So why should I trust him? Or worry about how he'd feel when I confronted him?

So I decided to just hit him between the eyes with it. I had no idea what he'd say. Maybe more to the point, I wasn't sure it'd matter what he said. The more I thought about it, the more it seemed like this might actually be the end of us. I was surprised at how painful that realization was.

I was in one sad, dark mood when I got back to the office. Alex was sitting on the edge of Michy's desk, showing her a YouTube clip on his iPad that had them both laughing. It's a measure of just how messed up I was that Alex took one look at me and shut it down.

Michy was immediately worried. "What's wrong, Sam? What happened?"

I filled them in on the latest news about Niko. "I can't believe he didn't tell me." I felt tears sting my eyes and blinked them back. "I mean, who is this guy? Definitely not who I thought he was."

Michy looked pensive. "I agree, it's not cool that he didn't tell you about that bar fight given what's going on right now. But I do get why he didn't tell you before. Don't you?"

Not really. "He was completely absolved. They never even filed charges. So why not tell me?"

Alex spoke gently. "Because it's embarrassing. Just because he didn't get tagged by 'The Man' doesn't mean he's cool with it. Niko's not a brawler—"

I interrupted. "How do you know?"

Alex continued. "He's an artist. It's obvious."

Michy knew this was exactly the kind of thing that would make me cut and run. She gave me a pointed look. "No, do not do this. We all have secrets." She knew more of mine than anyone else, but she was well aware she didn't know them all. "You have to give him a chance to explain."

I sighed. "Of course."

Michy raised an eyebrow. "No. I mean a *real* chance. The kind where you listen with an open mind. Not your usual kind, where you let him talk so you can pick out the inconsistencies and throw them in his face."

I was annoyed. "Since when do I do that?"

Michy and Alex replied in unison. "Always."

I rolled my eyes. "Whatever." I headed for my office. "Guess I'll go dig up someone to grill." I glared at the two of them. "Since that's what I always do."

I went into my office and closed the door. But I couldn't bear to turn on my computer. Worn out by my sadness and anger, I sat at my desk and stared dully at the black screen. After a few minutes, I gave up. I went over to the couch and flopped down, one arm over my eyes.

There was a soft knock on the door; then Michy said, "It's me, put down the gun."

She came in and sat down next to me. "I know you think it's over for you guys."

I dropped my arm and half sat up. "Well, don't you? How do we get past this?"

Michy looked at me with sympathy. "By talking and listening. That's what people in healthy relationships do."

I gave her a deadpan look. "Since when have I been involved in anything healthy?"

Michy didn't take the bait. She answered sincerely. "Since you've been with Niko."

"I really set you up for that one, didn't I?"

A little smile played on her lips. "Kind of." She continued on a more serious note. "You should go talk to Niko. Hear him out. A hundred bucks says you'll see things differently once he's had a chance to explain."

I sat all the way up. We made bets all the time. Usually for twenty dollars or less. "A hundred? For real?" Michy nodded. I held out my hand. "We'd better shake on this one. 'Cause I'm going to collect. No backsies."

Michy took my hand. "Fine. I'm happy to take your money. And I want a crisp hundie. No twenties." We shook. She went over to my desk, fished my cell phone out of my purse, and dropped it in my lap. "Here. Call him."

I stared at the phone. I was feeling a little better after Michy's pep talk, but I didn't trust my voice. What if he answered?

Michy folded her arms. "Now."

"Okay, fine. I'll text him." Michy waited while I typed. I said I had news and that we needed to talk. I held up the phone and showed it to her. "Done."

She nodded and headed to the door. "Good. I hope he gets back to you soon, because you're obviously not going to get a thing done until he does."

And with that, she walked out. I wished she weren't right. I wished I could just put all this out of my head and dive into work. I guess the truth is, I wished I didn't care so much. Luckily—or not, depending on how you look at it—Niko texted me back five minutes later, saying he'd be home in half an hour. He asked what I wanted for dinner. The honest answer would've been Tums. Or Pepto-Bismol. I just told him I'd be good with whatever he was in the mood for.

I lay on the couch for a while longer and tried to tell myself I'd be okay without him. I'd been single for thirty-five years, and it'd worked out fine. I didn't need a "real" relationship. Short-term was more my style anyway.

But I guess deep down, though I'd never admitted it to myself, I'd always hoped I'd find my forever guy. And I'd let myself believe that guy might turn out to be Niko. If I had to break up with him tonight, I'd be losing more than just this relationship. I'd be losing a dream. Because I knew I'd never let myself get in this deep again. It was too painful.

I finally dragged myself off the couch and went over to my desk, where I kept a mirror and some makeup in the bottom drawer. I took my time getting freshened up, fully aware that I was procrastinating. I looked at my phone. It was six o'clock. Niko had said he'd be home by now. It'd take me at least twenty minutes to get there at this time of day. I reluctantly packed up and left my office.

I saw that Alex's door was closed. I asked Michy, "Did he leave for the day?"

She snorted. "This early? Of course not. He's working on something related to Tanner; he didn't say exactly what." She took me in. "Nice touch-up job. I approve."

I gave her a wan smile. "Thanks." I headed for the door.

She said, "I want a full report by tomorrow morning. And don't forget my hundie."

I waved without turning back. "I'll take mine in twenties."

My stomach was in knots as I drove to Niko's place. What could he possibly say that would make me want to stay with him? What little faith Michy had kindled in me flickered and died as I pulled into his driveway. There was no way this was going to end well.

Niko answered the door looking particularly sexy—barefoot, in faded jeans and a black T-shirt. The smile on his face faded when he saw my expression. As I walked in, he said, "What's wrong, Sam?"

I can really pull off a poker face in court. But I pay for that skill by having zero ability to hide my feelings when it comes to my personal life. I walked into the living room and sat down on the couch. Niko had already lit the fire. I stared at the flames for a moment as he joined me. I clasped my hands together in my lap so he wouldn't reach for them and looked him in the eye. "You almost killed a man during a bar fight in Chicago. According to the police, you used the very same move on him that was used to kill Bryan. I wonder why I had to hear about that from the cops instead of you."

Niko looked stricken. He opened his mouth to speak, then closed it. It took a few moments before he could gather himself. "First of all, the cops are wrong. I chopped him in the neck, yes. When he came at me with a knife. The guy was crazy. But that was not an internal decapitation—which, by the way, is done from behind. I don't know where the police got that, but they're wrong. If I'd used that move, the guy would be dead."

I took that in. If true, it changed the picture I'd had—quite a bit. In that case, Niko hadn't lied—to the cops or me. And it'd be easy to verify whether the blow had been to the front of the guy's neck or the back. There'd be photos and descriptions of the injury in police reports. If Niko was telling the truth, it was one hell of a sloppy mistake to claim that the incident in Chicago bore any resemblance to Bryan's murder. But it sounded exactly like the kind of dumb thing O'Malley might do. Not Kingsford. He was pretty meticulous from what I'd seen. But right now, I had another question. "And you didn't tell me about this because . . . ?"

Niko dropped his gaze and swallowed. "It's not exactly my proudest moment. As a martial artist, I'm supposed to avoid confrontation. I shouldn't have gotten into it with that idiot. But he was hitting on this woman and wouldn't stop. She was getting scared. I told him to move on and leave her alone. He told me to fuck off and get out of his face. I stepped between him and the woman, and he took a swing at me." He stopped and sighed. "And you can guess the rest, but you don't have to. I'm sure you or Dale can get the police reports. It's all there." He hung his head.

If he was suggesting I get the reports, then he knew they'd back him up. So not only did he *not* lie about that fight, but the only reason he'd gotten into it in the first place was to protect a woman from a knuckle dragger.

Damn that Michy—and Alex—for being so right about him. And I had to admit that my reaction to the possibility of Niko's lying to me was beyond ironic. Although I'd never affirmatively lied to him, I certainly hadn't told him about any of my . . . extracurricular activities. I didn't even want to imagine how he'd react if he ever found out about the body count I'd racked up.

I needed to let him know that it was safe to tell me the truth, no matter how bad he thought it was. I looked into his eyes. "You get to choose what to share with me. I'm not one of those people who thinks couples need to live in each other's pockets. But whatever you do decide to tell me, just know that I'll never judge you." I paused and smiled. "Certainly not for pounding some asshole who deserved what he got—and a whole lot more."

The tension left Niko's face, and he smiled back at me. "You know, you're pretty amazing."

I felt anything but amazing. In fact, I felt guilty as hell for thinking the worst of him. "You're not so bad yourself." I took his hand. "And I'll get into it with Kingsford and O'Malley tomorrow."

Niko leaned in and kissed me softly. I returned the kiss with a little more urgency. I whispered in his ear, "About dinner. Maybe we can order in later?"

He smiled and stood up as he pulled me to my feet. "I was hoping you'd say that."

He held me by the hand as he led me into the bedroom. My kind of fairy-tale ending.

I'd been afraid to even let myself hope things would turn out this way.

TWENTY-ONE

I called Dale on the way to the office the next morning and told him what Niko had said about the bar fight in Chicago. "It was a chop to the front of the neck, not an internal decapitation. Can you pull the reports?" Dale said he'd do what he could.

Which turned out to be quite a lot—and fast. When I got in, Michy said, "You got an email from Dale with a few attachments." She gave me a smug look. "Judging by that—and the way you're floating on air—I'd guess you owe me some money."

I'd stopped at the bank on the way in, knowing I was going to suffer through a day of *I told you so*s. I dropped the hundred-dollar bill on her desk. "How long am I going to have to hear about this?"

Michy picked up the bill and gave it a snap. "Good question. Probably until it gets old—"

I interrupted, "It's officially old."

She smirked. "For me, that is. Until it gets old for *me*."

Alex came out of his office wearing a very similar smirk. "And me. So don't expect this to end anytime soon."

I shook my head. "You guys must lead really boring lives. I'd feel sorry for you, but I actually have to get some work done." I turned on my heel, went into my office, and closed the door behind me.

I sat down at my desk and opened the email from Dale. Sure enough, he'd already scored the reports from Chicago PD. Knowing Dale, he had a buddy in the department he'd been able to tap for a favor. Dale had buddies and connects everywhere. It's a good skill to have in general, but it's especially helpful for detectives. Having friends in the right places can save a lot of time.

I scanned the reports. And just as Niko had said, they clearly showed that the blow to the victim's neck bore no resemblance to the way Bryan had been killed. I called Dale. "Did you have a chance to read the reports?"

He gave a snort. "Yeah. It's not even close."

I was royally pissed off. That stupid mistake had sent me down a really bad spiral—and could've cost me a relationship. "What the hell made them think they could stretch that bar fight into anything remotely relevant to Bryan's murder?"

Dale sighed. "I can only guess. But I'd bet O'Malley talked to someone at Chicago PD who didn't bother to read the report and just jumped to the wrong conclusion."

I huffed. "And O'Malley ran with it."

He didn't sound happy about it. "Look, that's just my guess. But remember, you weren't even supposed to know about the whole Chicago thing. I'm sure Kingsford would've checked the report before saying anything to you."

"Right." And then I never would've known that Niko had almost killed a guy. All in all, I guess it'd worked out for the best. I'd always wanted to know all I could about him. That cooled my jets a little.

Dale interrupted my musing. "So what's your plan? You looking into the other investors?"

The good thing about this case was the long list of people with ample motive to want both Bryan and Tanner dead. "I was thinking your buddies Kingsford and O'Malley should be working on that. Any idea if they are?"

A phone started to ring in the background. "They'd better be. Look, that's my phone. I gotta bounce." He ended the call.

If the cops weren't checking out other investors' backgrounds and alibis, I'd be able to wrap that epic fail around their necks if we ever got to trial—and it'd crush them. Especially if Alex came up with a few investors who had no alibi. I was about to go talk to him about getting busy on that front when he knocked on my door. "Come in. Unless you're just looking for a chance to gloat some more."

Alex walked in. "I don't see why I can't multitask."

I made a shooing motion with my hand. "Out. I mean it."

He sat down in front of my desk. "Okay, fine. Spoilsport." He opened his iPad. "I've got news on Tanner."

I sat up. "You found him?"

Alex gave a curt shake of the head. "I wish. No. This is background info. But it's juicy. Apparently, Tanner got fired from a trading company in Philadelphia. They caught him doing some shady stuff."

So this cryptocurrency rip-off wasn't his first scumbag rodeo. "Shady stuff . . . as in?"

Alex glanced down at his iPad. "Seems he"—Alex made air quotes—"'accidentally' slipped investors' money into his own account. The boss threw him out and threatened to sue if he tried to work for any other trading company in the state. That's how he wound up here in California."

"Lucky us." I thought about how I could use this. "Did he lose any of that money?"

"No. The boss caught him before any real damage was done."

Damn. It was an interesting bit of information, but it wouldn't buy us any new suspects. "Have you started checking out our investors?"

Alex held up a hand. "Hang on. First things first. You wanted me to dig into Tanner and Bryan. I've got more."

"Excellent. Fire away."

He scrolled on his iPad. "Bryan got sued by his investors back when he was living in San Francisco."

This sounded promising. "What happened with the lawsuit?"

Alex frowned. "Nothing. It went away. From what I can tell, he managed to pay most of them back. Where he got the money . . . I have no idea."

"Someone must've been bankrolling him," I said.

Alex nodded. "A hundred percent. I'm trying to figure that out."

In addition to all the other items on his to-do list. "If Bryan did have a sugar daddy who expected to get repaid, and Bryan stiffed him, we might have something."

"Agree." He closed his iPad and stood up. "I'll keep digging into Tanner and Bryan, but it's time to move on to the investors."

"Yeah. I think I can get Dale to help out with some names and addresses." But that meant I'd have to spend a lot of time out of the office, because we'd have to meet with every single investor who didn't have an airtight alibi. It'd really put me behind with the rest of my case-load. But there was no choice. As Alex reached the door, I realized I'd forgotten to ask about his progress on another case. "What happened with Angelo?" Alex had gone to the jail to try and get Angelo to talk to him. "Did he come out?"

Alex rolled his eyes. "Oh, he came out, all right. But only because he thought someone else had sent me."

Then my theory had been right. I'd figured Angelo was being threatened about talking to the cops, because he got around and knew a lot about who did what to whom and why. "He thought you were sent by some gangbanger who's looking out for his homie in jail?"

"Not exactly. He thought I'd been sent by his brother, Tito."

I was perplexed. "Tito isn't in a gang."

"No, he's not," Alex said. "But he is a drug dealer."

I put it together. "Who's pretty big-time."

Alex nodded. "According to my sources. Which are pretty reliable."

Because he'd hacked into the LAPD database. Again. I had to get him to stop doing that. He was bound to get caught at some point. "So Angelo was planning to give him up to the cops."

Alex shrugged. "He didn't exactly say that. But when I told him I worked for you and that you needed to know what he could give the cops so you could make a deal for him, he gave me penny-ante stuff. A couple of car thefts, a burglary, some illegal weapons possession."

In other words, bubkes. The detectives would not be impressed. "Then his brother is the only real gold he had."

"Seems that way." Alex gave me a grim look. "So now what?"

I didn't see a whole lot of options. "Either he gives up Tito and we get the cops to give him protection, or he embraces his new home away from home—for a very long time."

Alex sighed. "Do you really think the cops can keep him safe?"

Neither of us was a big fan of the boys in blue. "It depends on how big Tito really is. Dale could probably find out for me."

His lips twitched in a little smile. "You know all this help from Dale is going to cost you."

I waved him off. "He'll want stuff from me regardless. May as well get what I need when I need it."

But I told Alex to close the door on his way out. If I wanted to give Dale a to-do list, I'd have to put him in the right mood. I texted him an invitation to dinner at Granville, a great restaurant in West Hollywood. It had a menu that went on for days, with lots of California cuisine as well as great burgers. And it wasn't as pricey as most places in the 'hood. It was one of our favorites.

He texted back, Sounds good. But whatever you think you're going to ask me to do, forget it.

Yeah, we'd see about that. I cleared out my in-box in anticipation of the hours Alex and I would be spending on the street and even got my time sheets done for Michy. By six o'clock, I was hungry and ready for a break.

I took my purse and iPad and went to Michy's desk. She was devouring a bag of one of those faux-healthy fried veggie snacks. "You know they're really just green potato chips."

Michy gave me an evil stare. "Better than what you eat, Miss Glazed Doughnut Queen."

I nodded. "That's fair."

She asked, "You heading out?"

"Yeah. And you can do the same." I told her I was taking Dale out to dinner.

She gave me a knowing look. "Good move. We could use his help."

"Exactly." I headed for the door. "He's useful. It's why I keep him around."

Michy snorted. "Bullshit. You two have a good time together. Admit it."

"Never." Though it was true. We did. When I didn't want to kill him.

I decided not to hassle with traffic and called for an Uber. For a change, I got there fifteen minutes early. Dale showed up soon after. Our table wasn't ready, so we took a seat at the bar. Granville makes some delicious specialty drinks, but I'm a vodka martini drinker all the way. Dale usually drank scotch, but he opted for beer—Stella Artois—tonight.

I raised my glass, and we clinked. "To your girlfriend, who has apparently widened your drinking horizons."

He gave me a grudging smile. "You're right. But it's really good." After we drank, he held out his glass. "Here, try it."

I made a face. "No, gracias. Beer makes me full after one sip, and I want to leave plenty of room for important stuff." I pointed to my martini.

Dale nodded. "Point taken."

We were off to a great start. And then I noticed Kingsford at the other end of the bar. He nodded at me, and I nodded back. Dale asked who I'd seen. I kept my voice low. "Guess who else is a fan of Granville?"

"Elton John."

Elton John is Dale's answer to everything. I told him that, shockingly, it wasn't Elton John. It was Kingsford. "What are the friggin' odds?"

Dale had a puzzled look. "What's he doing in West Hollywood at this hour?"

We didn't have long to wonder. Kingsford threw down a few bills and came over to where we were sitting. "Kind of weird meeting you guys here."

I raised an eyebrow. "A lot weirder to see you here. Your office is downtown. Mine is ten minutes away."

Kingsford took that in. "Got a couple of witnesses who live in the area."

I put down my martini. "You mean angry investors? If so, I'd call them suspects, not witnesses. Your suspect list has got to be about a mile long."

Kingsford glanced at Dale for a moment, then looked back at me. "We do have a lot of angry investors. But very few of them know how to kill someone in this particular way. Even fewer actually knew where Bryan lived—could've gotten access to his house."

I glared at him. "But I assume you're checking alibis."

He shrugged. "Of the few who fit the above criteria."

I didn't like where this was going. "And I'm sure you've considered the possibility that Tanner killed Bryan and then faked his own death so he could disappear with all the money. Right?"

He spoke with that condescending "I know more than you" tone all cops seem to have. "Of course we have. But I'll be honest with you. The best-looking theory so far is that someone killed them both. And the best-looking 'someone' is your client. You might want to tell Niko that as of now, we consider him a person of interest." He patted the bar between Dale and me. "Have a nice evening."

I turned back to the bar. "Asshole."

Dale's expression hardened as he stared after Kingsford for several long seconds, then met my gaze. His tone was both resigned and determined. "Okay, I'm in. Tell me what you need."

Kingsford had bombed my night. But I couldn't have asked for a better way to get Dale to lend me a hand.

Silver linings and all that, I guess.

TWENTY-TWO

Dale said he could give me the skinny on Tito by the next morning. And the list of investors with contact information wouldn't take much longer.

This is when having a dad who's a detective is awesome. It's a little less awesome when my clients find out about that. But there was one thing I'd decided to look into that I couldn't ask Dale to help me with.

I spoke to Alex about it privately the following morning. "I want to do a workup on Niko."

Alex's eyes widened. "I thought you guys were cool now."

"We are. I just . . ." It was hard to explain—even to myself. "I think I just need to know the truth about him."

He tilted his head and peered at me. "In what respect?"

I thought a moment. "I'd like to know more about his background, his growing-up years."

Alex frowned. "Hasn't he already told you about a lot of that? By our third date, Paul dredged up every memory he had since the age of three."

"He has. But he hasn't told me everything." I gave Alex a pointed look. "Obviously."

He nodded. "True." After a brief pause, he asked, "What are you not telling me?"

I realized in that moment what I really wanted. "I need to know whether he did it, Alex. Whether he killed them." I didn't like Kingsford's pronouncement that Niko was a "person of interest," but legally speaking, it didn't mean much. At this point, all they had were some loose circumstantial connections—and, of course, motive. They might never get any further with their theory. But we had access to more information about Niko than the cops would ever have. I knew we could figure out what, if anything, he'd done.

Alex stared at me intently. "Are you sure you want to know?"

It bummed me out to admit it. "Yes." I had to get to the truth. I just couldn't help it.

He stood up. "Okay, I'm on it." He started to leave, but he paused with his hand on the doorknob. "Assuming we find out he did . . . something. What are you going to do?"

I dropped my gaze to my desk. "I don't know."

Later that morning, Dale emailed me the list of investors. And he also came through with information about Tito. He delivered the latter via cell phone that afternoon.

As I answered the phone, I heard the roar of buses and cars honking in the background. "Where are you calling me from? A freeway median?"

"I'm heading for the churro cart on the corner. I smelled them on the way in this morning and couldn't stop thinking about getting one."

I laughed. "One? It'll be three by the time you're through. So you called to make me jealous? And hungry?" My stomach rumbled at the mention of those delicious cinnamony cylinders of perfection.

"Hang on." I heard him ask for two churros in Spanish. After he told the vendor, "Gracias," he was back on the phone. "Got information for you on Tito."

"Great. Spill."

He spoke with his mouth full. "No gig deal or his ory."

He was talking with a mouthful of churro. "I have no idea what you just said. You can't hold off on dessert for thirty seconds?"

I heard him swallow some water. "Obviously not. From what I can tell, Tito's not that big a dealer. At least, not the kind with enough reach to get to Angelo if the cops give him protection. That's the story according to Major Narco."

That was good news. Sort of. It meant Angelo could snitch and not worry about getting killed. But if Tito wasn't "that big," Angelo's information about him might not impress the cops enough to get him the deal I'd been hoping for. I'd just have to find out whether the cops would give him protection and what they'd be willing to give Angelo for his information. I thanked Dale for the info on Tito. "And thanks for the other stuff."

He paused. "What other stuff? I have no idea what you're talking about."

Mr. Paranoia didn't want any mention of the fact that he was helping me with an open investigation. One that happened to have placed my boyfriend in the ten-ring of the bull's-eye. "I just meant that list of great restaurants in Tuscany."

"Oh, yeah. Sure."

I almost laughed. But it really didn't hurt to be careful. "Go pound some more churros."

We ended the call, and I went over to Alex's office to tell him about Tito. "So here's the plan: you go talk to Angelo, find out what kind of information he can give up on Tito. Then I'll talk to the D.A. and the detectives and see whether they get excited enough to make a deal that's worth Angelo's while."

"Got it," he said. "In the meantime, I've been digging into Niko's history. Have you ever met his brother, Ivan?"

"No." He'd mentioned a brother but not much more than that. "I got the impression they're estranged."

Alex gave a humph. "And with good reason. He was a shot caller in the Rollin 90s."

I'd heard of them. So had every other cop and criminal lawyer. The Rollin 90s were about as bad as they came. Their game was mainly drugs. But they had virtually no limits when it came to protecting their territory or their product. Police estimate that gang was responsible for hundreds of murders and assaults over the past ten years. I could understand why Niko never wanted to talk about his brother. But it was hard to picture Sophia being able to handle a son with a lifestyle like that. I voiced the sentiment to Alex.

He opened his iPad. "I agree. But Sophia divorced the dad and moved out. Not sure when Ivan got jumped into the gang, whether it was before or after that."

I mulled that over. "Wasn't Ivan the older brother?" Alex nodded. That worried me. Younger brothers sometimes follow in their older siblings' footsteps.

He saw where my thoughts had taken me. "Remember, my brother was in a gang." He pointed to himself. "But I didn't go there."

True. Alex had come from some of the roughest beginnings, and joining a gang would've been a natural act of self-preservation. But he'd resisted the temptation. Maybe Niko had, too. "What else have you got?"

Alex was looking at his iPad. "It's weird, because it seems like the family was doing okay, and then all of a sudden, everything went down the shitter."

"What do you mean?"

He frowned. "No indication that the father lost his job or that he was abusive. And no indication that anyone got sick or died." He glanced up at me with a perplexed expression. "Everything was fine. Then, like, out of the blue, the parents got divorced, his father got busted for a hit-and-run while drunk driving—nearly took out a family of four—and then Sophia got sick. And a couple of years later, Ivan got busted for vandalism. Graffiti, actually."

I knew what that probably meant. "Gang graffiti?"

"Right. So by then he'd obviously joined the gang." He stopped and stared out the window behind me. "It just bugs me. I know I'm missing something."

How to learn more? I ran through the options in my mind. We had to be careful about who we contacted. I didn't want Niko to know I was investigating him. Ever. I could think of only one possibility. "Do you know where we can find Ivan?"

A look of disdain crossed his face. "Must we? He's a scumbag gang-banging loser. Even if he'll talk to us—a big if—he'll just spew bullshit."

I know it's hard to tell, but Alex has no love for bangers. I'm no fan, either. But I've known some who are okay people. Occasionally even helpful. They did a nice job helping me get rid of a homicidal cop. "He's our only shot. So yes, we must."

Alex sighed. "Yeah, I think I have an address for him. Assuming he didn't get busted in the past hour and a half."

"What's his rap sheet look like?"

He glanced down at his iPad again. "Actually, it's pretty minimal, all things considered. A couple of drug possession busts. A shoplifting charge—which he beat somehow." He scrolled for a moment. "I show an address for him in the Miracle Mile area. Looks like a house."

Not an apartment. The Miracle Mile area, in the Wilshire Boulevard corridor, is close to downtown Los Angeles. It'd fallen into disrepair in the not-so-distant past, but now some pretty pricey neighborhoods—with multimillion-dollar homes—were sprinkled among the middle- and lower-middle-income-bracket 'hoods. "Business must be good."

Alex gave me a sour but resigned look. "When do you want to go?"

I looked at my watch. It was only three o'clock. A perfect time to avoid evening rush hour. I stood up. "If you're waiting for me, you're backing up." He got up as slowly as he possibly could and slumped over to the door. "Your protest is duly noted."

He made a face. "We're taking your car."

When I told Michy who we were going to see, she said, "How did I know you'd have to do this?" She sighed. "Be careful."

"We'll make nice with Ivan. I'm not worried."

Michy shook her head. "I was referring to Niko."

Oh, that. I told her we'd make sure he never found out, and we headed for the elevator. Once we got into my car, I typed the address Alex gave me into Waze and pulled out of the garage.

On the way there, Alex made one remark about wasting time talking to an idiot banger, but otherwise we rode in silence. I was as curious as hell to meet Niko's brother. Although they were estranged now—and it seemed like that had been true for many years—Niko had spent his childhood with this man.

We were just twenty minutes away when I stopped musing and realized we'd need to come up with a cover story. "Who are we going to be?" Alex and I have a whole arsenal of personas to use when we want to talk to someone without letting them know who we are. "Real estate agents looking to list homes in the area?"

Alex shook his head. "I couldn't pull up the image of his place for some reason. If it's a dump, he won't buy it."

You never know. He might. But no need to take chances. "How about we're thinking of moving into the area? All you need to do is check your iPad for a house that's for sale nearby."

He gave a half smile. "Funny you should think of that. When I tried to pull up an image of his place, I saw a FOR SALE sign on the lawn next door. Assuming it's a recent photo—which we'll find out soon enough—that's a damn good choice."

I shrugged. "Sometimes I get lucky. But you know what I say."

"Yeah, I do. Because you say it all the time. So please don't—"

"I'd rather be lucky than good."

He put his hands over his ears. "Why must you always torture me?"

I gave him a beatific smile. "We only torture the ones we love."

He wrinkled his nose. "Now I'm going to vomit."

"Then please roll down the window." I turned onto Vista Street. "This is his block, right?"

"Yeah. Slow down." He pointed to a small beige ranch-style home on the corner with a redbrick walk and a charming set of bay windows that wrapped around the right side. Sure enough, the house next door had a **FOR SALE** sign on the lawn. It didn't look nearly as nice as Ivan's.

I parked around the corner out of the sight line of his house, in case we had to make a fast dash out of there. I looked at Alex. "Here goes nothin'."

He gave me a deadpan expression. "Probably."

We held hands as we moved up the brick walkway. Just two young newlyweds about to buy their first home together. Now *I* wanted to vomit. I couldn't find a doorbell, so I knocked. I didn't hear any movement or sound, and I worried that no one was home. I raised my hand to knock again, but then I heard the thud of heavy footsteps on wood. Someone was home, and they were coming.

The door opened, and a balding, heavyset man in his forties, a little over six feet tall, wearing skull stud earrings, peered out at us. "Can I help you?"

Could this be Niko's brother? I took in his worn jeans, faded Affliction T-shirt, and flip-flops. He didn't much look like a gangbanger. And he didn't look a whole lot like Niko—though he did have the same strong jawline. I smiled charmingly (I hoped) and leaned toward Alex. "Hi. I'm Sally, and this is Mark. We're hoping to buy the house next door, and we were wondering if you could tell us about the neighborhood?"

He sized us up for a moment, then stuck out a hand. "I'm Ivan. Come on in."

We all shook hands, and as we followed him inside, I felt a frisson of anxiety. I was going behind Niko's back to meet a brother he clearly didn't want in his life, or mine.

But as always, curiosity won out over decency, common sense . . . and guilt.

TWENTY-THREE

Ivan ushered us into a sparsely furnished living room. He gestured for us to sit on the sagging green couch and took a seat opposite us in a matching—and equally worn—recliner. I heard a television playing in a room toward the back of the house. Had he left it on? Or was someone else here? I didn't hear anyone moving around. We must be alone. Good.

Now that we were in closer quarters, I noticed Ivan had tats crawling up the back of his neck and letters tattooed above the knuckle on each finger. I couldn't make out what—if anything—they spelled without seeming obvious. But finger tats are a very typical gang thing.

We chatted about the neighborhood. Ivan said it was pretty peaceful, though "the assholes" were only a few miles away. He told us his house was on the fringes of the gentrified section, and the lower—and no—income neighborhoods were close enough for you to hit them if you "swung a dead cat." I didn't know why anyone would want to swing a dead cat, but I nodded and feigned a look of concern.

Alex wisely used that opening to talk about his own poor beginnings and how he'd been steeped in the gang life for years.

Ivan peered at him with narrowed eyes. "What gang was that?"

I hoped Alex had thought this through, because he had to be careful. He had to give the name of a real gang, but it couldn't be one Ivan might be able to access—and find out Alex wasn't a member.

Alex returned his gaze. "Calle 18."

Nice choice. 18th Street had started out as a Los Angeles street gang. But now it was a transnational gang that stretched across the United States and into Central America. From what I'd heard, it was one of the most violent gangs in the Southern hemisphere—which should get Ivan's respect—but even better, it had at least thirty thousand members. There was no way anyone in LA could tell Ivan whether Alex was a member. Especially since we'd given fake names.

Ivan began to probe Alex with questions about his gang life, and Alex was happy to oblige with gnarly—and authentic-sounding—stories. Stories he'd probably heard from his brothers, who really were gangbangers. It was a good strategy. If you want to get someone to open up about himself, you go first. And it seemed to be working. Ivan was nodding and leaning forward, eating it all up.

Alex finally said, "I'm going on and on. I hope I haven't bored you to death."

Ivan waved a hand. "No, man. I used to be in the life, too. Chosen Few MC." He stared off. "Me and my little brother."

His little brother . . . that couldn't be. I tried to sound pleasantly—not intently—interested. "You have a younger brother?"

Ivan's expression hardened. "Used to. We don't speak. Not since our little sister . . . died."

Little sister? Maybe this wasn't Niko's brother. Not only had Niko never mentioned being in a gang, he'd certainly never mentioned a little sister. "I'm so sorry. What happened to her?"

His expression turned bitter. "Drive-by shooting. Rival gang—Nazi Low Riders." Ivan shook his head. "I spent years looking for the pieces of shit who did it. That's why I stayed in Chosen Few. But not Niko. He bailed. Blamed me for her death. Hasn't spoken to me since."

A sister. One who died. Because a rival gang—as in a gang that was a rival to *Niko's* gang—killed her. What else was I going to learn about him? That he ran a high-stakes poker game in Dubai? That he laundered money for the Russian mafia? "Family gatherings must be pretty hard."

Ivan gave a short bark of a laugh. "They probably would be if we'd ever had one. Parents got divorced about a year after Kristina died. Dad drank himself into a fatal car accident, and my stepmom . . . she never forgave me. Haven't seen her since I graduated high school and moved out. She found a place somewhere on the west side and took Niko with her."

So Ivan was Niko's half brother. That's why they didn't look much alike. They had different mothers. I was trying to wrap my head around all this.

Alex could see I was reeling. He stepped in. "But Niko was in the gang, too. Why didn't they blame him?"

I thought that'd elicit a wounded remark about the injustice of it all. But Ivan gave a heavy sigh and hung his head. "Because it was my fault. I'd gotten into a beef with one of the Riders over a drug deal they screwed up for me. I beat the guy up pretty badly, put him in the hospital. My little sister was payback."

From the sounds of it, Niko had turned his life around after Kristina's death. I wouldn't be surprised if he was the one who'd suggested they move out of the area. "Did you ever find the person who killed her?"

Ivan's eyes darkened. "No. But the shot caller of the gang dropped off the face of the earth a few years later. People say he's dead. Cops suspected me for a while. I told 'em I wished I had killed him."

I asked, "Did they ever suspect Niko?"

"Not that I know of," he said. "He wasn't around. He'd been gone for a few years by then."

Right. That made sense. Niko would've been in college by that point, and he'd told me that he scored a scholarship to the University of California, Santa Barbara—which is where he'd taken his first martial arts class.

A woman wearing cutoffs and a Nirvana T-shirt that was at least three sizes too small came in. When she saw us, she ran a hand through pink-tipped black hair that looked like it hadn't seen a comb in months. "Ivan, the air-conditioning keeps cutting off. You said you fixed it."

Ivan turned to look at her. "I did. Just give me a few minutes."

She gazed at Alex for a long beat—as women so often did—then shifted her gaze to me. "Who are you?"

I introduced Alex and myself with our fake names and told her we were thinking about moving to the neighborhood. "Ivan's been kind enough to give us the pros and cons."

She nodded slowly. I didn't like the way she was staring at me. I stood up. "Well, we've taken enough of your time, Ivan. Thank you so much for—"

The woman pointed a finger at me. "I know who you are. You're that lawyer!" She turned to Ivan. "Babe, she's that lawyer who got her dad off for murder."

I moved toward the door. "I'm sorry, I think you've got me confused with someone else."

Alex reached out for Ivan's hand. "Thanks for your time. It's been a real pleasure."

But now Ivan was staring at me, too. He ignored Alex's outstretched hand. "Yeah, that's right. I knew you looked familiar."

I had my hand on the door, but the woman was moving toward me. "And you know what? She's Niko's girlfriend! I read it in *USA Today*."

Ivan stood up, his eyes blazing with fury. "What the hell are you up to?"

Alex stepped between the woman and me. "Nothing. Your wife is just a little . . . confused." He moved past me and opened the door.

Ivan didn't look persuaded. "I don't know what you're doing nosing around in my business. But I'll find out. And when I do, I'm going to find *you*."

I stepped out and said to Alex, "Come on, honey. We should get on the road."

We left the door open as we headed for the car and moved as fast as we could without breaking into a run. I jumped into the driver's seat, and Alex barely managed to get both legs in before I gunned the engine. I hoped to get away before Ivan could spot my car.

But he'd moved too fast. I was just about to make the turn when I glanced at my rearview mirror and saw him run out to the street. It looked like he was staring at my license plate. "Damn!"

Alex pulled down his visor and looked in the mirror. "Just be glad he didn't have time to go for his gun."

I drove to the freeway with one eye trained on the rearview, expecting to see Ivan in an F-150—because guys like that always have one of those monster trucks—bearing down on us any second. But when I reached the freeway and still hadn't seen him, I started to relax. He wasn't coming. Yet. "What do you think he'll do?"

Alex had been gripping the armrest. Now he let go and wiggled his fingers.

"Well, he doesn't strike me as the type to go to the cops."

No argument there. "But now he's bound to think something must be going on with Niko that made us look him up."

Alex nodded. "In which case, he might find out about Bryan and Tanner. And decide he has something to tell the cops."

Exactly my fear. "I haven't seen any press coverage yet. Have you?"

Alex was silent for a moment. "No. Not that I can recall. But I haven't been looking. Want me to call Michy and find out if she's seen anything in the news?"

I told him to go ahead and call her.

The call was brief. When he ended it, he said, "She hasn't seen anything so far."

But it'd only been a week since we'd found Bryan's body. The press was bound to get wind of this soon. The question was, if Ivan did hear about the murders, what would he do? There was clearly no love lost between them. Would he go so far as to give the cops damning information on Niko?

And if he did, what would that be? Would he lie? Or worse, would he even need to? After what I'd just learned about Niko, I couldn't say.

A gang history. A sister who'd been killed in a drive-by. And a shot caller who'd mysteriously gone missing. Right around the time Niko took his first martial arts class in college.

Anything was possible.

TWENTY-FOUR

By the time we got back to the office, it was almost six o'clock, and I knew I wouldn't get anything done. "I'm going to drop you off and head home."

Alex shifted to turn toward me. "I know you feel guilty, but we both know you were going to wind up digging into Niko with all that's been going on. And if it makes you feel any better, I would've done it on the sly if you hadn't asked me to."

I was surprised. "Are you serious? I thought it was just my usual pathological obsession with knowing the truth about everything."

He frowned at me. "Are *you* serious? This isn't just some rando client. This is the man you love. And seems to be the only man you've ever loved. If it were me, I couldn't go five minutes without digging into every corner of his life—murder investigation or no."

I relaxed a little. That was good to hear. "Thanks, Alex."

He stared out the windshield. "Of course, that doesn't mean we didn't potentially screw him by having our little chat with Ivan."

My tone was sarcastic. "Thanks, Alex." I pulled to the curb in front of my office building. "Get out."

Alex gave an indignant sniff and left. When I got home, I found a voice message from Niko on my landline saying he was sorry for the short notice, but he'd be flying out to New York tomorrow. He'd been putting off his next video shoot since Sophia had her stroke, but the media company had run out of patience. A fresh wave of guilt washed over me as I realized how relieved I was to hear that he'd be gone. But I needed time to absorb what I'd learned about him—and figure out what it meant that he'd hidden it all from me.

I understood his need to cover up the ugly and omit the embarrassing. I had a secret—or two hundred—of my own. But he was a prime suspect in a murder case.

And with every new revelation, I couldn't help wondering what else he was hiding—and whether that *else* included Bryan's or Tanner's murder.

I called Niko back and got his voice mail. I wished him a safe flight and said I'd be thinking of him. Truer words were never spoken. Exhausted by my own feelings of guilt and worried about what lay in store for Niko, I poured myself a double shot of Patrón Silver on the rocks and sank down on the couch. What I needed right now was a distraction. I turned on the television and flipped through my menu. I had two new episodes of *Better Call Saul*. Perfect.

At some point, I fell asleep on the couch at a weird angle and woke up with a sore neck. I rubbed it into submission as I sleepwalked to my bedroom, dropped my clothes on the floor, and fell into bed.

I dreamed that I was in a crowded airport, searching for Niko. It went on and on as I wound my way through the body-packed terminal, but everything around me was a blur. It was one of those dreams that are all about nonstop frustration and anxiety. My subconscious was so on the nose. I was happy when I woke up and put an end to it.

I took a shower and let the hot water beat down on my sore neck. I didn't have to go to court or meet with clients, so I dressed casually in slacks and a sweater. I'd just finished my second supersize mug of coffee and found my pulse when Alex called.

He sounded amped. "You about ready to go? I've got some investors who're willing to talk to us."

That was great news. "Who?"

Alex was in one of his hyperdrive moods. "Just come pick me up. I'll tell you on the way."

He can be incredibly bossy. He was still at home, which was about ten minutes away from my place, so I told him I'd pick him up there. I finished my caffeine fix and headed out.

The second I pulled up to his house, he walked out, iPad in hand. He got into the car and gave me an address in Bel Air—one of the priciest neighborhoods in the world. I typed it into Waze. "Is that north of Sunset?" Alex nodded. Houses in that lush, hilly area cost in the tens of millions. "Jeez. Whoever this is must've been one heavy-duty investor."

Alex read from his iPad. "He was. Gene Steier lost over one point five million to our favorite con artists, and he's pissed as hell."

Which was why he was willing to talk to us. He'd probably been talking to anyone who'd listen from the moment he found out he'd lost all that money. "Does he know who we are exactly?"

He closed his iPad. "Sort of. I told him you were a lawyer who was representing another investor."

And that sweetened the deal even more. The possibility of free legal help opens a lot of doors. Of course, he wouldn't be getting any. At least, not from me. But there was no reason to tell him that. "Does he know it's Niko?"

He shook his head. "He didn't ask, so I didn't tell. Should we?"

My involvement with Niko was no secret. I was sure that, by now, the cops had to know. "May as well. The investors will probably hear about it eventually anyway."

"True," Alex said. "And I don't see the harm in it. Niko lost a real fat stack. He's got a legitimate reason to hire a lawyer."

My voice was bitter. "You mean, besides the fact that the cops have just nominated him as their favorite suspect?"

Alex sighed. "Well, there is that."

We wove our way through the hills and pulled up to a sprawling beige compound surrounded by black iron gates. The style was meant to be Italian villa, but from what I could see through the gates, it looked pretty cookie-cutter. Just a large—okay, huge—version of the Mediterranean-style homes you can find all over the neighborhoods in upper suburbia. I rolled down my window and pushed the button on the intercom. A woman with a Hispanic accent asked who I was. I gave my name and Alex's.

She said, "Don't park in front of the garage."

Three seconds later, the gates swung open, and I pulled into a driveway that was the size of a football field. So, avoiding the garage doors . . . not a problem. Driveways that big usually have a fountain in the middle—that's frequently broken and filled with sludge. This one was no exception. A big, mushroom-shaped piece of concrete sat in the middle of a dry, moldy fountain. You'd think someone who bothered to put that thing front and center like that would want to keep it in good working order. But what do I know?

As I parked the car, I scanned the main building. The front door was a massive piece of wood with an iron-barred window at peephole level. It was flanked by two huge floor-to-ceiling windows of beveled glass. Pricey by any measure.

"What does our new best friend Gene do for a living?"

Alex was looking at the house with a smile. "Owns a national door and window company."

Of course. What else? As we got out and moved up the stone walkway, the mega-door opened, and a short, middle-aged woman in a maid's uniform appeared. I didn't think anyone made their housekeepers wear those things anymore. She gestured for us to come in and led us through a wide hallway with high ceilings that were punctuated by horizontal wood beams. Thick Persian runners covered the travertine floors. Everything I saw was tasteful enough, and certainly expensive, but there were no personal, creative touches.

After what seemed like a very long walk, she led us into a sunken living room that was the size of a ballroom. The ceiling—that felt like it was twenty feet high—carried through on the exposed-beam motif, and the room was so large, I figured there must've been twenty of those beams. I saw three different furniture groupings. I could tell that either Gene or his wife had told the designer to let them take over. Because this room had zero taste. All the sofas, chairs, and coffee tables were in various tones of brown. It felt like I was swimming in a sea of mud. The only bright spot was a random blue love seat that just made me ask, *why?*

The housekeeper motioned us to a brown (what else?) chenille sofa. Seconds later, a barrel-chested man with tufts of wiry red hair strode in. He was a ball of fast, nervous energy. I stood up and offered my hand. "Gene Steier? I'm Samantha Brinkman."

He gave me a limp shake with half his hand. "Yeah." He looked at Alex. "You the guy I spoke to on the phone?"

Alex nodded and held out his hand. "Alex Medrano. Nice to meet you."

Gene didn't return the sentiment. He perched on the arm of the double-size chair across from us, folded his arms, and lasered in on me. His voice was loud, as though he was projecting to someone fifty feet away. "My business manager says there's something fishy about that cryptocurrency trade. So what are you going to do about it?"

Clearly, this was a guy who did everything at full scream and warp speed. And he'd already managed to get under my skin. So I deliberately took a beat before I spoke—as slowly and irritatingly as I could. "I'm trying to gather information to find out what happened with the trade and where the money went."

He looked at me like I'd just said I didn't know how a thermos worked. "What happened with the trade? I'll tell you what happened. Those two idiots gave our money to a crook who was smarter than they are."

His business manager had smelled a rat, but Gene didn't know that the trade had never happened, that it was just a money grab. I probably could tell him now. The cops would eventually figure it out and tell the investors. But I didn't want him to get distracted. I needed answers of my own. I nodded—slowly. "So I understand."

He fired another question at me. "Where's Tanner? You got any information on him?"

I blinked—slowly. Then shook my head. "As I'm sure you know, the police are searching for him. Did they talk to you?"

His expression was disdainful, dismissive. "Yeah. Asked me where he might've gone, when I last saw him, yadda yadda. I told 'em I just did business with him. I didn't socialize with the little punk."

We definitely did agree on some things. "What about Bryan? Did you know him well?"

His tone was snide. "Well enough to know what he was."

An odd remark. "What do you mean?"

Gene made a sour face. "He liked the pretty boys."

So on top of everything else, our buddy Gene was a homophobe. Shocking. But I wasn't sure whether he literally meant "boys"—as in males below the age of consent—or just good-looking men. "You mean Bryan was gay?"

Gene snorted. "Total fag. Always had a bunch of kids around. Used to fly them places, take them out to fancy dinners. Bought 'em all kinds of shit."

Total fag? I felt my hand curl into a fist. I so wanted to slug this guy. But I needed information. Like, what Gene—who looked to be in his fifties—meant by *kid*. "How young were these boys?"

"Not one of them looked like they'd had their first shave," he said.

One glance at Alex told me that we both knew what this might mean. Alex asked, "Did any of their parents go after him?"

Gene shrugged. "Not that I ever heard. But who knows? I didn't hang out with the old fairy. Maybe someone did." He was annoyed. "Look, unless this has something to do with getting my money back, I really don't give a shit. He's dead. Moving on." Gene faced me. "So for the last time, how do you plan to get our money back?"

I wanted to tell him I had no such plan. That it didn't matter how much money he had, I'd never lift a finger to help a cretinous pig like him. But I decided not to burn this bridge, because you never know. I stood up. "I'm working on it, Gene. But the more information I get, the better chance I'll have to help you out. So if there's anything else you remember about either Tanner or Bryan, just give me a call." I handed him my card.

"All I'm gonna say is, *someone* better get my money back." He flicked my card with his finger. "And soon."

And with that, he got up and stomped out of the room.

TWENTY-FIVE

We waited until I'd driven out through the gates to talk about our meeting with the Olympic-level charmer that was Gene Steier. I started. "Too bad we didn't get to meet the missus. Bet she's a real gem, too."

Alex's lips twitched in a semismile. "You'll be shocked to learn that he's divorced. There is no Mrs. Steier. But do not shed a tear. A catch like him won't stay on the market long."

Sadly, I knew that was true. The biggest bastard becomes Prince Charming if his bank account is healthy enough. And Gene's was clearly the picture of health. "Much as I'd love to put him on our suspect list, nothing about this jerk smells like a murderer—or someone who hired a killer."

Alex gave a reluctant nod. "I don't see it, either. I'll check his alibi, just to be on the safe side, but yeah. We can move on."

But we hadn't come away completely empty-handed. "On a more optimistic note, if what he said about Bryan was true, we might have a whole other pool of suspects for his murder." An angry father—a mother seemed less likely given the cause of death—who found out that Bryan had been preying on his son had a pretty decent motive to take revenge.

Alex drummed his fingers on the armrest. "Agree. And we're about to talk to investors who might know the boys he was hanging out with."

I forgot he'd lined up other investors. "Who are they?" I pulled over and took out my phone. "And where are they?"

"Edie and Joey Franco." Alex gave me the address of a house in Holmby Hills—a neighborhood in Westwood that was slightly less pricey than Bel Air, but not by much. I put the address in Waze and headed for Sunset Boulevard.

Fifteen minutes later, I pulled up to another set of iron gates and spoke into another intercom. As I drove up the driveway, a white two-story house flanked by a set of imposing columns that held up a front balcony came into view. It kind of looked like the White House—only bigger. This time, the woman who opened the door was the owner, and she greeted me with a warm smile. As she ushered us into a marbled foyer, I thought she looked familiar, but I couldn't quite place her. I introduced Alex and myself.

She took my outstretched hand. "Pleasure to meet you. Do people call you Sam?"

Something about her just made me smile. "They do, and you should."

"Come on, guys." She motioned for us to follow her. "They're setting up for a shoot in the house, so we thought it'd be nicer to sit outside by the pool."

A shoot. I wanted to ask whether they were being interviewed for some show or had a show of their own, but it was risky. If they had their own show, she might be insulted that I didn't know about it.

She led us through a wall of accordion glass doors that opened out to an expensively furnished patio in a backyard that was the size of my apartment building. On the right side of the lawn was an iron sculpture of a grinning man and woman sitting on an upside-down house. Just ahead was a long teak dining table that was shaded by a large blue umbrella. A very tan, handsome man sitting at that table—who looked a lot like the iron sculpture man—waved to us. As we moved toward him, I realized why Edie looked familiar. Edie and Joey had turned a very successful house-flipping business into an even more successful cable show. Thus, the iron sculpture with the upside-down house.

Joey came over to us, and we shook hands. His smile lit up his whole face, and it looked genuine—not the usual broad, pasted-on type you see on most TV hosts. He nodded toward the house. "Sorry to have to talk out here, but it's crazy in there with the camera crew setting up. Can I get you something to drink?"

I sat down next to Alex and across from the Francos. "I'm good, thanks. And please don't apologize for meeting out here. It's a welcome change of pace." Not to mention, the perfect day for it. The sky was a piercing blue, and the pool sparkled under a sun that was warm but not too hot. The palm trees that lined the back of the property swayed in a gentle breeze. It was the kind of day LA is famous for—and the kind I seldom get the chance to enjoy.

Alex eased us into the interview with an open-ended question. "I understand you knew Bryan pretty well."

Edie looped her arm through Joey's. "He was one of our closest friends, and we just loved him. He really knew how to live, you know? We had such good times together."

Joey's smile was sad. "Bryan was the original bon vivant, and he liked to live large. Good food, nice clothes, fine art. He maximized the pleasure in every minute he had on this planet—and made sure everyone around him did, too."

This was a surprisingly benign view of someone who'd lost a lot of their money. And might well be a pedophile. "How much money did you lose on the cryptocurrency trade?"

Edie had been nodding and smiling as Joey extolled Bryan's virtues. Now, her face fell. "A hundred thousand. Which is a lot. But at least we have our business and the show. We'll be okay. Some others . . ."

Like Sophia, for example, who wouldn't be so okay. "Some are saying the trade was a scam all along."

Edie glanced at Joey, who sighed. "We've gone back and forth. But if it was a scam, I'm sure Tanner was the one who pulled Bryan into it."

Edie nodded. "Bryan was a prankster, but he never would've stolen from us."

I asked, "Prankster? What kind of pranks did he play?"

Joey gave a little laugh. "He'd score private planes for our trips to New York by pretending to be the owner." He shook his head. "How he managed to get the owner's information, I have no idea."

Edie seemed amused, too. "And remember how he got the owner of that art gallery to send him the painting he wanted COD?"

I raised an eyebrow. "And I assume he never paid." They shook their heads with a chuckle. For some reason, they seemed to think this was incredibly cute. I didn't get it.

Alex moved on. "We hear he hung out with a lot of young men. Mostly teenagers."

"He was like the Pied Piper," Joey said. "They just loved to be around him."

"Do you think it was sexual?" I asked.

Edie was adamant. "Absolutely not. He liked young people in general." She paused. "Actually, Bryan liked everybody. But the young ones really seemed to be drawn to him."

"Do you know any of the young boys who were close to him?" Alex asked.

Edie knitted her brow. "I can't remember anyone in particular. I know they all went to Rolling Oaks Academy. Joey?"

Joey stared down at the table for a few moments, then looked up. "Yeah, I actually do remember a couple of them. Christopher Monroe and Rafael Giovanni. Nice kids."

Joey confirmed they both attended Rolling Oaks. "Do you know how Bryan met Tanner?" I asked.

Edie tilted her head as she stared off. "I'm not sure. But I think one of those kids who went to the academy brought him to Bryan's house." She looked at Joey. "Right, honey?"

Joey shrugged. "Maybe. Makes sense." He turned to me. "You know what? You should check out the real estate guy in Beverly Hills. He invested big in the cryptocurrency trade. Really big. Tanner brought him in."

"Why? What do you know about him?" I asked.

Edie frowned. "He put in a lot of money. I'm pretty sure Bryan said he kicked in more than five hundred thousand. The thing is, from what we heard, we couldn't figure out where all that money came from."

Joey added, "He's not some hotshot real estate agent to the stars. Matter of fact, he's barely hanging on at the agency."

Edie nodded. "And we asked around. He doesn't come from a rich family. So where did he get that kind of money?"

It did sound sketchy. "What's his name?"

"Wesley Rogerian," Joey said. "Works at the Elite Homes Agency."

"But you never met him?" I asked.

Edie shook her head. "We just heard about him from Bryan." She pressed her lips together. "Tell you the truth, I think Bryan was a little jealous because he was Tanner's client."

Joey chimed in. "So we decided to check him out, because most of the really big investors came in because of Bryan. That's how we discovered there was something shady about him."

Edie teared up. "We were going to tell Bryan, but it was too late . . ."

Joey patted the hand she'd wrapped around his arm. His eyes looked watery, too. "We're really going to miss him."

Alex said, "We're sorry for your loss. You were obviously very close."

Edie nodded and wiped away a tear.

I'd been thinking I might tell them the truth about the cryptocurrency trade, because I really liked these two. But I didn't want to be the one to shatter their illusions that Bryan the Merry Prankster was actually just a thief—and possibly a child molester. They'd find out soon enough. Let them have their rosy memories for a little longer.

A man in torn—not fashionably distressed, I mean really beat-up—jeans poked his head out and called to the Francos, "We're ready when you are."

Joey took a deep, cleansing breath and recovered his winning smile. "Thanks, Dave. Be right there!" He turned back to me. "Sorry. Duty calls. But if you have any more questions, just let us know. We'll be happy to meet with you again."

We all stood up, and I shook his hand. "Will do. And thanks for your time."

Edie hugged me, then wiped away another stray tear. "I know we'll never see our money again, and I don't care. I just hope they catch the bastard who killed Bryan."

I told her I did, too. But as they ushered us out through the back-yard gate, I thought, *As long as that bastard isn't Niko.*

TWENTY-SIX

As we made our way back to the car, I thought about what our next step should be, but I decided to wait until we were a few blocks away before discussing my idea with Alex. Dale's paranoia was rubbing off on me. "I'd like to find out more about that real estate guy." If he really didn't have any visible means of support, then someone must be bankrolling him. And that someone had to be hiding behind a proxy for a reason.

Alex pulled out his trusty iPad. "Might be a laundering situation. Or it might be a tax evasion thing. If the real estate guy—what was his name?"

I had to think for a moment. "Wesley Rogerian."

Alex spoke while he typed. "If he was in a lower income bracket, which seems likely based on what the Francos said, he'd pay less taxes on the profit."

That was a distinct possibility, too. "My money laundering theory's more fun. Are you checking him out?"

"Just confirmed that he works at Elite Homes," he said. "But we can't go straight at him."

True. If he was fronting for someone, he wouldn't just fess up and say, *You got me*. We had to think of a way to finesse this. I started to ask for Alex's input, but he was typing away, intent on . . . something. "So what are you doing now?"

He kept typing for a few more seconds before answering. "Finding our two Lost Boys. Christopher Monroe and Rafael Giovanni."

Bryan's young protégés. "Any luck?"

Alex smiled at the screen. "Yep. Easy peasy. They should be in school today. We can try and catch them this afternoon when school's out."

I looked at the clock on my dashboard. It felt weird to have a car that actually told the correct time. My old car, Beulah, never got on board with Pacific Standard Time. Or any other time, for that matter. That's why I'd taken to wearing a watch, even though I hated it. Watches always feel like handcuffs to me. But now, wearing a watch had become a habit. Maybe partly because I kept expecting this car clock to go belly-up at any moment, too. No question about it. Beulah had scarred me for life. "It's one o'clock. They should be out around three. I assume you have their home addresses?" Alex nodded. "Do they live close?"

He read from the screen. "Looks like they both live in Encino. Rush hour's going to be an issue if we go back to the office before we head out there."

He was right. Encino was in the San Fernando Valley, and the traffic on any canyon road we could take to get over the hill would be backed up for miles. "Then why don't we head over the canyon now and grab lunch somewhere close?"

Alex grinned. "Always down for a free lunch."

"We're not getting paid for this case, remember? Find us a place that's cheap." I pulled away from the curb and headed for Beverly Glen Canyon. "Unless you want to pay."

He tapped a key on his iPad. "Cheap it is."

We made it over the canyon in just half an hour, and Alex guided me to Stacked Eatery—a casual breakfast and lunch place on Ventura Boulevard. He showed me photos of the food on Yelp. They made my mouth water. "The paninis look great."

Alex rubbed his hands together. "Yeah, I'm getting the one with chicken pesto."

I was thinking about doing the same, but when we sat down and looked at the menu, I fell for the Shroom Burger and fries. Alex chose the panini and passed on the fries. We traded bites of each other's food. "I'm happy with my Shroom Burger."

Alex stole a fry from my plate. "I'm happy with my panini."

I gave him a pointed look as he popped another fry into his mouth. "And my fries." It was time to talk strategy. "I'm thinking we can be up-front about who we are."

He swiped another fry off my plate. "Agree. And we should keep it simple. Just ask them to talk about Bryan."

I nodded. But I had a few follow-ups ready, just in case they didn't give us anything to work with on their own.

We lingered over lunch as we waited for the end of the school day. Our waiter stopped filling our water glasses and then finally gave up on subtlety and told us his shift was over. I pulled out my credit card. "Here you go. Sorry." I glanced at my watch. It was time to leave anyway.

We headed for the car, and I noticed a cloud bank approaching. A dark, wet cloud bank. If it rained before we could get back to the office, we'd be in for an ugly drive. As I slid into the driver's seat, I asked, "Which one are we seeing first?"

Alex got in and buckled his seat belt. "I think Christopher. He's closer to where we are now. Rafael's closer to the canyon."

We'd get a jump on the traffic that way. I applauded Alex's geographically strategic thinking. I noted that Christopher's house was north of Ventura Boulevard—a lower-rent area. I suspected he'd gotten into the academy on a scholarship, because Rolling Oaks was one of the most expensive prep schools in the country. When I pulled up to the curb in front of Christopher's tiny ranch house, my suspicion was confirmed.

It looked like an old-school suburban family home, so when I knocked, I expected his mother to answer. But Christopher opened the door. He was indeed a pretty boy. Curly golden hair, blue eyes, rosy cheeks. He looked like he was too young to be in high school.

I tried for a hip, young note. "Hi, I'm Sam. And this is Alex. You're Christopher Monroe, right?" He nodded as his eyes darted between Alex and me. I explained that I was representing one of the Gold Strike investors regarding the cryptocurrency trade that had wiped out a lot of them. "We heard you knew Bryan pretty well."

Christopher looked uneasy. "Uh, not that well. I mean, we kind of—"

Another young man appeared behind him and pulled the door further open. "Hey, we heard he was dead. How'd it happen?"

That told me the cops hadn't gone public with the news that it was a homicide. They were being unusually circumspect. Had to be Kingsford's doing. O'Malley wasn't smart enough to realize the benefits of playing it close to the vest. I introduced myself again. "And you are?"

Christopher made room for him, and he stepped into the doorway. "Rafael Giovanni."

I shouldn't have been surprised to see him here. He and Christopher went to the same school and hung out with the same pedophile. I mean, *alleged* pedophile. And why was I questioning a lucky break? "Nice to meet you guys. Mind if we come in? I promise not to take long."

Christopher didn't look too keen on the idea, but Rafael stood back and gestured for us to enter. "Sure."

I saw Christopher shoot him a dagger look as we stepped past them into the small living room. Alex and I sat on the brown-and-orange-plaid sofa that looked like it'd been there since the seventies. Christopher perched stiffly on the arm of the brown corduroy chair across from us. Rafael flopped down on the orange beanbag chair next to him. An effort had obviously been made to coordinate colors. I wasn't sure it was worth it.

I took a moment to size up the two boys. They were a study in contrasts. Where Christopher was fair-skinned and seemed to be wound pretty tightly, Rafael was olive-skinned and laid-back. But he was every bit as pretty as Christopher, with long, straight black hair and large almond-shaped eyes.

I decided to start with an innocuous-sounding question. "You both go to Rolling Oaks Academy, right?" They nodded. "What year are you in?"

Rafael replied, "Junior. How'd he die?"

I gave him a truthful, though incomplete answer. "They found him in the bathtub." I followed it up with a lie. "That's all I know. But there's talk that he might've committed suicide. Did he ever talk about ending it all?"

Rafael shrugged. "No, not to me. But I guess it's possible. My dad's a stock investment adviser, and he told me he heard some big trade went bad. Maybe Bryan felt guilty or something."

Good guess. But not helpful. "Christopher? What do you think?"

He had a sullen expression. "It's Chris. And I have no idea. Why would you think I'd know?"

Lots of hostility there. This was going to be tough. "Because you were friends. I thought maybe he might've said something."

Chris stared at me. "No, he didn't."

Okay, so much for that route. I changed tacks. "How'd you guys meet Bryan?"

Rafael said, "One of my brother's friends brought us to a party at his house a couple of years ago."

Alex asked him for the names of his brother and the brother's friend and asked whether his brother knew Bryan. Rafael said he didn't. I decided to try and loosen the boys up—mainly Chris—by getting them to talk about the parties, the trips, and the good times. Chris barely spoke. After half an hour, I decided it was time to get to the point. "Did Bryan have a sexual relationship with any of the guys?"

Chris's face hardened. "No. Absolutely not. Who told you that?"

I played it low-key. "I can't say. But that's fine. I hear you. Did you happen to know Tanner?"

Chris's jaw tightened. "I saw him at Bryan's a few times. But I didn't hang out with him. I thought he was kind of a jerk."

On that subject, there seemed to be unanimity. The good news was that I'd gotten Chris to start talking. "We've been wondering whether maybe it wasn't a suicide."

Rafael frowned. "You mean, like maybe someone killed him?"

I shrugged. "It's just a thought. Do you know who might've had it in for Bryan?"

Chris's face closed up again. "Other than all those people who lost everything? No."

I looked at Rafael. "You?"

He shrugged. "Same." He stood up. "I'd love to stay and chat with y'all, but I gotta jump." He reached out and fist-bumped with Chris. "Catch ya later, dude."

Chris was clearly a dead end. But I had a feeling Rafael knew more than he was saying, and he might be willing to tell us if Chris wasn't around. I got up. "We should get moving, too. Traffic's going to be brutal."

Chris followed us to the door. Probably less as a polite gesture than the need to make sure we were finally out of there.

I stepped outside and turned back. "Thanks for talking with us."

He grunted, and the moment Alex followed me out, he closed the door. I hurried to catch up with Rafael. "Hey, can we give you a ride?" I hadn't seen a car parked in front of the house, so I assumed he'd either taken the school bus or Ubered here.

Rafael stopped and turned back. "That'd be great. Thanks."

It was a self-serving favor. I hoped the time in the car would give us a chance to squeeze him like a juice box. We all piled in, and I asked Rafael for his address. As I'd suspected, he lived in a much more expensive neighborhood on the better side of town—south of Ventura Boulevard.

When we started to roll, I asked, "Did something happen between Chris and Bryan? He seemed kind of . . . angry."

Rafael blew out a breath. "You can't tell anyone I said this, okay?" I promised. "I think Bryan might've put the moves on Chris."

Alex said, "Then you think it was sexual with those guys who hung around with him?"

Rafael paused, then said, "For some of them, yeah. But I hung around with him, too, and I'm straight. All I know about the thing with Chris is that we all got drunk—I'm talking shit-faced—at Bryan's place about a month ago. And after that night, Chris never wanted to go back. I don't think he ever spoke to Bryan again."

That explained it. I was sure Rafael was right. Bryan was turning out to be quite the piece of work. A thief, a con artist, *and* a pedophile. "But you kept seeing Bryan?"

Rafael sighed. "Sort of. I always thought Bryan was kind of shady, but he could be fun, too. And he never tried anything on me." He looked out the window for a moment. "Anyway, he wasn't really the one I liked to hang with. Tanner was more my style. He's much more real."

How anyone could think something like that about Tanner was a real head-scratcher. Of all the things I could call him, *real* was the very, very last. But that wasn't my concern. "Are you still in touch with Tanner?" Maybe I could get a little daylight as to Tanner's possible whereabouts.

He looked upset. "No, I haven't heard from him in a while. I don't know what's going on."

Alex queried him about where Tanner might be staying. But no luck. Rafael only saw him at Bryan's house, and he never discussed any personal details—other than to brag about all his big "scores" and hot babes. Again, how did that equate with "real"?

I brought us back to the subject of Bryan. "How upset was Chris? Do you think he'd ever want to . . . hurt him?"

Rafael looked incredulous. "Chris? Go after Bryan? No way. That's so not him." After a moment, he said, "So you really do think someone killed Bryan?"

I shook my head. "I don't know. Like I said, I'm just wondering. But you seem pretty sure that if anyone killed Bryan, it wasn't Chris."

He was emphatic. "A hundred percent."

I had to admit, Chris really didn't seem to have that kind of violence in him. I had another thought. "Do you think Tanner ever had a sexual relationship with Bryan?"

Rafael gave a hoot of laughter. "Tanner? Ha! He's so straight, he wouldn't care if you called him gay. Every time we partied, he had a smokin'-hot babe on his arm. The last one was really on fire."

Alex asked, "When was that?"

Rafael replied, "Couple of weeks ago."

Only a couple of weeks ago. This "babe on fire" might be another source for us. "Do you know her name?"

Rafael's brow furrowed. "Uh . . . I think it was Angelina. Long blonde hair, these wild green eyes. And she was kind of short, but every inch was perfect. Like a Barbie doll, man."

Alex asked, "Did Tanner say how they met?"

Rafael pointed to a house on the right at the end of the street. It was one of those Mediterranean-style McMansions. "That's me. He said he met her at one of his parties. Tanner threw these crazy parties at his condo. Everyone in the building hated him. I remember her saying something about getting him to move to her neighborhood in Los Feliz, 'cause the neighbors were so much cooler."

I pulled to the curb in front of his house. "Did you go to all of Tanner's parties?"

"No. I only got to go to three." Rafael made a face. "Most of the time he'd act all Mac Daddy and say, 'This one's only for grown-ups.' He could be such a dick sometimes."

Those partygoers could be another source of information. "Did Bryan ever go?" If so, those partygoers might be able to tell us something about him, too.

Rafael reached for the door handle. "No. Matter of fact, he got super pissed off at Tanner because during one of those parties, a neighbor complained to him about the noise, and they almost got into a fight. It got so bad, someone called the cops." He paused. "Come to think of it, I should've known something shady was going on by the way Bryan got all bent out of shape about the cops being called. I remember him yelling at Tanner for bringing all that attention down on them."

I was intrigued. We might just have something here. "When did that happen?"

Rafael said, "About three months ago." He opened the door. "Anyway, thanks for the ride. But don't forget, I never said anything about Chris and Bryan."

I nodded. Albeit reluctantly. Ordinarily, I would've preferred to try and get Chris to press charges. But there was no point. Bryan was dead. And I was sure Chris had nothing to do with that. "Mum's the word."

Rafael had one foot out the door. He turned back with a quizzical look. "Huh?"

I sighed. "I promise, I'll never tell."

He got out and patted the roof. "Have a good one."

I'd lost one possible suspect. But that didn't mean we had to give up on the pedophile angle. Rafael's brother and his friend might be able to give us some names of other potential victims.

And there should be a record of that police contact at Tanner's party. Dale would be able to get us that easily. I could only hope it led somewhere.

TWENTY-SEVEN

We got stuck in the middle of rush-hour traffic and wound up crawling through the canyon. I could've walked faster. But it gave me time to call Dale (who groused that I seemed to have forgotten that he had a real day job) and ask him to track down any reports on Tanner's most excellent mondo condo party. And more than enough time for Alex and me to confer about what we'd learned and what to do next.

He said, "I'll get ahold of Rafael's brother and his buddy, but I have a feeling the pedophile track won't pan out."

I'd been thinking it might still be viable. "Why?"

He shrugged. "Because if Bryan had hit on a bunch of straight guys, I'd think at least one of them would already have either put him in the hospital or reported it to the cops. My guess is at most, we might find another Chris. A kid who got a little more than he bargained for but didn't really do anything about it."

And now wouldn't even admit there'd been a reason to do anything. "Fair point. But let's find out what the brother and his friend have to say. If they don't give us anything, we can put that theory on the back burner."

We marveled at the Francos' bizarrely benign view of Bryan and eventually segued into a more general discussion about the way people could deceive themselves into thinking just about anything if they wanted to.

After I dropped Alex off at his condo, I wondered whether I'd been deceiving myself about Niko. I could accept that there were large chunks of his past he preferred to keep hidden. I'd done the same in my own way. But was the Niko I fell in love with the person I thought he was? I kept coming back to that question.

And that question was still lingering in my mind as I climbed the stairs to my apartment. I'd just dropped my purse on the kitchen table when my cell phone rang. It was Niko. What timing. He asked how I was doing, and I brought him up to speed on what we'd learned so far. The revelation about Bryan rocked him.

"No way," he said. "I can't believe I missed that. What a scumbag."

I wasn't so surprised he didn't know. "How much time did you really spend with him? Wasn't Tanner your main connection?"

He admitted that was true. "But I didn't know anything about Tanner's wild parties, either. Which apparently were legendary."

Again, no surprise, that. "Why would he tell you? You're not the type who'd think those parties were a big attraction." Although now, I questioned everything I'd thought about Niko, though I knew for sure he was a relatively straitlaced workaholic. At least, he was now. No, I pictured older, much nerdier—or much scuzzier guys—as the prime target. Assuming those parties were intended—in part—to bring in business. A reasonable assumption, based on what I'd learned about Tanner.

He sighed. "I guess. It's just kind of . . . upsetting to realize how much I didn't know about those two."

Oh, the irony. "Yeah, seems they both had secret worlds. Anyway, I've been checking in with Sophia's doctor." I'd promised Niko I'd do the check-ins with the doctor, since the time difference between New

York and LA made it so hard to call at a normal hour. "He says she's stable. I'm planning to go see her tomorrow morning."

His voice was wobbly. "I really appreciate your help, Sam. But you don't need to go. I was calling to tell you we got done early. I'll be flying home tomorrow. I'll be back in time to see her myself."

I was glad to hear he'd be home soon. But I couldn't help being a little nervous, too. I didn't want to act differently with him. And I had a feeling—in spite of my mad crazy acting skills—I might. "That's great."

"And I can't wait to see you, too. I miss you so much."

I tried to keep the nervous edge out of my voice as I said I missed him, too. "But get some rest. You must've worked fourteen-hour days to finish this early."

He gave a heavy sigh. "More like twenty hours. But it's worth it. I'll get to be with you that much sooner." A male voice in the background called out to him. "I've got to go. I love you."

I told him I loved him, too, and as we ended the call, a wave of anxiety washed over me. I went to the liquor cabinet, pulled out the Patrón Silver, and poured myself a generous double shot. I didn't know how I was going to pull this off. Niko was a damn good bullshit detector, and he knew how to spot a phony at ten paces. I took a long sip of my drink. My only hope was that between his mother's precarious condition and his own jeopardy, he'd be too distracted to notice any difference in me.

I took my drink out to the balcony, but the night was cold and damp. The rain could come at any minute. I went inside and sat down on the couch. I turned on the television, but within minutes, my eyes started to close. The alcohol had hit fast. But this time, I knew better than to let myself fall asleep there. I took myself and my Patrón Silver to the bedroom and slid under the covers. I tuned my mini TV to a mindless home renovation show and turned off the light. I fell asleep before the first commercial.

I woke up to the sound of my cell phone ringing. It took me a few seconds to realize it wasn't on my nightstand. I'd accidentally left it in the living room last night. I turned off the television—which was now playing a baking show that featured obnoxiously cute kids—and hurried out to the living room. I dug through my purse just in time to see that the caller was Dale. And that I'd overslept. It was already eight o'clock. I tried to make my voice sound like I'd been up for hours. "Hey. What's up?"

He sounded amused. "Apparently not you until just this moment."

He never misses a thing, and he always lets me know it. "What? You never oversleep? I had a long day."

Dale said that no, he'd never overslept in his whole life. "I've got some info on the police response to Tanner's condo party. Apparently it never really got written up. The responding officers just filed an F.I. card and gave Tanner a warning."

Probably the neighbor didn't want to make the bad blood between them any worse. "Do you have the cop's name and contact information?"

He gave a *tsk*. "Oh damn. You need that, too? *Of course* I got it."

I wrote down the name—Deleon Washington—and his cell and office number. He worked in the Hollywood Division now. "Thanks, Dale. I know I owe you."

He heartily agreed. "But honestly, this time I'm glad to be able to help. Niko's a good guy. I'd like to see him get off Kingsford's radar."

I couldn't agree more. But as we ended the call, I wished I could tell him what I'd just learned about Niko. It'd help to get his point of view. The problem was, if I told him about the mysterious disappearance of that shot caller who might've killed Niko's sister, he'd wind up having the same suspicion I did. And that would only add to the suspicion that he'd killed again. This time to avenge what'd been done to his mother.

I knew Dale shared my belief in the need to give justice a helping hand now and then, but I wasn't sure how far that belief would take him—when he'd decide he had to be a cop and enforce the law. I decided that for now, I'd play it safe and keep what I knew to myself.

I called Alex and told him about my conversation with Dale. "I'd like to go talk to that cop ASAP."

Alex was way on board. "I'll get moving on it right now. If I get ahold of him right away, I'll call you. Otherwise, I'll just head in to the office."

I remembered that I had a court date fast approaching on another case. "I hate to ask you this, but have you had a chance to dig up anything useful for Jamie Stuart?" My credit card thief was facing a twenty-year sentence if I didn't find a way to get to Judge Raptor's cold, reptilian heart.

"Working on it. I might have something good. But I've been meaning to tell you. I just heard from Angelo."

I didn't like the way he'd said that. I'd been hoping Angelo had something good to trade so I could get the D.A. to cut him a lighter sentence. But when Alex last spoke to him, it turned out that all he had to trade was his big brother, Tito—who wasn't exactly a whale in the criminal ocean. "This doesn't sound good."

"It's not. I got a phone call from him yesterday. He said he wasn't going to talk. He'd just do the time."

Damn it. "Did you tell him I'd talk to the cops about getting him protection?"

"Yes, repeatedly. He doesn't buy it. He told me to tell you to just do your best."

Great. Beautiful. Now my only ace in the hole was the affidavit of the gangbanger who swore Angelo was just selling car parts out of his trunk—not assault rifles. Not exactly a winning hand. "He's hosed. But okay. It is what it is."

"I'll call you when I find the cop who filled out the F.I. card."

I told him that sounded good and headed for the shower. As I stood under the hot spray, I wondered how much Kingsford had found out at this point. From what Alex had been able to learn, Niko had never been busted. If that was accurate, then Kingsford might not be able to find out that he'd belonged to a gang. But he'd certainly know about Niko's brother, Ivan—who had been busted for drug possession—and the death of his sister, Kristina. What he'd make of all that was hard to say. One thing Kingsford would have to admit: Niko had managed to climb up and out of a really hard childhood.

I'd just finished toweling off when my cell phone rang again. Fortunately, this time I'd remembered to bring it with me. It was Alex. "You can't tell me you already got that cop."

"Okay," he said. "Then I won't. Except I did. Let's hit the road."

I told him I wasn't dressed yet. "I'll pick you up in half an hour."

He made an exasperated sound. "We don't have that kind of time. He's on morning watch. His shift ends in an hour. You get dressed; I'll drive."

I laughed to myself as I ended the call. Back when I had Beulah, he used to drive all the time. He—very rightfully—didn't trust her. But now that I had a spiffy new BMW, he was happy to let me be the chauffeur. Except at times like this, when he was hot on the trail and revved up to go. I wasn't sure this lead was worth that much excitement, but given our lack of progress so far, I didn't blame him for wanting to jump at the possibility of any kind of forward movement. To be honest, now that I thought about it, so did I.

I dressed as fast as I could, did a minimalist makeup job, and made it downstairs just as Alex pulled up. In a new car—a MINI Cooper. What the . . . ? I got in and belted up. "What was wrong with your Audi?" He'd only leased it a year ago.

Alex gave me a mischievous smile. "Nothing. I was just tired of it. But that's not what I told the dealership." As he backed out of the driveway, he offhandedly said, "Oh, and I might've used your name a little."

I rolled my eyes. "What did I supposedly threaten them with?"

He backed into the street and headed for Sunset Boulevard. "You don't need to know. It's over. He caved; I won."

I didn't really want to know anyway, so I let it go. Still, I worried that one of these days, Alex would run into someone he couldn't manipulate. On the other hand, it'd been three years since he started working for me, and it hadn't happened yet. So I let that worry go, too. "Where are we meeting Officer Deleon Washington?"

He made a right on Sunset Boulevard and pointed down the street. "Mel's Drive-In."

Mel's was one of the original drive-in restaurants. It was a hit when it opened in 1947, and it was still going strong. Best of all, it was just a few blocks away. I probably could've walked. Alex parked around the corner, and when we walked in, a young black officer in uniform waved to us from a table near the back of the restaurant. I walked over to him and extended my hand. "Samantha Brinkman. Thank you for taking the time, Officer."

He nodded. "You can call me Deleon."

"Hi, Deleon." Alex shook his hand. "I'm the one who called you."

As I slid into the booth, a waitress appeared at our table. She handed us menus. "Can I get you something to drink?"

I knew what I needed. "Coffee would be great. Deleon? Whatever you want's on me."

"I don't need the caffeine," he said. "About to go off shift. I'll just have water, thanks."

Alex ordered coffee, too.

I could see that this waitress moved fast, so I held off until she brought our drinks. Sure enough, she was back with them in twenty seconds and asked if she could take our orders. We all went with the standard breakfast fare of eggs (scrambled for me and Deleon, over medium for Alex), bacon, and toast. When she left, I asked, "Do you have a clear memory of the call at Tanner Handel's condo?" Cops see a lot of action. It was entirely possible his recollection of a minor-league incident like that was sketchy.

"I do. Partly because we got calls about that place a lot. Handel liked to party hard." Deleon squinted out the window for a moment. "I felt sorry for those neighbors."

Alex followed up. "You said *partly*. What else made you remember this particular time?"

Deleon's lips twitched in a tiny smile. "That woman." He looked up at the ceiling. "What was her name? Oh yeah, Angelina." He shook his head. "She's pretty hard to forget."

That was the woman Rafael had mentioned. "I've heard she's very attractive."

He chuckled. "She is that. And based on the accent, I'd guess she's a Russian national."

The waitress served our breakfast, and we all dug in for a few minutes. I took a sip of coffee to wash it down, then asked, "Was there anything else about her that struck you?"

Deleon nodded. "I got the feeling she was a pro. One of those girls who gets paid to whoop it up and keep the men happy."

"What made you think that?" I asked.

He gave a derisive half smile. "The men. They were all older than Handel. Looked like they had money but not the best-looking bananas in the bunch, if you know what I mean."

I nodded. "They were marks."

"Exactly," he said.

So my assumption had been right. Tanner was grooming the men, wining and dining them, so they'd invest with Gold Strike. "By any chance, do you have contact information for Angelina?"

Deleon gave a reluctant shake of the head. "Sorry. Wish I did. I hear Handel's gone missing."

I nodded. "Seems so." We chatted about Tanner Handel and Gold Strike as we finished our breakfast, but Deleon didn't have anything more to add. I thought his take on this Angelina woman was interesting. I wasn't sure she'd have any useful information for us, but I'd at least have liked to give it a shot. The only problem was, I had no clue how to find her.

We finished breakfast, and I picked up the tab and thanked Deleon. "If you happen to bump into Angelina again—"

"Oh, don't worry," he said. "I'll hang on to her."

But then Kingsford would get first crack at her. "Maybe you could give me a heads-up if you get her?"

Deleon studied me for a moment. "Sure, give me your cell number."

I thanked him again. He gave me a mock salute, then headed for his patrol car. Alex and I had just gotten into his MINI Cooper when my cell phone rang. Alex laughed. "He bumped into her already?"

I looked at the number on the screen. "It's Dale." Alex's eyes widened. We both knew what that meant. Something had happened. I answered. "Hi, what's up?"

Dale's voice was low. "They found a Porsche 911 registered to Tanner Handel."

A Porsche 911. Exactly the kind of car I'd expect him to drive. I didn't like the sound of this. "Where?"

Dale said, "In a ditch near the border of Arizona. Looks like someone was trying to hide it. The car was covered in dirt and branches."

I immediately reached for an innocent explanation. "Tanner could've buried it himself." I'd been saying all along that he'd probably faked his own death so he could disappear with the money he'd stolen.

Dale paused for a moment before answering. "Anything's possible, Sam."

"What condition was the car in?"

"Tires gone, hubcaps gone, it was almost completely stripped."

"Sounds to me like it got stolen by a pro," I said. Someone who had a fence for all those parts. "Tanner might've left it in a place where it was likely to get stolen. That'd sure help him set up his fake death."

His tone was skeptical. "I guess that's possible." Three beeps sounded on Dale's line. "I've gotta take this call. Maybe we should have dinner."

I swallowed hard. "Yeah, I guess we should."

We set the dinner for Sunday. I knew that meant we were going to have a serious talk about Niko and what he might've done. I could weave all the alternative theories I liked, but simple logic said there were easier ways for Tanner to fake his own death than to leave his car in a place where he could only hope it'd get stolen.

I couldn't deny it. This latest discovery made it far more likely that Tanner had been killed.

TWENTY-EIGHT

Alex saw my expression. "What happened?"

I filled him in. "They'll analyze every millimeter of that car."

He knew what I was getting at. "But even if they find Niko's prints or hair, that doesn't mean anything. He must've been in that car a bunch of times."

A big splotch of rain hit the windshield. Then another and another. It was going to start pouring in seconds. I stared at a girl who was mincing across the street in Daisy Dukes and five-inch-high pink platform shoes—Minnie Mouse in porn drag. She was about to get drenched. Right now, I wished I were her. I wanted to be anyone but me. "Depends on what they find and where they find it." Niko's prints on the passenger side door? No problem. Niko's prints inside the trunk, near bloodstains that came from Tanner? Big problem.

Alex started the car. "The only thing we can do is keep moving. And hope we come up with something that takes Niko off the hook."

We could make the former happen. It was the latter that worried me. Alex asked if I wanted him to drop me at home so I could get my car. "Nah, I'll just Uber home." I hated to drive in the rain, and it was a luxury I could afford. My office was only about ten minutes away.

When Alex pulled into the parking garage, he said, "What do you want to do about the Angelina angle? Think she's worth some time?"

I definitely did. "She seems to be pretty tight with Tanner. If there's any possibility he's still alive, she might know where he's hiding out."

He parked, and we got out. He armed the car alarm. "You want to talk to Niko, see if he knows anything about her?"

I nodded. So far, no one seemed to know anything about her other than her first name—that, and the fact that she was super hot. Not helpful. Niko was the only one I could think of who might know more. As we got into the elevator, I said, "I should be hearing from him any minute." I looked at my watch. "His flight lands in about an hour."

Alex blew out a breath. "Fingers crossed."

When we walked in, Michy was hard at work on her computer. "You writing an angry letter to the IRS? If so, can I help?"

She gave me a flat look. "I'm working on your billing." She tilted her head. "Want to make more jokes?"

I never mess with the person who's trying to get me money. I held up my hands. "What jokes? I was serious."

She raised an eyebrow. "So what's the latest?"

I told her about our interview with Deleon, what Dale had just told me, and what the discovery of Tanner's car might mean. "And I'll have to see Niko soon. Probably tonight."

Michy shrugged. "On the bright side, he might have some skinny on Angelina. And I assume you'll tell him about them finding Tanner's car." I nodded. "So that'll give you some cover."

I frowned. "Cover?"

"Yeah," she said. "For acting weird. Which you absolutely will be."

I had to smile. She knew me so well. "True. I guess that's something."

I went to my office and called the D.A. on Angelo's case. I tried to put the best spin on the matter as I could—starting with the sympathy gambit. "He's just too scared to talk. He's a sitting duck in that jail. He's bound to piss off someone if it gets out that he's cooperating—and we both know it always does. Unless you're willing to give him a deal for no time—"

The deputy D.A., Peter Shultz, interrupted me. "Not happening. Look, Sam, we know he doesn't have anything to give us on a rich target. The only question was whether we'd give him a little less time. If he's not talking, he either pleads to the sheet or we go to trial."

I'd had a feeling that would be his reaction. But if Angelo pled to all charges, he'd do more than eight years. His wife and children would be out on the street before he'd done six months. I played the only card I had left. "You're forgetting I have a witness—"

He interrupted me again. "Yeah, that shot caller—who also happened to be his customer? Pardon my arrogance for thinking I might be able to persuade the jury to agree that he's a little less than credible."

"You never know, Pete." Though we both did. Juries can be unpredictable at times—but probably not this time.

"Do yourself a favor and let this one go. If he pleads to the sheet, I won't ask for the max."

I hated to admit it, but he was right. That was probably the best I could do. "Okay, then. See you in court."

I ended the call, picked up my coat and purse, and went out to give Alex and Michy the news. When I finished, Alex said, "I can take another run at him if you want. But I don't think he'll budge."

"No, don't bother." This was do-or-die time. I'd have to handle this myself. I put on my coat. "I'll go talk to him. Hopefully, he'll sober up and realize he has to cooperate if he wants a deal."

Michy gave me a look of sympathy. "Seems unlikely. But good luck."

And on that cheery note, I headed for my Uber.

The traffic gods were with me. I got to Twin Towers in just under an hour. If Angelo refused to come out again, I'd just have to give him the news when we got to court. But this time, he agreed to see me. He looked surprisingly good for someone who was in fear for his life. He'd gained a few pounds, which filled out his otherwise bony, narrow face, and he'd cut his long, stringy—often greasy—hair. He sat down and picked up the phone. I picked up my phone and said, "You seem to be doing okay."

"Yeah, I guess I am."

I told him what the deputy D.A. had said. "Basically, right now, I think your best shot is to plead out and let me make a pitch for leniency. Unless you're willing to talk."

He shook his head. "No way. I'm not talking to no one."

I had a feeling he was going to say he wouldn't plead, either. In which case, the only option left was to go to trial. "I'm going to warn you. If we go to trial on a slam-dunk case like this, the judge will probably slam your ass when it comes time for sentencing."

But Angelo surprised me. "I'll plead. I don't want no trial. You can do your lawyer thing. Beg the judge or whatever. I'm good."

I stared at him. This was a big shift in attitude. "You do know you might do more than eight years, right?" He didn't blink. "I thought you were worried about your wife and kids."

He nodded calmly. "I was. But not no more. They'll be taken care of."

Then I understood. "As long as you don't talk."

"Exactly." He pushed his chair back. "So that's it?"

"Yeah. I guess."

He thanked me, hung up, and called to the guard to take him back to his cell. I watched as he left, thinking this had probably worked out for the best.

The ride back to the office was brutal. The traffic gods giveth and taketh away. I sat in a bumper-to-bumper stagnating line for an hour and a half. On the way, I got a text from Niko. He'd landed and was going straight to the hospital to see his mother. He asked if I could come to his place later. He'd make dinner. Even though, as Michy said, I had cover, I was still nervous about how I'd act now that I'd spoken to his brother, Ivan. But I had to bite the bullet sometime. I texted him back saying I'd pick up dinner at Greenblatt's Deli and get to his place at six o'clock.

When I got into the office, I told the troops about my visit with Angelo. "So, Alex, any sob-worthy story you can find in his past or present will be much appreciated." I didn't have the law card or the evidence card. All I had was the sympathy card. And hopefully Pete's word that he wouldn't ask the judge to max out his sentence.

Alex didn't look optimistic. "I'll get on it right now. But speaking of sob-worthy, I dug up some gold for Jamie Stuart."

I took off my coat. "Hit me."

"When he was fourteen, his mother died of leukemia. His father had been in the wind for years. And he had two younger sisters—ages six and eight. The state put them all in foster care, where, as you might guess—"

"They all got abused or molested." It was such an agonizingly familiar story.

Alex nodded. "Yeah, sadly. But when he turned eighteen, he got his sisters out of foster care. He was the sole support for the family for the next ten years. Then he got hooked up with a girlfriend who showed him the wonderful world of opioids."

"And thus began his life of crime." This really was a pretty harrowing tale. "Even Judge Heart of Darkness might go for this one." I'd ask for a probationary sentence that included rehab and community service, lean hard on the clear evidence that Jamie was someone who could pull it together, etc. It could work. "Nice job, Alex." I glanced at my watch. It was after five o'clock already, and I'd told Niko I'd get to his place by six. I said Niko had called and that I was bringing him dinner.

"You going to tell him about Tanner's car?" Michy asked.

Good question. "I'm not sure. I'll have to see what kind of shape he's in." And what kind of mood I was in. I wasn't sure I wanted to deal with it right now. I pulled out my phone. "I'd better get going. I have to Uber home and pick up my car."

Alex said, "I'd offer to drive you, but I want to get the workup on Angelo done."

I agreed. "I want you to get it done, too."

My cell phone pinged to say Uber was on its way. I told them I'd let them know how it went with Niko and left.

I pulled up the menu for Greenblatt's on the way home. It was still raining, so I thought chicken noodle soup would be a cozy choice. I scrolled through the menu to see what I should order for the main course. If I'd been alone, I would've ordered the jumbo turkey leg dinner with mashed potatoes and gravy and corn-bread stuffing. But I'd be with Niko, which meant I'd have to listen to lectures about carbs and cholesterol. I ordered us each the turkey breast sandwich with coleslaw on the side and tried not to feel resentful.

I was already late, so when the Uber dropped me off, I didn't bother to go up to my apartment. I got into my car and headed for Greenblatt's. I hate driving in the rain. The streets get oily and slippery, and no one seems to be able to see where they're going. By the time I got to Niko's place, I was tired, damp, and irritated with the world. I struggled up the walkway, dinner bags in hand, and tried not to fall on the wet concrete.

But when Niko opened the door and I saw his stricken expression, I forgot about all that. I set the bags down on the kitchen counter. "What's wrong?"

He pressed his lips together. "Mom's not . . . doing so well."

He told me that she seldom opened her eyes, and only for a few seconds at a time. And now she wasn't making any sounds at all. What little progress she'd made before had been temporary, and she now seemed to be slipping backward. "Niko, I'm so sorry."

He sagged against the counter. "It's all my fault. If I hadn't told her to invest with those con men, she'd be fine."

I understood his feelings of guilt, but he'd only meant the best for her, and he'd had good reason to believe she'd make a lot of money. He certainly had. "Niko, you've got to let it go. Come on, let's eat. You must be starving."

We took the food into the living room and lit the fire. After dinner, he seemed to relax. I'd been so focused on getting him out of his funk, I'd forgotten to worry about how I was acting with him and my own feelings of guilt at having gone behind his back to meet his brother. But now, my anxiety was mounting. I could feel my palms start to sweat. I glanced at Niko. Had he noticed? He was staring into the fire. I didn't think so.

After a moment, he rubbed his face and looked at me. "I just realized, I was so messed up, I forgot to ask what was happening with the case."

My stomach clenched. This was it. I hadn't been sure whether I should tell him about Tanner's car. But now, I knew I had to. I repeated what Dale had said about Tanner's car being found. As I spoke, I studied his face for any signs of fear that he'd been caught. But he seemed surprised. Genuinely? I couldn't be sure.

Shock spread across his face. "What do you think happened?"

I spooled out my theory about Tanner faking his own death, then knocked it down with the more logical explanation: that it was likely Tanner had been killed. "Obviously, this isn't great news."

He clasped his hands together. "I wish there was something I could do to help."

This was my opening. "Actually, there is." I told him what we'd learned about Angelina. "Did you ever meet her?"

He frowned for a moment. "I don't know. Maybe. I don't recognize the name, but I've seen Tanner with a lot of women."

Tanner was a player. But I already knew that. "You don't remember seeing him with one in particular? One who was a real looker and had a Russian accent?"

Recognition dawned on his face. "Oh wait. Yeah. I remember her."

But he didn't know her last name or where she lived or . . . anything else. I tried another tack. "Did you go to any of Tanner's wild parties?"

He made a face. "Yeah, once. In London."

I smiled. "Not your kind of scene, I take it."

He harrumphed. "To put it mildly. And I had no idea those parties were a regular thing with him. But if you're asking whether anyone I met there might know more about Angelina, the answer is: possibly. Liam Fallon. Tanner made a point of introducing us because Liam said he was a fan of mine. Liam manages a major hedge fund, and Tanner was trying to sweet-talk him into investing with Gold Strike."

That Tanner sure knew how to work all the angles. "And after meeting you, he did invest, right?"

Niko's expression was glum. "Yeah, he did."

I mentally reviewed the list of Gold Strike victims. "I don't remember seeing his name on any of the papers."

Niko shrugged. "Maybe we don't have all the investors' names yet."

I thought about that. "Or maybe he doesn't want his name out there." If Liam lost a bundle, he might be a viable suspect.

Niko frowned and shook his head. "No. Liam's a good guy. There's no way he'd ever kill anyone."

"Anyone can kill anyone. Especially when it involves the kind of financial hit people took in this case." I couldn't help but mentally add: *Or, say, when it puts your mother in the hospital.*

Niko gave a heavy sigh. "I guess."

I asked, "So where does Liam live? Do you have a number for him?"

He thought for a moment. "I think I remember him saying he lives in Westwood. His number . . . I think I might. Hold on."

Niko got up and headed for his study. I clutched my glass of wine and prayed he had it. We needed a break more than ever now. A few minutes later, he came back with a card in his hand. He sat down and looked me in the eyes. "He didn't do it, Sam. Trust me."

I took the card from him. "I do trust you." Well, sort of. "But I can't afford to trust anyone else." The card was made of heavyweight stock, and it was a buff cream color. The information on it was engraved. Everything about it said *money*, but in a classy way. I thought about how to approach a guy like this. "I need you to set up a dinner for the three of us."

Niko didn't look happy about it. "Just promise me you'll give him a fair shake."

I patted his knee. "Of course I will."

I'd give him a fair shake. And then go after him with everything I had.

TWENTY-NINE

Niko managed to reach Liam on the first try, which I took as a good omen—though not the kind of omen Niko would've liked. He set us up to have dinner at Catch—a great seafood and sushi restaurant in West Hollywood—for Sunday evening. I was relieved that it'd been so easy. And slightly cheered by the prospect of finding a new potential suspect.

But I'd been monitoring my behavior all night, worried that Niko might sense something different in the way I acted toward him. The constant vigilance made me feel like there was a rubber band inside my chest that might snap at any minute.

If he asked me to spend the night, I didn't know what I'd do. Luckily, he was exhausted. The bad news about his mother and the long flight had taken their toll. When I suggested we call it a night, he gave in without an argument.

Niko passed a hand over his eyes. "I am pretty tired. I'm sorry to be such lousy company."

I leaned over and kissed him. "You're wonderful company. Always."

He said he'd pick me up at my place at seven o'clock tomorrow night and walked me to the door. "I don't know what I'd do without you."

Maybe find a girlfriend who didn't suspect you of being a cold-blooded murderer? But I just smiled and said, "Me either." We hugged, and I headed for my car.

Once again, I hated myself for feeling the wave of relief that washed over me as I drove back to my place. I couldn't go on like this. We had to solve this case, and soon. Between my guilt trip about going behind his back and the unsettling feeling that the Niko I thought I knew was just a facade, I was becoming a real head case. That is so not my style.

And complicating everything was the fact that I knew I was being a hypocrite. So what if he'd killed Bryan? And Tanner, too? I'd probably have done the same. Besides, just because he may have lied to me about that, it didn't mean he'd lie about anything else.

Or did it? Maybe that was the problem. I couldn't be sure.

I needed to talk to Dale about all this. He'd been less willing to believe Niko might be the killer than I'd been—at first. But our last conversation told me he'd probably had a change of heart. And I wasn't sure what he'd do if he figured out that Niko had killed Bryan or Tanner. He'd covered for me in the past—or at least turned a blind eye to what I'd done. But I was his daughter.

We'd planned to have dinner tomorrow night, but dinner with a potential new suspect took precedence. I'd have to ask Dale to reschedule. As soon as I got home, I called him on my landline. He picked up on the first ring.

"I can't have dinner Sunday. How about the night after?"

"Let me check," he said. After a brief pause, he said, "That works. My place or yours?"

I'd feel better on home turf. "My place."

He generously offered to bring dinner. Actually, it wasn't generosity, it was self-preservation. "Is six thirty too early?"

It was. But I didn't want him to say he couldn't make it any later. "That works."

He replied, "Okay, see you—"

I interrupted. "I might have a new target."

"We're so not talking about this right now."

I sighed. Seriously? He couldn't even trust a landline? "Fine. Just don't form any opinions about . . . anything until we talk."

He paused. "Can't promise that. But I won't make any moves."

That was good enough for me. "Thanks." I hung up and headed for the shower. I was tired and more than ready for this day to end. When I got into bed, I told my brain to come up with ways to make Liam—or anyone else—a viable suspect. I've heard that if you tell your brain what to work on, it'll figure out creative solutions in your sleep. I drifted off, expecting to wake up with at least one brilliant idea.

Instead, I discovered that theory about telling your brain what to do was complete and utter bullshit. When I woke up the next morning, I had nothing. Sometimes I got bursts of inspiration on my days off. Doing boring things like vacuuming, mopping, and grocery shopping has led to surprisingly innovative ideas in the past. I threw myself into the drudgery of chores hoping that would work now.

It didn't. After a long weekend of drudgery, I still had no great plan as to how I'd put someone other than Niko on the hot seat. I'd just have to go to the dinner with Liam and hope to get lucky.

So I was glad for the interruption when Niko came over to pick me up Sunday evening. We didn't talk much on the ride over. He knew I was hoping to find cause to put Liam on the suspect list, and he didn't like it. "Remember, you promised to keep an open mind."

I held up my hands. "I'm totally open-minded."

He glanced at me. "And you're not planning to spring anything on him?"

I could answer that one truthfully—sadly. "I have no plans. None."

Since it was a Sunday night, I was a little surprised to see that the restaurant was packed. It seemed like the rain was going to start up again any minute, and Angelenos are notoriously terrified of dealing with rain.

A tall, well-built blond man in a navy blazer and black T-shirt waved to us. "Liam? Or just another one of your fans?"

Niko waved back and steered me toward his table as he whispered, "Does he look like a killer to you?"

I poked him in the side with my elbow. "Everyone looks like a killer to me."

Niko gave a fake grunt of pain. Liam moved toward us, and he and Niko shared a back-slapping bro hug; then Liam held a hand out to me. "Pleasure to meet you, Samantha. Niko's told me all about you."

I shook his hand. "I don't know whether that's a good thing or a bad thing."

Liam laughed, his blue eyes crinkling at the corners. "It's good, all good."

We sat down, and a waiter came over to take our drink orders. Liam held up his glass. "I went with a vodka martini. Grey Goose."

One of my faves. Damn, I had a feeling I was going to like this guy. Not that that'd stop me from going after him if I found anything I could use. I told the waiter I'd have the same. Niko ordered a glass of pinot noir. When the waiter left, I threw out the only line I'd managed to plan. "Niko tells me you guys met at one of Tanner's parties. Are they as crazy as I've heard?"

Liam made a face. "There's crazy good and crazy obnoxious. I'd only gone to the one where I met Niko. It wasn't my cuppa. Loud, shitty music; decent booze; and lots of women—none of whom I'd bring home to a pet snake, let alone my mother."

Niko laughed. "That's how we wound up bonding." He looked at Liam. "I think we weren't there more than an hour."

Liam nodded. "We took off and went to a pub, didn't we?"

Niko nodded. They segued from their mutual disgust with Tanner's party scene to Tanner's disappearance and Bryan's death.

I didn't know whether Niko was doing it on purpose, but he was definitely making it easy for me to get to the heart of the matter. "It's looking like someone killed Bryan—and possibly Tanner."

Liam shook his head. "Well, after that dumpster fire of a trade, I'd imagine there're a whole bunch of folks who'd be happy to see them both dead."

The waiter came back with our drinks. I usually propose some kind of toast, but I was too focused on what he'd just said to shift gears even for a moment. "You were one of the Gold Strike investors, weren't you?"

Liam took a sip of his drink. "I was. Or, rather, I invested with Gold Strike for some of my clients. But I got a hot tip on copper that looked like a more solid deal, so I pulled them all out before that cryptocurrency trade." He shook his head. "I feel so badly for those poor people who lost their shirts."

"So you pulled out before it went belly-up?" If he hadn't lost money on the sham cryptocurrency trade, he had no motive—which meant I'd just lost another potential suspect.

He put down his glass. "Yep. Now I'm wondering whether it collapsed because it was just a Ponzi scheme all along."

I couldn't tell him that it hadn't even been as superficially legitimate as a Ponzi scheme—that it was just a straight rip-off. But that didn't matter. What mattered right now was that I'd just landed back at square one. I needed to regroup. I picked up my menu. "I'm starving, how about you guys?"

We all agreed we were ready to eat. As I studied the menu, I tried to think of some other way to use Liam. The waiter saw us pick up our menus and came to the table. He looked at me first, but I'd been too preoccupied to focus on dinner. "Um, can I go last?"

Niko, who was obviously happy that his buddy was out of the line of fire, came to my rescue. "Why don't we split the crispy whole snapper?"

I put down my menu. "Sold."

Liam ordered the herb-roasted branzino and another martini. I held up my glass. "Me too. Thanks." I had an idea. When the waiter left, I asked, "Did you hang out with Tanner at all?"

He shrugged. "Some, yeah. Enough to keep good business relations. But we weren't, like, tight or anything."

If this didn't pan out, I was going to the ladies' room to bang my head against the wall. "Did you ever happen to see him with a woman named Angelina?"

He frowned at first, then slowly nodded. "Yeah. A few times. Matter of fact, she was the only one I saw him with more than once. The guy had a problem, you know? Always had to have some hot babe on his arm and almost never the same one. But Angelina was different."

I remembered what Deleon had said about her. "Did you ever get the impression she was getting paid for her, ah . . . time?"

He considered that for a few moments. "Not necessarily. And I doubt Tanner was paying her. That wasn't his style." He paused, then added, "But who knows what goes on behind closed doors?"

Hopefully I would, and soon. Time to go for the money shot. I crossed my fingers under the table. "By any chance would you happen to know her last name?"

The waiter brought our martinis. Liam picked up his glass. "Yeah. I'm good with names. I'm pretty sure it's Poranova. Why?"

I shrugged. "Just curious. Someone told me she was Russian. I was just wondering if that was true." Not my best lie, but he didn't really seem to care. I raised my glass for a toast. I finally had something to celebrate. "Here's to your good memory."

Now we had a chance of finding the much-heralded Angelina.

THIRTY

Niko had an early breakfast meeting the following day, so he took me back
to my place after dinner. As soon as we got into the car, he started in
with the *I told you so*s about Liam being innocent. I glared at him. "You
can let me out right here." I pointed to the corner up ahead.

He raised an eyebrow. "Really. You'd rather walk five miles in the
dark"—he pointedly looked at my shoes—"in four-inch heels than let
me get my gloat on?"

I waited for him to look my way before answering. "I'd rather crawl
on my belly over ground glass than listen to any more of this."

He laughed. "Okay, fine. I'm done." After a beat, he asked, "Do you
really think this Angelina woman knows something?"

I sorted through my feelings. "I'm not sure why, but yeah. I do."
Then again, it might just be the thrill of the chase. We'd bumped into
brick walls trying to get a line on her, and now that we'd found one, I
might just be feeling the triumph of success. For all I knew, Angelina
could turn out to be a dead end. "But we'll see soon enough."

We kissed good night in the car, and I promised to give him an
update after we talked to her. I hurried up the stairs to my apartment,
dropped my purse on the kitchen table, and pulled out my cell phone.

I had to call Alex and tell him we had a last name for the "smokin'" Angelina. My phone said it was only ten thirty. Alex should still be up.

When he answered, I didn't bother to say hello. "I got a last name. It's Poranova."

It took a beat for him to catch up, but then he said, "That's fabulous." In the background, Paul asked who'd called. Alex told him, "Who do you think?" Paul said to give me his best.

I harrumphed. "I do not believe for one second that I'm the only one who calls you after seven o'clock."

He gave an exasperated sigh. "You heard Paul. Obviously, you are. And by the way, is there some reason this couldn't wait until tomorrow?"

Probably not. "Yes. Because I knew you'd want to jump on this ASAP."

There was a moment of silence, then the sound of keys clicking. "I'm not saying you're right. But now that you've ruined my evening, I may as well see . . ." He trailed off.

I wanted to get out of my clothes. "Want to call me back?"

His voice was sharp. "No, I don't want to call you back. You were all on fire about finding this woman. You can wait."

I didn't want to undress until I could get in the shower. I sighed and lay down on the couch. "Fine. I'm putting you on speaker."

He kept typing. "Knock yourself out."

I put the phone on my chest and closed my eyes. I'd gotten sleepy all of a sudden. Those two martinis were getting to me. I made a mental note to never call Alex at night again unless it was a dire emergency.

But just five minutes later, Alex said, "Got her. She lives in Los Feliz, close to Griffith Park."

I knew the area. It was beautiful—very green, lots of trees, and the houses were charming and unique. Not a cookie-cutter style to be found. Whatever Angelina did for a living, it was working out well for her. "Can you find her place on Google Maps?"

There was a beat of silence. "Mm-hmm. She lives on King Street. Cool Spanish-style house, I think. But it's hard to see. The place is surrounded by an ivy-covered wall. Hang on." After a few seconds, he said, "Looks like you enter through a wooden gate. I'd guess she keeps it locked. I can't see an intercom, but there must be one."

I'd have to figure out how to get her to let us in. "I'll have to think on that. But nice work, Alex."

"Yay for me," he said, his voice sarcastic. "Now can I get back to what little I have left of my 'me' time?"

I said, "You know, you didn't used to be like this before you met Paul."

"That's right, Sam. This is what it's like when people live together. They enjoy each other's company." He paused and then, in a gentle voice, said, "You ought to try it."

Perish the thought. "Uh, sure. I have no problem with that."

Alex gave a short bark of a laugh. "Liar."

He was right, so I ignored him. "I've got Jamie Stuart's sentencing tomorrow, so I'll be downtown. Want to meet me there after and head over to Angelina's place?" I'd Uber to court. Save myself the hassle of slogging through the morning rush-hour traffic. Just the thought of that lifted my spirits.

Alex agreed. "And good luck with Jamie."

"I don't need luck with Jamie. I need luck with that friggin' demonic judge."

He wished me luck with the demon, and we ended the call. I headed for the shower and got into bed.

It was a pretty good night—for me, anyway. I got in a solid six hours of sleep and woke up feeling energized. I put myself together, gulped down a giant mug of coffee, and called an Uber. At the last minute, I realized I was hungry. I grabbed a bagel with cream cheese from the fridge and headed downstairs.

The car arrived in less than five minutes. As I slid into the back seat, I thought about how to approach Angelina. Should we use a cover? Pretend to be the "social directors" for some rich guy looking to hire girls for a big bash he was throwing on his yacht? That might be risky. What if she wasn't for hire? Liam didn't seem to think she was. But I trusted Deleon's instincts on this particular subject. Good cops have a nose for things like that.

I was still wavering when the car dropped me off. But I put Angelina out of my head. I had to prepare for battle with Judge Raptor—and maybe my client.

When I got to court, I asked the bailiff to let me into lockup. I found Jamie scrunched down in a ball in a corner of the cell. He looked so forlorn. I waved to him. "Hey."

After our last court appearance, I'd spoken to him on the phone about how dire the circumstances were with this judge, and he'd reluctantly agreed to plead guilty if he got a county lid—meaning, the judge couldn't sentence him to any more than one year in county jail. Most judges would've agreed to that. Not Judge Raptor. I'd had to explain that our judge wouldn't agree to anything less than a five-year lid. Jamie had been resistant, but he'd eventually caved. I'd asked a public defender I'd worked with back in the day to stand in for me to take the plea. That was the easy part. The real work was the sentencing hearing that would take place today. I'd filed a lengthy sentencing memo with the court, detailing Jamie's tragic childhood, and I planned to put the highlights of that memo on the record today—just to make sure the judge remembered them.

But I'd worried about how Jamie would feel today. Clients frequently have buyer's remorse after pleading guilty, and I was worried that Jamie might want to back out and withdraw his plea.

He came up to the bars, his expression fearful. "I know I gave you a hard time about taking a plea before." He glanced around behind me and lowered his voice. "But I've been hearing a lot of bad things about this judge. Like, really bad."

Ah yes. The county jail pipeline. Prisoners do a lot of sharing. It seemed that, for a change, it'd worked in my favor. "I tried to tell you."

"I'm glad I listened." Jamie licked his lips, then bent his head against the bars for a long moment. When he finally looked up, he said, "What do you think he'll do?"

"I honestly don't know. But you saw the memo I filed. I'm fighting for you. All we can do is hope he sees the light." I felt so badly for him. If I could get him into a rehab program, he was one client I knew would pull his life together. I went back out and waited for the case to be called.

I sat in the front row and watched as the judge hammered one defendant after another. When he finally called Jamie's case, I felt my throat tighten. I tried to take calming breaths as I moved to counsel table. The bailiff brought Jamie out and sat him down next to me. He'd lost weight in jail, and his jumpsuit hung loosely on his bony frame. All to the good. Nothing menacing about him.

The prosecutor was a decent sort. He said he left the sentence "to the discretion of the court" and sat down. The judge turned to me. "Ms. Brinkman? I've read your sentencing memo. Do you have anything to add?"

I didn't dare say much. He'd meant it as a warning not to waste his time. "Yes, Your Honor. Briefly, very briefly." I ticked off the major points: Jamie's mother's passing, his absentee father, his stint in foster care, and the burden he'd taken on so his sisters could get out of foster care and come home. "He took a wrong turn, Your Honor. But Jamie Stuart is a good man who just needs a chance to get his life back on track." I made a few more impassioned remarks like that, then sat down.

The judge fixed Jamie with an intense look. I wasn't sure what that meant. I swallowed hard. He glanced at the prosecutor, then at me before finally pronouncing the sentence. "I don't care for thieves. A lot of judges think it's a lesser crime, because it doesn't cause physical harm, and they impose lighter sentences for theft-related crimes. I don't agree with that philosophy. I think theft is a very serious crime, and it has very serious consequences for the victims."

Shit! He was going to give Jamie the max. I could feel Jamie's leg bouncing under the table. His face had gone deathly pale. I dug my nails into my palms to keep from screaming.

The judge continued. "But I do acknowledge that there are certain cases that deserve leniency, and I believe this is one of them. I'm going to go along with defense counsel's request that Mr. Stuart be admitted to rehabilitation and perform a hundred hours of community service. Probation will be three years." He turned toward Jamie. "Mr. Stuart, I don't know if you realize just how lucky you are to get such a light sentence from me. But I want to make it clear that if you wind up back here on a probation violation, I'll come down hard on you."

Jamie stammered, "I—I won't, Your Honor. I promise."

The judge raised an eyebrow. "We'll see."

I thanked the judge—and he ignored me and moved on to the next case. I patted Jamie on the back. "I'll be in touch."

He was still pale. "Thanks, Sam. I'll make it worth it."

I smiled. "I know you will."

I left the courtroom with a sense of satisfaction. Days like this were the reason I'd become a lawyer. I savored the feeling all the way down to the lobby. But when I saw Alex's MINI Cooper idling at the curb, I came back down to earth. On to the next problem.

As I trotted over to the car, I realized I knew how I was going to approach Angelina. "I say we tell her straight-up who we are. No cover stories."

Alex pulled out into traffic. "You're not worried that'll scare her off?"

I shook my head. "The opposite. I know Liam said he didn't think she was a paid escort, but my money's on Deleon. And if he's right,

Angelina's going to love the idea of having a defense attorney for a friend."

He headed for the freeway on-ramp. "Makes sense."

I scoped out the traffic and saw that the cars were moving. I hoped that was a good omen. "I assume you found a way to verify that she's home?"

Alex hit the gas and got into the fast lane. "Of course. I got her landline number and had Paul pretend to offer her an all-expenses-paid vacay in Bermuda if she'd just answer a few questions."

Smart move. It'd be bad if we got to talk to her and she recognized Alex's voice as the one who'd made her that phenomenal offer. "What'd she say?"

He gave a little smile. "She told him to leave her alone and that she was going to block his number. And then she hung up."

"Can't say I blame her." I hate those sales calls.

We talked about how to question her. I opted to start with open-ended questions. If she didn't give us anything, we'd get a little more pointed.

Alex navigated to King Street and parked in front of a very pretty tan stucco house. It had two balconies facing the street that were shaded by black awnings. Several tall palm trees swayed in the breeze at the front of the house. I saw the shrub-covered block wall Alex had described and the set of large arched wooden doors in the center. Thankfully, the rain had passed and the sun had peeked through the clouds. It was still chilly, but at least it was dry.

As Alex had guessed, there was an intercom next to the wooden door. I looked at Alex. "Here's hoping."

I pushed the button on the intercom, and an older woman with a heavy Russian accent answered. "Who is this?"

I didn't think this was Angelina. I gave our names and told her who we were. "I'm a lawyer. I represent Niko Ferrell. I'm here with my investigator, Alex Medrano. We'd like to talk to Angelina about Gold Strike."

The woman said, "One moment."

I looked around as we waited. The street was narrow and winding, and it was high up enough to afford the houses on this side quite a view of the city. I noticed, too, that Angelina's place was bigger than I'd thought. The front wall extended another thirty feet to my right, where there was a second set of double wooden doors, even wider than the ones where we were standing. Maybe that was the driveway.

Two minutes later, a younger woman with a less pronounced Russian accent spoke into the intercom. "You can come in."

I took the buzzing sound as my cue and pulled open the door. We walked through a drought-resistant garden filled with cacti and a variety of interestingly shaped rocks. As we approached, the oversize black lacquer door opened. And there stood a slender woman in a brightly colored kimono. She had one arm draped along the door and a cigarette in her other hand. Her thick blonde hair was swept up in a high ponytail with loose tendrils fetchingly pulled out to frame her face. And it was quite a face. Large, almond-shaped blue eyes; a perfect bow-shaped mouth; and high cheekbones. She peered at us through half-closed lids.

There was no mistaking who this was. I held out my hand. "Angelina, nice to meet you."

She took my hand as though it was an afterthought and looked me up and down. "You're the lawyer, yes?" I barely managed to confirm it before she turned her attention to Alex. And left it there as she gave him a slow, sexy smile. "You are Alex, yes?"

Alex—who was more than used to women falling for him—gave her a polite smile. Ordinarily, we used it to our advantage. But this time we'd agreed it'd be smarter to keep it professional and not give her any false hope. "I am, yes. Do you have a few minutes to talk?"

She stepped back. "Come in, come in."

Angelina led us into a sunken living room with dark hardwood flooring on which sat a very expensive-looking Persian rug. The furnishing was eclectic boho chic, with an overstuffed burgundy couch, vibrant artwork on the walls, and lots of throw pillows in unusual fabrics of all shapes and colors. The overall effect was warm, inviting, and luxurious in an unostentatious way. Kind of the opposite of Steier's monochromatic decorating hell.

Angelina sat on the couch and patted the space next to her as she beckoned to Alex. "Sit here by me."

I could easily imagine how every man she'd ever said that to would turn into a slobbering, stammering fool. But of course, not Alex. He declined, saying, "Thanks, but this looks so comfy." He took a seat on the chaise across from her. Then he very deliberately crossed his legs, woman-style.

Angelina's smile showed his message was received. She took a drag off her cigarette and tapped the ashes into a black quartz ashtray. "Irina said you want to talk about Gold Strike. I know very little about Tanner's business ventures."

I'd had a feeling she'd say that. I wasn't sure I believed her, but it didn't matter right now. "That's okay. What we'd really like to do is talk to him. But you know he's gone missing, right?"

Angelina's eyes grew wide. "No, I didn't know this."

This time I *was* sure. I definitely didn't believe her. "That's why we wanted to talk to you. It would help us figure out how to find him if we knew a little more about who he was. Like, did he have girlfriends or family in other states—or maybe even other countries—he might be staying with?"

Her smile was a mixture of amusement and derision. "Tanner has many girls. I would not call them friends. More like . . . business associates."

I raised an eyebrow. "You mean call girls."

She nodded. "Very expensive ones."

I was beginning to get a clearer picture now. "And you know they're call girls because they work for you, right?"

She peered at me through the cigarette smoke. "Why would I answer this question?"

"Because I'm a lawyer, and if you retain me, I won't be able to tell anyone what you say." The lawyer card was the only card I had to play. If she didn't bite, we'd be shit out of luck. "Give me a dollar."

She continued to peer at me for a long moment. I thought she was about to tell us to leave, but then she fished a wad of cash out of the pocket of her kimono, peeled off a five dollar bill, and gave it to me. "Now you are my lawyer?"

I put the bill in my purse. "Yes. I'm now your lawyer. Everything you say is privileged." She gave me a puzzled look. I explained. "I can't tell anyone what you say to me." I tilted my head toward Alex. "And that goes for him, too."

She nodded and took another drag on her cigarette. "Yes. The girls all work for me. Tanner would hire them to keep his investors happy. He paid me very well."

Time to drill down. "You know he scammed a lot of those investors, stole millions from them. That's why he's on the run."

She was unfazed. "I didn't know about that, but I'm not surprised. Tanner has his own . . . way of living. But I did not get involved in his other business dealings. I did not want to know."

I didn't buy that, either. But I'd come back to that the next time I sat down with her. For now, I needed to cut to the chase. "Where do you think Tanner might be?"

She waved the hand holding the cigarette through the air. "Who knows? He could be anywhere. Sometimes he even stayed here."

I leaned in and looked her in the eye. "You know him pretty well. You must have some idea."

She met my gaze with utter calm. "Tanner did not tell me where he went or what he did. He only talked to me when he wanted my girls or me."

I could see I was going to get nowhere with her. At least, not now. I let Alex take a crack at her, hoping she'd loosen up with him—but no luck. After another ten unfruitful minutes, we thanked her for her time and left.

We waited until we'd driven away from the house to share our reactions. I said, "She knows a lot more than she's letting on."

Alex was emphatic. "No doubt about it. We need to keep a close eye on her. And by we, I mean me. I scoped out her security system. I might be able to hack into it."

I hadn't even noticed a security system. Yet another reason why I can't live without Alex. "You're a genius."

But whether he managed to hack her security system or not, I had a feeling Angelina was going to lead us somewhere.

With a little luck, it'd be to Tanner.

THIRTY-ONE

We were just ten minutes from the office when Alex's cell phone rang. I read him the number.

He immediately steered toward the next off-ramp. "Yes! He took the bait."

I stared at him. "What on earth are you talking about?"

But Alex had already answered the call. "Hey, thanks for getting back to me."

He pulled onto a side street and parked the car. I didn't get much from his side of the conversation, other than the fact that he'd managed to sweet-talk someone into dishing the dirt on some guy named Wes.

I checked my email, deleted a bunch of junk, and texted Michy that we'd be there as soon as Alex finished his call.

When he finally did, he turned to me with a smug little grin. "That was my new best friend, Andrew. Who plays for my team and just happens to work at Elite Homes Real Estate Agency."

Recognition dawned on me as I realized who "Wes" was. Wesley Rogerian was the real estate agent who'd invested half a million in the cryptocurrency trade. I'd asked Alex to do some digging into Wesley.

Apparently he'd gotten lucky and found an agent who was willing to spill—and who apparently was gay. "The gay mafia is real."

Alex gave me a superior look. "Never doubt it. Anyway, according to Andrew, this Wesley guy is a total loser. Hasn't made a sale in a year. Total waste of a desk. No one can figure out why he hasn't been fired."

So Edie and Joey were right. They'd said there was something shady about him. "Then where'd he get the money to throw half a mil into the cryptocurrency trade?"

Alex frowned. "I scoured every database I could find. He's clean. No criminal record."

That made it pretty clear. "He's obviously fronting for someone."

Alex nodded. "The thing I haven't been able to figure out is who."

That was the question. And something else had occurred to me. "Did he make a stink about losing the money?" According to Dale, almost all the investors had contacted the police and asked about pressing charges.

He drummed his fingers on the steering wheel. "Not since I checked in with Dale last week."

I scrolled through the contacts on my phone. "I'll get an update right now."

I caught Dale on the way to lunch. He was with a couple of detective buddies and couldn't say much. I sometimes forgot that giving me inside information was a pretty dangerous thing to do. "I just need a yes or no. Does the name Wesley Rogerian ring a bell? He was one of the investors. Lost a bundle on the trade. Was he one of the investors who called the police?" It was a pretty unusual name. I was betting he'd remember it if he'd seen it on a report or heard Kingsford mention it.

He was silent for a few moments. "No, definitely not."

I thanked him. We'd planned to have a real talk, and now that I had some new information to contribute, I wanted more than ever to hear what he thought. "We still on for dinner later?"

He said we were, and I ended the call. I told Alex what Dale had said. The fact that Wesley Rogerian wasn't screaming bloody murder about losing that much money made a few things clear. "Whoever he's fronting for is hella rich."

Alex blew out a breath. "No kidding. And he—"

I interrupted. "Or she."

Alex nodded. "Or she has got to be dirty."

Probably using money he—or she—had hidden from the IRS. I wasn't sure how it'd help solve the murder case, but I wanted to find out who this mystery millionaire was. "I think it's time we paid a visit to our Underachiever of the Year. Where's the agency?"

Alex started the car. "In the heart of Beverly Hills. Very high-end."

Which meant the agents were probably very high-end, too—and plenty pissed off about having to endure a loser like Wesley. I felt kind of sorry for him.

Alex got us there in just fifteen minutes. Quite a feat considering it was the lunch hour, when everyone and their dog was out on the streets. The building was one of those understated types, and the sign that read **ELITE HOMES REAL ESTATE AGENCY** was brass with sleek, minimalist block letters. The front door was made of heavy, tinted glass inset with a simple wrought-iron design.

And the inside was just as elegant. Every desk looked like an antique, and each was big enough to seat two agents with room for their desktops. But the floors and lighting were ultramodern. I wouldn't have thought the mix would work, but it did. The place was gorgeous. I counted eleven agents, all of whom appeared to be hard at work—either on the phone or on their computers. And they all looked like they'd been dressed by a stylist—a really good one. Even the men looked très chic.

I saw an older woman with stylishly cut gray hair approach us. Her smile was slightly sharky. I whispered to Alex, "Do you see Wesley?" Alex had pulled up his photo, but I'd forgotten to look at it.

He shook his head as he moved toward the woman and poured on the charm. "Good afternoon. We're here to see Wesley Rogerian."

Her smile faded. "Are you sure there's nothing I can help you with?"

Her voice held a note of exasperation. No doubt, she was thinking we'd be yet another sale Wesley failed to make. Andrew had been dead-on. "Thank you, but no. Is he not in today?"

At that moment, a man with slicked-back blond hair and a hook nose emerged from the back of the office. Unlike the other men, who were perfectly turned out, his tie was loosened and the top button was unbuttoned. I noticed he was wearing shoes with squared-off toes, which only made his already oversize feet look like skis. It had to be our man. But I waited for Alex to give the cue.

He nodded toward the man. "I believe we've found him. If you don't mind . . . ?"

I could see the woman very much minded, but she tried to be graceful about it. "Of course." She reached into the pocket of her navy-blue blazer and pulled out a card. "Please don't hesitate to call if you still have any questions."

Wesley had taken a seat at the desk that was against the wall toward the back of the office. Unlike the other two-man desks, this one was barely big enough for a single adult. I had a feeling that neither the desk nor its placement was an accident. But that setup gave us some privacy. Exactly what we needed. As we headed toward Wesley, I saw Alex give a little wave to a handsome young man in a Tom Ford suit. "Your new best friend, Andrew?"

Alex gave me a brief nod. "Want me to start off?"

That'd give me a chance to get a bead on Wesley. "Sure."

We reached Wesley at his desk, and Alex introduced us. Again, we'd decided not to use a cover story. There was a strong chance the cops would go public with the case very soon, and when they did, the press would be all over Niko. And that meant I'd get some attention, too. If Alex and I lied about who we were, everyone we'd spoken to would find out. We didn't need to make ourselves yet another target for a lot of pissed-off investors. It was very likely we'd want to talk to some of them again. Besides, I was still looking over my shoulder and expecting Ivan to be standing there. With a gun. I definitely didn't need another enemy.

Alex glided up to Wesley with one of his most disarming smiles. He told Wesley who we were and that we were talking to all the investors who'd lost their shirts on the cryptocurrency trade with Gold Strike. "We're hoping to file a lawsuit to recoup some of the money, and we thought you might need our help, too. We hear you lost quite a bit of money yourself."

The bit about the lawsuit wasn't true, but it was a safe enough lie. We *could* file a lawsuit. We just wouldn't. I don't do civil practice. It bores me to death.

Wesley's face tightened. "That's none of your business. And I don't want to get involved in any lawsuits."

Alex took a few more runs at him, but Wesley wouldn't budge. Sometimes it takes a light touch; other times it takes a battering ram. I decided it was time to haul out the battering ram. "Look, Wes—can I call you Wes?"

He gave me a flinty look. "No."

I smiled. "So, Wes. I'm going to level with you. The cops are going to come knocking on your door sooner or later. And when they do, they're going to have a few questions for you. Like how someone who makes less than fifty thousand a year managed to invest five hundred thousand with Gold Strike." I paused for effect. "But they won't stop there. Because once they start looking, they're going to find out that this isn't the first time you've sunk a wad of cash into a Gold Strike portfolio. And when they do . . . well, I suppose you can guess what happens next. Can't you? Wes?"

His lower lip began to tremble. "I—I can't tell you . . ." He seemed to run out of breath.

He was on the hook. Now I just had to reel him in. "Listen, I'm a lawyer. If you tell me who gave you the money, I might be able to help you." In fact, I was already imagining the argument I'd make for him. But the truth was, I'd probably never have to make a case for dear old Wes. Because the cops had their hands full with the mob of investors who actually wanted their attention. They'd be happy enough to let sleeping dogs lie for those investors who weren't complaining.

He looked at me with desperation. "You will?"

I nodded. "Absolutely. And everything you tell me will remain confidential. I promise." Sort of. Depending on whether the name he gave me turned out to be a viable murder suspect—in which case, I'd blast that name to every cop and reporter I could get my hands on.

His Adam's apple bobbed. "Okay. You're right. I'm fronting for someone. But the money's clean. I swear!"

I stared at him. "Then why use you?"

His words tumbled out in a rush. "Because he didn't want anyone to know he was getting into some of the riskier trades."

That was weird. "Why would he care?"

Wesley shrugged. "He owns a lot of real estate agencies. Does a lot of big land deals. I think he doesn't want the banks to get the impression he can't be trusted."

I wasn't sure I bought that explanation. But that was a conundrum for a different day. I needed a name. "So who is this millionaire real estate mogul?"

Wesley corrected me. "Billionaire. You might've heard of him."

The name he gave made the blood rush from my head to my toes. A roaring sound filled my ears. I felt myself growing faint. I had to grab the edge of the desk to keep from falling.

Because I'd heard of that billionaire all right.

He was the monster who'd raped me almost every night for the better part of a year when I was twelve years old. The beast who'd starred in all my nightmares ever since. Nightmares I woke up from screaming and drenched in a cold sweat.

Yes, I knew Sebastian Cromer very, very well.

THIRTY-TWO

I'm sure Wesley didn't notice my reaction. He was too busy worrying about his own skin. But I knew Alex had seen my reaction, because he immediately stepped in and continued the questioning.

I did my best to pull myself together and tried to focus on what they were saying. But I felt like I was watching them through a telescope.

A few things did penetrate my haze. Wesley said Sebastian Cromer had been investing with Gold Strike for the past year. Until now, he'd made quite a bit of money with them. And although he'd taken a bath on the latest cryptocurrency trade, he'd ordered Wesley to lay low until he decided how to deal with Bryan and Tanner.

The latter piece of information made me sit up like I'd been stuck with a cattle prod. There was no way Sebastian would kill anyone himself, but he certainly could've hired someone to kill Bryan—and maybe Tanner. Could I really get that lucky? I tuned back in and asked, "So what did he decide to do? Did he tell you?"

Wesley's gaze drifted toward the door—where he undoubtedly wished he was right now. "Yeah, he decided to meet with Bryan."

This was almost too good to be true. "And did he?" Wesley nodded. "When?"

"The night before Bryan died," he said.

I asked, "How do you know?"

Wesley squirmed in his seat. "Because we all had dinner at Sebastian's house."

That was weird. "Sebastian took you with him? Why?"

He stammered, "I-I guess—I think to make Bryan nervous."

I raised an eyebrow. Wesley looked the type to get an ass kicking. Not the type to give one. "Why would your being there make him nervous?"

Wesley dropped his gaze. "Because I had evidence that Bryan was . . . into boys. Photos. And a couple of voice mails. Sebastian threatened to give everything to the police if Bryan didn't get his money back."

My soaring hope of finally getting to serve that bastard plummeted to the ground. The only way Sebastian could get his money back was to hold the threat over Bryan's head. He had nothing to gain and everything to lose by killing Bryan. My next words came out dry and flat. "I assume Bryan promised to get all his money back."

Wesley nodded. "In fact, he went back to his place that night and got a hundred thousand out of his safe. Gave it to Sebastian."

I wanted Wesley to stop talking. Every word he said made it more impossible to paint a target on Sebastian's back. "What about Tanner? Did you or Sebastian ever make contact with him?"

"No," he said. "Not that I know of. Sebastian didn't really deal with him. He only dealt with Bryan."

I let Alex take back the reins for the next fifteen minutes, but Wesley had nothing new to add. Other than the fact that Sebastian paid him five grand a month to be his front man. Seemed like a pretty lousy deal for Wesley. I was sure the money Sebastian was using to invest came from some shady source, and although I didn't think the cops on the murder case would find out, that didn't mean other authorities—like the IRS—wouldn't. And if they did, Wesley was in for some very uncomfortable encounters.

Alex eventually thanked Wesley for his help, and I gave him my card. "Call me if you think of anything else. And if the cops come knocking, don't talk to them until you talk to me first. Got it?"

Wesley did an almost audible gulp. "G-got it. Th-thanks."

He really wasn't cut out for a life of crime. Even the fringe-y kind of thing he'd gotten himself into. When we got back to the car, Alex turned to face me. "Do you want to tell me who Sebastian Cromer is to you?"

I hesitated. I had to tell him something. The question was, how much? Michy already knew he'd been my mother's boyfriend, and she knew he'd been abusive. But I'd never shared the details. I decided I could tell Alex that much. "He was my stepfather for one dark, horrible year. Left me pretty messed up for most of my teenage years . . . and maybe a little beyond." To put it mildly. Very mildly. But it was enough for Alex to get the drift. "Sorry if I acted weird. It was kind of a shock to hear his name come up."

Alex's eyes were full of sympathy. "I'll bet. Too bad he didn't pan out as a suspect. I'd love to see his ass in maximum security."

I gave him a sad smile. "No, general population. That would be the dream. He'd be dead in an hour." Maybe less, once I told some of my clients in prison that he was a child molester. It's a badge of honor among inmates to kill pedophiles. "But I love that he got fleeced by Bryan and Tanner."

Alex returned my smile, then started the car. "There is that. Kind of weird that he wound up involved in this Gold Strike disaster."

I'd thought so, too, at first. But actually, it wasn't. "Sebastian's always been heavy into trading, and he usually went for the big, risky hits. That's how he grew his real estate business so fast." I added, "That, and probably some gnarly tax fraud."

We made it to the office just in time for our usual late lunch and found Michy standing behind her desk, purse on her shoulder. She said, "I need to get some fresh air. Want me to bring something back for you guys?"

It was a beautiful day, and after the rain and wind, the air really did smell fresh. The idea of getting out was extra appealing after the morning we'd had. "Tell you what, let's all go out. But first I have something to tell you."

As I recounted our conversation with Wesley, Michy let her purse slide down her arm and sank into her chair. When I finished, she said, "Oh my God, I can't believe it. Sebastian Cromer. I never thought I'd have to hear that horrible name again."

I couldn't agree more. "The only good thing is knowing that he got burned—and bad—by Bryan and Tanner."

Michy knitted her brow. "But if he's using dirty money, can't you get him busted for . . . something?"

I'd considered that. "I'd imagine so. But he's not stupid. He's probably hidden his tracks pretty well. It'd take time to dig out enough evidence to make a case. And a white-collar conviction wouldn't be worth it. He probably wouldn't even do any time."

Michy sighed and nodded. "You're right. Someone needs to kill that guy."

I swung my coat over my shoulders. "Amen to that. Now let's get out of here and go have lunch."

We opted for Mardi, a mellow outdoor restaurant on Holloway Drive that served light California-style cuisine. I had the chopped salad with chicken, but Michy and Alex were more adventurous. She ordered the Sicilian fusilli—which, of course, I took bites of until she threatened to stab me with her fork—and Alex ordered the grilled salmon, which also looked good, but I couldn't fend off fork attacks from both sides.

Michy shook her head. "Why don't you just order what you really want?"

I finished chewing the forkful of her fusilli I'd just speared. "Because I didn't know that's what I wanted until you got it."

We never talked shop in public. Anything we said would be privileged, and if someone overheard us, we'd have breached the privilege—which meant it could be repeated in court. So Alex told us about the Danube River cruise he and Paul were planning. And Michy talked about how her boyfriend, Brad—an associate at a white-shoe law firm—was trying to persuade her to go on a cruise to Alaska. She was wavering. "I know it's beautiful and all, but it's friggin' freezing."

I had other problems with the whole cruise business. "It's awfully close quarters. I think I'd go nuts if I had to spend that much time with Niko nose to nose."

Alex smiled. "I think that's part of the charm. But how's he doing? How's his mother?"

I said Niko was trying to hang in, but he was stressed. His mother wasn't in great shape. "She seems to be getting worse."

Michy's voice was angry. "Those two assholes. If she dies, it'll be all because of them."

Alex nodded. "Speaking of those two assholes, I have another investor for us to meet."

I'd been pleasantly distracted by our lunch. Now, the darkness and pain that'd flooded through me when I'd learned that Sebastian was involved in the case came rushing back. I pushed away my plate. "Who?"

Alex saw my reaction. "Don't worry. This one's a sweetheart."

Alex told me about her on the drive back to the office. Margaret Vanderhose was the president of a charity that provides meal service for the disabled and elderly.

We went to see her that afternoon at her home. A cozy, three-bedroom cottage-style house in Beverlywood, a neighborhood just south of (and a few income levels lower than) Beverly Hills.

According to the bio Alex had read me, she was in her late fifties. Maybe it was her full, rosy cheeks and warm, vibrant personality, but she seemed at least ten years younger. Margaret was utterly devoted to her cause, and her eyes misted over when she described her "family"— which was how she referred to her clients.

When we entered, she led us to the banquette in the breakfast nook. "I'm sorry to squeeze you in here, but I'm remodeling. The rest of the house is all torn up." She cast a worried look in the direction of what I presumed was the living room. "And now I'm not sure we'll be able to finish, what with the big hit we took because of Gold Strike." She shook her head. "If we have to finish it ourselves, it'll be very bad news. Not that Steven—my husband—isn't handy. But he's never actually built anything before."

Living with that kind of mess and chaos would drive me nuts. "I'm so sorry."

Margaret waved a hand. "It's nothing compared to what my family is going through. I've had to beg the food banks for donations just to make sure they get something to eat."

How could those jerks rip off someone like this? But then again, given what I'd seen of them, I shouldn't have been surprised. I posed the real question. "How did you happen to get involved with Gold Strike?"

Margaret folded her hands on the table. "Our vice president is a friend of Edie and Joey. I don't know if you've heard of their show." A smile flitted across her lips. "I just love them. I watch them every day. Anyway, they told her about Gold Strike and how much money those men had made for them."

Edie and Joey might have blinders on when it came to Bryan, but they'd be plenty upset to know what he'd done to a wonderful woman like Margaret and her charity. "Did your vice president ever meet with Bryan and Tanner?"

"She said she didn't need to," Margaret said. "But I thought it was important to see them face-to-face and get a sense of who they were." She shook her head, her voice bitter. "I guess we all know how that worked out."

I gazed at her with sympathy. "They must've impressed you at the time."

She sighed. "Oh yes. They really did. Promised me I'd get a huge return in just six months." Margaret bit her lip. "The thing is, I know that if something sounds too good to be true, it probably is. But the foundation had hit a rocky patch. Donations were slowing down. If I didn't do something, we'd have to cut back our services. Some of our family would be left out in the cold." She looked sorrowful. "I was desperate."

I felt badly for her—and her "family." But I was in search of a suspect, and Margaret clearly didn't fit the bill. "Did your husband ever meet with Bryan or Tanner?"

She sighed. "No. He blames me for all this. He warned me all along not to get into business with them." Margaret paused. "Ordinarily, I would've listened to him. But then I met Tanner's mother."

Tanner's mother. Wait a minute. "You met his mother? When?"

Margaret looked out the kitchen window. "A year ago? Something like that. We had lunch. She was such a sweet woman. And, oh my, did she ever love her son. Went on and on about how he'd been a child prodigy. Won leadership awards in elementary school and high school. She said he actually started studying the stock market in third grade. Very impressive."

Sure it was. If any of it had been true. But Alex had found Tanner's school records. Tanner had never won an award of any kind. More to the point, the woman Margaret had met couldn't have been Tanner's mother. She'd died of leukemia ten years ago. "Did you just meet her the one time?"

"No," she said. "We actually had lunch a few times."

I had a hunch about where this was heading. "Had you invested with Gold Strike yet?"

She sighed. "No, I hadn't. In fact, the last time I saw her was the day I finally did invest." Margaret met my gaze. "I know. It's all so obvious now."

She'd been suckered all right, but Tanner had really worked her hard. And desperation can make fools of all of us. "Do you by any chance have a phone number for her?"

Margaret opened a drawer and took out a pad of pink Post-its. She wrote down the "mother's" name and phone number and passed it to me. I saw that the name she'd written was Louisa Hunsecker. I gave her a puzzled look. "Tanner's last name is Handel."

She nodded. "She told me she'd taken back her maiden name." Margaret drooped in her chair as her voice filled with sadness and defeat. "I tried calling her when I heard we'd lost all our money, but she never called back."

That woman—whoever she was—had befriended Margaret for the sole purpose of getting her to invest. And she was every bit the con artist Tanner was.

I'd represented some of the most vicious murderers imaginable. But few were as despicably immoral as Tanner Handel.

THIRTY-THREE

When we got back to the office, I told Michy about our meeting with Margaret.

She made a face. "So he literally robbed the poor and elderly. What a scumbag. Is there any chance Louisa Hunsecker is her real name?"

Alex shook his head. "No way. I'd bet everything she told Margaret was a lie—like that story about him being a child prodigy and all the awards he never really got. But I'll check out her name, just to be on the safe side."

As Alex headed to his computer, I turned to Michy. "You know, I'm really hoping that asshole is dead."

"Except for one minor detail." She raised her index finger. "What that'll mean for a certain guy you seem to like."

I sighed. She was right. If it turned out someone had killed Tanner, Niko would be number one on the list of suspects. But that thought led me to an idea. "I wonder if Tanner ever said anything to Niko about his mother."

Michy gestured to her phone. "Easy enough to find out. Care to place a bet? Five bucks says the answer is no."

I put a hand on my hip. "Why on earth would I take a shitty bet like that?"

She gave an impish smile. "Same reason you've taken my other shitty bets. Because you can't resist."

"Then consider this a first." I headed for my office and called Niko.

And as we'd expected, Niko said Tanner had never made any kind of reference to his mother. "I kind of got the impression both his parents had passed away."

I asked Niko about his own mother. "Have there been any changes in her condition?"

His voice was tight. "No. But the doctor keeps telling me she'll decline again soon, and then it won't be long . . ."

Doctors. Don't get me started. "Why does he feel the need to repeat that over and over? It's not like you're going to forget."

There was a heavy silence for a few beats. "I think he's afraid I'm in denial about her chances. He just wants to prepare me."

I had a few thoughts on that doctor's helpful reminders. Like, there's no such thing as "preparing" anyone for so huge a loss. And why knock denial? Isn't it better to live with hope, regardless of how unrealistic, for as long as possible? After all, medical miracles do happen. Not very friggin' often, but still. No matter how "prepared" he was, Niko was going to suffer—terribly. But this was no time to rant about the doctor. What Niko needed right now was a shoulder. "I get it. You going back to the hospital tonight?" He'd taken to spending all his free time at his mother's bedside.

"Yeah," he said. "I know it's crazy, but I feel like she can sense my presence."

"I don't think that's crazy at all." I'd heard stories about coma patients who said they'd known—and appreciated—the people who stayed with them. "Want some company?"

"That's kind of you, but no. All I do is sit there like a zombie anyway." Niko said he missed me and I said I missed him, too—though to be perfectly truthful, I thought the fact that we weren't seeing much of each other right now was probably for the best. The digging I'd done on him and the questions raised by what I'd learned weighed on me. So I was relieved when we ended the call without making plans to get together.

Just ten minutes later, Alex appeared in my doorway. He rapped on the doorframe. "Ready to fall off your chair with shock?"

I gripped the arms of my chair. "Go for it."

He sat down on the couch and opened his iPad. "The phone number Louisa Hunsecker gave Margaret has been disconnected." He made air quotes. "'And there is no new number.'"

I glanced down. "Still in my chair."

Alex held up a hand. "Wait, it gets better. The address she gave belongs to Furry Friends. A pet grooming service."

Maybe it was Alex's wry delivery. Or maybe I just needed a laugh. But this non-news was kind of funny. I spoke earnestly. "Well, then I'm sure she must've worked there."

Alex widened his eyes. "That's what I thought. But no. Can you believe it? When I spoke to the manager, he said no one by the name of Louisa Hunsecker had ever worked there."

I stared at him. "Well, now I really am about to fall off my chair."

He held up his hand again. "Then get ready to hit the floor. Because the name Louisa Hunsecker? Belongs to a thirty-two-year-old junkie. Who died of an overdose in Kansas City—ten years ago."

Another dead—quite literally—end. I told him Niko had never heard Tanner talk about his mother. "So now what?"

Alex frowned. After a moment, he said, "I can only think of one place to go if we want to chase this down."

I'd had the same thought. "Angelina." He nodded. I looked at my watch. It was almost six o'clock. I was supposed to have dinner with Dale tonight. But this was more urgent. "Think it's too late to hit her up?"

Alex raised an eyebrow. "Her? You're kidding, right?"

I deadpanned him. "They're not literally ladies of the night. For all you know, she's an early riser."

He shook his head. "So many jokes come to mind."

"Please don't share them. First, let me cancel with Dale."

As it turned out, Dale had been about to cancel on me. He'd gotten pulled into helping to serve a search warrant. We agreed to talk the next day and pick another night. I ended the call and said, "Okay, all set. What's her number?"

I pushed the buttons as Alex read it to me. Someone with a thick Russian accent answered. "Poranova residence. Who is speaking?"

I recognized the voice as that of the older woman who'd first answered the intercom at Angelina's house. How to play this? As super important and urgent? Or laid-back and casual? I didn't want to sound desperate and give Angelina the impression she had the upper hand. But if I played it too low-key, she might blow me off. I landed on urgent. I told her who I was, then said, "I need to speak with her right away."

The woman paused. "You can tell me what is this regarding?"

I was curious. That was awfully personal. She had to be a relative. But even so, Angelina was a grown-ass woman, entitled to some boundaries. I wondered if she knew this woman asked questions like that. Regardless, my answer was the same. "No. I can't." I purposely added a touch of menace. "And I don't think she'd want me to."

She gave a loud harrumph. "Angelina is very busy right now. Give me your number."

I gave her my number and ended the call. I sat back. "And now, we wait."

Alex loved waiting about as much as I did. Which is to say, he really hated it. He crossed his legs and bounced his foot up and down. "Why don't we just go over to her place?"

The idea had occurred to me, too. "If we have to, we will. But it'd be better to get her to respond." She was the key link to Tanner. If we wanted to get her to open up about him more, we had to make her feel like she had a say in how and when we made contact. That wouldn't happen if we went and banged on her door without warning every time we wanted to talk to her.

Luckily, as it turned out, we didn't have to wait long. Seven and a half minutes later (but who's counting?), Angelina called me back.

I put a smile in my voice. "Hey, thanks for getting back to me so—"

She interrupted me. Her husky voice was even deeper than usual. "I was going to call you. We need to talk."

A hundred possibilities fired in my brain. Did we just get lucky? Was she about to admit she'd been hiding Tanner? Did she know who had killed Bryan? "Of course. We can come by now if you want."

Her speech was rapid, pressured. "I—uh—it might be better if you come later."

I took a guess. "When we'll be alone?"

She whispered, "Yes."

I knew I should wait till we saw her, but I had to see if she'd give me a clue. "Does this have to do with Tanner?"

She lowered her voice. "I'll tell you when I see you."

Angelina said I could come over at eight o'clock, and I agreed. I ended the call and told Alex what she'd said and how she'd sounded. "Do you think she knows where Tanner is?"

Alex drummed his fingers on the arm of the chair. "Maybe. And if so, I wonder why she's suddenly willing to tell us." He frowned. "I'm also wondering what's up with that older woman. I thought she was just a housekeeper, but if she's the reason Angelina didn't want to talk just now . . . Did it sound like she was scared?"

I shrugged. "I couldn't tell. But it might not be that she's afraid of the housekeeper. She might just be afraid to let anyone else hear what she wants to tell us."

Alex met my gaze. "You mean, like, confess to a crime?"

I voiced the answer I hoped for. "Yeah. Like maybe the fact that she's hiding Tanner. Because he killed Bryan."

He gave a little chuckle. "Wouldn't that be perfect."

I held up my hands. "A girl can dream, right?"

But I secretly crossed my fingers. They say dreams—not just nightmares—do come true. Why not this one?

THIRTY-FOUR

It was dark by the time we headed out to Angelina's house, and as Alex made the turn onto her street, a sparkling array of city lights spreading all the way to downtown LA came into view. Beautiful.

I'd been trying to keep my hopes for this meeting in check so I wouldn't crash and burn if it didn't pan out. But my sweaty palms and thumping heart made it clear I wasn't succeeding. I needed to calm down. I told myself to take deep breaths, to consider the possibility that what she wanted to tell me might be the worst possible news—that Niko had killed Bryan, or Tanner, or both. But that only made me more nervous. As we walked up to the outer door of her house, I dried my palms on my jacket. I couldn't remember whether Angelina was a handshaker, but I wanted to be ready just in case. I tilted my head toward the intercom. "Hit it."

Alex licked his lips and took a deep breath before he pushed the button. It made me feel better to see that he was nervous, too. Angelina answered. "Who is it?"

I leaned in. "It's us."

A buzzer sounded, and we walked through the courtyard. Angelina appeared at the door. She was barefoot, in fashionably shredded skinny jeans and a white crop T-shirt. I tried to read her expression for some hint of what was to come. She seemed more somber than last time but nowhere near as freaked out as I'd expected.

She headed toward the living room and waved for us to follow her. As we entered, I saw that the floor-length drapes—which had been closed before—were open now, which exposed a bank of windows that afforded a view of the city. She'd left a lit cigarette in a black ashtray that was shaped like a cupped hand. Between the mesmerizing view and the tendrils of smoke that floated up toward the high ceiling, I felt like I'd stepped into a noir fifties movie. Angelina sat down and picked up her cigarette.

Alex sat on the paisley ottoman across from her, and I took the overstuffed burgundy chair to his right. Now that I had a chance to study her more closely, I could see that she was agitated. She was ready to get down to business. So was I. I dug my nails into my palms to keep my hands from shaking. "Tell us why we're here."

She took a drag from her cigarette and blew out the smoke in a fast, long stream. "I need you to do something for me. It's about my sister."

Her what? I'd been so sure she was going to tell us something about Tanner, I had to take a moment to regroup. "Older or younger?"

Angelina tapped the ashes off her cigarette. "Younger, much younger. Fifteen years old. Eliza was what our mother called a surprise baby."

Angelina had to be at least ten, maybe even fifteen years older. She was probably more like a second mother to Eliza than a big sister. Eliza must be in some kind of trouble. This was good news for me, because Eliza was a minor, which meant that unless she'd killed someone, I could probably get her out of doing any time. And it wouldn't take much work. A nice, easy-peasy way to earn brownie points with Angelina. "What's going on with her?"

She rubbed her forehead. "Eliza knows she has to call me before she comes over. I don't allow her to be here when I have . . . guests. But two weeks ago, she came without calling. She'd just had a fight with her—how did she call it?" She tapped her forehead. "Her, uh . . . bestie. I wouldn't have let her come if she'd called. I had a big party going that night. Many men Tanner and Bryan were trying to do business with. Ordinarily, I would have sent her home immediately, but she was so upset." Angelina paused and put down her cigarette. "I had to let her stay."

I'd heard about Tanner's parties. I hadn't known she threw them, too. "Were those parties a regular thing?"

She picked up her cigarette and studied it for a moment. "Yes. But not usually here. Most of the time, we used Tanner's condo."

I had a bad feeling about this. "What happened?"

She bit her lip. "I couldn't really talk to her, and the party was getting very loud, so at about ten o'clock—maybe a little before that—she called for a Lyft and went outside to wait. The next thing I knew, she was back and pounding on the door." Angelina seized the neck of her T-shirt and pulled. "She was crying. Her blouse was torn; her hair was a mess. She said she'd gone outside to wait for the car, and someone came up behind her and grabbed her around the waist. He put a bag over her head, tied her hands behind her back, and dragged her into the back seat of a car, and . . ."

I closed my eyes for a brief moment. This one hit a little too close to home. "And raped her."

Angelina nodded. Her hand trembled as she took a long drag off her cigarette. "I asked her if she could remember anything about him. Was he tall? Was he old? Young? Did he speak?"

Good questions, all. "And?"

She shook her head. "All she could say was that he seemed older, because when she tried to fight him off, he was breathing very hard."

That wasn't much. "Did she remember anything about the car? Whether it seemed new? How big it was?"

"She just said the seats felt like leather." Angelina's tone was bitter. "It's nothing. She knows nothing."

I could feel the guilt coming off Angelina in waves. "But you think it was someone who'd been at your party."

She nodded. "It must have been. This neighborhood, sometimes homeless people who live in the park roam around. But this man does not seem like a homeless person. The problem is, Eliza doesn't want anyone to know, and I can't go to the police anyway. If it was one of my clients . . ."

They might decide to tell the police what Angelina did for a living—if only so they could use it to discredit Eliza. "So you and Tanner were business partners?"

Her face hardened. "Not partners. But yes, it was all business between us. He paid me to keep the men happy so they'd invest with Gold Strike."

And now I could see that she hated herself for it. "Then I take it Bryan and Tanner were at the party that night?"

Angelina flicked the end of her cigarette in the direction of the ashtray. The ashes fell to the floor. "Of course. But I know it wasn't either of them. They never left." A look of anger crossed her face. "Too busy working their targets."

That figured. "Do you keep guest lists?"

She pointed to her head. "I keep them in here. I can give you the names of the fifteen men I personally invited."

I could hear a *but* coming. "Were there more than fifteen there?"

"Many more," she said, her tone despairing. "The problem is, I always allow them to bring a plus-one."

Of course. "A plus-one who has money to invest."

"Yes," she said. "And they often stretch the plus-one to a plus-two. There were at least thirty people at the party—maybe more. I don't know."

I thought about that. "Maybe your caterer knows?"

Her shoulders slumped. "He might have an estimate. But I always serve buffet-style."

Alex said, "Because you never know how many there'll be."

"Exactly," she replied.

Alex opened his iPad. "You can rule out Bryan and Tanner. Anyone else?"

She thought for a moment. "Yes. Three of the men I personally invited. I know them very well."

He nodded. "Tell you what, just give me the information for all fifteen you personally invited. The three you ruled out, too. Someone might've seen who left around the time Eliza did."

She nodded. "But I must warn you, the names may not be real. Email addresses, phone numbers, yes. Names, no."

I said, "And you don't know who any of the plus-ones were." She shook her head. Terrific.

Alex looked up from his iPad. "What about your security camera? Have you checked the footage on it to see if it showed a man leaving the party right after Eliza?"

Angelina's expression was grim. "Of course I did. But my camera only shows the courtyard, and two of the lights in the courtyard were out. I couldn't see anything."

Alex asked, "Would you mind if I took a look? Fresh eyes . . ."

She stood up. "Come with me."

We followed her into an office that was just a few steps from the living room. She tapped a key on the desktop computer, and it whirred to life. Then she sat down and typed for a few seconds. A dark image that showed the outlines of the courtyard at the front of the house appeared on the screen. She moved aside and waved Alex over. "This is from the night of the party, just before Eliza left."

I watched over his shoulder as he played the footage. Angelina was right. I could see figures moving around, but I couldn't even tell who was male and who was female. And it was impossible to see if anyone left. The front gate was shrouded in darkness. Alex rewound the footage and played it again more slowly, but it was no use.

He pushed away from the computer. "You need to upgrade your equipment."

Angelina gave him a flat look. "This is not news."

This was going to be a daunting bitch of a hunt. "We'll do everything we can to find this guy. But just out of curiosity, what're you going to do if we find him?"

Her eyes turned to slits. "Don't worry about that. That will be my problem."

I had a feeling that man—whoever he was—would wind up sleeping with the fishes. I was A-OK with that. In fact, it was downright inspiring. I'd move heaven and earth to get that bastard. "We'll need to meet with Eliza." We might be able to ferret out more information than Angelina had. Not just because we were experienced at getting witnesses to talk, but also because witnesses—and especially sexual assault victims—can be more comfortable talking to sympathetic outsiders than to family.

Angelina pressed her lips together and frowned. "I don't think she will want to talk to you. She doesn't want anyone to know about it."

Of course not. Because, as I knew from vast experience, she blamed herself. Sadly, that attitude was common. "Then she doesn't know you told us." Angelina shook her head. "It'll really help if we talk to her. Tell her we'll keep it confidential. It won't be like going to the cops."

She bit the inside of her lip. "I will try. No promises."

I'd pushed it as far as I could. I'd just have to hope she could persuade Eliza to cooperate. But now it was time to get what I'd come for. I told her about Margaret and the woman who'd posed as Tanner's mother. "She gave the name Louisa Hunsecker, which we know is fake."

Angelina sighed. "Oh yes, the mama. Tanner has used her with others. She is, what you say, a fake. The name I know her by is Iris Falls."

She gave me an address in North Hollywood and a cell phone number. I studied it. "How long ago did you get this contact information?"

She stared out the window for a brief moment. "A year ago? But Tanner called her a few weeks ago, and I think that's the number he used. It should still be correct."

Alex asked her to give him the names and contact information for the men she'd invited to the party. She gave him the names from memory, but I noticed she pulled out her cell phone to get the rest. "Why don't you give us your cell number? That way we won't have to go through your housekeeper."

Angelina stared at us, then frowned. "She's not my housekeeper. She's my grandmother."

As I'd suspected. "Does she live here?"

"Sometimes," she said.

I asked, "By any chance, was she around on the night of the party?"

Angelina looked at me like I'd grown another head. "Are you crazy?"

"Yeah, I am." But it was worth a shot to find another witness. Angelina gave me her cell phone number, and Alex made sure he'd gotten the contact information for the guests. I told her to let us know what Eliza said and stood up. "We'll be in touch."

She walked us to the door, and just as we were leaving, she said, "I really don't know where he is. Tanner. Believe me, I have no clue."

But I didn't. And probably wouldn't—until they found his body.

THIRTY-FIVE

When Alex dropped me off at my car, it was after nine o'clock. Niko was probably still at the hospital. But he'd said he didn't want me to come, and besides, I didn't have anything good to tell him.

That train of thought led me to a review of what I'd learned so far—about Niko and the case. I'd asked Alex to keep digging after our meeting with Niko's brother, Ivan, but he hadn't come up with anything new. It seemed we'd plumbed the extent of Niko's hidden past.

Which didn't at all mean we'd uncovered the truth about his present—or rather, his more recent past. Our efforts to find a viable suspect for Bryan's murder—and potentially Tanner's—hadn't exactly yielded great results so far. The angelic charity worker Margaret and Bryan's steadfastly loyal buddies Edie and Joey were out. And Gene Steier, though a real dick, had a pretty decent alibi. Alex had tracked down his whereabouts before and after Bryan's murder. He'd spent the entire time in a luxury room at the Hotel Bel-Air—with a young masseur named Esteban. Gene Steier, the guy who'd called Bryan a "fairy" and a "fag." It's a kind of hypocrisy I find particularly loathsome. But bottom line, we were batting a big, fat zero on the alternate suspect scoreboard.

I sighed. But the fact that I couldn't give Niko any good news was no reason not to call him. I pulled my phone out of my purse and pressed his number. When he answered, his voice was muted. I asked, "You still at the hospital?"

"Yeah. The doctor came by when I got here at six o'clock." His voice was heavy with sadness.

I dreaded the answer to the question I was obliged to ask. "What did he say?"

"He said—" There was a catch in his voice. "He said her vitals were declining."

I felt my chest tighten. From the sound of this, Sophia could pass any day now. "I'm so sorry, Niko. Want me to come be with you?"

A nurse said something to Niko I couldn't make out. A chair scraped, and there was a pause; then he said, "Thanks, Sam. But no, that's okay. I'll be leaving pretty soon. I think I'll probably just go home and crash. You're not missing anything, trust me. I'm a drag to be around."

He sounded drained. "I don't believe that—ever. And you know I don't care what kind of mood you're in. But I understand. I'm sure you're exhausted. Just please let me know if there's anything you need, anything I can do."

He said he would, and we ended the call with a promise to try and get together that weekend. But as I drove out of the parking garage, I realized something wasn't quite right. Something in his voice, or maybe the fact that he'd said he'd *try* to see me this weekend—when he usually said he *would* see me. Was he avoiding me? I didn't want to think about what it'd mean if he was.

For the first time, the fact that this might be how it ended—with each of us avoiding the other because of the secrets this case might reveal—felt more real than ever. If the case went unsolved—or somehow unresolved—I'd forever be wondering who he really was. Worse, I'd always wonder what else he was keeping from me.

And then, knowing myself, my little foray with Ivan would only be the beginning. I'd take over for Alex and personally go after every lead I could find to figure out whether he'd killed Bryan and/or Tanner, and anything else I didn't know about him. Which would ultimately prove impossible and leave me feeling frustrated, guilty, and even more suspicious. Because there's no way you can know everything about anyone. And slowly, over time, I'd pull away. Or maybe, as he started to feel my suspicion—or began to suffer too much from his own guilty secrets—he would.

My thoughts had taken me to a very dark, sad place, and by the time I got home, I was tired and miserable. I decided to take a shower to wash off the day, pour myself a stiff enough drink to knock myself out, and bring this unhappy day to an end.

I felt better after the shower, and with a double shot of Patrón Silver on the rocks in my hand, I was ready to call it a night. I'd just crawled into bed and turned on the television when my cell phone rang. It was ten o'clock. Who'd call me this late? I looked at the screen and saw it was Dale. My heart gave a fast, hard thump. This had to be bad news. I put down my drink and answered in a tight voice. "Hey. What's up?"

"Just reporting in," he said. "You okay?"

I'd forgotten that after seeing Angelina, I'd texted him to ask if he could check and see whether a serial rapist had been reported in the area of her house. I didn't think that's who'd attacked Eliza, but I had to make sure. "Yeah, it's just been a rough day." Only then did I realize that part of the reason I was in such a shitty mood was because Eliza's rape had triggered my own issues. I wondered for the millionth time whether I'd ever get past them.

Dale said, "The database doesn't show any recent reports of a serial rapist."

I moved on to the greater likelihood. "Can you maybe check to see if there are any registered sex offenders in the area?" They live among us—a lot more than most people realize.

"I can," Dale said. "Want to tell me why you need me to? And while you're at it, maybe clue me in as to why today was so rough?"

I wouldn't have minded telling him about Eliza. But I couldn't do that without telling him about Angelina, and that would violate the privilege, since I'd made her a client. I opted for a partial truth. "I guess I'm a little worried about the noose that seems to be tightening around Niko's neck."

There was a rush of air over the phone as Dale blew out a breath. "Yeah, I know they're running hard on that video footage of Bryan's back door."

I'd known they would. The moment they'd seen the jacket in Niko's closet that looked like the one in the video, they'd acted like it was a smoking gun. "But no one's saying they can identify Niko in that video, right?"

"Not so far, no," he said.

I could tell by his tone of voice that he thought that could happen any time now. "What's going on? Do they have something new?"

There was shouting in the background. "I've gotta jump. The guys are ready to hit the road. But no, not that I know of. It's just that . . ."

Niko was still looking like the most viable suspect. "Got it. Can you do dinner tomorrow night?"

"Checking my calendar." There was a pause. "Yep, we're on. Your place. Eight o'clock. I'm bringing the food."

I said, "Sounds good," but he'd already ended the call.

For some reason, I felt better knowing I'd be seeing him tomorrow—though I'd cut off my right arm before I ever told him that. I took a long pull on my drink and tuned the TV to *Atlanta*, one of my favorite shows. But I was too tired to enjoy it. Depression and fatigue had my eyes closing before I could take a second sip.

I guess, after the day I'd had, I should've expected it. But I didn't. Somehow, I never seem to know when the nightmare will hit. And that night, it hit with a vengeance. Sebastian's ironlike claws bit into my arms and lifted me up to the giant black maw that was his mouth as I screamed and writhed in his grasp. As he pulled me closer, I felt blood running down one of my arms.

A low, guttural choking sound—which turned out to be my own voice—woke me up. And my left arm was soaking wet. I saw that the drink I'd left on my nightstand was on the floor. I must've flung my arm out during the nightmare and hit the nearly full glass. Now what was left of my drink was all over my arm.

I looked at the clock. It was only four thirty. Damn. I'd never get back to sleep. But I was still exhausted. I had to try. I took another shower and climbed back into bed. I managed to drift off by about five thirty. Not bad for me. Not so great was the fact that I wound up oversleeping. It was almost nine thirty a.m. when I woke up.

My cell phone showed two text messages from Alex. One at eight a.m. saying that he'd found a location for Tanner's "mother," Iris Falls, and that he'd meet me at the office at eight thirty. Another at eight thirty-five asking, Where are you?!

I called him. "Sorry, I had a bad night. So where'd you find the fake mom, and how are we going to get her to talk to us?" Someone who was working scams for Tanner wasn't likely to be all that friendly.

He sounded impatient. "She works at one of those places where they register you for TSA PreCheck. It's in West Hollywood. She'll be stuck behind a desk."

A captive audience. Just the way I liked them. "So she's close by. Want to pick me up?"

"No. But I want to get moving, so yes. You can pay for gas."

That seemed only fair. "Happy to."

He warned me to be ready by ten o'clock or he'd fill up at the station on South Santa Monica in Beverly Hills—a landmark that provides the most expensive gas in all of Los Angeles. Thus incentivized, it took me just twenty-five minutes to shower, get dressed, put on makeup, and get downstairs.

Alex was already idling in the driveway. When I got into the car, I said, "So how do you plan to get us face-to-face with Iris? Those TSA PreCheck places are pretty busy. It took me three weeks to get an appointment."

He gave me a superior smile. "I just told her Tanner sent me. Told me to ask for her specifically."

Very, very smart. "And since he must be paying her to do shady things for him, she figured your visit was worth more than her usual minimum wage." He nodded. "Nice."

"The question is, do we want to stick with that story once we start talking?" he asked.

We might not be able to. "Let's play it by ear."

Alex turned left on Beverly Boulevard, and after a couple of minutes, he pulled into an underground parking garage beneath a nondescript two-story strip mall. Alex led the way as we walked up two flights and turned left down a corridor that ended at a suite of offices named Identifast, Inc.

As we entered the very full waiting area, Alex held out his cell phone, and I saw a photo of a smiling brunette in a short bob. She had somewhat heavy features—a strong jawline and thick lips—but she was not unattractive. "Iris Falls, I take it?"

Alex nodded, then scanned the cubicles that filled the room. I spotted her first, in a cubicle near the east window. I whispered, "She's over there, to your left." We'd gotten lucky. There was no one in the chairs in front of her desk. She was between customers.

He looked in her direction, then smiled and waved to her. The motion caught her eye, and when she turned to face us, Alex called out, "It's me, Iris! Tanner's friend."

She cast a nervous glance at me, then motioned for us to come over. As we made our way toward her, I decided to drop the ruse. The minute I started asking questions, she'd know we weren't just here to do some sketchy deal. In a low voice, I told Alex to let me do the talking.

As we sat down, I looked her in the eye. But she couldn't return my gaze for more than two seconds at a time, as her eyes rapidly shifted back and forth between Alex and me. That was all it took to let me know she was in deep with Tanner and worried about it. Excellent. Just what I needed. "Let me start by telling you that Tanner is not our buddy. We know what he's been up to and, more specifically, what you've been up to with him. We just met with Margaret. Remember her? The woman who ran that great charity for the sick and elderly? The one you lied to so she'd buy into Tanner's cryptocurrency scam?"

Iris's face froze. "I—I never lied. Tanner told me it was a good deal. I believed him."

I drilled her with a look. "And how about you being his mother? Did Tanner make you believe that, too? Don't bullshit a bullshitter, Iris. You lied your ass off. And you knew damn well that so-called 'investment opportunity' was a total rip-off. The minute Margaret invested, you headed for the hills. How much did he pay you? What's your going rate for scamming decent people out of their hard-earned cash?" I watched her body sag, inch by inch, with every word I said. "Relax. I'm not a cop, and I'm not coming for you. I'm coming for Tanner."

Iris gave me a pleading look. "I need you to know I'm not that person. Really. But I got in a car accident a few years ago. Smashed into a parked car—a Maserati. I couldn't call the police because I didn't have insurance. And I was on Oxy because I'd thrown out my back. I'd just been laid off from my job as a bank teller, and I had no savings. If I'd had to pay for the damages, I'd go bankrupt."

I wasn't sure why she felt compelled to tell me all this, but now that she'd started, I had to hear the whole story. "So what does all this have to do with Tanner? Was it his car?"

She shook her head. "The story about being his mother? It's not entirely a lie. I'm his aunt."

Now that she mentioned it, I could see a slight resemblance in the strong jawline. Which of course helped sell the story that she was his mother. And now I had a feeling how this story ended. "You were panicked, and you knew Tanner would find a way to cover it up for you, right?"

She sighed. "Yes, well. I knew he could be . . . resourceful. I took him to the area where I got in the accident, and he saw that there were home security cameras everywhere. One of them would've caught my license plate for sure. So he filed a report with the cops saying my car had been stolen earlier that morning, before the accident. Then he took my car to a chop shop and bought me a Prius."

And bought her along with it. "So you've been working for him ever since?"

Her eyes widened. "No! The setup with Margaret was the only time. And I'll never do it again!" She swallowed and looked away. "It was a terrible thing to do—especially to someone like her."

It wasn't a bad act. It probably would've worked on most people. But I was used to being lied to. My clients did it all the time. So I was pretty good at spotting liars. And Iris was an accomplished one. That car accident, her bad back, getting laid off. Lots of detail. Too much detail. And very little of it true. Plus, she'd worked Margaret hard—and very effectively. No novice could've pulled that off. That said, I didn't think Iris would've done it on her own. Besides, she wasn't my problem. Tanner was. "Since you're Tanner's aunt, you must know him pretty well."

"Actually, I don't," she said. "I barely ever saw him when he was growing up. His father was a major league asshole. I hated him. Cheated on my sister constantly. So I'd get together with my sister, but I never went to the house. I only really got to know Tanner when he moved out here, around ten years ago."

Alex asked, "Did your sister move out here?"

Iris's face clouded. "No. She got leukemia, died ten years ago. I blame that toadstool of a husband."

I knew that much was true—Alex had found out that Tanner's mother died of leukemia. Maybe we could get something useful out of her after all. "When was the last time you saw Tanner?"

She stared off for a moment. "A month ago? Maybe more."

Alex asked, "Is it unusual not to see him for that long?"

"Not really. We don't run in the same crowds."

I'd bet they did—when there was money involved. "If he were trying to lay low, where do you think he'd go?"

Her brow furrowed. "The last time I saw him, he told me about a friend who bought a villa near Puerto Vallarta."

This sounded promising. "Do you know who the friend was? Did he mention a name?"

"No," she said. "But I'd imagine it was someone he'd done business with before."

The problem was, that could be a very long list. "Did he say where in relation to Puerto Vallarta?"

"No," she said. "But he showed me a photo. It looked like it was pretty isolated. I remember him saying that his friend had asked him to come down to talk about some new business idea." She paused for a moment, then added, "I can't say whether that was true. But I don't know why he'd lie about it."

Not to her anyway. Why bother? And I had to admit, if he wanted to disappear, a villa in a remote area outside Puerto Vallarta would be a good choice. Alex asked her to describe what she'd seen in the photo and took notes. Her memory was surprisingly detailed.

But how to find him there, with no clue as to who his friend was or exactly where the villa was located, was a whole different problem.

THIRTY-SIX

We thanked Iris for her help. She tried to smile and nod as she said, "My pleasure." But her wary expression told me that was yet another lie.

As we headed for Alex's car, I said, "Can you do anything with her description of that villa?"

Alex hit the remote, and the double beep of his car alarm bounced off the walls. "I'd say there's a fifty-fifty chance. At best."

Not great. "So we just have to hope we get lucky."

As we got into the car, he threw me a sarcastic smile. "But as someone likes to say way too often, I'd rather be lucky than good."

I gave him a look. "Shut up."

When we got back to the office, I saw that Michy looked all spiffed up in a low-cut black sweater. And her dark-blonde hair was down, *sans* the habitual Scünci. "Wow, what's the occasion? Are you and Brad actually going to have a real date, like grown-ups?"

They both worked long hours, but the sweatshop that called itself a white-shoe corporate law office worked him to the bone. Nights off— even on the weekends—were few and far between. Consequently, their dates usually consisted of ordering in pizza.

Michy reflexively reached up to adjust the Scünci that wasn't there, then lowered her hands and smoothed the back of her hair. She made a face. "We're having dinner with his parents at Craft."

I was puzzled. "I thought you said you liked them."

She gave an impatient sigh. "I do. It's just that we never get any time alone, and now that he finally has a night off, I'd like it to be just us."

I didn't blame her. "Well, dinner doesn't last all night."

She rolled her eyes. "Yeah. We'll see whether Brad can stay awake."

True, that was a long shot. "But you'll be happy you put up with all this when he makes partner."

"If he survives that long," she said. "Anyway, enough about my anemic love life. Angelina called back. She said Eliza's willing to meet with you."

I'd given up on the possibility. "That's fantastic." I paused for a moment. I didn't want Angelina to be there when we talked. "Can we cut Angelina out of the loop and meet Eliza alone somewhere?"

Michy nodded. "I had a feeling you'd say that. I asked Angelina for her number, but she didn't want to give it to me. So I told Angelina to give Eliza our number."

"I hate to leave the ball in her court. I guess we'll just have to see if she hits it back over the net."

Michy gave me a triumphant smile. "Actually, she already did." Michy touched the space bar on her keyboard and woke up her computer. "Eliza didn't leave a number, but she asked if she could come in this afternoon. She said she'd call back at lunch."

"Excellent. A happy surprise, for a change. I'm going to go listen to our interview with Angelina." I wanted to review what she'd said about the rape.

We always secretly recorded our interviews with witnesses. I didn't want them to know, because I've found it makes them self-conscious and—worst of all—cautious. But I needed to let them see that I was memorializing what they said in case I had to confront them with inconsistencies later, so Alex always pretended to take notes. That never seemed to bother witnesses the way a glowing red light on a recorder did.

"I'm going to finish my workup on Angelo," Alex said.

I'd been on my way to my office, but now I stopped. His next hearing—when he'd plead guilty to all charges—was coming up, and I'd asked the judge for immediate sentencing. Angelo wanted out of county jail yesterday. Prison is much nicer, believe it or not. "And? Have you found anything heartwarming?"

Alex gave me a despairing look. "Not a thing so far. And it's not looking good."

I nodded. I'd had a feeling we'd come up dry on this one. The only argument I could make was that Angelo had saved everyone the hassle and expense of a trial. But the Honorable Sally Thomsky was a new judge. I didn't know how she felt about guns—especially illegal ones— or the people who sold them. "Thanks for trying, Alex. Let me know if you happen to get lucky."

He said he would—with zero enthusiasm—and I went into my office and closed the door.

I'd nearly finished listening to Angelina's interview when Eliza called. Michy put her right through. I could hear teenage voices in the background. She was calling from school. I made my voice as warm and nonthreatening as I could as I told her that I'd be happy to see her this afternoon. "And I promise, everything you say will be confidential."

Eliza spoke in a fast, shaky voice. "Thanks. Um, then is two thirty okay?"

"Sounds great." I considered offering to pick her up, then realized that having any of the kids at school see her getting picked up by some stranger was the last thing she'd want. "And I'll cover your Lyft. Or Uber."

I gave her my office address, and she typed it into her phone, then read it back to me. "It'll just be you, right?"

I always prefer to have Alex with me during interviews. If a witness decides to go south when he testifies in court, I can't take the stand to contradict him. A lawyer can't testify in her own case. So I need an investigator, i.e., Alex, to do it. But this case would probably never see the inside of a courtroom. I could do this one alone. "If that's what you want, absolutely."

She whispered, "Okay, later."

As we ended the call, the shakiness in her voice made me worry she might not show. But she did. Half an hour early, in fact. I went out to the reception area to greet her.

Although she wore no makeup, Eliza was a stunner. She was taller and a little less voluptuous than Angelina—I guessed the latter would change in the next few years—but there was no mistaking the family resemblance. Eliza's cheekbones and jawline weren't as pronounced as Angelina's, but she had the same generous mouth and large blue eyes as her sister. Her blonde hair was twisted in a long braid that hung down to the middle of her back. I noticed that unlike so many in her generation, she had no visible tats or piercings. The overall effect was soft and innocent. It made her seem even younger than her fifteen years. I got the feeling that nothing remotely like that hideous rape had ever happened to her before.

It made me that much more determined to get the asshole who'd done it. I put out my hand. "Hi, Eliza. I'm Sam." I tilted my head toward Michy. "And that's my boss and best friend, Michelle."

Michy gave her a warm smile and waved. "Hey, Eliza."

Eliza shook my hand, then gave me a confused look. "She's your boss? Aren't you the lawyer?"

My lips twitched. "Yes, but Michy is everything else. Paralegal, bookkeeper, receptionist, occasional investigator . . . you get the picture."

She gave a little smile and nodded. "And she's your bestie. That's cool."

Alex came out of his office, his hand outstretched. I'd warned him he might not be welcome in this interview. Very often, female victims aren't comfortable talking to men—no matter how "woke" or how sympathetic. "Hi, Eliza, I'm Alex, her investigator. Thanks for coming in."

Everything about him was perfect. His voice was gentle and warm, and his smile was kind. But I could see it didn't matter. She shook his hand, but she did it reluctantly. As she turned back to me, I caught his eye, and he nodded to let me know he understood. He said, "I've got to get back to work, but it was nice to meet you. Let me know if you need anything, okay?"

Relief spread across her features. "Sure. And thanks."

I gestured to my office. "Want to come in?" I let Eliza take the lead and followed her inside. "We can sit anywhere." I swept an arm toward the couch and the chairs in front of my desk. She opted for the couch. I had an idea. "Would you like Michy to join us?" I'd seen that she'd sparked to my BFF right away.

Eliza tucked a stray hair behind her ear. "Yeah, that'd be cool."

I poked my head out of the door and waved for Michy to come in. She pointed to herself and whispered, "Me? Really?"

I nodded. Michy shrugged, then came in and joined Eliza on the couch. I turned one of the chairs around to face them. I started by reminding her that this conversation would be confidential and explained the law regarding attorney-client privilege. "You're officially my client now. So none of us in the law firm can tell anyone what you say."

Eliza pulled her braid over her left shoulder and hung onto it. "What if the cops ask you questions?"

I shook my head. "Doesn't matter. They can't make me tell them anything. And unless you've reported what happened, they have no reason to ask me." I paused. "Have you? Reported it, I mean?"

"No." She let go of her braid and looked down. "I feel bad about that. He's still out there. If he did it to someone else, it'd be all my fault."

I leaned in. "Eliza." I waited for her to look at me. "Whatever he's done or will do is *his* fault and *only* his. Not yours. It's very important you know that." She nodded, but I could see it'd be a while before she let herself off the hook. "The only thing we can do about it right now is try and find him."

She gave me a searching look. "And then what? If we don't go to the cops, how do we stop him?"

I had no doubt Angelina would deal with him much more swiftly—and finally—than any judge. But I didn't know how well Eliza knew her sister. "I don't want you to worry about that right now. Just know that we do have a plan." Sort of. For the briefest of moments, a knowing look flashed across her face. But in an instant, it was replaced by a solemn expression. It happened so fast, I wasn't even sure I'd seen it. Maybe it was just wishful thinking. But I'd be glad if she knew her big sister would make sure he got stopped. Permanently. "Are you ready?" She nodded. "Let's start with what he looked like. I know you didn't see him. But did he seem to be tall? Short? Thin? Fat?"

She stared at the window behind me. "He seemed . . . average. Definitely not fat. Taller than me, and I'm five foot six."

Michy asked, "How much taller? Would you say he was six feet tall?"

Eliza thought for a moment. "Around that, maybe."

"What about his hair?" I asked. "Could you tell whether he was bald or had long or short hair?"

Eliza's brow furrowed. "He definitely wasn't bald. I remember smelling some kind of hair product. And I didn't feel it on my . . . on my body. I'm pretty sure it was short." She paused for a few seconds. "And he smelled like he'd been drinking."

"Could you tell what kind of drink?" I asked. "Scotch? Whiskey? Tequila?"

She wrinkled her nose. "Wine. Red wine."

Maybe we were getting somewhere. "Do you remember whether Angelina was serving red wine at the party that night?"

"I know she was." Eliza glanced from me to Michy. "I snuck some."

I smiled at her. "Sounds like something I would've done. Do you remember what kind you drank? Did it smell like what you'd been drinking?"

She sighed. "No. I don't even remember what I was drinking. I just know it smelled like red wine."

Too bad. If I'd been able to pin down the kind of wine, I might've had a chance to narrow down the list of suspects. But this was a step in the right direction. "Do you remember who you were talking to at the party?"

She shook her head. "A bunch of people but no one in particular. It's all pretty much a blur." Eliza quickly added, "But I wasn't drunk or anything. I only had one glass of wine, and I didn't even finish it."

I could see it was yet another thing she was blaming herself for. "I didn't think it was because of the wine, Eliza. It's a blur because of the trauma. I'm going to keep saying this as long as it takes: none of this was your fault." She nodded and dipped her head. I gave an inward sigh. It was best to move on for now. "Could it possibly be an ex-boyfriend who was looking for payback?"

She shook her head. "Not . . . No. We broke up a year ago, and it was pretty mutual."

I had a hard time believing that any guy would want to break up with someone like Eliza, so the "mutual" part was debatable. But a year is an awfully long time to wait for payback. I scratched the ex-boyfriend theory off my list. "Are you seeing anyone now?"

"Uh, not really." She glanced at me, then quickly shifted her gaze.

Eliza might be good at a lot of things, but lying wasn't one of them. She was definitely seeing someone, and it had to be a person she didn't want anyone to know about. And then I was struck with a possible answer—not one I liked. "Tanner, right?"

She swallowed hard, then nodded. "But it wasn't, like, a regular thing. We just hooked up once in a while." She gave me a pleading look. "Please, you can't tell Angelina. She'll kill me! She never wanted me to be there when he came around."

I'd kill her, too, if she were my little sister. Was there any woman or girl Tanner knew who he hadn't had sex with? Apparently not. I didn't get it. His "charm" completely eluded me. But this told me our little Eliza wasn't exactly the Snow White she'd appeared to be. "Of course I won't tell her. I can't, remember? But I guess by now you know she was just trying to protect you."

Eliza looked down at her lap, where her fingers were interlaced. "Oh, I knew it then, too." She paused, then said, "After I'd been with Tanner a couple of times, he asked me to have a three-way with him and Bryan."

Huh? The Bryan who had hot-and-cold-running boys on tap? "I thought Bryan was gay."

She nodded. "He was. I actually saw him in the VIP section of a bar on Santa Monica dancing with a much younger guy." Eliza met my gaze. "But I said no. I wouldn't do it. I just want you to know that."

I was happy to hear it. "Do you think Bryan and Tanner had a thing going on?"

Eliza shrugged. "I don't know. I guess it's possible. But I definitely got the impression by the way Tanner asked that it wasn't the first time he'd tried to get a threesome going."

Might this news open up another avenue? "Was Tanner bisexual?"

She shook her head. "Didn't seem like it. I never saw him with a guy, and he never asked me about doing a threesome again, so . . ." She shrugged.

I took that in for a moment. I'd chew on this new information with Michy and Alex later, but I had a theory about what Tanner was doing with that threesome proposition.

I turned the questioning back to the assault. "And you're sure the guy who attacked you wasn't Bryan or Tanner?"

"Yeah," she said. "A hundred percent. I know it wasn't either of them."

We asked for more details about the assault, about exactly where she'd been when he first attacked her, about her attacker's clothes, his car, about . . . everything we could think of. But not only had she been blindfolded, her memory was compromised by the trauma. We couldn't dredge up anything new.

It was going to be another nutcracker of a case. Perfect.

THIRTY-SEVEN

Eliza left at three thirty, and I asked Alex to come join Michy and me so we could fill him in on the interview and talk about what we'd learned.

He looked incredulous when I told him about her liaisons with Tanner. "Seriously? Is it just me? Because I really don't get what all these women see in that guy."

Michy looked from Alex to me. "I don't get what you guys don't get. I've seen his picture. He's hot, and he's got bad-boy charm." She glanced at me. "I'd have thought you in particular would see that in a heartbeat."

She was right. I usually did go for jerks like him. I raised my palms. "What can I say? Consider it good news."

Michy smiled. "I do. Maybe you're finally getting to see what it's like to be with someone who's good for you."

The mention of Niko brought a wave of uneasiness. *Was* he good for me? He certainly had been so far. But I couldn't be sure of anything about him at this point. And the longer this investigation continued, the more time I had to question whether I really knew him. I didn't like the way I was feeling, and I didn't want to talk about him right now. I moved us back to the subject of Eliza. "In any case, bad-boy hottie or not, I definitely didn't see Eliza hooking up with him."

Michy shrugged. "Seems like typical teenage rebellion to me. Big sister tries to keep her away from him, so he immediately becomes the one thing she's gotta have."

Alex nodded. "Fair point. But what do you make of that three-way proposition? I have pretty decent gaydar, and Tanner had nothing but hetero vibes coming off him."

I offered my theory. "I think you're right. Tanner's straight. But it's a great way to control Bryan. And Tanner's all about whatever gives him control."

Alex tilted his head. "That fits."

Michy asked, "Are we a hundred percent certain Eliza's attacker had been at the party?"

I wished I could say yes. "No. We're not. It seems likely, but red wine isn't exactly a rare item."

Michy sighed. "You know, I don't usually say this, but I'm glad she doesn't want to go to the police. I doubt they could do anything with what little she gave us."

It said something that Michy—who'd been brutally attacked herself and was adamant that everyone should call the police—thought it wasn't worthwhile in Eliza's case. I looked from Michy to Alex. "Anyone have any doubts or concerns about her story?"

Alex shook his head. "None."

Michy nodded. "Same."

I didn't, either. "Then I think the next step is to canvass the neighborhood." I'm all about the latest technology. Concealed cameras, Ring cameras, motion sensors, whatever. But in the end, there's only one way to do a decent investigation, and that's by door knocking the area and asking questions face-to-face.

Alex heaved a sigh and stood up. "I assume you want to start tomorrow."

I would've said I wanted to start right now, but Dale was coming by for dinner. I glanced at my computer. It was already after six o'clock. I had to get home fast if I wanted to clean up the place enough for my neat-freak father. Seriously, his kitchen looks like an operating room. I always tell him it's compensatory behavior for the dirty job of being a cop. His typical response has something to do with dirty defense lawyers, but I can never remember what it is because I never listen.

I stood up and grabbed my coat and purse. "Yeah. Check out the 'hood and let me know how early we can get going." We had to time the canvass for when the maximum number of residents was likely to be home.

Michy pushed her body off the couch as though it hurt. "I'd better get going, too. Don't want to keep the 'rents waiting."

I had to smile. "Buck up, sunshine. The 'rents won't want to hang out that late. Brad might actually manage to stay awake long enough to go back to your place."

She headed for the door. "Please stop. It only makes it worse to get my hopes up."

Alex put an arm around her as they moved toward the reception area. "If he crashes and burns, you can come over and hang with Paul and me."

Michy gave him a wan semismile. "Paul does make a great martini. I might just do that. Thanks, Alex."

He patted her shoulder. "We've got your back."

And on that note of sad camaraderie, we locked up and left. Just another day in paradise at Brinkman and Associates.

I stopped to buy a couple of bottles of pinot noir and a jumbo-size bottle of Patrón Silver. Alcohol was a must for this particular dinner, given what we'd be talking about. When I got home, I surveyed my apartment. It was pretty neat by normal standards. I don't love to clean, but I do it once a week. And I'm not one to leave things lying around.

But I had to admit, the place wasn't up to Dale's standards. I dropped my purse on the kitchen table and pulled out the mop.

By the time Dale arrived, I'd vacuumed the living room, used the hose to vacuum the couch and wing chair, dusted the coffee table and end tables, and scrubbed down the kitchen. But I hadn't had time to freshen up.

When I opened the door, he glanced at my flushed, sweaty face. "I feel bad about putting you to all this trouble." His tone was sarcastic.

I gave him a flat look. "What trouble? I was just doing yoga."

His lip curled in a half smile as he held up the bag of food and a bottle of what I recognized as a very good cabernet. "Where do you want these?"

I gestured for him to put it all on the kitchen counter. "You know, if you weren't such an OCD screwball, I wouldn't have to sanitize every inch of the apartment just so you'd sit down."

He ignored that and went to the cupboard to survey the glassware. "What are you drinking?"

I started unpacking the bag and saw that he'd gone for a simple dinner of steaks, baked potatoes, and steamed garlic spinach. The cabernet was a perfect choice. "I'll start with a Patrón Silver on the rocks."

Dale opened the cabernet to let it breathe and poured us each a shot of tequila on ice. We took our drinks to the living room, and he sat on the wingback chair—as usual—and I sat down on the couch—as usual. I held up my glass for a toast. "Here's to us catching up."

He raised his but said, "I don't think you're going to want to toast to that."

Shit. I gave him a dour look, but we clinked and drank. "Okay, hit me."

He set down his glass. "Kingsford and O'Malley have been talking to all Tanner's friends and acquaintances about that jacket the man in the surveillance video wore."

"Figures." Dale had warned me they were lasered in on that footage.

"None of Tanner's friends or business contacts has ever seen him in a jacket like that."

I was relieved. It wasn't good news, but it was nowhere near as bad as it could've been. "How would they know? That video was so dark, you can't even make out the color."

Dale spread his hands. "Apparently, they zeroed in on the style and fit."

I raised my glass again. "Well, here's to you giving me not such bad news."

This time, he shook his head. "Not done. They got Tanner's and Bryan's cell phone records."

My mouth went dry. "And?"

"Bryan's last call was to his mother," he said. "No surprise—everyone talked about how close they were. She said he'd sounded depressed but hadn't mentioned being threatened by anyone."

So far, so good. I forced myself to ask, "Did he say he was expecting any company that night?"

"No," Dale said. "The thing they're focused on is Tanner's last call. It was to someone at a company called Voltech. Sound familiar?"

I shook my head. "Not even remotely."

Dale picked up his drink. "You might want to ask Niko about it."

We both knew that was exactly what I planned to do. "Have they found Tanner's cell phone?"

"Not yet," he said. "But the cell records show there was no activity after the night he disappeared."

That might—or might not—be an ominous sign. "I know Kingsford's thinking that means someone killed him. But if Tanner's in hiding, there's no way he'd keep using that phone."

Dale cradled his drink in his lap. "I don't disagree." He regarded me with a steady gaze. "But let's be honest. Things are starting to stack up in a way that's not great for Niko. I have a feeling you've been doing a little . . . background checking on your own. Care to share?" He saw my hesitation. "Look, Sam. This is one case I wouldn't mind letting go unsolved. I think you know that. Whatever you tell me stays between us. I swear."

I had a choice to make, and it wasn't an easy one. Because if I confirmed that I'd dug up new information on Niko—even though what I'd learned didn't prove he'd killed anyone—Dale would know I wasn't about to stop until I'd found some real answers. And he'd keep asking me what I had. Eventually, I knew I'd come up with *something*—and it might well be the nail in Niko's coffin. If Dale decided he couldn't keep that to himself, Niko would spend the rest of his life in prison, and I'd be to blame. So if I told him what I'd learned, this might be the beginning of a very slippery slope.

On the other hand, if I confided in Dale now, I'd be in a better position to get his help with whatever I did come up with—even if that only meant his advice and support. But most likely, it'd be much more than that. Dale's help had been instrumental in the past. It could be what saved Niko now. I'd been going through this mental tug-of-war ever since Tanner had disappeared. It was time to make a decision. I either trusted Dale or I didn't. I took a deep breath and told him what I'd learned—both from Ivan and from Alex's investigation.

Dale took an occasional sip of his drink as I talked, but he listened without comment until I'd finished. He took a beat before answering. "None of this proves he killed anyone. But you already know that. My take? You're more bothered by the fact that he didn't tell you than what you've learned."

I'd long since accepted that possibility. "But that shot caller who fell off the face of the earth without explanation . . ."

Dale nodded. "Is—and isn't—a worry. The asshole might not have personally killed his sister, but he was certainly responsible for it. We both know that no one would've made a move like that without his say-so. Whether Niko killed him is neither here nor there. You have no proof and neither does anyone else. And since when do we care about a punk like that shuffling off this mortal coil?"

His matter-of-fact tone was just what I'd needed to hear. "So it doesn't bother you that he basically hid a possible murder, an attempted murder, and his whole childhood from me?"

Dale sat up and rolled his shoulders back. "The attempted murder— I assume you mean that bar fight in Chicago?" I nodded. "That was a bullshit rap, and you know it." He gave me an amused look. "Have you never heard the old saying about people in glass houses? I'm going to go out on a limb and guess that you haven't exactly been forthcoming with him, have you?"

I'd known that was coming. I tossed my head. "It's not the same."

"It's exactly the same. So let me know when you decide to tell him all about your childhood—and what you've been up to since Michy got attacked. Then you can get upset about what he hasn't told you." He rattled the cubes in his glass. "Now we can either have dinner or have another drink. Your choice. But I'm warning you, if I have another drink on this empty stomach, I'll probably get drunk."

I stood up. "God knows I don't need to see that."

Dale followed me into the kitchen and took my elbow. "Listen, Sam. I don't mean to make light of it. If Kingsford and O'Malley catch wind of Niko's past, it'll be trouble. But it's hardly a smoking gun. I just think your personal feelings about Niko kind of . . . skew your judgment." He paused. "And I'm sure it would do the same to me."

Although it helped to hear that he didn't consider Niko's secrets as ominous as I did, I still thought my fears about his legal jeopardy might be well justified. But maybe I was too close to the situation. Dale probably had a more balanced perspective. "Are you getting worried about what else Kingsford will come up with?"

Dale emptied his glass in the sink and put it in the dishwasher. "Honestly? Yeah. I'm worried as hell."

I wished I hadn't asked.

THIRTY-EIGHT

I was tired and depressed by the time Dale left, but I was too keyed up to sleep. What I needed to do was take a hot shower, calm down, and try to get some rest.

Instead, I went to the kitchen and opened my laptop. Niko had told me about a personal Facebook page he kept under another name. We'd used it to share photos and links. But since Bryan's death and Tanner's disappearance, I'd been surfing around on it whenever I got the chance. I hadn't told Alex about it, because it was meant to be a private page, and there was only so much guilt I could handle.

The funny thing is, surfing that Facebook page had turned out to be a kind of self-soothing behavior. As I read one innocuous posting after another, I could reassure myself that I had nothing to worry about. And now, as I read Niko's funny postings about the taping in New York, I felt myself relax. A half hour later, I was yawning and ready for bed.

For a change, I had a peaceful night's sleep and didn't wake up until eight thirty—a real coup for me. I stretched and enjoyed the luxury of feeling rested . . . then had a full-on panic attack. I was supposed to be in court today—wasn't I? Heart thumping, I grabbed my phone and checked my calendar . . . and sagged with relief. My day was clear. I didn't even have any office meetings scheduled. I got myself a cup of coffee—love those automatic coffee makers—and took it back to bed. I watched a home makeover show until nine a.m., then called Michy. I wanted to get an update on her evening with Brad and his parents. "So how'd it go last night?"

She spoke softly. "Actually, it's still last night—if you know what I mean."

I chuckled. "I think your pet iguana knows what you mean. But that's awesome. See? What'd I tell you?"

She sighed. "Okay, let the I-told-you-sos begin. How'd it go with Dale? Was he helpful?"

It was hard to know how to answer that. "Sort of. I'll tell you about it when we have some 'us' time."

"I'm free tonight," she said. "You?"

"Yeah." Which was pretty out of the norm. Niko and I usually spent at least one weeknight together. "I know he's got his hands full, what with work and his mom, but it's starting to feel kind of . . . deliberate. You know?"

Michy took a beat before answering. "I don't necessarily agree with you, but I get why you'd feel that way. Let's talk about it over dinner. Want to go out? Or order in?"

I never liked to talk about personal things in public, so we agreed to hang at her place—a great little condo on Westmount Drive, just seven minutes away from my apartment—and order in.

I did some errands on my way to the office, then spent the day catching up on the usual boring stuff of daily lawyer life, i.e., emails, paperwork, time sheets, and letters to clients who were in custody. Michy wanted to take off early so she could clean up before I got there. I gave her an incredulous look. "Clean up what? A stray hair that fell out when you left this morning?" Michy is the only neat freak I know who might actually give Dale a run for his money. "You know you really might be on the spectrum."

Michy held up a middle finger. "I've got your spectrum right here."

I laughed and told her to get going, then put my head down and forced myself to finish the time sheets. By the time I got out, it was almost six o'clock. I called the Bao Dim Sum House and placed our orders, then got dressed and headed out. No makeup and I barely brushed my hair. It was the beauty of a girls' night in.

I picked up our dinner and a bottle of pinot grigio at a liquor store nearby and got to Michy's condo right on time at seven o'clock. She answered the door looking freshly scrubbed, with her hair piled up in a topknot. "God, that smells good. I've been craving Bao's and dim sum for weeks."

I entered and put the bags on the kitchen table. "Where're we sitting?"

She pointed to the low-slung coffee table in the living room, where she'd laid out two place settings. Her living room opened onto a balcony that offered a view of the west side. It was a full moon, and its silvery glow bathed the city in a soft white light.

We talked about Brad, his crazy work schedule, and what a great night they'd had. She refilled our glasses as she said, "I think he might actually be ready to leave that torture chamber."

I held up my glass. "I'll drink to that."

Michy raised hers, and we clinked. "Amen." She took a sip of wine. "Your turn. When we left off, you said you felt like Niko's avoiding you. Here's what I wanted to say about that. One: sometimes a cigar is just a cigar. He might just be thrashed. He's definitely got good reason. But two: let's assume he is avoiding you. Are you worried that it's because he killed Bryan or Tanner?"

That was pretty direct—even for Michy. "I, uh . . . I guess so."

She gave me a shrewd look. "And if he did, that'd be the end for you?"

Was she actually asking—or rather, outright saying—what I thought she was? "You think I'd stay with him even if he killed one of them—or both?"

She put down her glass. "Sam, don't you think it's time we stopped pretending I don't know what you did for me?" She put her hand on mine. "Because I do. I know you killed him."

I felt the blood drain from my face. "Wh-what are you talking about?" She couldn't possibly know I'd killed the man—my former client—who'd stalked and attacked her. Not for sure anyway.

She studied my face for a moment. "I'm talking about your reaction when the police told me he'd been killed in a hit-and-run." She let go of my hand and smiled. "You're a good actress, but you can't fool me. Never could."

For a moment, the world seemed to tilt. It made me a little dizzy. But now I knew she had no hard proof. I had a decision to make. If I admitted she was right, she'd have to live with the knowledge that she'd been complicit in the cover-up. I didn't think that'd sit well with her. It was one thing for her to live with an educated guess about what I'd done. That still left room for doubt. But it'd be a whole different world if I told her she was right—and removed all doubt. I lived with what I'd done—to her attacker and many others—very comfortably. But Michy wasn't me. I knew she'd suffer if I confirmed her suspicion. I couldn't do that to her. I owed her the peace of mind of uncertainty.

I smiled and gave her hand a squeeze. "I'm flattered that you think I'd do that for you. I'd like to think I would, too. But the truth is, I didn't. That hit-and-run . . ." I shrugged. "We just got lucky. Sometimes the universe does the right thing and coughs up some justice."

She gave me a skeptical look. "I don't know, Sam. I remember the look on your face when the police told us. You weren't surprised. You were so calm."

"I was so *happy*." I gave her a meaningful look. "And you seemed pretty okay with it, too, as I recall." Her expression told me the seeds of self-doubt were starting to take root. Perfect. Now I just needed to play it cool and let them grow. I decided to segue back to the matter at hand. "But what made you bring that up now?"

Michy had been staring off. It took her a moment to shift gears. "Because . . . well, even if you didn't kill that guy, I think eventually you might have. And it'd be a shame to let go of a great guy for doing something you—well, maybe you wouldn't do yourself, but you sure wouldn't blame him for it."

I couldn't really argue. "In other words, you're calling me a hypocrite."

She frowned. "Actually, no. I don't think you'd dump him for killing those con artists. I think you'd dump him for not being up-front with you." She gave me a frank look. "Because you know how you get."

I did. It was a matter of trust—as in, I didn't have much to spare. And being with someone who held out on me tweaked the hell out of me. "It's starting to look dicey for Niko." I told her what Dale had reported—and what he'd thought.

Michy stared down at her wineglass for a moment. "I don't know, Sam. The police may get closer, but I'm not sure they'll ever solve this one. The question is, if they don't—and they can't clear him—what will you do?"

I'd been thinking about that. "I don't know." But I had another question. "What if the cops can't solve it, but I do? Then what?"

She sighed and shook her head. "I guess you'll have to burn that bridge when you get to it."

I nodded. I looked at her across the table and—for the millionth time—acknowledged the wonderful person Michy was. Though she hadn't been certain whether I'd killed her attacker, in her heart, she believed it might well be true, and she'd kept the secret all these years—without telling me—for my sake. "You are probably the best person I'll ever know. I couldn't love you more."

She smiled. "Back at ya."

Closer than sisters. That's what we used to say when we'd first become besties in junior high. And I knew we always would be.

When I got home that night, I got a call from Alex. "I've got it."

I couldn't resist. "Shouldn't you be sharing that news with Paul?"

He ignored me. "The place Iris told us about."

"The villa in Puerto Vallarta? How in the hell did you do that?"

He reminded me of how much detail Iris had given us—which was true. "And I had a little help from my friend Google Maps."

It must've been more than a little help. But still. No one else could've pulled that off. "Where is it?"

"It's in a town called Fresnillo," he said. "The owner's name is Sergio Paz. His dad's a billionaire. From what I can tell, Sergio seems to be your typical do-nothing rich kid. Daddy paid for everything. Including the villa."

That sounded promising. "If his daddy owns the villa, then how do you know he's the guy?" Tanner's business associates, AKA suckers, came in all shapes, sizes, and ages.

"I'll explain later," Alex said. "But the profile fits, don't you think? Rich kid who wants to show Daddy he can make money, too. Throws in with a flashy jerk like Tanner."

It did fit. And I'd get a trip to Puerto Vallarta out of it. Win-win. "So what are we waiting for? Book the flight."

Alex tsked. "Sorry to burst your vacay dream bubble, but he also has a place in Carmel Valley, San Diego, and according to his Facebook page, that's where he's staying now."

Bummer. And it was a three-hour drive, so I knew what was coming next. "I suppose we're taking my car."

"Damn straight," he said. "I've done my share."

He had. "Fine, but you drive on the way back."

Alex said, "Happy to. We should get an early start. Pick me up at seven a.m."

Ugh. I hate early mornings. "Why so early? What's wrong with nine o'clock?"

"Traffic," he said. "It'll take us twice as long if we leave that late. And I want to make sure we catch him before he gets started on his day. I'll give you a wake-up call."

Wake-up calls make early mornings even worse. They feel like a dousing with ice water. "No, thanks. I can manage."

But as we ended the call, I had a feeling he'd do it anyway. So I set my cell phone for a quarter to six.

A good thing I did. Alex called at five minutes to six the next morning. I was glad to be able to sound legitimately awake—and get the jump on him. "I'm just about ready to leave, so get the lead out." I wasn't, but I knew it'd chap him to be rushed.

And it did. He was clearly—and unpleasantly—startled. "What? You're lying." I told him I definitely wasn't. He said, "Fine. I'll be waiting outside."

Ha. Gotcha. But I had to race to finish dressing and fill my giant travel mug with coffee. Just to be a gracious winner, I filled a regular-size travel cup for him.

True to his word, Alex was ready and waiting at the curb when I got there, his own travel cup in hand. He glanced at the one I'd brought for him. "I guess it doesn't hurt to have a backup."

I was willing to bet we'd wind up fighting over it. Alex slid into the passenger seat and typed on his cell phone. "I just put the address in Waze. We should get there in about three hours."

We clinked travel cups and headed for our meeting with Richie Rich.

THIRTY-NINE

Carmel Valley is arguably the richest neighborhood in San Diego, a city that sports a number of high-end communities. As we drove through the hills on the way to Sergio's house, I got a panoramic view of the city and gorgeous coastline. The wide streets were lined with palm trees and mini mansions, and I noticed that many of the homes looked relatively new—and very expensive. "Fair to say Daddy paid for this place?"

Alex was looking out the windows at our surroundings. "For sure. As far as I could tell, Sergio specializes in a lot of nothing—other than living off the family money."

We hadn't met him yet, but Alex's guess that Sergio saw Tanner as a proving ground for his own business acumen seemed dead-on. "Do we know where the family money came from? Is it literally Daddy's? Or did Daddy inherit it, too?"

"I didn't get into that," he said. "I figured if it turned out to be important, Sergio might give us some answers himself."

Probably true. It didn't matter right now. I'd just been curious. "So now tell me, how'd you figure out Sergio was the friend Tanner mentioned to Iris? Why not the father? He owns the place in Fresnillo."

Alex gave a dismissive wave. "Please, piece of cake. Sergio likes to chat. A lot. The boy's got nothing but time on his hands. Among Facebook, Twitter, and Instagram, I could map out his whole life for the past five years if I wanted to."

That figured. I was no fan of social media myself—I'm a classic noncommunicator—but it had definitely made my life, and especially Alex's, a hundred times easier.

Alex told me to turn left onto Torrey Hill Lane and gave me the address number. After a few seconds, he told me to slow down, then pointed to an amber-colored Spanish-style house with a red-tiled roof. The heavy wooden garage doors were closed and the driveway was empty, but I parked at the curb in front of the house. Better not to take a chance of blocking someone in or out—and better if we needed a fast getaway.

As we headed up the tiled walkway, I noticed a variety of palm trees—large and small—that filled the front yard. It didn't get much more maintenance-free than that. A possible testament to Sergio's lack of either the skills or the interest in upkeep. I glanced at my cell phone as we approached the windowless double doors. It was ten thirty. If Sergio was a partier, this might be the middle of the night for him. I whispered to Alex, "Do we happen to know what Sergio was up to last night?"

Alex whispered back, "According to his Facebook page, it was a beer and pizza night at home. We should be okay."

We'd decided to play two concerned friends of Tanner's who'd invested with Gold Strike and were worried about where he'd gone. I'd see where that took us and adjust accordingly. I reached for the black iron knocker, but Alex shook his head and pointed to the Ring doorbell. He pressed it and looked up at the camera.

The voice of a young male with a mild Spanish accent asked, "Who are you?"

Alex gave me room to step closer to the camera. Sergio was an out-and-proud hetero, so I'd been designated to run point on this one. I smiled. "Hi! I'm Samantha, and this is Alex. We're friends of Tanner's, and we're kind of worried about him. He told us all about you, so we thought maybe you'd know what's going on?"

There was a long pause; then he said, "I'll be down in a minute."

It was more like five minutes. Long enough for me to wonder whether last night was more than just beer and pizza. Or whether he was going for his gun. Alex and I exchanged a look. Maybe this was too risky. I'd just jerked a thumb toward my car when the door finally opened. The photo Alex had found of Sergio on Instagram had shown a dark, brooding type with heavy eyebrows, thick black hair, and the clichéd five-o'clock shadow. But the photo hadn't done him justice. He was an eleven on a scale of ten. Sergio was model-level handsome, and his V-shaped body—revealed to great effect by an open white linen shirt and tie-waist linen pants—showed a great deal of devotion to the gym.

He gave Alex a passing glance, then raked his eyes over me from head to toe before motioning for us to come in. We followed him into a simply furnished but spacious living room with glass accordion doors that provided a view of the ocean and access to a beautiful infinity pool, built-in separate hot tub, and outdoor kitchen. On a sunny, clear-sky day like this, it was a distracting place to do an interview. But we'd just have to muscle through.

Alex and I sat on the couch. Sergio sprawled on the chaise across from us. His expression was guarded. "How do you know Tanner?"

I gave him our prepared spiel about having met him at a party he'd thrown and hanging out together a few times, then becoming investors. I didn't want to overplay the friendship angle. He might wonder why Tanner had never mentioned us. Or why Sergio had never seen us at any of Tanner's parties. I wrapped up by saying we hadn't heard from him in a month or so, and we'd really taken a bath on our last investment. "Frankly, we're not just worried about him, we're also kind of pissed off that he left us in the lurch like this. Didn't say a word, just totally ghosted on us." We'd decided that story was the best way to get him to open up and air his own gripes with Tanner. From what we'd seen so far, it seemed a fair guess that everyone involved with Tanner would have *something* to bitch about.

But Sergio didn't take the bait. "I haven't seen him in a few months myself."

Technically, in terms of being in the same physical space, that might be true. But it was a dodge. We knew they'd been in close contact via Facebook and Instagram. Alex pinned him down. Gently. "Yeah, Tanner gets around a fair amount. We're just wondering if you've heard from him."

Sergio stretched out on the chaise, offering an extended view of world-class abs. "Not really. I mean, not, like, in real time."

Two could play this game. I leaned back and crossed my legs. The move hiked up my skirt a bit, which got his attention—as I'd intended. He was acting pretty cagey. "You mean, not on the phone?" He nod-ded. "How about Facebook? Or Twitter? Did you guys DM?" Direct messaging on Twitter was just about as fast as talking on the phone. But again, technically, if that's how they communicated, it was true. It wasn't in real time. Still, his reaction was pinging all my bullshit meters.

I heard a buzzing sound. Sergio pulled a cell phone out of his pants pocket, gave it a quick glance, then put it back. "Yeah, we DM'd a few weeks ago."

Alex asked, "You mean just before he disappeared?"

A flash of anger crossed his face. "I don't know exactly when he fell off the map. I just know the last time I heard from him was right after that friggin' cryptocurrency deal went south."

So Sergio was pissed off. If my guess about the reason was correct, this visit could turn out to be much more productive than I'd expected. "Did you invest in that trade? Because we did, and we lost a bundle."

There was a look of real fury on his face now. "Yeah, I sunk two hundred K into that damn thing. Lost every penny."

That wasn't the biggest outlay of all the investors, but it wasn't the least, either. I wondered why his name hadn't shown up on any of the investor lists. "Have you been contacted by the cops?"

He shook his head. "No, why? Have you?"

It was probably safe to lie to him about this. "Yes. But I'm sure they'll get to you soon. Did Tanner tell you he was planning to go somewhere when you last DM'd him?"

He sat up, plainly agitated. "No, he never said anything about that." His jaw tightened. "I don't know where that jerk is, and I don't care. That cryptocurrency trade was supposed to double my investment. I was finally going to be able to pay for my share of the place in Fresnillo—show my father that I could make money on my own. Now, thanks to that asshole, I look like a fool." He shifted his gaze between Alex and me. "So if you guys find out where he is, I'd sure like to get some goddamn answers."

A very angry investor. One who was young and strong—and one who had money to pay for his revenge if he didn't want to exact it himself. Sergio was looking like a better suspect with every word out of his mouth. "We all would, believe me. By the way, where were you when you last DM'd with him?" If Sergio had been here in Carmel Valley, that'd put him close to Tanner right around the time he dropped off the radar.

He paused a moment before answering. "I was in Puerto Vallarta."

He might not be the sharpest knife in the box, but he'd figured out where I was going. I had a feeling this interview was at an end. And I was right.

Sergio stood up. "I don't know where Tanner went. So you two—whoever you are—can get out of here."

I held up my hands. "Hey, no offense. I didn't mean to accuse you or anything like that. We're just trying to get our money back."

"Yeah? Well, me too." Sergio's flat expression said he wasn't buying it. He gestured to the front door. "I've got things to do, so . . ."

So much for my dreams of shrimp on that massive barbie and cocktails in the hot tub. Alex and I left. Swiftly but with dignity.

When we got back to the car, I handed the keys to Alex. "You promised you'd drive back."

He said, "I'll be glad to drive. But don't you want to know whether Sergio lied about being in Puerto Vallarta when Tanner went missing?"

I sighed. I did. I got into the driver's seat. When Alex settled into the passenger seat, I asked, "How are you going to manage that from the car?"

He picked up his iPad. "It's a three-hour drive, and I've already got his cell phone number." He gave me a sidelong glance. "Don't ask me how."

I pulled away from the curb. "I wouldn't dream of it." He'd hacked into cell tower databases before, so if he had the number of Sergio's cell and the name of the service provider, he could certainly do it again.

It took the better part of the drive, but as we crossed the boundary into Los Angeles County, he raised a hand to high-five me. I shot him a look. "You know I won't do that." It feels so lame when I miss. "What've you got?"

Alex sighed, then said, "Our friend was most definitely not in Puerto Vallarta."

"Was he in Carmel Valley?" That'd be good. Very good.

Alex smiled. "No. He was in Beverly Hills. At the Four Seasons."

So he'd been close to both Tanner and Bryan. And he'd lied about it. That was better than good. That was great. Finally, we had a viable straw man. I raised my hand and gave Alex a palm-stinging high five.

FORTY

We took a long lunch on the way back to the office and spent the whole time talking about what Sergio might've been doing at the Four Seasons. I thought about a best-case scenario. "Would it be too good to be true that he was hanging out with Tanner?" If so, I could make a credible argument that he'd visited Tanner after Niko left.

Alex gave a short laugh. "Probably. But may as well dream big."

It was after six o'clock when I pulled into the parking garage and dropped Alex off at his car. "Go home and have a nice dinner with Paul. You've earned it."

He tucked his iPad under his arm. "I've earned a hell of a lot more than that."

True, but I had no intention of admitting it. "Has anyone ever told you humility is not your strong suit?"

Alex smirked as he opened the door. "You're confusing self-awareness with arrogance." He put one foot out, then paused. "Hey, have you asked Niko about that Voltech place yet?"

The place Tanner had last called. I hadn't. Because I'd been avoiding Niko just as much as I thought he'd been avoiding me. "I'll call him tonight."

Alex got out and leaned down, his expression sympathetic. "We'll get our answers, Sam. They may not be the answers we're hoping for, but I have a very strong feeling that you won't have to be in limbo forever."

That was a sort of comfort—I supposed. "Thanks, Alex. I'll let you know if I find out anything useful."

He turned to go, then stopped and leaned down again. "Almost forgot. You have Angelo's plea and sentencing on Monday, don't you?"

I checked the calendar on my phone. "Yeah." I wasn't looking forward to it. I hate to let a client plead straight-up. I took in Alex's flat expression. "I'm guessing you didn't find anything helpful."

"Not a thing. Want me to go with you?"

"Nah. Why should both of us suffer?"

Alex sighed and headed to his car. As I drove out, I decided I may as well call Niko now. If he was at the hospital, I could do what any decent girlfriend would do and go keep him company. Lately, my last couple of calls had gone to voice mail. This time, he picked up.

"Hey, Sam. Sorry I've been a little MIA. Work's been crazy, and I've been spending every spare second with Mom."

His tone was light—but was it forced? I couldn't tell. "No worries. How's she doing?"

He sighed. "About the same, I think." His voice dropped. "But the doctors think she might've slipped a little more in the past couple of days."

"Are you with her now?" I assumed that's why he'd lowered his voice.

"No," he said. "I'm at the editing facility. Trying to wrap the last video."

I noticed he didn't ask what I was doing later. Even though I wasn't keen on seeing him, it made my heart sink to realize the feeling was probably mutual. I did my best not to let my sadness show. "I need to ask you a question. Have you ever heard Tanner mention the name Voltech?"

"Voltech?" He paused. "No. Sounds like some tech company. Why?"

I wasn't surprised he didn't know. Tanner seemed to have played everything as close to the vest as possible. Except for those bacchanalian parties. "It was the last number he called."

"Huh," he said. "Interesting. Well, let me know what you find out."

Still no invitation—to lunch, to dinner, to anything. "You mean what Alex finds out. That's way above my pay grade."

He chuckled; then his voice grew softer. "I've been missing you. Seems like I haven't seen you in about a year. What about this weekend? Are you busy Saturday night?"

I was elated and panicked at the same time. He sounded like his old self. Maybe I'd just been misdirecting, projecting my own feelings of distance on him. I needed to stop worrying about acting weird around him. "Not yet. Want to have dinner?"

A sexy smile was in his tone. "At least that."

I hadn't realized until that moment just how much I'd missed him. "I'm in."

This time, I suggested we get together at my place. But Niko insisted on making dinner. "Don't worry, it won't be quinoa and tofu."

Thank God. "I'm not worried. If that's what you want, I probably won't get home until around ten thirty."

He laughed, and I told him I wasn't joking. When we ended the call, everything seemed so . . . normal. Maybe it really was all in my head. And maybe Niko had nothing to do with Bryan's death—or Tanner's possible death.

It'd been a long day, and I was plenty tired by the time I got home. But I felt more relaxed than I had in quite a while. I hadn't realized how much my worries about Niko had been weighing on me. I didn't have any court appearances or meetings, so I decided to let myself sleep in.

When I strolled in at nine thirty the next morning, Michy raised an eyebrow. "Did someone get lucky last night?"

I laughed. "No, but someone might this weekend."

She gave me an amused smile. "That sounds promising. You feeling better about what's going on with him?"

I didn't want to jinx it. "For now."

I was just about to walk into my office when Alex emerged from his. "*Some* of us got in early, because *some* of us like to get things done."

I turned to face him. "And because *some* of us are OCD." He folded his arms and glared at me. I realized he must've found something, so I changed tacks. "A highly prized trait for which some of us are very grateful."

He nodded. "Much better. I checked out Voltech."

"You did?" I told him Niko had never heard Tanner mention it.

He pulled up the old secretary's chair and sat down. "Turns out the company is just one guy. Chuck Montrey. He's an IT consultant. And I just happen to know him, because one of his clients was the BMW dealership where I used to work. Chuck is the one who got me into IT."

I stared at him. "You've got to be kidding."

He lifted his palms. "I know, it's crazy, right? I couldn't believe it, either. Though, to be fair, it's not as big a coincidence as you'd think. Chuck has clients all over LA."

Even so, it was nice to get a little boost from the universe once in a while—instead of the usual kick in the ass. "Does he know about your . . . legal issue?" Meaning, about how Alex stole two 750Lis and almost wound up in prison. Since Chuck had worked for the dealership when Alex stole the cars, it might make him less excited about helping Alex now.

Alex nodded. "He knows it all. And he was cool with it. So cool, in fact, he told me all about his last contact with Tanner."

I wasn't sure where this was going. "Am I going to be happy or sad when I hear this?"

He shrugged. "You be the judge. He said Tanner asked him to come over to the condo that night."

"Before or after Niko saw him?"

Alex frowned. "Chuck couldn't remember what time he went. But he did remember that he headed over there right after he got Tanner's call, and according to the phone records, Tanner called him at six thirty-five in the evening."

I replayed what Niko had said about when he'd gone to Tanner's condo. "Then Chuck was there well before Niko." Alex nodded. "So what happened?"

Now Alex smiled. "Tanner asked Chuck to destroy his hard drive. And he asked Chuck for a new phone."

"Did Chuck destroy it?" I prayed the answer would be no.

Alex sighed. "Unfortunately, yes. But still . . ."

Yes, still. We were on a roll. We had a viable suspect in Sergio—who'd lied about where he was. And now this.

Clear evidence that Tanner was planning to run.

It was a good day. And now that I'd get to share this fabulous news with Niko, it was going to be a great weekend.

I told the troops this new find deserved a celebratory dinner. "I'd set it up for Saturday, but Niko's coming over, so it'll have to be next weekend." It occurred to me I'd need to fix up the place. "Michy, remind me to pick up some Pledge."

Michy gave me a thumbs-up. "Cleaning the place twice in one week. That's gotta be a record for you."

I shot her a dagger. "No it's not."

She leaned back in her chair. "Okay, when was the last time you did that?"

I couldn't remember. She was probably right. "Uh . . . some other time. I'll think of it."

As I retreated to my office, she said, "Yeah, let me know."

When I got to my desk, I actually spent a few minutes trying to remember, but I had nothing. I gave up and got down to work. It always went faster when I had something to look forward to. The first time I looked at my computer, it was noon. The second time I looked, it was five thirty. I love when that happens.

I shut down for the day and went out to Michy's desk. "Adios. I'm outta here."

She gave me a half smile. "Didn't manage to remember any other times you cleaned up twice, did you?"

I sailed past her. "I will, don't worry. Wish me luck."

She called after me, "Luck."

As I headed for my car, I thought about what to wear tomorrow night—something that looked like I hadn't thought about it. The jeans and sweatshirt that were ripped in all the right places would do the trick: sexy, but believably "I just threw this on" looking.

The next day, I shopped for flowers—an uncharacteristically girlie thing for me to do, but it felt right for some reason—bought some good wine, and picked up some fancy cheeses and crackers for appetizers. I thought I'd given myself more than enough time to do everything, but as they say, plans were made to be ruined. The lines at the wine store were ridiculous, and I hit really bad traffic. By the time I got home, I barely managed to vacuum the living room and bedroom and wipe down the kitchen before rushing into the shower. And of course, Niko showed up early. My hair was still wet and my makeup was faded and smudged. Perfect.

I was self-conscious as I answered the door. "Hi, you. I'm a mess. I thought I left in plenty of time to get everything—"

Niko grabbed me by the waist and gave me a long, lingering kiss. "You look absolutely beautiful."

I closed the door, and we kissed again. And I—of course—melted. Niko, as usual, managed to look like he'd stepped out of a magazine, even though he was simply dressed in low-slung jeans and a long-sleeve black T-shirt.

When we came up for air, I noticed he'd set down a grocery bag. "Want me to unpack?"

He stroked my face. "I've missed you so much. And no, I don't want you to do anything. Except open the bottle of wine and pour for us."

I ran my hand through his hair. "I've missed you, too."

We hugged for what seemed like five minutes; then he picked up the bag and moved into the kitchen. "I made most of it in advance. I just need to get the rice going."

"What are you making?" I tried to keep the note of apprehension out of my voice.

He heard it anyway and smiled. "Your favorite. Lamb stew."

"Fabulous." I could eat myself into oblivion with that stew. It was delicious. And he'd picked up a bottle of Opus One. Wow. Probably the most expensive wine I've ever had. I got the opener out of the drawer. "We're really styling tonight."

Niko laughed. "Yep. Uptown all the way."

I poured us each a glass. He spooned the stew into a pot to heat up and got the rice cooking. It only took a few minutes for the smell of rich spices to waft into the air. "If I keep standing here, I'm going to grab a fork and eat out of the pot."

His eyes sparkled. "I love an appreciative audience. But let's get you out of here."

We took our glasses to the living room and snuggled on the couch. I'd forgotten to eat lunch, and it only took two sips for me to feel the buzz. I curled up next to him and laid my head on his shoulder. But the calm was suddenly shattered by someone pounding a fist—hard and repeatedly—on the door. I jerked up. "What the hell?"

Niko stood up. "I take it you weren't expecting—"

A booming male voice interrupted. "Brinkman! I know you're in there! If you don't open this goddamn door right—"

I recognized that voice. And the look of fury and alarm on Niko's face showed me he did, too. He crossed the room in two strides and yanked open the door. "What are you doing here?"

Ivan's frame filled the doorway. He glared at Niko, then shifted his gaze to me. "Ask that little bitch girlfriend of yours!" He pushed past Niko and started toward me. "Why'd you fucking sic the cops on me?"

My throat was so tight, I could barely make the words come out. "I d-didn't. What are you talking about?"

Niko put out an arm and barred his path. "Yeah, what the hell are you talking about?"

Ivan, who was shaking and red in the face, pointed at me. "Ever since she came around asking questions about you, they've been all over me."

A look of shock crossed Niko's face as he turned toward me. "You . . . went to see Ivan . . . about me?"

I swallowed hard. I wanted to speak, but I couldn't find the words. Really, there was nothing I could say that would make it look like anything other than what it was. I'd been snooping around behind his back. Because I thought he might be a murderer. I finally managed to say, "I'm so sorry. If you just let me explain . . ." But I knew that any explanation I came up with would just make matters worse.

The look of shock on Niko's face turned to hurt. But Ivan continued to rage. "That little snitch-bitch of yours has a big mouth. And if you don't close it, I—"

Niko turned back to Ivan and grabbed him by the neck. "You heard her—she didn't talk to the cops! And don't you dare threaten her, you piece of shit!"

Ivan tried to pull away. "Her dad's a cop, you fool!"

Niko shoved him toward the door. "Get the hell out of here. And don't you ever come near her again!"

As Niko opened the door, Ivan twisted away. "Or you'll do what? Kill me? Break my neck like you did to that shot caller?"

Niko spun him around, put a foot on Ivan's back, and pushed him out the door with so much force, he stumbled and fell flat on his face. He picked himself up, but he didn't come back for more. He gave me a menacing look—somewhat undermined by the scrapes on his nose and cheekbones—and limped away. Niko slammed the door behind him, but he didn't turn around for several seconds. When he did, he had an anguished look on his face.

I wanted to die. "Niko, I just needed to find out . . . I mean, you never told me about that bar fight in Chicago, and I needed to know . . ."

His glance slid off my face. "Whether I killed them." He stood staring at the floor for a few moments, then went to the kitchen table and picked up his keys. "I understand. I guess I should've known."

No! This night could not end this way! I moved toward him. "Niko, I'm sorry. But you have to know how hard I'm working to clear you. I'm going to clear you! I've got evidence that Tanner's in hiding. And I found someone else who might've gone after him, too!"

Niko slowly nodded, but he didn't look at me. "I do know how hard you've been working to help me. And I appreciate it. I really do. But I . . . I just have to go. I'm sorry." He moved toward the door. "You should turn off the rice in about five minutes."

And then he left. I stared after him, feeling as though someone had taken a bat to my whole body. I guess I should've realized that this day might come. But the brothers lived in such separate worlds—seemingly by mutual agreement—I'd thought the odds of Niko finding out were almost nil.

But odds don't always play out the way they should. I turned off all the burners, went to bed, and sobbed myself to sleep.

FORTY-ONE

That night, I discovered that devastation and heartache have an upside. Between the misery, the self-loathing, and the ocean of tears, I was so exhausted, I actually slept through the night.

But I couldn't make myself get out of bed. I lay there and replayed last night over and over, wishing I could find a way to make things right again. And wishing I hadn't been so hell-bent on digging into Niko's past. But even now, as worn out and shredded as I was, I knew I couldn't have done anything differently. I had to know the truth. It was in my nature. And it didn't matter that the person I was investigating for murder was Niko. I believe anyone is capable of committing murder—especially when they have a good reason for it.

Admitting that to myself made me feel even worse—doomed, actually. I'd ruined the best relationship I'd ever had—or would ever have. I doubted I'd ever be able to make it work with anyone. I may as well get myself a dozen cats and chenille bathrobes right now. There'd be no happily-ever-after endings in my future. I turned onto my stomach and pulled the pillow over my head. I spent the rest of Sunday in some version of that position.

But the next morning, the question I'd had the night before came back to me. Why *had* the cops started circling Ivan all of a sudden? The shot caller had gone missing—probably gotten killed—more than ten years ago. Ivan's appearance last night made it clear no one had come knocking on his door since then. Now the cops were all over him.

Neither Alex nor I had said a word to the cops, and I'd only told one other person about that shot caller's likely demise. Dale. Would he have tipped off the cops? After promising me I could trust him, after swearing he'd never repeat anything I told him? I couldn't believe he'd do it on purpose, but maybe he'd accidentally let something slip. I had to find out.

That—and the fact that I belatedly realized I had to be in court for Angelo's case at ten thirty—got me out of bed and into the shower in ten seconds flat. I washed my face with cold water and did the best makeup job I could to cover the puffiness of my tear-filled night, then poured myself a vat of coffee and headed to my car. I called Dale as I merged onto the freeway. When he answered, I went straight to the point. "We need to talk."

There was a note of surprise in his voice as he said, "I've got witness interviews scheduled after breakfast." The din of voices mixed with the clatter of dishes in the background. "How about tomorrow night?"

I guessed he was at The Pantry. He liked to have breakfast there. It was a landmark downtown restaurant that was almost a hundred years old. I love their simple home-style food, but I had no appetite today. "No. Now. I'm about fifteen minutes away." I wasn't exaggerating. For a change, the freeway was working the way it was supposed to. Probably because it was late enough to miss the morning rush hour. I was flying— with one eye on the rearview because . . . cops.

After a long pause, he said, "Okay. Meet me in Pershing Square on the Fifth Street side by the fountain."

Pershing Square was a small park in the middle of downtown Los Angeles. It was a perfect place for us to hide in plain sight. And if anyone noticed us, it wouldn't look strange. The Police Administration Building, where Dale worked, was just blocks away, and so was the courthouse.

I got there in just under twelve minutes and found Dale sitting on the concrete surround for the fountain. There weren't many people at the café tables nearby, but I supposed he was being extra careful. Fine by me. I sat down next to him, and he studied me for several moments.

I'd worn the biggest, darkest sunglasses I could, but they didn't fool him. "What happened?"

I told him the whole story. "So I just need to know. Did you tell anyone about Ivan?"

He shook his head. "Absolutely not. Not a chance. Why would I risk saying anything about Niko's past—to anyone, let alone a cop?"

He was right. It didn't make sense. Dale was way on Niko's side. "I just thought it might've . . . I don't know, slipped out by accident."

Dale lifted my sunglasses and lowered his head to look me in the eye. "Nothing slipped out accidentally. You know me better than that."

I pulled back and readjusted the lenses. "Don't do that." The bright sunshine blinded me. "I'm sorry. I just don't understand why they suddenly hit him up out of the blue."

"Because you're too upset to think clearly," he said. "It's pretty obvious. They want to use Ivan to get something on Niko."

I really must've been a mess not to think of that. Even if they didn't know Ivan and Niko were estranged, they had past police reports that showed the shot caller's disappearance was still an open case—and that both Ivan and Niko had motive to kill him. If Ivan could give them anything that helped prove Niko had killed the shot caller, that would help fuel their case against him for Bryan's murder. Especially if there was evidence the shot caller had been killed in the same bizarre way as Bryan.

Something else occurred to me. "That must've been what happened, because Ivan accused Niko of killing that shot caller by breaking his neck. How would he think of something like that? That shot caller disappeared. No one knows his cause of death. The cops must've told him about Bryan."

"Right." Dale had an expression of disgust. "Such cheesy police work."

"And let me add to that—it's also stupid. It'd be hard to find someone with less credibility than Ivan." Not only did he have a big, obvious ax to grind with Niko, but he also had a motive to frame him if he could. Because Ivan could have easily killed the shot caller himself. He had just as much motive and much easier access. Niko was an undergrad at the University of California, Santa Barbara at the time the shot caller went missing. Ivan was in pocket, at home in Los Angeles. That didn't mean Niko couldn't get down to Los Angeles. It's only an hour away. But still. Who'd take the word of a jerk like Ivan over . . . anyone?

Dale shook his head. "It's a pretty dumb move. Typical O'Malley."

"Agree," I said.

He put an arm around my shoulder—which surprised me. We almost never touched. "I know it doesn't feel like it right now, but I'm sure Niko will come around. He's going through a tough time, between his mother's condition and the murder case. You've got to cut him a little slack."

"I'd be happy to cut him all the slack he wants." I swallowed hard and blinked back the tears that were threatening to fall. "Why couldn't I just leave well enough alone? Why did I have to go snooping around behind his back?"

Dale had a look of understanding. "Because you need to know the truth, and because you realized he wasn't inclined to give it to you."

That was only partly true. "The thing is, I already had my doubts before I found out about the bar fight in Chicago."

"I'd probably have had a few myself if I were you," he said.

"Really?" I asked. "If what's her name—your girlfriend, the criminalist—was a murder suspect, you'd be thinking she might've done it?"

He hesitated for a moment. "Well . . . maybe not quite as much as you are. You're a little further out on the spectrum."

I shot him a look. "If that was supposed to make me feel better—"

"Sorry. But that's hardly news."

I reluctantly nodded. "True."

Dale gave my shoulder a squeeze. "I just have a feeling it's going to be okay. You're a lot to lose, Sam. He'll figure it out."

It was as close to a normal father-daughter moment as we'd ever had. And I was stunned by how good it felt. "I don't know. You didn't see the way he looked at me." As much as I was enjoying this new intimacy, it was making me a little uncomfortable. I stood up. "But I guess we'll find out."

He tilted his head toward the underground garage. "You park down there?"

I nodded, and we headed for the elevator. "So what about the Ivan issue? Can you find out why they're talking to him?"

"I'm pretty sure I can," he said. "Especially if it was O'Malley's play."

We reached the elevator, and I pushed the button. "It has to be. And it'd be great if you could find out what Ivan told them."

The elevator dinged, and he put out a hand to hold the doors for me. "That's the plan. I'll be in touch." He gave me a reassuring smile. "In the meantime, don't worry about Niko. He'll be back. Trust me. I'm a guy. I know how guys think."

I managed to give Dale a half smile. But as the doors closed, I leaned my head back against the wall to keep the tears that'd filled my eyes from falling. It was over for Niko and me, and it was all my fault.

The parking garage was dark and strangely isolated for a weekday. The echo of my footsteps felt like every clichéd story where the lone female gets raped / murdered / beaten / robbed. I hurried to my car, jumped in, and hit the gas. It didn't occur to me that I had a much more specific threat to worry about until I was flying down the freeway. Since

Ivan knew where I lived, he could certainly follow me and wait for me to land in an ideal assault-friendly locale—like that parking garage. But Niko had given him a good ass kicking. I felt pretty sure Ivan wouldn't want to risk facing him in round two.

I had to hustle to make it to court on time for Angelo's case. The last thing he needed was for me to show up late. I managed to make it by 10:25 and checked in with the clerk, who said the judge was running right on time. And she was dead-on. The judge called our case at ten thirty on the dot. I moved up to counsel table as the bailiff went to bring Angelo out of lockup. I'd expected him to be scared, worried, maybe even angry. But he walked out with a calm expression and a confident step. When the bailiff seated him, I leaned down and whispered, "Are you sure you want to do this?"

He nodded. "A hundred percent. I gotta take care of my family."

What the hell had Tito promised him? It had to be more than just protection for Angelo and his wife and kids. Tito must be paying him off—enough to ensure that Angelo's family would keep a roof over their heads. That he was willing to face a stiff prison sentence to make that happen was kind of noble.

The D.A. took the guilty plea, and true to his word, he left the sentencing "to the court's discretion." I gave him a nod of thanks, then made an impassioned plea for leniency based on the lack of violent crime in Angelo's history and the fact that he'd saved the court a lot of time and money by pleading guilty. I then veered into total fantasy. "My client has tremendous remorse for what he's done, and he fully intends to make time to counsel young adults on the perils of owning firearms when he gets paroled." Out of the corner of my eye, I saw the prosecutor cover his mouth to hide a smile.

Judge Thomsky asked, "Is there anything else, Counsel?"

I decided to lay it on even thicker. I mean, why not? What did we have to lose? "Just one more thing, Your Honor. Angelo Lopez is a devoted family man, and I can promise the court he'll not only be a model prisoner, but he'll turn over a new leaf when he gets out. He's got a real entrepreneurial gift that he intends to use to create a legal business so he can give others like himself—who made a few mistakes—a chance to start over. So all I ask is that you give Angelo Lopez a sentence that lets him begin that good work sooner rather than later—and lets him rejoin his family, who love him and will miss him terribly." I gestured to the gallery, where his tearful wife and two adorable young sons were sitting. I always make it a point to have the family in court—and hopefully in tears—for sentencing.

I sat down and watched the judge flip through the probation report. Angelo gave me a look of appreciation. He whispered out of the side of his mouth, "You done good. But did I really say all that about remorse and starting a business and shit?"

I turned toward him so the judge wouldn't see my face. "Shut up."

Judge Thomsky finally looked up. "While I do appreciate the fact that Mr. Lopez has saved the court the expense of a trial, I cannot ignore the fact that this was not his first rodeo. And I take a very dim view of the possession or sale of illegal firearms. They're the scourge of our society, where mass shootings have become an everyday occurrence. Accordingly, I'm imposing the sentence of six years in state prison." The judge turned to me. "Counsel, I believe you've said your client wants a forthwith?"

Meaning, immediate transfer to state prison. "Yes, Your Honor."

Judge Thomsky made the forthwith order, calculated Angelo's time credits, and we were done. I signaled the bailiff to give me a second with him. "I'm sorry. I was hoping for midterm."

Angelo shrugged. "Four years would've been better. But it could've been eight, so . . . I'll get good time, work time. Pro'lly get out in three."

I wasn't sure about that calculation, but it'd be what it'd be. And he was right: it could've been worse. I appreciated his philosophical take. The bailiff stepped in. It was time to go. I wished Angelo luck, and as the bailiff took him into lockup, he waved to his wife and sons. They all waved back, his wife now openly crying. I could only hope Angelo meant what he'd said about keeping it together so he could get paroled as soon as possible. I walked out with the family, gave them the most optimistic version of what to expect, then headed to my car.

Angelo's hearing had distracted me from the wreckage that was my life. But now, alone in the car, the misery settled over me like a shroud. As I neared the office, I thought about what I'd say to Alex and Michy. I dreaded having to retell the story and get a giant *I told you so* from Michy. I parked and moved toward the elevator with leaden feet.

The moment I walked into the reception area, Michy saw that something was wrong. "What happened?"

I tilted my head toward Alex's door. "Is he in?"

She had a worried look as she nodded. "He's been in since seven thirty."

I went to his office and knocked. I spoke through the door. "Got a minute?"

Alex appeared, his expression confused. "No lame joke? What's going on? Are you sick?"

I sighed. "Kind of." I gestured to my office. "Come on in, guys. I need to tell you about last night."

I saw Alex and Michy exchange an uh-oh look. We settled in—Michy and me on the couch, Alex on a chair—and I told them the whole sorry tale. When I finished, I swept a hand toward Michy. "Have at it." I sat back and waited for the *I told you so*.

She frowned. "Have at what? I love Niko almost as much as you do, but fuck him."

I sat up, stunned. "Why?"

She looked at me with disbelief. "Because you never would've gone digging into his past if he'd been up-front with you to begin with."

I told her what I'd admitted to Dale. "But I was suspicious before that."

She rolled her eyes. "You're suspicious of that stapler." She tilted her head at the one on my desk. "It's just who you are. But you didn't *do* anything until you found out about that attempted murder charge in Chicago. So I repeat: fuck him."

Alex nodded. "Same. Stop beating yourself up. He needs to start thinking about secrets and what they do to a relationship. I know I said that I understood why he'd want to hide a past he wasn't proud of. But then I got to thinking. I remembered that I'd told Paul about getting convicted for stealing those BMWs on our third date."

This was not at all the reaction I'd expected. "Thanks, guys."

Michy continued. "Sure. And here's another thing. I'll bet you gave him the spiel you always give your clients about telling you everything." I nodded. "Well, he didn't listen. I never expected to say this, but if he doesn't get his head straight about this, you should move on. You can do better."

Alex said, "I think so, too. Matter of fact, I remember getting that spiel from you myself. You were just trying to do the best job you could for him."

I shook my head. "Hold off on my sainthood. It wasn't just that. It was for myself, too. I had to know the truth."

Alex's tone was sarcastic. "Yeah, and no one ever has mixed motives. Enough with the self-hatred. If he doesn't come around, I say good riddance."

I appreciated this support from the troops, but the pain of losing Niko was too sharp—and maybe it always would be. "I wish I could feel that way."

The room fell silent. Alex peered at me. "You know what you need?"

"A bullet in the head?" I said flatly.

He gave me one of his classic exasperated looks. "A distraction. And I have just the thing. Remember Angelina said there were three guys at the party she totally trusted?" I nodded. "I lined up interviews with them."

Smart move. That way we could decide for ourselves how trustworthy they were. "Great. But we'll need a cover story for this situation." Angelina didn't want anyone to know about Eliza's rape, so we needed a good excuse to ask questions about the night of the party.

Michy stretched her legs under the coffee table. "How about telling them someone stole something from Angelina's house during the party? Something valuable but small enough to slip into a pocket. Like jewelry or some little art thingy."

I gave her a thumbs-up. "Nice. That works."

Alex gave her an appreciative smile. "You're good."

She lifted her chin. "I'm great."

He said, "At lying, I mean."

She picked up one of the pillows on the couch and threw it at him. I had to admit, Alex was right. The distraction was helping. "Alex, check with Angelina so she can give you an idea of the kind of thing she'd have. But tell her it can't be anything she really has." In case someone from the party had seen it in her house since then.

He gave me a salute and stood up. "I'll go call her now." He paused at the door. "And we're set to meet with the guys tomorrow. Starting at nine thirty a.m. sharp. You can pick me up at nine."

"Thank you for the privilege," I said.

Michy stood up and stretched. "Speaking of driving. You two need to hand in your mileage and gas for the month." She saw me roll my eyes. "Unless you don't care about the tax write-off."

Oh, well, there was that. "I'm all over it." Michy and Alex headed for the door. But a question occurred to me. "Do you think Niko will even want me to keep representing him?"

Alex narrowed his eyes. "Only if he wants the best."

Michy lifted her palms. "He's right, but I see your point. It could get pretty awkward." She saw my face fall. "Let's not borrow trouble, okay? The story with you two hasn't ended yet."

I wanted to agree. But I just couldn't. They left, and I pulled out my travel expense sheet, glad to have something mundane to keep me busy. I'd been at it for a couple of hours when Michy came back in. She picked up the remote and turned on my television. "Someone leaked to the tabloids about Bryan's death."

I sat back and watched. Sure enough, the five o'clock news anchor was saying, "Police have played it very close to the vest on this case, but multiple sources have confirmed that Bryan Posner was the victim of a homicide. And the cause of death is one of the most bizarre we've ever heard: internal decapitation. When asked if there were any suspects, the LAPD spokesman declined to comment. We'll update you on this breaking news story as more information becomes available."

The police were being pretty tight-lipped about it. For now. But I knew that wouldn't last. Those leaks from "multiple sources" would force their hand. "The cops are going to have to get out in front of this now."

Michy turned off the television. "Yeah, I bet they hold a press conference by tomorrow."

And that meant it wouldn't be long before Niko's name surfaced as a "person of interest." When that happened, he'd need a full-time lawyer on hand—if only to deal with the press. If he intended to fire me and get someone else, he'd have to do it soon. The thought sent a lead weight into the pit of my stomach.

Because then there'd be no more doubt about it. We'd be through.

FORTY-TWO

I forced myself to finish my monthly travel expense report, but once I had, I was totally depleted. There was no point even trying to get anything else done. But the thought of going home and sitting alone where I'd have nothing to distract me from the endless replay of what I'd done and why I'd done it and how it'd probably ended any chance I had for a relationship was so depressing, I couldn't make myself turn off the computer.

I leaned back in my chair and closed my eyes. I don't know how long I sat there before Michy said something—I didn't catch the words—and made me lift my head. "What?"

"I said, you should call it a day." She gave me a long look. "How about I come over and hang with you for a while?"

As always, she knew exactly what I needed. "Thanks, Michy. But I can't let you ruin a perfectly good evening with the Mistress of Doom."

"That's funny, I see your mouth moving but I don't hear any words." She waved a hand toward the door. "Come on. Get up. We're outta here."

I picked up my purse and followed her out. Alex met us in the reception area. "You're leaving? Good. Get some sleep. We need to charm the hell out of those party animals tomorrow."

"You should pack it in, too." I knew he'd been putting in very long hours for the past couple of weeks.

"I am," he said. "In fact, I was just about to ask if you wanted to come over for dinner."

I gave him a grateful smile. "Thanks, Alex. But I'm going to take my droopy ass home."

Alex glanced at Michy. "Are you going with her?" She nodded. "Perfect."

We all headed out, and as we walked to our cars, Alex said, "Why don't I pick you up tomorrow? You can sleep in a little longer."

It was a kind offer, but I knew sleep wouldn't be on the agenda tonight. Letting Alex pick me up would only make a long night longer. "That's okay. I want to bank some driving credits. So gas up and get ready. It's going to be your turn for a while after tomorrow."

Alex shook his head. "Well played." He opened the car door. "But enjoy it while you can. I'm planning to get a motorcycle."

I couldn't picture perfectly coiffed Alex jamming a helmet on his head. "No you're not."

He got into his car. "I guess you'll see soon enough."

Michy looked from Alex to me. "You two. Honestly." She turned to me. "Get in and get going."

It was pretty silly, this game we played about who had to drive. But I wouldn't have been surprised if Alex did show up with a motorcycle just to spite me. We all drove out, and as I steered toward home, I reminded myself how lucky I was to have such great friends. And how much worse I'd be feeling if I had to go through a time like this alone.

Michy made a command decision on the way to my house and picked up a pizza—the perfect no-fuss comfort food—and we had a real girls' night. We talked a little about Niko and my fear that there'd never be another man in my life. But for the most part, we watched movies on Netflix and chilled out. It was all I could manage and exactly what I needed.

When Michy left a little after midnight, I didn't want to go to bed—where I knew I'd just lie awake or, worse, have my usual nightmare. So I found another movie—some lame rom-com—and fell asleep on the couch. That gave me a few hours of rest. But at four a.m., I rolled over and landed on the floor. I conceded defeat and dragged myself into bed. I was so tired, my whole body hurt, but I couldn't stop thinking about how—and why—I'd lost Niko and what the future did—and didn't—hold for me. At six o'clock, I gave up trying and headed for the shower.

I was dressed and ready to go by seven a.m., which gave me plenty of time to power through my mega-size travel mug of coffee. I needed every drop of that four-cup monster to get my brain in gear. And I was hungry, but all I had in the fridge was leftover pizza. Not an option. Not after eating six slices last night.

I turned on the television and surfed the local news shows to see if the LAPD had made any more announcements about the case. Not so far. I left at eight thirty and stopped at my favorite bagel shop on the way to Alex's. By that time, I was starving. I couldn't even wait to get to Alex's place. I slathered on the cream cheese and ate in the car.

When I picked him up, he pointed at my face and made a circle. "What's going on there?" As he got in, he spotted the bag of food on the passenger side floor. "Ah. I see we're now eating animal-style."

Damn. I quickly wiped my mouth with a napkin. "I brought some for you, so make nice."

He fished a sesame bagel out of the bag. "Have I told you lately how ravishingly beautiful you are?"

I gave him a look. "Why no, I don't believe you have. Now where are we going?"

He pulled his cell phone out of his pocket. "Beverly Hills. Dayton Drive. 'Hair by Andress.' We're meeting with the man himself. Andress Violini. He's Angelina's hairdresser."

I turned onto Santa Monica Boulevard and headed west. Ten minutes later, Alex spotted the two-story floor-to-ceiling-windowed building that housed the upscale salon. I gave our names to the receptionist. I assumed it'd take a while before Andress appeared, so I moved toward the chairs in the waiting area. But I hadn't even had the chance to sit down before he came out and greeted us—with a two-handed shake for me. His eyes traveled over my body like a pair of hands. "I assume you're Samantha." He exuded sensuality.

I felt a little *zing* of excitement. "I am."

After I introduced Alex, Andress said, "Come into my office. It's too noisy out here." He led us through the packed salon—not an empty chair in the place—to a room at the back that was tastefully furnished in a sleek, modern style. I noticed abstract oil paintings on the wall that'd probably cost a fortune. Clearly, business was healthy at Hair by Andress.

And the space must've been soundproofed, because the din of hair dryers and chatter disappeared the moment he closed the door. As Alex and I sat on the couch, I had a feeling this room saw a lot of action that had nothing to do with the business end of things.

I spooled out our cover story—that someone at the party had stolen a diamond-and-gold cuff bracelet that'd been custom-made for Angelina by Paloma Picasso. "We're thinking that person probably left the party shortly after dinner, at about ten o'clock. Do you remember seeing anyone leave around that time?"

Andress gave us a bleak look. "I hate to disappoint you, but everyone there was in and out of the house all night long. Before and after dinner. Angelina doesn't allow smoking—or drugs of any kind—inside the house."

Not helpful. "I assume you see a lot of the same people at Angelina's parties?" Andress nodded. "Did you happen to notice anyone new? A man you hadn't seen before?" I was betting our rapist hadn't been to any of Angelina's parties before. I was sure he would never go again.

"There were a few." He paused. "There was an older guy who was obsessed with horses." He took in my puzzled look. "Horse racing. Talked nonstop about his day at Santa Anita." He paused, then added, "Oh yeah, and I finally met some of the younger guys who work for Angelina."

That was news. "I didn't know she hired men, too."

"Neither did I," he said. "But I assumed they worked for her, because I've never seen men that young at any of her parties."

Based on Eliza's description, we could probably rule out those men. "Anyone else you remember?"

He tapped his fingers on the arm of his chair. "A man who owned a chain of Dairy Kings." Andress chuckled to himself. "I remember him because he looked like Humpty Dumpty, and someone told me he was into B&D." Andress shook his head. "All night I kept picturing him on all fours, wearing a dog collar."

"Anyone else?"

He shook his head. "I was more interested in the women, to be honest."

I took one last shot. "Did you see Eliza at the party?" I thought that maybe if he'd noticed her, he might remember having seen a man follow her out of the house.

Andress frowned. "Who?" I described her. "Sounds like a pretty girl, but no."

I raised an eyebrow. "I'm surprised. I thought you said you were focused on the women."

He looked annoyed. "Yeah. Women. Not little girls."

Score one for Andress. He didn't know how much I appreciated hearing a man say that. But there was nothing more he could tell us.

Our next stop was a jewelry store on Wilshire Boulevard. The owner—Stan Busker—hadn't noticed anyone leave right after dinner. Because he'd had one too many hits of weed and passed out in the backyard before the appetizers were served.

Our third and final witness for the day owned a famous—and famously expensive—seafood restaurant in Pacific Palisades. Allen Forman was a tall, bald man with a soft voice and kind eyes. He hadn't seen anyone leave the party after dinner, but he had seen something. "I do remember seeing a young girl come into the house as I was leaving. She looked very upset." I described Eliza and asked if that sounded like the same girl. "Yes, that sounds about right."

"Did she say anything to you?" Alex asked.

"No." His expression was sad and worried. "But she seemed out of breath, like she'd been running. And I think she might've been crying. Did something happen to her?"

For a moment, it flashed through my mind that Allen Forman might be our rapist. How'd he just happen to be leaving when she came back? Then I remembered that Eliza had said her attacker definitely wasn't bald. But maybe . . . "Did you take any photos that night?"

He gave me a direct look. "I know this is important, so I'll show you. It's just a couple of selfies with the guys. But you've got to promise not to tell Angelina. Because we're not supposed to."

I crossed my heart and hoped to see that Allen had a full head of hair that night. But when he pulled out his phone, I saw his gleaming pate. Alex and I asked him about the men who were in the photos with him. Just more rich guys who were obviously willing to pay serious cash for a good time. And none of them had left the party early. He said, "Why would they?"

As Alex and I headed for the car, I said, "This was a waste. I say we take a pass on the partygoers for now."

Alex nodded. "Everyone was moving around way too much. Even if someone did see a man leave right after dinner, it could take us weeks to find that person."

And then we'd have to get incredibly lucky for that person to be able to identify who that man was. "We might have to revisit the guest list, but for now, I say we door knock the neighborhood."

We reached the car. "I think so, too," Alex said. "Let me finish getting all the info on the neighbors."

Alex always liked to find out as much as he could about who they were—and when they'd be most likely to be home. I just had to hope we'd find a decent witness in the neighborhood.

Because I was starting to think it might be our only chance of solving this case.

FORTY-THREE

We'd done a lot of driving around, and it'd eaten up most of our day. By the time we got to the office, it was after four o'clock. We told Michy what we'd learned—which was, at best, mildly entertaining—and then I headed into my office.

Alone, without Alex or witnesses to distract me, my thoughts circled back to Niko. I fired up my computer, hoping to dive into work to take my mind off him, but I found myself navigating to his Facebook page. Although I'd initially told myself I just wanted to see if it revealed anything that might help with the case, I'd eventually admitted that it was a feel-good activity. But now that we weren't even together, I was forced to admit that my motive was even more pathetic. Surfing through his Facebook page let me feel like I was still connected to him.

I usually started in present time and worked backward. When I'd last left off, I'd gotten as far as six months back. Intending to spend only a few minutes, I picked up there and began to scroll. But half an hour later, I was still at it.

I'd gone back another two months when I noticed a posting about a man named Mark Kennar. I remembered Niko telling me how he'd met him on a dirt-biking trip when he stopped for lunch at a nearby café called On the Road. The place was in the middle of nowhere—which made sense, since it was close to dirt-biking trails—but according to Niko, the food was great. They'd become dirt-biking buddies ever since. I scrolled down further and found a photo of Mark and Niko standing in front of the café in their dirt-bike gear, holding their helmets. I stared at the hills behind the building and tried to recall where it was. Wait. Now I remembered. It was in Soledad Canyon.

My heart gave a painful, heavy thump. It was the perfect place to dump a body. And it wasn't just that. Something else had been bugging me. I remembered that the night before we'd found Bryan's body, I'd called Niko, but he hadn't answered. And he hadn't called me back until the next day. I'd assumed he'd been at the hospital and that the cell reception there was lousy. But that couldn't be right. He'd used his cell phone to call me from the hospital several times, and I'd been able to reach him there, too. So where had Niko been? And why hadn't he called me back until the following day?

That was right around the time Tanner had disappeared. Niko could easily have killed Tanner that night and dumped his body in the canyon. The timing definitely worked.

I stopped and pushed back from my computer. I was making one hell of a leap—from a friend in Soledad Canyon and a missed phone call—to murder. I needed to get a grip. Besides, the cops had gotten a search warrant for Niko's car at the same time they got the warrant for his house. In fact, they'd even taken his car to the lab for a few days so they could swab it for blood and trace evidence. It was almost impossible with today's technology to wipe it all away. They obviously hadn't found anything. And they definitely would have checked his GPS, too. If he'd driven to Soledad Canyon on a night when Tanner might've been killed, they'd have been all over it. Unless, of course, he'd used another car.

Was I leaping to the worst conclusion so I could vindicate myself?

But . . . the questions nagged at me. The dots might connect. I might not be crazy. What I needed right now was a reality check. I went out to Michy's desk and called for Alex to join us.

He emerged with an annoyed look on his face. "If you want to start canvassing those neighbors tomorrow, I need to be able to finish checking them out."

"This won't take long." I gestured to the old secretary's chair in the corner. "Have a seat."

Michy, still focused on her monitor, held up a finger. "Just a sec. I'm downloading an update." After a few seconds, she sat back. "Okay, done. What's up?"

I told them about my searches on Niko's Facebook page and what I'd been thinking. "Am I just reaching for a way to prove I was right?"

Michy adjusted her Scünci—royal blue to match her fashionably distressed sweater—and shrugged. "You might be. But it's not a completely crazy idea. The thing is, like you said, he had to have used another car or the cops would've picked up something when they searched."

"But I've never seen another car at his place, and he's never mentioned having one." My theory wouldn't hold any water unless that second car existed.

Alex leaned back and folded his arms. "There is a way to find out."

I hesitated. Once I started down this road, there'd be no stopping. Did I really want to know? On the other hand, why not? What did I have to lose? Niko and I were through. "How?"

He stroked his chin. "I'd start with cell phone tower records and see if he made any phone calls near Soledad Canyon that night."

I thought about that. "Seems unlikely he'd take that risk."

He nodded. "But you never know. People who aren't contract killers don't necessarily think all that clearly when they're disposing of bodies. Anyway, it can't hurt to start there, and it's easy enough to do."

I was sure the cops had already checked Niko's cell phone records. But that didn't necessarily mean they hadn't found any calls near Soledad Canyon. The case hadn't been filed yet, so they didn't owe me discovery. Still, I gave it a low probability of success. "And if you don't turn up anything? Then what?"

"Then I make up some excuse to see him, swipe his cell phone, and install spyware to see if there's anything on his phone that shows where he was that night," Alex said.

I didn't want to go there. It was one thing for us to snoop around by talking to his brother or checking out his Facebook page. It was a whole other world to make up a lie and steal his phone so I could spy on him in real time. "Not loving that idea. Let's see what you find in the cell tower records."

Alex said, "I get that you're feeling ambivalent, but I can't do this if you tie my hands."

Of course I was ambivalent. But I also wanted to know the truth. I just wasn't ready to go to DEFCON One quite yet. "One step at a time, okay?"

Alex rolled his shoulders back and stood up. "Fine by me. Do you want me to finish with Angelina's neighbors or crack into Niko's cell phone records?"

Now that there was a possibility of an answer about Niko, I was anxious to get it. But I also wanted to get moving on the interviews. "How much more time do you need for the neighbors?"

"About an hour, maybe a little less," he said.

It was already after five o'clock. He'd probably want to stay late and get into Niko's cell records tonight, but I could wait another day or so. "Finish the neighbors, then go home. I can wait on Niko's records for a couple of days."

Alex started to head to his office, then paused. "Did you ever get that sex offender information from Dale?"

Right. I'd asked Dale to see if there were any registered sex offenders in Angelina's 'hood. He'd promised to send them to me. I'd been so focused on Niko's Facebook page, I'd forgotten to check my email. "Michy, can you log in for me?"

She hit a few keys and scrolled. "There it is. I'll forward to Alex and print it out."

The printer whirred to life and spit out a page. There were only three names on the list. Not bad. I'd seen supposedly kid-safe suburban communities with many more than that. I handed the page to Alex. "Decent place to start."

Alex scanned it. "Not much here. But I'll take all the help I can get."

Fatigue hit me all at once. True, it'd been a busy day, but I suspected my newly discovered theory about Niko's guilt was probably more to blame. "Guys, I think I'm going to call it a day. Alex, if you can't finish within the hour, just bail." I gestured to the page of sex offenders in his hand. "Between those ex-cons and whoever else answers their doors, we'll have more than enough to do for one day."

Alex waved to me as he headed into his office. "Don't worry. And I'll drive tomorrow. But we need to get there by eight a.m., so be ready by seven thirty. Most of the residents are going to be gone by eight thirty."

Since I probably wouldn't be able to fall asleep anyway, I didn't mind the early pickup. As I went to my office to get my purse and jacket, Michy followed me. "Want some company?"

I looked at her with love. "Michy, you're the best. But I've got to start getting over him. You've done enough babysitting."

"It's not a chore, you know." She gave me a little smile. "I thought it was kind of fun to hang out on a school night. We haven't done that in so long."

We were all working way too hard. "When we wrap up this case, we should plan a vacation." Unless Niko fired me. In which case, we could take that vacay a lot sooner.

Michy said she had a few things to wrap up, so I left her to it. I was so tired, I couldn't wait to take a shower and curl up in bed.

But for some reason, when I got home, I couldn't bear the thought of getting into bed. I poured myself three fingers of Patrón Silver, grabbed a blanket, and settled on the couch. I felt numb as I sipped my drink and watched the television with unseeing eyes. Would I ever see Niko again? I might not. He could fire me via email, and his new lawyer could meet with Alex to get up to speed on what we'd found. The thought that Niko might get a new lawyer led to the even more painful thought that he'd find a new girlfriend. Just the idea of him kissing another woman—touching her face, holding her hand, sleeping with her—was unbearable. I took a long slug of my drink. Then another. I got up and poured myself another. I fell asleep after the second sip.

This time, I spent the whole night on the couch—and woke up with a stiff neck and enough of a hangover to remind me why drinking the night before an early-morning wake-up was a very bad idea. I dragged myself into the shower and brought my vat of coffee into the bathroom so I could take sips to clear my head while I put on my makeup.

I'd thought I did a pretty good job of covering up last night's bad behavior, but when I got into Alex's car, he gave me a long look. "I'd ask how your night was, but I don't need to."

I let my head fall back against the headrest. "Don't worry, I'm good. Almost."

Alex gave me a skeptical look. "Look, Sam. No judgment. I'd be a zombie if Paul broke up with me. Just know that you're welcome to come spend the night whenever. It can be hard to go home to an empty place at a time like this."

He'd hit the nail right on the head. "Thanks, Alex. I'll keep it in mind."

He merged onto the freeway. "I guess you didn't have a chance to check the news this morning." I told him I hadn't. "Good thing I did, then. The cops did a presser on Bryan's murder this morning."

I usually turn on the news while I'm getting ready. But with my throbbing head this morning, I couldn't bear the noise. "Did they mention any names?"

"So far they only named Gold Strike. They said Bryan's death occurred shortly after Gold Strike did a major trade that cost investors millions. I guess they still haven't figured out that the so-called 'major trade' was actually a scam."

"Or they're just playing it safe for now." But this wasn't as bad as I'd feared. I'd been worried they'd say something about having a person of interest. The minute they did, the press would go full bore to find out who it was—and it wouldn't take long for someone to leak Niko's name. "This case is too juicy for the press to ignore. They'll keep pushing." And the harder they pushed for answers, the more the cops would feel they had to show some progress. "It's just a matter of time."

Alex gave me a sidelong glance. "Do you think Niko knows that?"

"Definitely," I said. "Because I told him to expect it."

We drove on in silence. Alex got off the freeway at Los Feliz Boulevard and drove to King Street. I pointed to a spot down the block from Angelina's house. "How about there?"

Alex turned left and found a parking space just steps away from the first house we planned to hit. I looked up and down the sidewalk. "I don't see any street surveillance cameras, do you?" LAPD was expanding the reach of its wireless network, and some residential neighborhoods—albeit usually the ones that had a homeowner association—had begun installing them, too. Alex shook his head. Scratch that option.

He consulted his cell phone, then nodded toward a small bungalow across the street. "Jennifer Arbagian is a stay-at-home mom with two kids. Our only hope is that she's so bored, she's desperate enough to want to talk to two strangers."

But it was much more likely that she'd refuse to come to the door. Safety first. Especially with two young children. Surprisingly, boredom won. Jennifer answered the door with a harried expression. I could hear a baby crying in the background. I'd decided I could tell these neighbors a version of the truth. After introducing Alex and myself, I said, "We're hoping you can help us. Two weeks ago, a man assaulted a young woman on this street. By any chance, do you remember hearing or seeing anything unusual? It would've been around ten p.m."

She gave a short laugh. "Ten o'clock? I haven't managed to stay awake past eight since my first kid was born. I'd love to help you, but I'm sorry. By that time, I was dead to the world."

I scanned her front doorstep. "Do you have any kind of surveillance camera?"

She shook her head and sighed. "We really should. We talk about it, but somehow we never get around to doing it. You should check with the others on the block, though. I'm sure someone else does."

She was right. A few neighbors actually did. But their camera range was either limited to the porch and a few feet of the front walkway or picked up too little of the sidewalk to be of use. And Jennifer's response—that she hadn't seen or heard anything unusual—pretty much set the tone of the answers we got from everyone else as we moved up the street. At least, those who answered the door. A lot of them didn't.

All in all, the neighbors we did speak to were a friendly lot—with one exception: the registered sex offender, who'd been busted during his senior year in college for taking part in a group gangbang of a semiconscious sorority girl. I didn't really consider him to be a likely suspect. I was pretty sure that whoever attacked Eliza had been a guest at Angelina's party, and she'd told me that none of her neighbors were ever invited to her parties—for obvious reasons. But I couldn't completely rule out the possibility that Eliza's attacker had been someone who didn't attend the party. And a registered sex offender who lived on the block where the assault was committed made for an interesting suspect.

I'd been planning to subtly ferret out his alibi, but he took the matter right out of my hands when I asked him if he'd seen or heard anything on the night in question.

"No, I didn't fucking see or hear anything. Want to know why? Because I was in the hospital! For three fucking days! Some shit-for-brains dad saw me talking to his little princess and almost ruptured my spleen."

I was delighted to hear it. "I'm very sorry."

But he wasn't finished. "What kind of insane, uncivilized world are we living in nowadays? I mean, all I did was say hi to that girl, and this Neanderthal asshole jumps me." A disgusted look crossed his face. "She wasn't even that hot."

Alex would check to see if he really had been in the hospital at the time, but his story—and the heated, spontaneous way he'd volunteered it—felt legit. As we headed across the street, Alex said, "I don't think that father hit him hard enough."

I wholeheartedly agreed. "Yeah, I was tempted to kick him in the spleen myself."

I'd noticed that, as we moved up and down the street, Alex was taking photos. Now, as he paused to take yet another one, I asked, "What are you doing?"

He raised an eyebrow. "It's a crime scene. A good investigator always takes photos of a crime scene."

He'd been reading one of those damn *Investigations for Dummies* books again. "I told you to knock it off with those stupid How To's. They're written by wannabes who never were."

Alex gave me a superior smile. "You're so going to regret saying that."

I didn't think so, but I saw no point in arguing. We hit the other side of the street. It was no better. I pointed to the last three houses we had left. "I say if no one else has anything for us, we forget about the door knocking. If no one on this block saw or heard anything, then I can't imagine that anyone who lives farther away would have."

"Yeah, this is pretty much a bust." He consulted his iPad. "The next house is . . . another sex offender." He looked at me. "Please try not to piss him off."

I punched him on the arm. Our sex offender's house, like many others on the block, had a Ring doorbell. I motioned for Alex to step back, and when I pushed it, I stood as close to the camera as possible. I had a feeling that our buddy Ken Lorimar—who'd been busted for statutory rape of a sixteen-year-old girl—would be more likely to answer if he thought a lone woman was at the door.

I stared for a moment when Ken opened the door. He was as close to a mouse as a human could get. Short, slender, thinning hair worn slicked back, and tiny eyes behind wire-frame glasses. He had a half smile when he saw me, but it vanished when he noticed Alex standing a few feet away. He pushed his glasses up the bridge of his nose and stammered, "C-can I help you?"

He was so nervous, I wondered why he'd answered the door. "We're investigating an assault that took place two weeks ago on this block. A young girl was attacked. There was a big party going on across the street at the time. Can you tell us if you saw anything unusual that night?"

He licked dry lips. "No, I didn't see a thing. I—I was busy. I'm a day trader. I was at my computer all night."

That he'd been home—and maybe on his computer that night—was believable. In any case, I wasn't concerned about his alibi. He didn't fit the description of the attacker. But he was suspiciously shaky. He had to be hiding something. I took a quick look at his home—what I could see of it over his shoulder. And spotted the reason for it.

There was a telescope in the kitchen window that was positioned to face the street. "Really?" I pointed to the telescope. "Seems to me you had a perfect view—and one you enjoy an awful lot."

Ken blinked rapidly. "There's nothing illegal about watching the street! It's a public place."

I looked him in the eye. "True. But I bet your probation officer would love to talk to you about it." I'd had a hunch that the reason he'd opened the door was because he thought I might be a probation officer. "Especially after I tell him about the girls who hang out there."

Beads of sweat popped out on his forehead. "Okay, okay. I do watch that house. But I've never gone over there!"

Still, it didn't look good for him, and he knew it. "What did you see, Ken?"

He rubbed the back of his neck. "It's just . . . I don't want to have to go to court."

On that score, I could reassure him. "You won't. I promise."

He peered at me between more rapid blinks. "I thought I heard a sound like a scream, but soft. Like someone had a hand over their mouth. I couldn't tell whether it was a guy or a girl. I turned the 'scope to try and see who it was, and that's when I saw a tall guy get out of the back seat of a Bentley."

A Bentley. Our attacker had definitely been at the party. "Can you describe the man?"

Ken bit his lip. "Tall, a little over six feet. Medium build. That's about it. I only saw him for a few seconds."

Alex asked, "Where was the Bentley parked?" Ken pointed to a spot a few doors down, on the same side of the street as Angelina's house. "Can you describe it?"

Ken thought for a moment. "It was white, and it looked fairly new."

I had to ask the next question, though I had little hope of hitting pay dirt. "Did you happen to get the license plate number?"

Ken shook his head. "I wasn't really sure what had happened. Weird stuff happens all the time up here."

I knew that was true. It was a great neighborhood, but it was still Griffith Park. A public place that all kinds of people had access to. "Can you describe the girl?"

He stared out the window. "I couldn't really see her. When she got out of the car, she ran up the street." He pointed toward Angelina's house. "That way. She was kind of bent over, and she had her arms wrapped around her waist. It all happened really fast."

I went back to the attacker. "Did you notice what the man was wearing?" Ken shook his head. "What about his hair? Anything unusual?"

"Just that he had some," he said. "I didn't notice the color."

Which probably meant it wasn't white or silvery gray, or it would've stood out. "Did you get a hit on his age? Did he seem young, like in his twenties? Or older?"

Ken pondered that for a moment. "Definitely not twenties. Maybe forties? I don't know. I'm not a good judge of age."

That's probably the story he tried to sell the cops when he got busted. Alex and I asked a few more questions, but we couldn't get anything more out of Ken. I thanked him for his time. "If you think of anything else, give Alex a call." The less contact I had to have with this creep, the better.

We door knocked the few remaining houses, got nothing from the one person who answered the door, and headed back to the car. Alex turned to me as he tucked his iPad under the driver's seat. "Well, at least we know the rapist drives a white Bentley. Think Angelina might know who owns one of those?"

I shrugged. "We're here. May as well ask." But I wasn't optimistic. She wasn't personally doing the valet service. So why would she know what cars her guests drove?

We caught her in another one of her pricey kimonos in the midst of getting ready to go out to dinner with a client—whom she refused to name. "He is very famous and very married."

I was puzzled. "Then why not just have him come over?"

She lit a cigarette. "We usually do, but sometimes he needs a change. We go to safe places, private places. Tonight, we go to the Bungalows."

The San Vicente Bungalows was all that and more. A private club in West Hollywood that admitted only the most famous, most wealthy, and most in need of a place to go where no one could ask for a selfie—camera phones were disabled at the door with a sticker over the lens. Angelina's client had to be a very big fish indeed. I asked her whether any of her guests drove a white Bentley and got the predictable answer.

She squinted at me through the smoke. "That's the car that belongs to the man who raped Eliza?" I nodded. She waved an impatient hand in the air. "How would I know this? No one talks about what car they drive. Is that all you've learned?"

"That, and the fact that the attacker had definitely been one of your guests at the party." She looked unimpressed. I couldn't blame her. Our lack of progress frustrated me, too. But without an accurate guest list, it was impossible to build a list of viable suspects. The three men we'd spoken to had clearly shown that the guests were an unreliable source at best. I needed to find people who'd attended the party who weren't drunk, stoned, or looking to get laid. Then it hit me. "You said you used a caterer?"

Angelina nodded. "Actually, a chef. Boris Moseyev. He's a genius, and he brings his own crew to serve and clean. I use him for all my events."

Finally, a ray of hope. I got his contact information.

Between Boris and his servers, someone must've seen *something*.

FORTY-FOUR

"Nice move," Alex said as we got back into his car.

I snapped on my seat belt. "Desperation always inspires me. But we really need this to pan out, because that's all I've got. You?"

Alex pulled out and steered toward Los Feliz Boulevard. "I've got nothing."

Tired of all the brick walls we'd hit on Eliza's case, I shifted gears and took stock of where we stood with Bryan's murder and Tanner's likely murder. I remembered I hadn't gotten an update on our favorite alternate suspect. "What's happening with Sergio?"

"Nothing. As in, he's off the list. He's got an alibi."

Of course he did. "Let me guess. He spent the night praying with two priests and seven nuns."

Alex sighed. "Better than that. He had dinner at the Bungalows with a bunch of celebrity A-listers, then played poker with them all night."

It was one hell of an alibi. Somewhere in the back of my mind, I'd known he wouldn't pan out.

When Alex dropped me off, I told him to go home. "We've squeezed our brains enough for one day."

Alex looked unhappy. "I'll probably just do a little workup on that chef." I started to shake my head. "From home. Okay? I just need to remember what it feels like to make some real progress."

I had to smile. "Fine. But have dinner. Relax. Don't screw up your whole evening. I don't want Paul on my ass for being a slave driver."

He shifted into reverse. "Don't worry. He knows who he hooked up with."

Alex backed out, and I headed upstairs. It was weird. I'd lived alone my whole adult life, and it'd never bothered me. To the contrary, I'd reveled in the freedom. But now, after having been part of a couple—a happy one for a change—my once-prized solitude felt lonely and isolating. The apartment I'd found cozy and comforting now felt like an empty box, and I wandered from room to room like a ghost.

Sleeping on the couch had become a habit. The bed only reminded me of nights with Niko. I showered, poured myself a stiff shot of Patrón Silver, and swore to myself that I'd start cutting back, then lay down on the couch. How long would it take for me to get back to normal, to being my old self? Would that ever happen?

I didn't remember falling asleep, but I must have dozed off, because I woke up to the *ding* of a text message at six thirty the next morning. I had to admit, depression had its benefits. I'd never slept so much in my life. And I'd learned how to avoid falling off the couch. So many great accomplishments.

I rubbed my eyes and picked up my phone. This had to be either Alex or Dale. No one else would reach out that early. The only real question was whether it was good news or bad.

It was from Alex. I got a weird hit on Niko's cell phone records. Call me when you're up. After a message like that, I was plenty up. I called him. "Did you find a call in Soledad Canyon?"

"No," Alex said. "But he made a couple of calls from up by Tehachapi. Who does he know there?"

Tehachapi? I had to think for a moment to remember where that was. I knew there was a prison there, because I'd had a few clients who'd been sent there. From what I knew, it was just a really small desert town with not much going on. And it was at least two hours north of LA. "I can't think of anyone. He never mentioned the place to me. Can you tell who he was calling?"

"Not yet," he said. "It's too early to call and work my magic. But I will in about an hour."

I was going to grouse that he could've waited another hour to call me, too, but I had to admit I probably would've done the same. Those calls might not mean anything, but they seemed a little . . . odd. "What's the time frame?"

"The first one was a couple of months ago. But the second one was the night of Bryan's murder."

I could feel my pulse speed up. "Call me after you've reached that number. I'll get ready to go." Hopefully, Alex would be able to "work his magic" and get us a meeting with whomever Niko had called.

As I got into the shower, I tried to sort out my feelings. I'd been worried that Alex might find phone calls that showed Niko had been in Soledad Canyon when Tanner disappeared. He hadn't. But Tehachapi had miles of empty desert. It could work just as well as the canyon for a dumping ground. I was getting more anxious by the second. I dried off and got dressed with shaking hands.

I'd blow-dried my hair, put on makeup, and was on my second tub of coffee by the time Alex called me back. "What've you got?"

His voice was tight. "The number he called was for a security guard who works at a private airfield."

A what? "Did he know who Niko was?"

"I couldn't get into that," he said. "I was selling auto insurance at the best rates in the state."

Not one of Alex's best cover stories, but he was reaching out into the void. He'd had to keep it generic. "Did he tell you where that airfield is?"

"He didn't have to," Alex said. "There's only one. You ready to do this?"

My heart was pounding. I had no idea where this would lead. A part of me didn't want to find out—but the much bigger part, the one that'd already gotten me into so much trouble—had to know. "Yeah, I'll pick you up. Leaving now."

I didn't wait for him to tell me whether he was ready. Boys don't need time to get ready. And I didn't bother to stop for bagels, doughnuts, or Egg McMuffins. I brought a couple of bottles of Dasani for the road and called it good. We had no time to lose. I knew Alex was feeling the same way.

He was waiting on the curb when I pulled up, and he had his cell phone already programmed to Waze. "I'll navigate. It'll be fastest if we take the 14 Highway."

I headed for the 101 Freeway north. "How're we going to pry this guard open?"

Alex tapped his cell phone and studied the directions. "Um, tell him your boyfriend probably killed a guy and you'd like to see if he buried the body nearby?"

I glared at him. "You're a laugh riot."

He sat back and stared through the windshield. "Give me a minute. I'll come up with something."

We spent the better part of the next two hours trying to come up with a believable story. But it was hard to make up a story when we didn't know why Niko had called the guard or what he was doing at a private airfield in a little desert town. We still hadn't settled on a plausible story when I got off the freeway and turned onto the road that would lead us to the airfield. "I hate to say it, but we'll just have to play it by ear."

Alex raised an eyebrow. "You mean, wing it?"

I shot him a dagger for that terrible pun. "Apologize. Right now."

He sat forward and pointed to a sign up ahead. "That must be it."

It was. As I got closer, I saw that it said **Tehachapi Airfield**. I followed the arrow on the sign to an open gate. "That security guard isn't exactly working overtime."

"Then again, how many people are dying to get into this place?" Alex said.

A fair point. I pulled in and drove slowly toward the hangars. They were all pretty small. "Must only be for single engines." Alex nodded. I kept rolling forward, looking for signs of life. The place looked deserted. "Where is this security guy?"

Alex was scanning the area, too. "Maybe it's his day off?" After a few seconds, he said, "Wait! That looks like an office, doesn't it?"

I looked to my right and saw a little shack with windows on three sides. "Must be." I drove toward it and parked far enough away to give us a running start if things got hairy. I'd been relatively calm during the drive. The effort to come up with a story had distracted me. But now, my palms had started to sweat, and I could feel my heart racing. I tried to act nonchalant. "Let's see what happens."

Alex hesitated, one hand on the door handle. "I wish I knew what we were in for."

He didn't get nervous often, but he was now. I looked at him. "Me too." I tapped the steering wheel. "So what the hell are we going to tell this guy?"

Before Alex could answer, a bowlegged man with a potbelly who looked to be in his fifties exited and came toward us. He was wearing a khaki security guard uniform.

I swore under my breath. "Shit!"

A few seconds later, he was standing at my side of the car. "What can I do for you folks today?"

I opened the door, and as I got out, I said the first thing that popped into my head. "My boyfriend's buying a Cessna, and I wanted to rent him a hangar as a birthday present. Can you tell me what your rates are?" Not bad considering I'd come up with it on the fly. So to speak.

He scratched his head. "Usually around two seventy-five a month. Another hundred for the tie-down gear. But we can't handle anything bigger than a single engine." He gestured to the fleet of hangars behind him. "As you can probably see."

I put on my most charming smile. "I can. Would you mind showing me one?"

"Sure," he said. "Come on. I'll give you a ride."

We followed him to the back of the guard shack where a golf cart was parked and got in. He drove across the field to a hangar at the far end. He parked, and as we moved toward it, I had an idea. The guard unlocked the padlock on the door and pulled it up. I didn't know how hangars were supposed to look, but there wasn't that much to see. Just a bigger version of a garage, minus all the broken toys, bikes, and junk that's usually piled inside.

I took a few seconds to look around and act interested. "You know, I'm a little worried that my boyfriend may already have found the one he likes. It'd be bad if I chose the wrong one."

The man shrugged. "I think they're all pretty much the same."

I gave him a conspiratorial smile. "So do I. But my boyfriend can be a little . . . picky." The guard returned my smile. Good. This had to work. "His name is Niko. If you don't remember his name, I can show you his picture. Maybe you can let me see which one he looked at?"

The guard frowned. For a second, I thought he was going to say no. But instead, he said, "I'm not great with names. Let me see that photo." I pulled up a picture of a smiling Niko and showed it to him. The guard gave me a sad look. "I hate to break it to you, ma'am, but he already rented himself a hangar."

I feigned upset. "No. You're kidding! I don't believe it. Which one?"

He pointed to a hangar two slots to the left. "That one right there. Got it just a few weeks ago."

A few weeks ago. The paperwork would show exactly when, but I knew it was right around the time Tanner had gone missing. This was feeling more ominous by the second. I memorized the location of the hangar as I put on a hangdog expression. "Well, hell. I'm going to have to dream up something else to get him."

The guard led us back to the golf cart and dropped us off at my car. "Sorry about that. Does he golf?"

I sighed. "No, just likes to fly." I got out and moved toward my car. "But thanks for your help!"

He waved to us and motored back to the guard shack. As we drove off, Alex asked, "We're coming back tonight, aren't we?"

"Oh yeah. Most definitely."

I had to know what the hell Niko was doing with an airplane hangar. And why he'd never told me about it.

FORTY-FIVE

We headed into town to do some shopping. For picklocks, electric drills, and bolt cutters—though Alex doubted we'd be able to find cutters heavy-duty enough to get through the padlocks he'd seen on the hangars. "For once, I wish I would've brought my car."

He always kept a completely stocked toolbox in the trunk of his car. I offered an alternate suggestion. "If all else fails, we could roofie the security guard and steal his keys."

I'd been kidding, but Alex seemed to be giving it some thought. "That'd be a great Plan B if we could find someone else to do it for us."

"Someone else . . . who'd immediately point the finger at us." I pulled up to the mom-and-pop-style hardware store Alex had found on the app AroundMe. How did we live before we had these little pocket-size computers?

He gave a reluctant nod. "Let's hope they've got a decent selection of picklocks."

Actually—a bit alarmingly—the little place did. I'd expected to find electric drills and even bolt cutters, but they had entire sets of picklocks. Alex had a field day deciding which one to get. "We probably only need this twelve-piece set. Those padlocks are pretty simple. But we'd be safer getting the twenty-six-piece set. Why take chances?"

I agreed. "I have no desire to make a second trip up here." Tehachapi was nice—if you were into miles of nothingness.

As we moved toward the cashier, Alex said, "I assume you have flashlights in your car."

I stared at him. "No. Why would I?" I held up my cell phone. "I have this."

He rolled his eyes. "Because that won't be worth a damn in a big, dark hangar." He muttered something that included the word *ridiculous* and headed back to the shelves.

After Alex made his purchases, we found a little diner, where we lingered over an early dinner and waited for the town—and hopefully the airfield—to shut down. The manager of the diner kicked us out at eight p.m., which I took as a sign that it was late enough to go scope out the area.

I drove down the road to the airfield slowly. If it was still open, I didn't want the guard to see us. I wouldn't be able to explain why we'd come back after finding out Niko already had a hangar. But when I reached the gate, I saw that we were in luck. It was closed. I pointed to the padlock. "Want to take your new toys for a spin?"

He scanned the area. "Kind of. But I think the fewer locks I mess with, the better. The fence is low enough to climb over. Just drive a little farther away so we can stay out of range of the camera."

I hadn't seen one, but now that he mentioned it, I noticed an old-school surveillance camera mounted on a fence post just behind us. I didn't see any lights that indicated it was working. "I'm not sure that thing is even on. But no reason to risk it." I drove around the perimeter to an area where there were some bushes and cacti I could park behind.

I climbed over the fence first, and Alex handed me his tools, then joined me. We paused and looked around to make sure we didn't have company, then hurried to Niko's hangar. Alex took a pick out of the kit, and I used the flashlight on my phone to illuminate the padlock as he went to work. He jiggled it this way and that, but it didn't budge. I glanced around behind us. We were clearly visible from the road. If someone drove by, we'd be in big trouble.

Alex took out a second pick and tried again. Still no luck. I was starting to get nervous. "We need to make this happen soon, Alex."

He glared at me. "Does it look like I'm playing tiddlywinks?"

"Sorry." I took a deep breath and tried to calm myself.

But the second pick didn't work, either. Now I was seriously getting worried. I watched as he worked with the third pick and prayed it would be the charm. It wasn't. "Maybe it's time to try the bolt cutters."

He lifted the heavy padlock. "They'll be useless on this thing." He picked up the drill.

I'd never noticed how loud those things were. I glanced over my shoulder again—and saw headlights in the distance that hadn't been there before. Were they getting closer? It sure looked like it. "Alex, someone's coming! We've got to bail!" I turned off the flashlight on my cell phone.

And at that moment, the padlock popped open. With my heart hammering in my chest, we slid open the door, hurried inside, and closed it as quietly as we could. Alex had been right. The cavernous space was so pitch-black, I couldn't even see him, and he was standing next to me. But I could hear him breathing—fast and hard. My breath was just as labored. We stood there in the dark with our backs against the door, listening. Sure enough, seconds later, we heard the sound of a car engine approaching. I whispered to Alex, "If this place has a guard on night shift . . ." We'd be screwed. Alex had left the open padlock in the door. It'd take a guard two seconds to see it'd been broken.

He looked up at the ceiling and closed his eyes. I thought he was praying, but he whispered, "I wish I could blame you for this one."

As the car drew closer, I thought my heart would burst through my chest, it was beating so hard. But just when I thought the car was going to enter the gate, the sound of the engine began to recede. It was passing by. I was so light-headed with relief, my knees almost buckled. We leaned back against the hangar door and caught our breath. When the sound of the engine faded into the distance, Alex turned on his flashlight.

I'd expected to see a small single-engine plane. But all I saw was an SUV. A black Denali. Alarm bells immediately went off in my head. "Who pays for a hangar to store a car?"

Alex nodded. "And up here in the middle of nowhere?"

As we moved closer, I noticed it was covered in dust and dirt. Did it even belong to Niko? Maybe he was storing it for a friend? Maybe his buddy who had the café in Soledad Canyon. What was his name? Mark Kennar. But why keep it a secret? "I'd like to find out who it's registered to." I tried the driver's side door. It was locked. "Shit. Do any of those picks—"

Alex brandished a slim piece of metal and slid it into the space between the window and the door. I heard a *click*, and he tried again. It opened. "It's scary how easy that was." Alex hit the button to unlock the other doors and walked around to the passenger side. He reached inside and opened the glove compartment. Other than an old travel-size package of Kleenex, some loose change, and gum wrappers, it was empty. I glanced around inside the car. "I probably shouldn't do this, but . . ."

Alex climbed in. "But we're going to."

If there was trace evidence—even small drops of blood—we might be destroying it right now. But I had to know. As carefully as we could, we began to search, examining every inch with our flashlights. Now that the car's dome light was on, my cell phone flashlight, with its pointed beam, worked well. Inside, the car was somewhat dusty but not enough to say it'd been sitting untouched for months. Weeks, maybe. I was nervous as we pored over seats and floors, searching for any traces of blood.

But after half an hour, I was ready to give up. It was weird that he'd store some random SUV here, but maybe it was just a dirt-biking thing.

Tehachapi seemed the kind of place where dirt biking would be huge. I got out and went around to the back of the SUV and lifted up the door. I shined my flashlight around the rear cargo area. It didn't seem dirty enough for a car that carried dirt bikes. Then again, Niko was a neat freak. I was reaching up to pull the door back down when something in the right side well behind the back seat caught my eye. I leaned in and picked it up. When I saw what it was, my stomach lurched.

It was a Sex Addicts Anonymous chip. Just like the one that'd fallen out of Tanner's pocket. And it took very little effort to imagine how it'd gotten there. Like most SUVs, the back seat folded down to create a bigger cargo space. It'd be much easier to get Tanner's body into the car if the back seat were down. The chip must've fallen out of Tanner's pocket when Niko lifted him into the SUV. And after he'd disposed of the body, when he'd pushed the seat back up, the chip had fallen into the well.

I showed Alex the chip and told him how I thought it'd gotten there. "The only way that theory doesn't work is if the car belonged to Tanner."

Alex shook his head. "No way. This thing is so not his style. And besides, he didn't rent this hangar."

No, he hadn't. Niko had. At just about the time Tanner had gone missing. It wasn't proof beyond a reasonable doubt—but it was proof enough for me. And I was sure that if the cops got their hands on this car and started swabbing, they'd find the fibers, hairs—and probably even blood—that *would* be proof beyond a reasonable doubt. I felt sick. "He did it, Alex. Niko killed Tanner."

Alex nodded. "It doesn't look good."

So now I knew. Or at least, I was pretty sure. Was there any way to keep the cops from finding the car? We'd already created a reason for suspicion by breaking the lock, although when we talked about it at the diner, Alex had said he could put it back together well enough so it wouldn't be obvious unless someone really yanked on it. And I couldn't think of a way to dispose of the car without pointing a finger right at Alex and me. Not now that the security guard could identify us. In any case, I had no idea where to put the car that would keep it out of the cops' hands. The ocean? I'd have to find a cliff to drive it off. I didn't know where that might be. A lake? It'd have to be remote enough to be sure no one would see me do it. I didn't know of any lakes that'd fit that bill. No doubt this was why Niko had hidden it here in the first place.

But if we found the car, the cops would, too—eventually. Especially now that the cops were looking hard at Niko. And if they did, they'd probably get enough evidence to convict him. I couldn't possibly wipe down the car well enough to get rid of all the little pieces of hair and fiber and . . . whatever. But I could get rid of one piece. I pocketed the SAA chip.

Alex was staring at me. "We need to get out of here, Sam."

I nodded. "But first, let's take some photos." I wasn't sure what I'd do with them. I just knew I'd regret it if I didn't. Alex and I took photos from every angle, inside and out, including the license plate and VIN. Then we did our best to wipe down the areas we'd touched, crept out, and quietly slid down the door of the hangar. I stood guard while Alex put the padlock back in place. It actually looked pretty good from where I was standing.

Then we hurried back to my car. I didn't stop to think about what I'd just learned until we were rolling down the freeway and Alex asked, "What are you going to do, Sam? Are you going to confront him?"

That queasy feeling came rushing back. "I don't know."

FORTY-SIX

I was filled with questions about the Denali. "I can't see him secretly buying a car and hiding it just in case. He must've already had it." And if he'd had it before he met me and was keeping it in storage somewhere, I wouldn't expect him to tell me about it. He might not even have remembered he had it. Being rich means you can forget things like that.

Alex added, "You mean he already had it when he killed Tanner?" I nodded. "I think you need to slow your roll. You mean *if* he killed Tanner. I'm with you, it looks bad. But Niko might be hiding the Denali for someone else."

The car behind me flashed its brights, distracting me. I looked at my speedometer. I was already doing seventy-five miles per hour. Who was this nutbag? I changed lanes and let him fly by, then processed what Alex had said. "The person who really did kill Tanner." I couldn't keep the note of doubt out of my voice.

Alex tapped my shoulder. "Hey, Skeptismo. Aren't you the one who says keep all possibilities on the table until you can't? Until we know more about that car, we can't rule that one out."

I supposed that was true. "So how do we find out more about that damn car?"

He said, "There is an easy way to do that."

I knew he meant asking Dale. But that would mean sharing the most damning evidence against Niko yet. I trusted Dale, but . . . it made me nervous. "I'll think about it."

"You could call him now." His voice was impatient. "It's after ten o'clock. He's probably home."

I shook my head. "He won't talk about anything on the phone, remember?"

Alex slid down in his seat. "Right. My bad. I forgot about Mr. Paranoia. I just really want this thing to get resolved." He gave me a sidelong glance. "I know you don't care much."

I gripped the steering wheel. I knew he was being sarcastic, but there was a part of me that really didn't want to resolve it. It was a small part. One that was doomed to be overridden at every bend and turn. But still. It was there. I handed Alex my cell phone. "Text him and see if he can get together tomorrow."

Alex began to type. "I'm being you, right?" I nodded. He typed some more. A few minutes later, he said, "Dale wanted to talk to you anyway. He'll come by the office in the morning."

"Perfect. Tell him yes and find out what time." But Alex hesitated. "What?"

"I set us up to talk to Angelina's chef and his team tomorrow," he said.

I didn't want to wait to find out about that Denali any longer than I had to. And besides, I was losing hope on the Eliza front anyway. I was close to deciding that was one mystery I'd never be able to solve. Sadly. "We don't need to do all the interviews together. You can start without me. Take the servers first. I'll catch up with you after I talk to Dale."

Dale texted that he'd be at the office no later than eight thirty a.m. Which meant he'd most likely show up around eight a.m. He was always early. In this case, the acorn fell about ten miles away from the tree. I was always late. But as I dropped Alex at home, I promised that this time, I'd try to be prompt. "And I'm sure whatever Dale has on his mind, it won't take long."

Alex picked up his iPad. "He does get right to the point. You have the chef's address?"

I checked the calendar on my cell phone. "On Melrose Boulevard, close to La Brea?"

He nodded. "And you should keep those tools we bought in your trunk. Especially the flashlights."

I gave him a look of disbelief. "You're kidding, right? As if I'd ever be able to pick a lock. Take them. I'll keep the flashlights. I'm pretty sure I can work those."

I popped the trunk to give him access. Alex sighed and got out of the car. He took the set of picklocks and bolt cutters and slammed the trunk. As I pulled away from the curb, I could feel my energy start to ebb, and my eyes burned from hours of staring at the road. I drove home; took a long, hot shower; and, for the first time in a while, got into my bed. I didn't want to believe Niko was guilty. But the feeling that I was finally closing in on the truth gave me some relief. I hadn't been sure whether it'd be better to know if it meant he was guilty. But now I did. And it was. I needed resolution. Questions don't sit well with me—even if I don't like the answers.

I set my alarm for seven a.m., made sure it said "a.m." and not "p.m."—a mistake I'd made in the past—and fell asleep within seconds.

I woke up relatively refreshed given the fact that I'd only had six hours of sleep. Forty-five minutes later, showered, dressed, made up, and caffeinated, I headed for the office. When I pulled into the parking garage, it was five minutes to eight. I rode the elevator up to my floor feeling victorious. I was sure I'd gotten here before anyone else.

And I had. No one else was there—except Dale, who was waiting outside the door. I fished my key out of my purse. "Thanks for stopping by."

He gave me a little smile. "Thanks for trying to beat me here."

I opened the door. "I don't know what you're talking about." Why did he always have to bust me?

We went to my office and sat on the couch. I said, "I've got a favor to ask. But you go first."

Ordinarily, he'd have made a crack about my always asking him for favors. This time, he didn't. "First of all, I confirmed that it was O'Malley who gave the order for the cops to go bang on Ivan's door. I hear Kingsford wasn't happy about it. For all the reasons you'd think. I had a friend set Ivan straight about that. So I don't think you'll be hearing from him again."

I knew Dale had been in the gang unit back in the day and still had some street, i.e., gangbanger, connections. After the ass kicking Niko had given him, I doubted Ivan would darken my doorway anyway. But threats from another—and equally lethal—source couldn't hurt. "Thanks." I studied his expression. It was grim. "I have a feeling that was the good news."

His gaze was direct. "The white-collar unit checked out Tanner's accounts. There's a fair amount of money still there. From the looks of things, none of them were cleared out."

I was right. It wasn't good news. If Tanner were on the run, he would've taken all the money. But given what I already knew, it didn't come as a shock. It was just another piece of the puzzle that'd fallen into place. "Got it. My turn?" He nodded. "I need you to find out what cars are registered to Niko and run a VIN for me."

Dale raised an eyebrow. "Why?"

This was going to be the hard part. "I can't tell you . . . yet."

He studied me intently. "I don't like doing favors in the blind. And it's annoying that you still think you need to hide things from me."

I didn't blame him. But I'd decided to give the long-shot possibility—that Niko was hiding the car for the real killer—this one chance. But as soon as I closed this loop, I knew I'd have to tell Dale. "It's not like I'm asking for that much. Running a VIN and checking Niko's registrations isn't that big a deal." I met his gaze. "I promise I'll tell you everything. I just need to see the whole picture first." I paused. "Can you please, just this once?"

"You say that as though it's the first time you've asked me to do something for you without telling me why. We both know it isn't." He shifted his gaze to the framed photo of Niko on my desk. "I'm going to cut you some slack because it's your boyfriend."

I interjected. "Ex-boyfriend."

He sighed. "Whatever. But I'm warning you right now. This will be the last time."

"Fine by me," I said. I wasn't planning on getting into bed with any other murder suspects.

Though I guess, as they say, never say never.

FORTY-SEVEN

My mood was bleak as I headed out to join Alex, who was interviewing Chef Moseyev's servers. What little doubt I had left about Tanner's death and Niko's role in it was rapidly fading. But as I navigated through the traffic toward Beverly Boulevard, I found myself getting angrier and angrier at the way Niko had played me—the way he'd acted as though I had no right to suspect him. Yes, I'd taken it further than that. I'd actively investigated him on the down low. But I never would've had to do that if he'd been honest with me to begin with.

By the time I parked under the low-slung building that housed Chef Boris Moseyev's business operations, I was fuming. If I didn't calm down, I'd scare off the servers and blow any shot we had at getting information. I took a few deep breaths and envisioned myself on a sun-drenched beach . . . which only led to thoughts of my fantasy vacation with Niko. I gave up. I'd just have to try and keep it together.

The office was as plain wrap as the building—except for the framed reviews for Chef Boris Moseyev, all of them raves. Among other things, he was touted as "God's gift to the culinary arts" and "one of the most creative, versatile chefs in the business." Those food critics could really gush. I walked up to the receptionist—a young millennial with stretcher ear piercings—and gave him my name.

He snapped his fingers. "Oh right. You're the lawyer." He tilted his head toward the hallway behind him. "Second door on the left." The phone rang, and as he picked it up, I thanked him and moved down the hall.

I knocked softly. "Alex, it's me." I hoped I wasn't interrupting something important.

Alex opened the door. Behind him sat a twentysomething woman in torn jeans and an off-the-shoulder oversize black T-shirt. His expression was one of suppressed frustration, but he kept his voice light. "Hey, Sam. Violet and I were just wrapping up."

The young woman stood up. "Then we're done?"

Alex summoned a tight smile. "We are. Thanks. You can send in the next person."

When the door closed behind her, I said in a low voice, "What's wrong? Are they stonewalling you?"

He blew out a breath. "No. They just don't know anything. All they do is keep the buffet trays filled, freshen the drinks, and mop up the messes. They don't talk to the guests. At all."

That seemed strange. "Why not?"

Alex shrugged. "Beats me. Whatever the reason, no one remembers seeing who left when. One of them saw Eliza leave. He guessed it was around ten o'clock."

Not much, but it helped corroborate the approximate time of the rape. "Did he see her come back?"

"No," Alex said. "And neither did anyone else. They all said they were too busy. Chef apparently is one tough taskmaster."

I pondered that for a moment. There was a knock on the door. Our next server was reporting for duty. "Skip the servers. Let's go straight to the top."

"Moseyev?" Alex asked. I nodded. He went to the door and told the server he could leave. "Are you the last one?" He said he was. Alex thanked him for his time, and the server left.

We went out and asked the receptionist to tell Boris we were ready to talk to him. The receptionist told us to have a seat and gestured to the orange molded plastic chairs that lined the wall. We sat down, and Alex nodded at the chairs as he leaned toward me. "Not all midcentury modern is created equal."

I glanced at them. "Chuck E. Cheese must've had a fire sale."

We had to wait almost twenty-five minutes to get an audience with "God's gift to the culinary arts." Chef Boris Moseyev came out in person, and he was an imposing sight. Well over six feet, a solid rectangle of a body, and a thick head of white hair that looked like the end of a broom. He beckoned to us. "Come to my office."

We followed him down the hall into a medium-size, bare-bones office. There were a few framed photos of him shaking hands with some celebrities I recognized—Ben Affleck, Charlize Theron, Tim Burton— and some I didn't. But other than a laptop that sat on a very messy desk and two wire-frame chairs, the office was virtually unadorned. I guess that made sense. His real office was the kitchen. I introduced Alex and myself. He already knew why we were there, so I got straight to the point—and pursued my hunch. "Do you instruct your servers not to talk to the guests?"

He grunted something that sounded like "yes." In a heavy Russian accent, he said, "I cook for many famous people. I do not want my servers to bother them."

That's what I'd thought. "But you must do a little mingling. You're famous, too." It was true. Also, big egos—because I sensed he had one—always enjoy a little ass kissing.

He spread his hands and sighed. "They always want to shake hands and take . . . how do you say . . . selfies?"

I nodded. "Did any of the guests make an impression on you? We're focusing on a tall man, medium build, dark hair."

He gave me a perplexed look. "This is a description for many men. And I must tell you, I did not spend much time with any of the guests at that party. All of them were the same."

"In what way?" I asked.

He wrinkled his nose as though he'd smelled a dead rat. "Assholes. All of them. Rich, stupid assholes."

I decided I liked Boris Moseyev—chef to the stars. Given his attitude, it seemed very unlikely that we'd get anything useful out of him, but just for fun, I asked, "Were there any assholes in particular who stood out?" I'm a sucker for a great story.

He frowned, then nodded. "One. He treated me like a servant. Told me to make him special drink. Terrible drink, with Prosecco, vodka, and orange. Idiot."

That did sound disgusting. "Do you remember whether he left the party shortly after dinner?"

He shook his head. "He may have. But I was working. Not watching what assholes do."

He was pretty funny. Useless to me. But funny. I was ready to wrap up, but Alex had a question. "Can you describe him?"

Chef Boris pressed his lips together. After a moment, he said, "Tall. Not as tall as me. Only thing I remember is his ring. On this finger." He held up his right pinkie finger. "Very expensive. Big square diamond set in white gold, maybe platinum. Looked very old-style."

Recognition hit me like a frying pan to the face. I recognized that ring. I asked for a piece of paper and pulled a pen out of my purse. I drew as good a facsimile as I could and showed it to Boris. "Did it look like this?" My heart pounded as he peered at my crude drawing.

After a long moment, he said, "Yes. Like that." He looked at me. "You know this man?"

"No, but I think I've seen this ring before. Probably some online consignment store." My tone was deliberately offhand.

We chatted for a few more minutes, learned nothing more, and thanked Boris for his time. I'd played it as cool as I could, but I felt sweat begin to trickle down the back of my neck as Alex walked me to my car. But when I fished out my remote, I saw that Alex was staring at me.

He said, "You do know the man who wore that ring, don't you?"

I nodded, unable to trust my voice. "I need you to do something—and I apologize in advance, because it's risky. I'd ask Dale, but I've pushed him to the limit already."

"Of course. Whatever it is, I'll take care of it." He looked concerned. "You okay?"

I wasn't, but I said, "Yeah. No worries. I need you to hack into the DMV database."

He smiled. "Is that all? Sure, no biggie."

But it was. "Just because you got away with it once doesn't mean you won't get caught this time. And I won't be able to make any more deals for you." Which is why I'd sworn I'd never ask him to do it again.

He gave me a sly look. "Who says it was just once?"

I stared at him. "When did you . . . Never mind, don't tell me." But it was kind of reassuring.

"Does this have to do with the owner of the white Bentley?" he asked.

I nodded. I could barely choke out the name. "Sebastian Cromer."

Alex's face froze. "Oh my God."

"Yeah." Sebastian Cromer, the featured player in my nightmares. My tormentor. And the murderer of my childhood.

It might just be a coincidence. Maybe that ring wasn't one of a kind. But it was distinctive. And I'd recognized it from Boris's description because I'd seen it every night for a year, when Sebastian came into my bedroom.

FORTY-EIGHT

My guts were churning as I drove back to the office, my head filled with *what-ifs*. What if Sebastian owned a white Bentley? What if it turned out to be the car where Eliza had been raped? What if we could prove it was in fact Sebastian who'd raped her?

But those were a lot of *ifs* to resolve. Even if Sebastian did own a white Bentley, how would we prove it was *the* white Bentley? Ken Lorimar hadn't gotten a license plate number. And even if we could prove that was Sebastian's car, how would we prove the man in question was Sebastian and not some guy who'd either broken into the car or gotten Sebastian's key somehow? Eliza couldn't identify anyone.

And yet, it seemed obvious to me that Sebastian was the one who'd raped Eliza. Everything about it was his style. The cruelty, the aggression, and his choice of victim—a young girl. But I knew him. Angelina didn't. And I had no intention of telling her how I knew him.

So the question was, how much proof would Angelina need to activate her hit man? Which brought me to another *what-if*. What if I got enough proof to satisfy me—I was close to being there right now—but it wasn't enough for her?

Then I might just have to kill him myself. Because I wouldn't be able to stand it.

I was a tangled mess of frustration. Too many questions swirling and too much anxiety about the possibility that they might never be answered. By the time I got to the office, I was so stuck in my own world, I didn't even notice that Michy, the phone cradled between her head and her shoulder, was waving to me until she stood up.

She looked at me as she spoke into the phone. "Great timing, Dale. She just walked in."

I hurried into my office and closed the door. This had to be about Niko's car registration. I picked up the phone. "Hey, what's up?"

His voice was tense. "I need to make this fast. Our friend only has the one car you know about. The other one's listed as salvage. According to the record, the last owner totaled it in a major collision. There's no current owner listed."

"No way." I hadn't noticed any damage to the Denali. "Can someone fake that?"

Cars honked in the background. "Why not? You could probably pay someone to fake the paperwork on anything."

In which case, it had to have been someone else's car. I couldn't imagine Niko wanting—or even thinking of getting—fake paperwork to keep his name off a car registration. I couldn't imagine why he would need to. But Tanner? Most definitely. I could easily see him doing something like that. So maybe the Denali belonged to Tanner after all. But that only begged the question: What was Niko doing with it? "Yeah, true. Okay. Thanks, Dale. I owe you one."

There was obvious irritation in his voice as he said, "An explanation, to start with."

I knew that was coming. "Just pick a day and time."

Voices now mixed with the sounds of traffic. "Tomorrow night, my place."

Dale lived out in Porter Ranch. A nice suburban neighborhood, but it'd take me at least an hour to get there. If Alex managed to make some progress, I didn't want to have to leave the office early enough to make it for dinner. "I'm pretty swamped right now. I'll get back to you."

"You'd better. And soon." His tone of voice told me I'd better pony up with the whole story or there'd be hell to pay.

After we ended the call, I leaned back in my chair and closed my eyes. The fact that the Denali was listed as a salvage car with no registered owner—other than the insurance company that'd declared it a total loss—told me it likely had been Tanner's car. It seemed like the kind of thing he'd do. Keep an unregistered car around, just in case. And that would've been a good thing if it were still a possibility that Tanner was on the run. It would explain away the SAA chip and any other trace evidence that showed Tanner had been in the car.

But now, knowing that he hadn't cleared out his accounts, in addition to the fact that his Porsche had been found in a ditch, made it much more likely that he was dead. So the probability that the Denali belonged to Tanner only made matters worse. It would've been a lot easier—and safer—to transport Tanner's body in an SUV, especially one that belonged to him and was right on hand, than to try and stuff it into a regular car.

A car, say, like Niko's Maserati.

I went to the couch and lay down. I had too much crashing in on me at once. There was a soft knock on the door. I half sat up. "Michy?"

She opened the door. "Yeah, and what's his name." I saw that Alex was standing behind her. "He told me about Sebastian."

I motioned for them to come in. "I've got news from Dale on Niko, too."

Michy sat on the couch and put my feet in her lap. Alex turned around one of the chairs in front of my desk and leaned forward as he sat down. "Good or bad?"

I sighed. "Bad."

He shook his head. "You're having one hell of a day. What did Dale say?"

I filled them in. "Tanner has to be dead, and I think he must've told Niko about that Denali at some point. Where he kept it, the fact that it was unregistered."

Michy and Alex were both silent for a long beat. Then Michy said, "But Niko can't be the only one he told about that car."

"She's right," Alex said. "I still think it's possible Niko's hiding the car for someone else."

As they say, anything's possible. The question is, what's most likely? I couldn't think of any other investors who had no alibi, had the skill and strength to kill a healthy young man, and were friendly enough with Tanner to have known about the Denali.

Before I could give voice to those thoughts, Michy said, "And you're assuming the Denali belonged to Tanner. It could've belonged to someone else."

I supposed that was true, too. "Can you think of a better suspect than Niko?"

She shrugged. "I might be able to if I knew all the people Tanner had screwed over. But that list is so long. How could you even find them all?"

I held up my hands. "I give up. You're right. We may never know who did it for sure." I couldn't think about this anymore. "Alex, let me know when you've figured out whether Sebastian owns a white Bentley."

He had a smug smile. "Already did. And he does."

I sat up. "What? How on earth did you hack into the DMV database that fast?"

"I didn't." He opened his iPad and tapped the screen. "I Googled him. Found a photo of him getting out of a white Bentley on his way to a big fund-raiser."

He handed me the iPad. I studied the photo. The sight of Sebastian made my stomach clench. I had to force myself to read the caption.

Sebastian Cromer, Mimi Goldstone, and Joseph Overton attend a star-studded fund-raiser for Greenspace. The date showed it'd been taken just one week ago. I handed the iPad back to Alex. "Nice work. So now, how do we figure out whether that was the car our registered sex offender saw?"

He pulled out his cell phone. "Remember I took pictures when we canvassed Angelina's 'hood?"

Uh-oh. If those damn things actually did wind up being helpful, I'd never hear the end of it. "Sadly, yes. I do."

Alex pursed his lips. "You should be sad. Because you were wrong. I was right to take them." He tapped his phone and spread two fingers apart to enlarge an image, then held it out to me. "See?"

I stared at the photo. "All I see is the roofline of a house."

He pointed to a shiny spot. "That's a surveillance camera on one of the homes on Angelina's street. And it's high enough to take in the spot where the Bentley was parked."

I replayed the memory of our conversations with the neighbors we'd spoken to. "I thought no one had a camera with a range farther than their front porch."

He nodded. "But we only got to talk to about half of them. I found three houses where no one answered the door that have cameras like this."

I was confused. "That's cool, but how's that going to help? They wouldn't answer the door before, so why would they now?"

He put his phone back in his pocket. "I can try and get the IP addresses for those cameras and see if I can hack into their home computers for the date we want. It was only a couple of weeks ago. Most cameras nowadays store the images for a month before they start recording over the footage."

That sounded like a tall order. "You think you can hack into their hard drives?"

He shrugged. "You'd be surprised how many people still use lame passwords—like their street address or birth date."

It was worth a try, I supposed. "May the Force be with you."

FORTY-NINE

After Alex retreated to his office to do his dirty work, Michy patted my foot. "How're you holding up? This is an awful lot to deal with. First Niko, now Sebastian."

Now that I could relax for a bit and let Alex do his thing, I felt my eyelids drooping. "I'm so tired all the time. I can keep the motor running while we're working, but by five o'clock, all I want to do is crawl into bed."

She gave me a worried look. "It's the stress, and probably depression. Honestly, I don't know how you manage to keep going."

I was about to say I didn't have a choice, but I supposed I did. "I think we're close to the end of the line on Eliza's rape. I'll hand over the evidence to Angelina and let her have at Sebastian. And Niko . . . I guess I have as much closure on that case as I'll ever get. I should just let it go."

Michy didn't look convinced. "Then you aren't going to tell him what you found out?"

I'd gone back and forth on that so many times. "Whenever I think about confronting him, I just wind up asking myself, why bother? Nothing good can come of it." He'd get angry with me for investigating him . . . again. And I'd get angry with him for lying to me.

She gave my foot another pat and stood up. "I'm not sure I agree. But obviously, it's your call."

I looked up at her. "Since when has that stopped you from telling me what to do?"

Michy gave me a little smile. "That's fair. Okay, here's my two cents' worth. I think you should tell him everything and see what he says." She moved to the door. "You're right. It could get ugly. Or not. And it's still possible he didn't kill anyone." She paused at the door. "Not that that really matters to you." She left, and I closed my eyes.

I couldn't argue. Michy was right. It was possible Niko hadn't killed anyone. But I had no desire to go through another night like our last one. If he got that upset just because I'd contacted his brother, I could only imagine how bad it'd get when I told him all I'd done since then.

And besides, I was just too damn tired to deal with anything more. I must've drifted off, because when I opened my eyes, I looked through the window and saw that the sun was near the horizon. I pulled out my cell phone. It was almost six thirty. I decided I may as well call it a day. I put on my jacket, got my purse, and walked out to find Michy shutting down her computer. "I'm on my way out, too. Give me a sec to check in with Alex."

I knocked on his door. "Hey, we're taking off. You ready to pull the plug?"

Alex came to the door. "I won't say I miss those bad lines you usually throw at me, but this normal behavior is really getting worrisome."

I could barely make myself smile. "Any progress?"

He looked dejected. "Not so far. I did find one genius who used the word *password* as his password. But it looks like his camera was offline for the past month. I'll keep at it, though. I'm not ready to give up yet."

"Don't push it, Alex. If this doesn't pan out, we'll just have to find another way."

Alex went back to his computer, and Michy and I headed for the elevator. I told her what Alex was working on as we rode down. She shook her head. "Why does he need to hack them?"

The elevator reached the garage, and we walked to our cars. "Because they wouldn't answer the door."

She shrugged. "Maybe I'm just too old-school, but if it were me, I'd give the door knock another chance."

I'd just raised my remote to unlock my car, but now I stopped. "Because they might not have been avoiding us? They just might not have been home?"

She nodded. "Or in the bathroom, or in the shower, or on the phone." She sighed. "You guys always jump to the worst conclusion."

I had to laugh. "But we're usually right, you've got to admit."

She deadpanned me. "No, I don't." Michy got into her car and drove off.

Apparently she didn't have to admit it. On the way home, I thought about whether we'd succeed in getting any of the neighbors who had the long-range cameras to open the door—and if they did, what their footage would show. If it was good enough, I'd be able to make a strong case for Angelina. And then . . . I forced myself to rein it in. Better to not get my hopes up.

As I climbed the stairs to my apartment, I was so preoccupied, I nearly fell on someone who was sitting on the top step. I grabbed the railing to steady myself, and when I saw who it was, I stared in shock. "Niko? What are you doing here?"

He stood up. "I won't blame you if you say no. But can we talk? Please?"

I was struck by how good—and how painful—it was to see him. A part of me wanted to push him down the stairs. But the rest of me wanted to put my arms around him. He obviously had something to tell me. But did I want to hear it? Only if he planned to tell me the truth. I felt pretty confident I'd know if he lied to me. Especially given all I'd learned. And if he did, I could always throw him out. "I guess so."

I walked past him and led him into the apartment. I didn't offer him anything—not even water. I dropped my keys and purse on the kitchen table and gestured to the living room. I sat down on the wing-back chair, deliberately avoiding the couch so I wouldn't have to sit next to him.

Niko sat on the couch and leaned forward, his elbows on his knees, hands clasped. "I owe you an apology. Maybe the most profound apology I'll ever owe to anyone." He stopped and took a deep breath. "I didn't want you to know about my past. It's a terrible embarrassment to me. I'm not that guy anymore. And really, I never was. I thought that if you knew I'd been a gang member, lived that kind of life, you'd never see me the same way again."

This was it? This was what he'd come here to tell me? His past was the least of my issues. If that's all he had to say, it was going to be a very short conversation. "You know what I do for a living. You know how I met Alex. And yet I hired him, and I trust him with my life. Why on earth would you think your past would matter to me? You sure don't give me much credit."

He looked down at his hands. "It's not about you. It's about me. My shame. My disappointment with who I was." He raised his head and met my gaze. "Anyway, I'm only telling you that to explain why I acted . . . the way I did when Ivan showed up. He represents everything I detest, everything I tried so hard to put behind me. Seeing him here, in your place . . . I lost it. I acted like a fool."

I gazed at him coldly. "Okay, thanks for sharing." I started to get up.

He raised his hand. "Wait. Please. I'm not done." I sat back down. He looked me in the eye. "The thing is, I'd been planning to tell you about . . . Tanner. But every time I tried, I got scared. I was afraid I'd lose you." His shoulders slumped. "And now I've lost you anyway. So I'm here because I thought the least I could do is tell you the truth."

Still angry about all the hell he'd put me through, I refused to be moved by his sadness. I braced myself for what he was about to say. "Okay, let's hear it. What about Tanner? And Bryan, while you're at it."

He stared at the floor as he spoke. "I didn't kill Bryan. But I found out that the so-called cryptocurrency trade was just a straight-up scam—that there was no trade, that it was just a heist."

I'd suspected the same thing. "And you think Tanner realized that Bryan was about to take off with all the money?" Niko nodded. I reflected on the way Tanner had behaved when we'd gone to the Gold Strike headquarters. "So that night we went to their office, when Alex found the BYO holding company on Bryan's computer and Tanner acted so freaked out—"

He shook his head. "It was all bullshit. I didn't know it at the time, of course. And I can't prove it, but now I think Tanner set up the holding company and pretended to be all shocked when Alex found it so he could point the finger at Bryan and claim he'd stolen all the money."

I'd have to ask Alex about the feasibility of that. But it sounded plausible enough—for two sociopaths like Tanner and Bryan. I remembered the surveillance video footage showing a man near Bryan's back door. "Then you think Tanner killed Bryan? He was the man in the video?"

He nodded. "It must've been. I know it wasn't me."

That video footage had never been clear enough to say who that man was. But I'd always thought it could've been Tanner.

When Niko continued, his voice was bitter. "It wasn't a bad plan: kill Bryan, frame me by using the internal-decapitation move, and take off with all the money. Of course, I didn't know he'd killed Bryan and framed me when I went to see him that night. I just knew he'd lied and ripped everyone off, and I was furious—"

"So you decided to kill him." Not that I blamed him.

He sat up, his expression anguished. "No! I never meant to kill him. I went to his place to confront him. For some stupid reason, I thought

I could shame him into admitting what he'd done—and that I'd either get him to turn himself in or I'd go to the police and tell them what'd happened." He rubbed his eyes. "Even now, I can't imagine what made me think for one second that would work. The only thing I can say is that I was really messed up."

I guess that *was* all he could say. Because the very idea that someone like Tanner might have enough of a conscience to confess was ludicrous. But was that the truth? Had Niko really just meant to persuade Tanner to confess? I studied him for a long moment. His tortured expression, his woeful tone, his abject misery. My gut told me it was the truth. He'd been too shattered to think clearly. So he'd projected his own morality, his own psyche onto Tanner. Niko knew that if he'd killed someone, he'd have felt compelled to admit it—as he was, in fact, doing right now. And so he'd hoped Tanner would do the same. "Go on."

Niko swallowed hard. "I know I was pretty steamed when I confronted him. And Tanner didn't deny he'd scammed us all. He just . . . he completely lost it. He attacked me, immediately went for my throat. I tried to stop him, kept trying to back away, but he just kept coming at me. I got worried someone would hear the noise and call the police. I tried to get out of there, but when I went for the door, he grabbed me and put an arm around my neck—like a choke hold. I managed to break free. But I knew I'd have to knock him down to get out of there. So I threw a punch, hit him hard right in the chest." Niko paused, his brow furrowed. "I must've hit him in the heart, because he went straight down and just lay there. He wasn't moving. I couldn't believe it. At first, I thought he might be trying to fake me out. But then I saw that he didn't seem to be breathing. I took his pulse and . . . he was dead." He lifted his head, his expression showing he was suffering with the memory. "I didn't mean to kill him. I really didn't. It was an accident. But I knew no one would believe that. I fight for a living."

He glanced at me briefly, then looked away. His shoulders sagged, misery etched in his features. And I could see that he'd lost weight. His face was thin and drawn. A lot of that had to do with his mother. But now I could see that Tanner's death, and lying to me about it, had also been weighing on him.

At first, I'd listened with a healthy dose of skepticism, reluctant to believe almost anything he said after he'd lied to me for so long. But I could picture it all so easily. I'd seen so many homicides go down that way. A stray bullet, a lucky punch, a blind knife thrust. And his tone and body language showed utter sincerity. Had Niko not been a martial arts expert, he'd be in the morgue—and Tanner would be sitting on a pile of cash a thousand miles away.

So I had no doubt. Niko had told me the truth. Finally. And now, I needed to follow suit. I told him about finding the Denali and Tanner's SAA chip in the rear cargo area. "That was Tanner's car, wasn't it?"

There was a look of shock on his face. "How did you figure all that out?"

I shrugged. "It's what I do. Alex and me, that is."

He nodded slowly. "Yes, it was Tanner's car. He'd bragged about scoring an unregistered SUV. I never did know what he'd planned to use it for." He paused. "I think I do now."

To make his escape after he killed Bryan. "But didn't you say he bought it a while ago? You're not saying he planned to kill Bryan all along?"

He spread his hands. "No. I think when he first bought it, he just wanted to have it around—in case. But when he dreamed up that cryptocurrency rip-off, then . . . yes. I think it became part of the plan to take the money and run."

That sounded about right. But now I was curious about the logistics of it all. "Okay. So how'd you get Tanner's body out of the condo and into the Denali without anyone seeing you?"

He took a deep breath. "That was really just luck. I knew he kept the Denali in the condo parking garage. The only thing I could think to do was wait until it was late enough that no one was likely to be around—after two in the morning—then I put his arm around my neck and stood him up next to me so it'd just look like I was helping my drunk friend get home."

So simple—at least for someone as strong as Niko. And since Tanner wasn't bloodied, the story would be believable. "Then you were the one who took his comforter?"

He nodded. "I used it to cover his body after I put it in the Denali. I told the police about it because I knew someone would notice that the blanket on the bed was different. I thought I may as well front it to the police myself." He had a look of resignation. "Other than that, I thought I'd straightened the place up pretty well before I left. But that wineglass, the lamp . . ." He shook his head. "I screwed that up big-time."

Because he really wasn't a killer. And even so, he'd covered his tracks better than most. I had another question. "Why did you get rid of his Porsche? To make it seem like he'd gone on the run?" Niko nodded. "How'd you manage to get it all the way to Arizona?"

"I didn't. I just drove it to a dark street in Koreatown, left the doors unlocked, and let nature take its course."

He hadn't calculated the killing, but he'd done a pretty impressive job of figuring out how to get away with it. "Then you knew Tanner was dead when you told the police that you'd been with him on the night Bryan got killed."

He nodded. "I can't believe the things I did to get away with Tanner's . . . death."

"Guess your gang life came in handy after all." I could see he didn't love that observation—no matter how true it was. "So did you dump the body in Tehachapi?"

He briefly closed his eyes, as though to block out the memory. "No, in Malibu Canyon."

Niko dropped his gaze back down to the floor. I wasn't sure how to feel. I was glad he'd finally told me the truth. But he'd put me through hell. My heart felt bruised, battered. "I wish you'd told me all this to begin with. I get that you were afraid of how I'd react. But you don't have much faith in me."

He jerked up and looked at me with tears in his eyes. "No! Please! I do have faith in you. But don't you see? That's not the point."

It hurt to see him so upset, but that pissed me off. "No? Seems like it to me."

He shook his head. "There's no way to predict how either of us will deal with something as bad as this. I can sit here and tell you all day long that there's nothing you've done or ever will do that will make me feel differently about you. But can you honestly say that you wouldn't still be afraid of how I might react?" He gave me a searching look. "Can you?"

His point flew straight to the center of the bull's-eye. I was a hypocrite. A big, giant hypocrite. Which was pretty much what Michy had said in a gentler—but no less accurate—way. The thought shook me out of my self-righteous anger and hurt. He was right. Would I ever tell him about all that I'd done—or even what I might do in the future? At this moment, I couldn't say that I would. "No. You're right."

Niko's expression was filled with pain. "The real issue is that I was a coward. I never thought I'd hear myself say those words." He paused and blinked back the tears. "I don't expect you to take me back, Sam. I just wanted to tell you that I know I was wrong. That I should've manned up and told you the truth and dealt with the consequences." He swallowed hard. "And that I'm going to turn myself in. I can't live with this." He stood up.

I was stunned. I couldn't believe what he'd just said. I went over to him and grabbed him by the shoulders. "You can't do that!" The thought of him spending the rest of his life in prison—of never being able to be together again—was unbearable. "I . . . I love you."

He put his hands over mine and gazed into my eyes. "I love you, too. But I have to do this, Sam. These past weeks have been torture for me."

I was desperate to find a way to talk him out of this. "Before you go to the police, I need you to just . . . wait. Give me a little time to . . . figure out how to handle this." If I set it up right, I might be able to get the D.A. to let Niko plead to a manslaughter. Given all the circumstances, I might even get a deal for low term—or even probation. Maybe. "I get that you feel you need to pay for this, but you shouldn't have to overpay."

Niko looked uncertain. "I don't know . . ."

I felt a spark of anger. "Listen, Niko. You didn't kill a choirboy. You killed a sociopathic con artist who ruined dozens of people's lives and who put your mother in a coma. Exactly how much penance do you think you have to do for offing a maggot like that?"

A smile briefly tugged at his mouth. "You have such a way with words."

I could see I was fighting a losing battle. But I wasn't about to give up. There had to be a way to get through to him. "And what about your mother? You'll be leaving her all alone. I mean, I'll visit her—and I'm sure her friends will, too. But still . . ."

He sighed. "I wasn't planning to go to the police until she passes. But the doctor says it won't be long now. Maybe a few days at most."

I needed to buy more time. "Just give me a week, okay? That's all I ask."

He stared out the window for a few seconds, then looked down at me. "Okay. A week. But then I'm going to the police."

I nodded, but I couldn't stop the tears from falling. I'd never been more sure that I wanted to spend my life with Niko—or more certain that I wouldn't get the chance.

FIFTY

Niko stayed the night, and though it was wonderful to be back together, it was bittersweet. I tried to savor every moment, aware that there likely wouldn't be many more. But that awareness meant every moment was also tinged with pain. After he fell asleep, I lay awake for hours as I tried to figure out a way to keep him from turning himself in. But I couldn't think of a single thing.

I told myself that my brain would work on it while I slept and that I'd wake up with an idea. That's happened for me many times before. Not this time. When I woke up, all I had was a massive headache—and an empty bed. I stumbled out to the kitchen and found a note on the table.

Had to go to the studio. Call you later. Love, Niko.

I needed to clear my head and figure this out—fast. I showered, dressed, and poured myself a gallon of coffee as I turned over one idea after another. But every one of them basically came down to my begging Niko not to confess. That clearly wasn't going to cut it. And I knew from experience that the more I forced the issue, the harder I tried to find a solution, the more I pushed away any chance at finding it. I needed to give my brain a rest.

And then I remembered that I'd planned to do something today. Something important. What was it? After all that'd happened last night, I'd been thrown off track—to put it mildly. I searched my memory. After a few moments, I remembered what it was.

I looked at the clock on the oven. It was early, just seven thirty. Not to mention a Saturday. But I was sure Alex would be up. And I needed to make something happen. I was feeling stymied by Niko. Taking action—even if it didn't have anything to do with him—would help.

I called, and, sure enough, Alex sounded wide-awake. I told him what Michy had said about the neighbors who hadn't answered the door in Angelina's neighborhood. "They aren't necessarily avoiding us. Why not take another run at them?"

Alex said he hadn't had any luck trying to hack into their hard drives. "Unfortunately, people are getting a little smarter about security. Such a drag. So yeah. Sure. We may as well give it a try."

"Great. I'll be at your place in twenty minutes." I have no patience under the best of circumstances, but now? Forget it.

Alex grumbled about the insane hours on this job, but he said he'd be ready. I filled my travel mug with coffee, though I was already on a jittery caffeine high, and headed for my car.

When I picked Alex up, he noticed I was unusually amped. But I'd decided not to tell anyone about Niko's confession. At least, not yet. And if I persuaded him not to go to the police, then maybe never. So I said, "I went a little overboard on the coffee situation. Also, I'm anxious to see what we get from these neighbors."

He opened his iPad and tapped the screen. "To be honest, I'm not terribly optimistic. Out of the twelve houses where no one answered the door, only five had cameras that looked like they might pick up the area where the Bentley was parked. Not great odds."

They weren't. But I'd take them. "It's better than nothing. And besides, we only need one to come through."

Alex didn't look persuaded, but I couldn't afford to go along with his negativity. I had to keep hope alive, or I'd sink into a depression that would send me to bed for a month.

The traffic wasn't as bad as usual. We made it to Angelina's neighborhood by eight thirty. I just had to hope that the people we needed to see wouldn't be at their kids' early-morning soccer games. As I parked at the end of the block, I felt my stomach tighten. There was so much riding on this. For Angelina and Eliza, and for me. It had to go right.

But no one answered the door at the first two houses. I could feel the anxiety spread from my stomach to my chest. We knocked on the third door. An older, very tanned man in Ralph Lauren jeans, loafers, and a button-down shirt answered the door. He even combed his white hair like Ralph Lauren—with a deep part on the side. His glance slid off me, drifted over to Alex—and stayed there. Our new best friend, the Ralph Lauren wannabe, was probably gay. That meant Alex would do the talking.

Alex introduced us and told him about the young woman who'd been assaulted on the night of the party. "I notice you have a surveillance camera mounted above the door. It might have captured some part of it. Would you mind letting us take a look?"

He gave Alex a warm smile. "Not a bit." He stood back and opened the door wider. "Come on in."

But it turned out the camera had malfunctioned a few days before the rape. Our pseudo Ralph Lauren hadn't known that until he tried to access the footage. He was very apologetic. To Alex. "I'm so sorry. I wish I could help you out."

I had a feeling help wasn't the only thing he wished he could give. But as we thanked him, I found myself taking shallow breaths. We only had two more houses left. No one answered the door at the next house, and when I peeked through the transom, it looked empty.

As we headed up the walkway of the last house, I wiped my sweaty palms on my thighs. I knocked on the door. If this one didn't pan out, I wasn't sure what I'd do. I didn't have a Plan B. Ten seconds passed. Then twenty.

Alex started to turn toward the street. "Sorry, Sam. I guess—"

But at that moment, the door opened. A young woman who looked very businesslike in a pinstriped skirt suit asked, "Can I help you?"

I forced a smile. "I sure hope so." I made the introductions and told her about the assault. "It's possible your surveillance camera picked up something. Would it be okay if we took a look at the footage for that night?"

She frowned. "I was home that night. I'm pretty sure I would've heard something if it'd happened close enough to be within range of my camera . . ." She trailed off, her expression uncertain as her gaze shifted between Alex and me. I tried to send her calm, reassuring, we're-not-serial-killer vibes. Finally, she said, "But I'd like to help. So come on in." As she led us to her computer, she said, "I don't have a lot of time. I've got a meeting with a client."

I promised her we'd be fast—or rather, Alex would. She'd forgotten how to access her footage, but Alex knew how, and he gave her a quick tutorial as he searched for the night in question. When he found it and hit play, I held my breath. The picture was grainy and distorted, and it took a good fifteen minutes, but as I stared at the monitor, I saw a white Bentley pull up and park at the curb at the very edge of the screen. The camera had just barely picked it up.

I stared at the screen so hard, my eyes watered as the driver of the Bentley straightened the car into position against the curb. The seconds felt like hours as I waited to see who would get out of the car. At last, the driver's-side door opened, and a man stepped out. As he stood up and locked the door, I took in every detail I could. He was tall, over six feet, medium build. And he was dressed in jeans and a V-neck sweater. Was it him? Was it Sebastian? It *could* be. But it might not be. The picture wasn't clear enough to tell.

He moved away from the car and out of camera range. Alex fast-forwarded to a few minutes before ten p.m. I folded my arms across my stomach and clutched my elbows. This was it. If Ken Lorimar had told the truth, we'd see the man drag Eliza into the Bentley.

But the screen suddenly went black. I almost groaned out loud. "What happened?"

Alex tapped a few keys, then hit play again. The time code at the bottom showed that it was now after eleven p.m. "Did you have a power outage?"

The young woman stared off for a moment. "Oh yeah. We did. I forgot. I think it was a fuse? Something like that." She couldn't miss the anguish in my expression. "I'm so sorry." She looked at her watch and sighed. "I've really got to leave."

I couldn't speak; all I could do was nod. But Alex had more presence of mind. "Would it be okay if we copied some of that footage?"

She looked worried. "How long will it take?"

Alex said, "Two seconds. Three tops." She nodded, and his fingers flew over the keyboard. A few seconds later, he stood up. We thanked her for her time. We'd gotten what I'd hoped and prayed for. Maybe.

As we headed back to the car, I tried to manage my disappointment. We didn't get the image of the assault I'd hoped for, but we did get a shot of the Bentley and the driver. The question was whether the shot was good enough. "Can you enhance the footage at all?"

"I'll try," he said. "But you saw how bad it is. And how far away."

This footage could make or break the whole case. If Alex couldn't do some major improvements, I'd be back at square one.

We got into the car, and I drove to the freeway. I merged and steered into the fast lane. Alex gripped the dashboard. "Would you slow down? You're driving like a maniac."

"No, I'm not." I looked at the speedometer, thinking it'd show I was doing sixty-five, maybe seventy miles per hour. I was doing eighty-five. I eased up on the gas. I had to get a grip. But I was dying to see what Alex could do to that footage. On the way back to the office, I called and told Michy that her idea of trying the door knocking again had paid off and what we'd found—or rather, what we hoped we'd found. She barely let me finish before saying, "I've got to see this. I'm coming in."

Michy was already at her desk when we got in. I waved to her and followed Alex to his office. He stopped in the doorway and gave an exasperated sigh. "It won't help to have you breathing down my neck."

"Are you kidding?" I gave him an incredulous look. "Of course it will."

Alex threw up his hands. "Sure. Why not invite your mother, father, and pet iguana, too?" He pointed to us and gave us the evil eye. "No one says a word until I'm done."

I pretended to zip my lips, and we all trooped into Alex's office. I sat on the edge of my seat across the desk from Alex, and Michy sat next to me.

But ten minutes later, the office phone rang. "Tell me when he's done." She ran to take the call.

It was another half an hour before Alex sat back in his chair and said, "I'm done." He turned the monitor around. "Have a look."

I leaned forward and stared at the screen. Alex had grabbed still shots of the car and the best shot the camera had gotten of the driver. I focused on the photo of the driver. It wasn't great. If I'd had to use it in court, it would've been a problem. But it was good enough for me. "That definitely looks like Sebastian."

Alex nodded. "I know it is." He pointed to the still shot of the car and enlarged the image. "See the license plate?"

I peered at the screen again. "Yeah." I looked at Alex. "It's his?"

"It is," he said.

I looked at him with gratitude. And relief. "Nice work, Alex."

He gave me a smug smile. "I know. You going to take it to Angelina?"

A frisson of excitement ran through me. "I am."

And Angelina would take it to the man—or woman—who'd end Sebastian. I'd dreamed of this day for so many years. The day I'd finally see him dead.

I could already feel the gaping wound in my psyche begin to heal. I left Alex's office with a smile.

FIFTY-ONE

I called Angelina and told her I had good news. "But I need to tell you about it in person. And Eliza should hear it, too. Can I meet with the two of you this evening?" It was already after four p.m., and the Saturday night traffic was in full swing. I wouldn't be able to make it back to her neighborhood before five thirty at the earliest.

There was a long pause before she answered. "Does it have to be tonight?"

I was taken aback. People don't usually put off hearing good news. "Yes, it really does." I didn't want to wait a second longer to put a bullet in Sebastian's head.

Angelina sounded annoyed. "I have a dinner party in Bel Air, and I have to be there by eight o'clock."

I assured her it wouldn't take long. "How does six thirty sound?"

She reluctantly agreed, and we ended the call, but I was perplexed by her cavalier attitude. She'd given me the impression that finding Eliza's rapist was an urgent matter. Now, it seemed to be about as urgent as getting a teeth cleaning. But then again, she didn't know what "good news" meant. For all she knew, it might only mean that I had a new lead.

When I told Michy about the phone call, she agreed. "I'd bet she doesn't want to get her hopes up. I know I wouldn't." She looked up at me with a smile. "You're practically floating on air. I can't imagine what this must mean to you."

I could barely wrap my arms around the enormity of it myself. "It feels incredible."

She grew more pensive. "And you don't know what Angelina's going to do with the information?"

"She didn't exactly say." But I had a pretty good idea.

Michy gave me a shrewd look. "Whatever it is, I'm guessing we'll all be okay with it."

I shrugged. "I definitely have a preference."

She nodded. "I don't blame you."

I went back to my office to kill some time until we could leave for Angelina's. For the better part of an hour, I tried to read the latest published opinions in California, but I couldn't concentrate worth a damn. I decided it wouldn't hurt to leave a little early and shut down the computer.

I found Alex sitting on the secretary chair next to Michy's desk. He asked, "Want me to go with you?"

I waved him off. "No need. I've put you through enough the past few days. Go home and let Paul cook you something fantastic."

He raised his arms over his head and stretched. "I am pretty beat. Okay, have fun."

I turned to Michy. "And you too. Get out of here. Save what's left of your weekend."

She nodded. "Okay, but call me later. I want to hear all the deets."

"Will do." I sailed out the door on a cloud.

I got to Angelina's house fifteen minutes early. I hate when people show up early at my place, so I waited in the car and imagined how she and Eliza would react when I gave them the news.

At six thirty on the nose, I walked up to the wooden gate and pressed the intercom button. A voice I recognized as Angelina's responded. "Who's there?"

"It's Sam," I replied. A second later, there was a buzz. I pushed open the gate and moved up the walkway. Angelina came to the door, cigarette in hand, dressed in skintight jeans and another one of her exotic kimonos and motioned for me to follow her inside.

She led me to the living room, and I saw that Eliza was already there, seated on the couch. She gave me an apprehensive smile. "Angelina said you have good news. We're not sure what that means exactly."

Michy had guessed right. I sat down next to her and nodded. I waited as Angelina pulled a furry white ottoman closer to us and sat down. "I think we've found the man who attacked you." I opened the folder that held the still photos of the driver and the white Bentley and showed them to Eliza. "I know you never got to see him, but could this be the man who assaulted you?"

Eliza stared at it for a long moment. "I think so . . . He seems like the right size."

I pointed to the Bentley. "And could this be the car where it happened?"

She took another long beat. "It could be, yeah."

I showed the photos to Angelina. "Do you know who this is?"

Her expression was icy cold as she stared at them. "I do not know him. But I know who he is. He was at the party that night."

Eliza looked from me to Angelina, her expression anxious. "So now what?" Her voice rose with tension. "I don't have to go to court, do I? You promised I wouldn't!"

Angelina shook her head. "No, you will not go to court. But Samantha and I have to talk now. Why don't you go watch television?"

Eliza looked relieved as she stood up. "Can I watch the one in your bedroom?"

Angelina waved her cigarette toward the second floor. "Of course, but close the door."

Eliza turned to me. "Thank you, Sam. I'm really glad you found him." But as she headed for the stairs, I wasn't sure she meant it. Now that I'd found the rapist, there was a real possibility that someone might decide it was time to file a police report—and that was clearly something she didn't want to do.

When I heard the upstairs door close, I faced Angelina. "I can tell you where to find him. Or would you prefer that I talk directly to your . . . ah, connection?"

Angelina's expression hardened. When she spoke, her voice was cold, bitter. "My connection just got deported. Right now, I don't have anyone else."

My heart began to pound. "Are you kidding?" I couldn't believe it. My soaring spirits abruptly came crashing down. "Can't you find someone else?" She struck me as someone who had the kind of tentacles that could reach as low as they come.

She angrily flicked her cigarette ash on the floor. "It's not as easy as you think. I have to find someone who knows how to . . . take out the garbage and will not cause me . . . problems later."

Problems—meaning blackmail. She needed someone who could be trusted. I got that. Still, there was another option. "Look, I get that Eliza doesn't want to testify. But she might not have to. He might make a deal." I knew, though, that it was unlikely. Pedophiles very seldom want to admit what they are. But I just couldn't bear the thought that Sebastian would get away with it . . . *again.*

Angelina set her jaw. "I want him to be punished just as much as you do. But I cannot let her testify."

Not only because Eliza didn't want to but because that would expose too much about Angelina's life. I was furious. "So you're just going to let this monster go free? How could you?"

She stood up. "I will take care of this. But not until I find the right person."

I knew I was being dismissed. "And who knows when that will be? Maybe never, right?"

Angelina drilled me with an icy dagger. "It will be when it will be. If that's never, then it's never. Eliza is my sister, not yours. If I can live with it, so can you." She turned and headed for the stairs. "You must leave now. I have to get ready."

I stood there, unable to move, my body shaking with fury. A thousand ugly retorts came to mind, but none of them would do me any good. As Angelina disappeared up the stairs, I noticed a solid-looking hand-painted vase on a nearby side table. It was all I could do to keep myself from picking it up and throwing it at the wall. I hurried out of the house before I could lose my battle with temptation.

When I got into the car, I pounded on the steering wheel as tears of frustration and anger coursed down my cheeks. That evil motherfucker walked away again, and I was powerless to stop him. This could not be happening! Not again!

And on top of that, a wonderful man like Niko was about to go to prison. Maybe for life. I gritted my teeth. Nothing about this was right.

I wasn't sure why, but I needed to drive to Sebastian's house—as I had on a few other occasions over the years. The last time, though, a neighbor had reported my car as a suspicious vehicle. Luckily, Dale had intercepted the call and came to warn me. He'd told me to stop, that we'd find a way to get Sebastian, but lurking around his house like this would only get me in trouble.

The thing is, that was more than a year ago, and we still hadn't found a way. And now, when I finally thought I had, he'd won . . . *again*. I pulled to the curb across the street from his mansion and peered through the gates. I'd been sitting there for half an hour when a slender blonde woman dressed in a black jersey dress I recognized as a Prada design came out and headed for a black Tesla that was parked in the gargantuan circular driveway. She looked like the type who'd be his latest wife, i.e., pretty enough to be a trophy and narcissistic enough not to care what he did to little girls. Basically, a high-class beard.

I supposed it wasn't fair to assume she knew that he was a violent pedophile. If she didn't have any young daughters to serve up to him on a silver platter like my mother had, she might not know. I was just sick to death of hearing the stories about the ridiculously clueless wife, who managed to live with a despicable predator and have no idea about what was going on in the basement / attic / storage closet. And regardless of what she might or might not know, I had a hard time believing that any halfway decent human being would want anything to do with a soulless monster like Sebastian.

I wrote down her license plate as she drove off just for the hell of it. I wondered whether Sebastian was still at home or if she'd gone off to meet him somewhere. I decided to wait and see if he emerged. After twenty-five minutes with no action, I'd decided to pull the plug when I saw an older-model red Mercedes minivan pull into view. It must've been parked farther back, where the trees and shrubbery blocked the view. That wasn't Sebastian's kind of car. As the gates opened, I spotted the license plate and wrote down the number. Then I noticed that the driver was an older Hispanic woman. Probably his housekeeper. I glanced at my dashboard. It was eight o'clock. Either she started late or she kept really long hours.

I waited for another half hour, but no one came or went. I drove home, thinking about that housekeeper. I wasn't sure why. Maybe it was just something to do to keep me from going crazy. But it gave me a thread to pull—albeit a seemingly useless one. I called Alex from the car and told him what'd happened with Angelina.

He was almost as enraged as I was. "So that's it? Nothing happens to him? He just walks?"

I commiserated with him for most of the drive home. But when we'd beaten the subject to death, I thought of something for him to do.

"Can you do me a favor? I need Dale to run a couple of license plates for me. But I might've leaned on him a little too much lately. He'll probably feel more inclined to do it if you ask."

He harrumphed. "I'm not sure you're right about that. But why? What's this for?"

"Honestly, I'm not sure."

And that was the truth.

FIFTY-TWO

I drove home with two thoughts circling endlessly in my brain: How to get Sebastian. How to stop Niko from turning himself in. And they continued to run through my brain nonstop as I picked up dinner at my favorite drive-through, Taco Bell; got home; ate my tacos and quesadilla; showered; and got into bed. And as I turned off the light, I fully expected to dream about them in some form. That kind of obsession was standard operating procedure for me. It's one of those traits that's both a blessing—it makes me a good problem solver—and a curse—it drives me and everyone around me crazy.

So I fully expected my usual nightmare featuring the odious beast on two feet, AKA Sebastian, to destroy what little sleep I might manage to eke out. Oddly, it didn't. But that was probably because I spent most of the night wide-awake, trying to figure out how to answer those two questions—and all of Sunday, too. I did my chores in a fog of distraction as I worked through every possible angle. But I had no inspiration, and the prayer that my sleeping brain would turn up answers that night went unanswered. To add insult to injury, I slept even less than I had the night before.

When dawn finally broke and freed me from the obligation of even pretending to sleep, I was relieved. I jumped out of bed, already wired and ready for action. It's the upside of my obsessiveness. I can't sleep, but I also don't need to. Which should've made me cut back on my coffee habit and limit myself to three or four cups. It didn't.

By the time I got into my car, I was so amped, I could've flown to the office on my own. And now, the only thing I wanted to do was stake out Sebastian's house. What I thought I'd accomplish by doing that, I didn't know. I guess it was just the need to feel like I was taking action—and any action would do.

When I got in at eight thirty, Alex emerged from his office. I asked, "Did you reach out to Dale?"

"Reached out and got an answer," he said.

I never could've gotten Dale to do it that easily. "See? I told you he'd be nicer to you."

Alex gave a little smirk. "Honestly? I think he only did it for me to piss you off."

That sounded about right. "So what'd he get on those license plates?"

Alex motioned for me to come into his office. He walked around behind his desk and fired up his computer, then tapped a couple of keys. "The Tesla belongs to Marjorie Gorsuch, age thirty-nine, registered address 708 Ledo Way in Bel Air." Alex looked over his monitor at me. "Sebastian's place, right?"

I nodded. Marjorie still used her maiden name, so maybe they weren't married. He'd probably wised up and stopped marrying his beards. "What about the old Mercedes minivan?"

Alex scrolled for a moment. "That one's registered to Sebastian, his address."

He'd probably bought that car for the housekeeper. Knowing him, that meant she was a live-in. He wouldn't take the chance that she'd drive it to her house every day and maybe get in a wreck. But why would he need a live-in for just him and Marjorie? I had an awful thought. "Can you find out who that housekeeper is, and whether either of them has children?"

Alex nodded as he began to type. "Just give me a minute."

I sat down in front of his desk. He shot me a look of irritation. I said, "I won't bother you." I held up my phone. "I'll just sit here quietly and go through my emails."

His expression was skeptical, but he went back to typing. Half an hour later, he sat back. "As far as I can tell, Marjorie has no kids. The housekeeper—Theresa Gomez—her children are all grown and on their own."

So there were no children living in the house. Thank God. "Great. Thanks, Alex." I stood up to go.

"Mind telling me why you're investigating Sebastian's female occupants?" he asked.

I paused. "I'm not really looking into them. I'm just . . . looking." For something, anything.

Alex gave a nod of understanding. "I feel the same way. It's just so wrong that we can't get him. You don't think Angelina will ever come through?"

I raised my palms. "Who knows? She might. But right now, it doesn't look good."

Alex's face fell. "Is there anything we can do?"

I sighed. "Working on it. But I'm open to any and all—and I do mean all—suggestions."

I headed out to the reception area and saw that Michy was going through my time sheets. I'd called her last night right after I'd spoken to Alex and given her the bad news about Angelina. When she saw me, she gave me a despondent look. "I was up all night thinking about that asshole. Makes me wish I knew some hit men of my own."

It was a miserable day at the office for all of us. "No you don't. They're a really bad liability." Hit men usually wound up getting busted for something, because most killers for hire aren't the brightest bulbs in the chandelier. And once they did, they grabbed on to anything they could find to make a deal. The name of the person who hired them would be top of mind.

I went into my office and did my best to focus on work, but my mind kept wandering back to the same two questions: How could I get Sebastian? And how could I stop Niko from turning himself in? I forced myself to stay at my desk, but by three o'clock, I had to concede it was a losing battle.

I picked up my purse and walked out to Michy's desk. "I'm useless. I think I need to get out and clear my head."

"I don't blame you," she said. "I'll probably be able to get these bills out by five o'clock. Mind if I pack it in then?"

I could see she was almost as depressed as I was. "Sure, no problem." I headed for the door. "I'll call you later."

I'd intended to do some errands, a little grocery shopping, then go home and make myself a healthy dinner for a change. But instead, I found myself driving down Sunset toward Bel Air. I pulled over and parked. What on earth was I doing? I had no plans, no ideas, no reason to think anything would come of staking out Sebastian's place. Except maybe getting myself busted for loitering. But it was the only thing I could think of to do, and I needed to do *something*. I decided it was pointless to resist. I pulled out into traffic and continued on to Sebastian's mansion.

This time, I made sure to drive to a spot a little farther away and parked under a tree with low-hanging branches. I sat there until almost eight p.m., when sheer fatigue and hunger forced me to pack it in. But as I drove away, I made a decision—to stop pretending I'd be able to do anything else for the next four days, the deadline Niko had given me.

I'd been hoping he might extend it. We hadn't been able to see each other since our last night together, because now he was basically living at the hospital. But we'd been in phone contact, and during our last call,

Niko told me that Sophia was declining fast. The doctors said it could happen any minute now. And if she passed before my week was up, he wasn't sure he'd be able to wait. He wanted to go to the police and get it over with. My deadline might actually get moved up.

That's why my decision to go all out, drop everything else, and focus on my surveillance was my only choice. There wasn't much hope it'd yield anything. But at least I'd know I went down swinging.

I spent the next three days staking out Sebastian's mansion. I'd get there at eight a.m. and stay until eight or nine p.m. I was careful to pick different parking spaces and drive to the nearest intersection every few hours in case any of the neighbors decided to look out their window and noticed me hanging around. But after all that time, all I'd learned was that Theresa left the house for a few hours in the afternoon two of the three days, that Marjorie did a lot of lunches and dinners and had an extensive designer wardrobe, and that surveillance is hell on your stomach and bladder.

By the third day, I was feeling desperate. Something had to give. So this time, when Theresa left the house at three thirty, I decided to follow her. I'd worried that I might miss something or that maybe I should wait and follow Marjorie. But given what I'd seen of her, I doubted she'd lead me to anything more useful than a pricey place to shop or have lunch.

When Theresa pulled out through the gates, I waited for her to get to the intersection, then began to follow her at a discreet distance. I noticed that she sat low in the driver's seat, which meant she was short. That was good. It'd be harder for her to look at the rearview mirror.

Theresa headed west on Sunset Boulevard, then took the 405 Freeway south. She was a nervous driver who liked the slow lane. Also good. It was a lot easier to hang back and follow a slow driver than to have to weave through traffic to keep up with a fast one. She took the 405 to the 10 Freeway west all the way to the Pacific Coast Highway. I figured she must be heading to Malibu.

But after twenty minutes, she turned left onto Malibu Canyon Road and headed away from the beach. She was either on her way to a place in the canyon or somewhere on the other side—like Calabasas or Hidden Hills or . . . There were a lot of possible options. As I followed her into the canyon, I began to get nervous. It was a one-lane road. If she'd noticed me behind her before and saw me now, she might figure out I was following her. But I couldn't afford to hang back and let someone else get in front of me. There were a lot of winding streets on the north end of the canyon. If she turned onto one of those and there was even one car between us, I'd lose her for sure.

I gripped the steering wheel and tried not to imagine what might happen if she spotted me and called Sebastian. He had a lot of connections—many of them in high places in the LAPD. And I was doing exactly what Dale had warned me against: giving Sebastian the rope he'd happily use to hang me. I was starting to think I'd taken a big risk that had very little chance of reward when Theresa put on her right turn signal. I glanced in that direction and saw that the road she was about to turn onto led to a huge vineyard that covered the entire hill—except for the very top, where there was a beautiful lodge-style house surrounded by gardens. The sign at the bottom of the hill said CORRELO VINEYARD. A sign below it said NOT OPEN TO THE PUBLIC.

I'd reached the end of my travels with Theresa. As she drove up the hill, I continued for another mile down Malibu Canyon Road, then pulled over. I Googled the vineyard. As I'd suspected, Sebastian owned it. He probably used that mega lodge for his staycations.

I looked out at the pastoral setting around me. A family of mule deer was grazing in a field on the left. Above me, a red-tailed hawk gracefully rode the air currents—a lovely thing to watch if you forgot it was hunting little furry things like bunnies. I felt my body wind down from the adrenaline high of the past few days and leaned back as I closed my eyes.

Seconds later, I bolted up in my seat. Maybe it was because I'd finally let my brain relax. Or maybe that hawk had inspired me. But I had an idea. Okay, correction. A crazy, risky idea. Still, it was better than nothing. Maybe. I picked up my cell phone and called Alex.

"So you're alive," he said. "How many masseuses have you driven crazy?"

I'd told him and Michy that I was taking a few days off to chill out. I wanted to give them plausible deniability if my surveillance efforts landed me in jail. "Only three. Today. I have a question. That Mercedes minivan, does it have GPS?"

"Hang on, let me check." The sound of rapid typing came over the line. "It was a 2004 ML350, right?"

I know zero point zero things about cars. Once we get past the color, I'm out. "You're asking *me*?"

"No, you're right," he said. "That'd be ridiculous. Yeah, that's the model. And no, it doesn't have GPS."

So far, so good. "Okay, thanks." There was just one more thing I needed him to do, and I needed it fast.

When I told him what it was, he said, "I can have that for you in an hour—two max. But can I just ask, what's the name of that spa you're at?"

I heard the suspicion in his voice. "Okay, thanks."

I ended the call. He'd be even more suspicious now. But better suspicious than provably complicit. If I wound up taking the fall for what I was about to do, I had to make sure I didn't take anyone down with me.

FIFTY-THREE

Knowing that the Mercedes minivan didn't have GPS was a crucial first step. Now, all I could do was hope Alex could deliver on the last task I'd given him.

As I drove down Malibu Canyon Road and headed for the freeway, I tried not to think about how it would shred my plan if he gave me the wrong answer. I turned on the radio and tried to distract myself with a podcast, but I couldn't keep my mind from wandering back to the problem. I played *Kind of Blue* by Miles Davis, but that didn't help, either. Finally, as I was getting off the freeway at Laurel Canyon, Alex called me back. When he gave me the answer, I let out a "Booyah!"

He sounded worried as he said, "Sam, what're you up to?"

"Nothing. Forget I asked you. Please." I wished I hadn't needed his help. But I could take it from here.

I ended the call and thought about what I needed to get now. That was a problem. I noticed my gas tank was near empty. I pulled into the Mobil gas station. As I filled up, I tried to figure out how to solve it. When I got back in my car, I sat there and racked my brain. My plan had a lot of critical junctures, and it'd crash and burn if any one of them didn't work out. Had I already hit an impassable roadblock? I stared out the windshield. Suddenly, a man with a heavy Russian accent honked at me and yelled, "Get out of the way! What are you doing?"

Yanked out of my reverie, I realized I was still parked at the pump. And then it hit me. That angry Russian had just given me the answer. I waved to him, yelled, "Thank you," enjoyed the confused expression on his face, and pulled out onto Laurel Canyon Boulevard. I picked up my cell phone and placed a call. "Hey, Angelina, I have to ask you a favor. And it has to stay just between us."

She was hesitant. "What is it?"

I took a page out of Dale's book. "I can't tell you on the phone. But I think you're not going to mind helping me out."

She told me she'd be home for another hour, and I said I'd be there in half that time. But her tone had been suspicious. When I got to her house, she glanced up and down the street before letting me in.

This time, she told me to follow her upstairs. "You will have to talk while I get ready."

"No problem." She looked ready to me. Perfectly made up, hair carefully tousled, and dressed in black leather leggings and a sheer, flowing chiffon blouse. But what do I know about these things? I was lucky if I remembered to zip up my jeans. When we got to her bedroom, I told her what I needed.

She gave me a puzzled look, but she said, "I think there is something here."

She gestured for me to follow her, and we went to a guest bedroom. It was spare but tastefully decorated with a view of the hills behind the house. She paused with a finger to her lips, then led me to the en suite bathroom. She pulled out the drawers on either side of the vanity.

And there it was. Exactly what I needed. I asked Angelina for a pair of tweezers and a paper bag. "A grocery bag will work."

She thought for a moment, then left the room. When she returned, she had a Barneys shopping bag in her hand. "This is all I have."

Of course it was. Barneys was only one of the most high-end retailers in the country. "That's perfect, thanks."

As I used the tweezers to put the items into the bag, she stood and watched, arms folded. "Why do you need these things?"

I folded over the top of the bag to seal it. "It's better if I don't tell you." Though I knew she'd figure it out very soon if everything worked as I hoped it would. Involving her was a risk, but a necessary one. All I could say was, I felt as confident as one can, in a situation like this, that she'd keep my secret.

She asked if I needed anything else. "I must finish getting ready now."

"Not a problem," I said. "I'm all set. And thank you." She waved me off with an impatient gesture and led me out of the room. I stopped in the hallway. "I can see myself out, save you some time."

"Good." She headed for her bedroom, and I headed to my car.

I was elated as I drove home. Tomorrow, the plan would be set in motion. Then there'd be nothing to do but wait—and hope it all fell into place. But as I unlocked the door to my apartment, my cell phone rang. It was Niko. My heart gave a hard thump. I dropped my purse and keys on the kitchen table and tried to keep my voice steady. "Hi, Niko. How's it going?"

He spoke softly. "Th-the doctor said she's not going to make it through the night."

I could hear the tears under his words. "I'm on my way."

I picked up my purse and keys and headed to my car. I was filled with conflicting emotions: heartbroken for Niko and panicked that he wouldn't give me any more time before turning himself in. But I only needed one more day. He had to let me have it.

I found him sitting next to Sophia's bed, holding her hand, his head bent. I went over to him and squeezed his shoulder as I searched for the right words to say. But all I could come up with was, "I'm so sorry." I couldn't say that I knew what he was feeling, because I definitely didn't. Then again, does anyone really know how another person feels—particularly about a loss like this?

He leaned his head to the side and laid it on my hand. "Thanks for coming, Sam."

I pulled up a chair and sat next to him. I did what I could for him—which wasn't much. Brought him water, rubbed his back, and listened with sympathy when he shared memories of happier days with Sophia. But for the most part, we sat in silence as we waited for the inevitable to happen.

We'd both grown drowsy as the hours passed, but suddenly, one of the many machines hooked up to Sophia began to make a loud beeping sound. As we startled awake, doctors and nurses ran in and pushed us away. They worked feverishly, but within minutes, I heard the long, unbroken signal that warned the patient was flatlining. They kept working for a few minutes more, but finally, they stopped. I heard one of the doctors announce the time of death. Sophia was gone.

Niko collapsed into my arms and wept while the nurses performed the postmortem rituals. As I held him, I thought about the despicable, self-dealing minions from hell who'd ended Sophia's life and brought Niko so much pain. And who'd both so richly deserved to die.

I helped with the paperwork and made the arrangements to send her body to the crematorium he'd picked out. It was late—past midnight—by the time we left the hospital. Our footsteps echoed loudly in the empty corridors. When we got into the elevator, I asked where he wanted to spend the night—my place or his. "But if you'd rather be alone, I'll totally understand."

He put his arms around me and laid his cheek on my head. "No, I need to be with you. Do you mind staying at my place? I'd like to spend one last night there with you."

I pulled back and shook my head. "I'm not letting you turn yourself in."

His expression was kind but determined. "Sam, this isn't really up for discussion." He pulled out his cell phone. "I took an Uber here. You can ride with me. I'll take you back to your place tomorrow, okay?"

The finality in his voice made it clear that I needed to do something drastic to change his mind. But what? I needed some time to think. "Actually, I need to stop at my place and pick up a change of clothes."

He nodded and walked me to my car. I told him it wouldn't take me long. But I drove home as slowly as I could to give myself time to think of a way to talk him out of going to the police. When I got to my apartment, I threw clothes into my duffel bag at random, barely seeing what I was packing. But no matter how hard I tried, I couldn't think of the right words to say, the winning argument that would change Niko's mind. Maybe because I couldn't understand why Niko was so hell-bent on confessing when the so-called victim was such a waste of flesh.

And that, I supposed, was the fundamental difference between us. I suffered zero pangs of guilt for disposing of trash. Niko ascribed to a much higher moral code. I didn't know how to persuade that kind of person that he shouldn't get punished for killing someone.

The answer continued to elude me as I threw my duffel bag into the trunk and headed for Niko's house. But finally, as I was pulling into the driveway, the answer came to me. I knew what I had to do, and I hated it. On top of that, I was going to hate myself for doing it. It went against my every instinct. And I couldn't even be sure it would work. But it was the only way I could think of that stood even a slim chance of success.

I wouldn't do it tonight. Not after all he'd been through. And all I needed was one more day. I felt sure I could buy myself that much time.

But that'd probably be all Niko would give me. I was miserable as I pulled my duffel bag out of the trunk and headed for the door.

Tomorrow, I was going to have to tell Niko the truth.

It was a long, tear-filled night, but eventually, sheer exhaustion forced us to sleep.

I woke up at a little past five a.m. the next morning—by design. I had a lot to do, and I wanted to get going before Niko could wake up and start asking questions.

I picked up my clothes, tiptoed out, and dressed in the powder room. As I stepped out of the house, I closed the door as quietly as I could. I winced at the beep as I hit my remote to unlock the car. I took a quick look back to make sure Niko hadn't woken up, then slipped into the driver's seat, put the car in neutral, and coasted down to the street. After one more glance in the rearview mirror to make sure the coast was clear, I fired up the engine and took off.

As I drove, I steeled myself for what was coming. The next few hours were going to be a waiting game, and waiting was not a strength for me. After that, it'd all be a matter of luck and timing. When I arrived at my destination, I plugged in my earbuds and listened to a podcast. And then another. And then another. I was starting to get worried.

But by noon, my quarry had emerged. Now things were going to move quickly. I put my car in drive and took slow, deep breaths to calm myself as I pulled away from the curb.

It was on.

FIFTY-FOUR

I watched Theresa drive through the gates and waited until she'd made it halfway to the intersection before following her down the street. I had to be careful. If she spotted me now, my whole plan would go up in smoke. But if I hung back too far and lost her, that would blow my plan, too. I had to remind myself to breathe as I slowed down to let her get a couple of car lengths ahead.

She turned left on Sunset. Great. I had plenty of traffic to hide in. If she followed the pattern I'd seen in the past few days, she should be on her way to do errands and, hopefully, grocery shopping. I gripped the steering wheel and tried not to think about how screwed I'd be if she was just going to fill her gas tank or to the dry cleaner's. That. Could. Not. Happen. Neither of those chores would give me enough time to do what I had to do.

I saw her right turn signal blink as she approached Doheny Drive, and I dropped back another car length to give myself cover. But when I made the turn onto Doheny, her minivan was nowhere in sight. *What the . . . ?* Where had she gone? Fear blurred my vision. How could I have lost her? Frantic, I scanned the cars ahead of me. I screamed, "No! This is bullshit!"

I was raking my hand through my hair when the bus that'd been in the left lane turned onto Santa Monica Boulevard. And like sunshine pouring through a cloud bank, there she was. Theresa, my savior. In her little minivan. Still slowly heading south on Doheny. This time, I wasn't taking any chances. I pulled into the left lane right behind her, my eyes glued to her rear window.

When we got to the light at Beverly Boulevard, she put on her left turn signal. If luck was with me, she was headed to the Ralph's grocery store on the corner. I followed her as slowly as I could and prayed she'd turn into the parking lot. When she put on her right turn signal at the entrance to the parking lot, I hit the steering wheel and hissed, "Yes!" This was perfect. Exactly what I needed.

I stayed behind her as she searched for a parking space. This Beverly Hills grocery store was always crowded, and today was no exception. I hung back and watched as she found a space along the far edge of the lot, then drove past her and parked two spaces down. I pulled out the devices I'd seen Alex use.

Getting into a car is easy—if you know someone like him. He'd used the Signal Amplification Relay Attack, one of the simpler ways to break into a car. It intercepts the remote locking signal. All you have to do is get the transmitter close to the car and one other device close to the key fob. I slung my extra-large handbag over my shoulder and moved as close to her car as I could while I waited for her to get out. The moment she did, I took a few more steps toward her. Then, as she hit the remote, I pushed the buttons on my devices.

As soon as she entered the store, I checked to make sure no one was watching, then walked up to the passenger side of the minivan, snapped on a pair of latex gloves, and reached for the passenger door handle. This had to work. I pulled, and . . . it opened! I glanced around one more time to make sure I was safe, then took out the "goodies" I'd gotten from Angelina's guest bathroom: Tanner's hair, his bullet-style cork snorter (such a douchey thing to have—it figured), and—surprisingly—his handkerchief. I didn't know anyone who carried a handkerchief anymore. But whatever. Thanks to Angelina, I had a treasure trove of DNA. And one more item—my personal contribution: Tanner's SAA chip, the one I'd found in the Denali. As I carefully placed the items, my heart was pounding so hard, I was afraid I'd stroke out.

When I'd first come up with the idea to plant evidence in Theresa's car, I'd thought maybe Tanner's SAA chip would be enough. But after a few moments of thought, I realized that might not suffice. Who knew whether any of Tanner's DNA was still on it? And even if it was, there was bound to be DNA from a lot of people on that chip. That wouldn't do the trick. I needed to find things that could only have come from Tanner.

At that point, I'd thought my plan was toast, because I didn't know where I'd be able to find them now that the cops had cordoned off his condo. It'd taken that impatient Russian guy at the gas station to make me remember Angelina—and the fact that she'd said Tanner sometimes stayed at her place. I mentally thanked Angelina again as I went to the back of the minivan to plant the last two items—also my personal contributions. Unregistered guns are so useful. I'd known they'd come in handy one day, but I hated to part with them. I'd have to see if the connection who'd sold them to me would come through again. I placed them under the carpet in the cargo area, with just the tip of the butt of one gun showing. Hidden just enough that Theresa wouldn't notice it—but not too hidden if the right person looked.

I closed the door and hurried back to my car. According to my phone, the whole operation had only taken a minute and a half. It'd felt like an hour. And as I leaned back in the seat to catch my breath, I could feel that my hairline was damp with sweat. But so far, so good.

I settled into my car and waited for Theresa to come back. The next step was going to be the fun part. Twenty minutes later, she emerged. I followed her all the way back to Sebastian's house, to make sure her car would be there, then drove a few blocks away and called 9-1-1 with a burner phone. "I need to report a crime. I saw someone selling guns out of a Mercedes minivan. I took down the license plate, and I followed the car for a while. I think he lives in Bel Air." I'd deliberately chosen that story because the cops had busted someone for selling a huge cache of firearms out of a house in Bel Air just two weeks earlier. They'd have to take my call seriously.

Then I drove back to Sebastian's street to wait for the not-so-fun part. I had to hope for a lucky break. I knew Theresa would deny having sold any guns—because she hadn't. But would she let the cops search the car to prove she was innocent? I was counting on it. If she didn't, I'd have to hope the cops would try for a search warrant. Given the neighborhood and the person the car was registered to, I sincerely doubted they'd do it. Sebastian was too big a fish to mess with—especially when all they had was a 9-1-1 call from someone they'd never be able to contact. And that would be the end of my one and only plan.

I parked across the street in my favorite hiding place, under a large jacaranda tree, and tried to calm myself with deep, cleansing breaths. It didn't work. All I managed to do was make myself hyperventilate. Dizzy and a little nauseous, I gave up on the deep breathing.

Finally, two cops in a patrol car arrived. I watched as they approached the gates, then drove in. A few seconds later, I saw Theresa come to the door. I couldn't hear what the cops said, but I saw her shake her head vigorously. I held my breath. This was it. Now or never. If she didn't let them search, my whole plan would go down the drain. And Niko would go to prison.

I dug my nails into my palm to keep from jumping out of my skin, but then a few seconds later, I saw her step out of the house. And she did it! She led the cops to the minivan. They pulled out their ginormous flashlights, and the taller of the two cops searched the passenger side, while the shorter one searched the driver's side. I whispered, "Look in the back, damn it. Look in the back!" The taller one moved to the rear passenger seat, waved his flashlight from one side to the other, then shook his head. Shit! They were about to give up! He walked over to Theresa. Probably apologizing to her for the intrusion. I dropped my head on the steering wheel. It was over. But I couldn't stay here. I sat up and reached for the start button on my car, then noticed that the shorter cop had moved to the back of the minivan. He was opening the hatchback! I stared at him. "Find it! Fucking find it!"

After thirty painful seconds, I saw him flip up the carpet and heard him shout something to his partner. He'd found it.

I let out my breath and sagged against the seat. Now they'd swab the guns, find Tanner's DNA (because I'd made sure of it), and realize this car was involved in a lot more than just gun sales. And once they got a criminalist in there with his Q-tips and tweezers, he wouldn't be able to miss the rest of the evidence I'd planted. Then Kingsford would start turning over all the stones. He'd figure out that Sebastian had lost a bundle to Gold Strike and that he had a house near a great dumping ground—Malibu Canyon. And he'd realize that Sebastian had no alibi for the time of Tanner's disappearance. Something else I'd made sure of with a little help from Alex, who'd tracked Sebastian's movements and found out that he'd been off the radar and alone. And if I really got lucky, when they searched Malibu Canyon—as I was sure they would—they'd find Tanner's body.

The sound of sirens in the distance yanked me out of my reverie. The place was going to be swarming with cops in two minutes. I had to get out of there. I pulled away from the curb and forced myself to drive at a leisurely pace. It'd be a very bad time to attract attention. As I headed toward Sunset, I was cautiously optimistic that this would all play out the way I'd hoped.

But now came the part of the plan that I'd been dreading: telling Niko that I'd framed Sebastian—and why. That it was not just for his sake but for my own, as well. I hated having to tell him about the hell of my childhood—almost as much as I hated having to use it to manipulate him into going along with the setup. But I knew that was the only way to persuade him to let Sebastian take the fall for Tanner's murder. And I had to do it fast. Niko had said he was going to turn himself in today. But he'd promised not to do it until I could go with him. I called him on his cell.

"Hello? Sam?" The sound of a local news program played on a television in the background.

The news. Another reason why I had to get to Niko right away. All that police activity in a place like Bel Air was going to get media attention in a heartbeat—even if they didn't know exactly what was going on. "Hi. Are you at home?"

"Yeah. How come you're not? I thought you said you didn't have to go to court today. I was hoping we could spend a few hours together before I . . ." His voice trailed off.

Before he turned himself in. "Don't move. I'm on my way over. I—There's something I need to tell you."

There was a long pause. He sighed. "Sam, I told you. I've made up my mind."

"I understand. Just hear me out, okay? I'll be there in ten minutes."

He said he'd listen, but his tone of voice made it clear that he thought there was nothing I could say that would change his mind.

I hoped he'd be wrong. He had to be.

FIFTY-FIVE

When I walked in the door, Niko took me into his arms and hugged me for a long moment. Then he held me at arm's length. "Sam, if you want to help me negotiate a plea, that's fine. I appreciate the help. But you have to accept my decision."

I saw the determination in his eyes. This was going to be even harder than I'd thought. But I was equally as determined to stop him. I nodded toward the couch. "Let's sit down."

As we settled in, I prepared myself for the most important closing argument of my life. I'd spent hours mapping out everything I wanted to say and gone over it a hundred times. But now, as I sat next to him, I found myself utterly tongue-tied. I cleared my throat and felt panic rise in my chest as I struggled to find the words. Niko watched me with a mixture of concern and curiosity. Finally, I forced myself to speak. "I've told you my childhood was a bit . . . chaotic." Niko nodded slowly. "Well, it was actually more than just a bit chaotic. When I was twelve, Celeste—"

"Your mother, right?"

"Right." He'd never met her, and I seldom spoke of her. And he couldn't get used to the way I refused to call her "Mother." My tongue felt like it was wrapped in cotton as I continued. "She married a billionaire real estate mogul, Sebastian Cromer. We moved in with him just one month after they'd met. But as it turned out, Celeste wasn't the reason their relationship moved so fast." I had to look away. "I was."

Niko blanched. "You mean . . . ?"

I nodded. "Sebastian was a pedophile." I told Niko all the gruesome details. How Sebastian had given me a beautiful bedroom at the back of the house—so no one would hear me scream. How he'd come to that bedroom every night for nearly a year. How he'd violently raped me at least once a night. And how I'd eventually managed to force Celeste to leave him. Then I told him about Eliza—an example of the countless other girls he'd likely raped and who'd probably been afraid to report someone as powerful and connected as Sebastian.

Niko's expression had gone from sucker punched, to anguished, and then to furious. By the time I'd finished, his expression had turned downright thunderous. I worried that he might go hunt Sebastian down that very moment. When I finished, it took him a while to calm down enough to speak. "Is it too late for you to tell the police about him?"

I nodded. "The statute of limitations ran out long ago." I paused. That wasn't the whole truth. "But honestly, even if there were a way around it, I just . . . I couldn't do it. I don't want the whole world to know." I saw the pain and sadness in his eyes as he nodded his understanding. "Anyway, it's not just about my own revenge. What about all the other girls? He's never going to stop. That's why I did . . . what I did." I told him about how I'd framed Sebastian for Tanner's murder. Afraid of his reaction, I talked at warp speed.

Niko stared at me in shock. His mouth moved, but no sound came out. Finally, he said, "Sam, you can't . . . I mean, I get why you did it. But it's not right."

I took his hands. "It *is* right. Think of what he's done—to me, to Eliza, and to so many other girls we'll never know about."

Niko frowned. "But he didn't kill Tanner. Sebastian is a monster, but he needs to go down for what he did. Not for what I did."

I exploded in utter frustration and anger. "But he won't! Don't you see? Guys like him never do! That's the problem!"

His features twisted in confusion. "I do see. But . . . that's not justice. Him taking the fall for something he didn't do."

"Is it justice that you go to prison for ridding the world of a narcissistic sociopath who trampled on and shredded other people's lives—and basically killed your mother? Is it justice that a rich and powerful predator who's ruined the lives of so many young girls and will certainly go on to ruin many more never pays the price? In fact, gets to enjoy a life of incredible luxury? Is *that* justice?"

Niko teared up. "I—I don't know, Sam."

I put a hand on his cheek. "If you can't do it for yourself, then do it for me." I felt like a shitheel for saying it. But I was desperate, and that was the only argument that seemed to have a chance of swaying him.

Niko looked away. After a long moment, he sighed. "I have no choice."

I stared at him. Was he still going to turn himself in? "Wh-what do you mean?"

"I'm not going to the police. I can't."

He put an arm around me, and I leaned into his shoulder, relieved that now, we could be together without the fear that the police might come knocking again.

I just hoped he wouldn't wind up resenting me. Because he was right. He really didn't have a choice. I'd boxed him in but good. And it did ping my conscience. But not much. After all, I'd only forced him to do what was best—for everyone. Maybe he'd even thank me one day. Probably not. But only time would tell.

It wasn't a magical evening. Niko was still suffering from Sophia's death, and my revelation about Sebastian had rocked him. But we held each other through the night and talked about . . . everything.

The news of Sebastian's arrest for the murder of Tanner Handel broke the next day. The police had moved faster than I'd expected. Though, given the amount of evidence I'd left for them, I shouldn't have been surprised. I was at home, packing up for an extended stay at Niko's when the local news came on. I'd been monitoring all the news programs since the moment the police found the guns in Sebastian's minivan. So now, when I saw the BREAKING NEWS! banner, I grabbed the remote and turned up the volume. A young blonde anchor was saying, "The spokesperson for the LAPD has announced that Tanner Handel has been declared a murder victim and that the suspect has been taken into custody. Sebastian Cromer, a billionaire real estate mogul, was allowed to surrender at the Beverly Hills Police Station . . ."

I threw the remote in the air and yelled, "Yes! Motherfucking yes!" Justice. Finally. I walked out to the balcony and stared down at the city as I savored the victory. This might just be the best day of my life. I had to share the news. I texted Michy and Alex to tell them—and got a rousing reply: "We just saw! Are you going to the office?"

I texted them that I was, and they texted back saying they'd join me. Then I called Niko—both to let him know and to get a sense of how he was dealing with his decision. When he answered, I was suddenly nervous. "Have you seen the news?"

There was a beat of silence before he said, "I have. So it's really happening."

Was he having regrets? He couldn't change his mind. Now, more anxious than ever, I said, "Are you okay?"

"Yeah, I'm all right."

But his voice was a little shaky. "We'll talk tonight?"

His tone seemed forced as he said, "Sure."

I was worried about his state of mind. Was he going to back out? Go to the police after all? I didn't think so. He wouldn't blow everything up. But would the decision I'd basically forced him to make ultimately end us? Now, after speaking to him and hearing the way he'd sounded, I had to admit it might. But I couldn't say I had any regrets. I'd had to do it. I'd had to seize the chance to put Sebastian away. I'd never get another one—of that I was certain.

If Niko and I broke up, I'd have to accept that was the price of justice—as painful, even agonizing as that would be. Right now, though, in this moment, I didn't want to dwell on the impending doom of our relationship. I'd dreamed of getting my revenge since the first night Sebastian had come to my bedroom. If only for this one day, I wanted to revel in the satisfaction and joy of it all.

When I got into the office, I found Alex and Michy watching the news on my television. A bottle of Dom Pérignon was on the cabinet behind Michy's desk. I laughed. "You guys sure work fast. I'd say it's a little too early, but what the hell. Let's pop that sucker open and get this party started."

Alex did the honors, and we talked about the wild—and fabulous—turn this case had taken. I lifted my glass for the first toast. "To truth and justice!" As we all sipped, I thought, *Maybe not truth. But justice for sure.*

Michy and Alex had both remarked on the coincidence of Sebastian—the man who'd made my childhood hell and who'd raped Eliza and God knows how many others—being arrested for Tanner's murder. And yet, it'd made sense. He'd been fleeced big-time, and Alex talked about how angry some of the other investors—who'd lost a lot less than Sebastian—had been. I saw a cloud of suspicion briefly cross Michy's face, but neither she nor Alex had any idea how I—or anyone else—could've managed to set Sebastian up. Maybe more to the point, neither of them really wanted to question it. A horrifying creature had gotten what he deserved. As Michy put it, "Case closed, and good riddance."

Dale would undoubtedly guess that I'd had something to do with Sebastian's arrest. But there was one person who knew *exactly* how this beautiful coincidence had happened. Angelina. I wondered whether I'd be hearing from her.

Dale showed up at the office at noon. As I'd expected. I'd known he'd want to make contact. I heard Michy greet him as he entered the reception area. "Hey, Dale! You going to join us for lunch?"

Dale said, "No, wish I could. I just need a few minutes with Sam. Rain check?"

Michy said, "Anytime. She's in her office."

Dale walked in without knocking and closed the door. "Pretty amazing news about Sebastian." He sat down in one of the chairs in front of my desk and spoke softly. "Couldn't have happened to a nicer guy."

I met his gaze. "It is kind of perfect. What are you hearing from Kingsford?"

He had a satisfied expression on his face. "Just that the case looks good so far. And they're going to try and get Sebastian to talk to them about Bryan Posner. He's about the same size as the man in the surveillance footage."

I doubted Sebastian would talk to the cops about anything. And I knew he had an alibi for the night of Bryan's murder. But I didn't mind keeping that tidbit to myself. If they could find a way to pin Bryan's death on Sebastian, I was all for it. "Any progress in the search for Tanner's body?"

"They're using canines, but it's a lot of ground to cover." Dale gave me a pointed look. "Be nice if they knew what area to focus on."

I knew he was hinting that I should get the information from Niko. Dale was well aware that this kind of perfect justice didn't just happen on its own. And although he didn't know how I'd done it—and probably didn't want to know—he knew I'd done something. And predictably, he was way okay with it.

I thought about whether I wanted to ask Niko where he'd dumped Tanner's body. It might help get Sebastian convicted if they found it. "No body" homicides are notoriously hard to prove. But I wasn't sure I wanted them to find it. Although it was unlikely any of Niko's DNA would be detectable now that the body had been out in the elements all this time, I couldn't be 100 percent certain the cops wouldn't find *something*—no matter how small.

So I gave Dale a noncommittal answer. "Maybe you'll get lucky with some hiker." That was actually a real possibility. I can't believe how many times I've heard about random hikers finding bodies.

Dale absorbed my underlying message—a maybe not—then asked, "How's Niko doing?"

"It's been a pretty rocky time. But I think he'll be okay." Maybe. I hoped.

"And how about you? How're you doing? The world look a little different to you now?"

Sebastian was behind bars, where he'd belonged for decades. That felt good. No, correction. It felt great. But that wouldn't erase the damage he'd done. I shrugged. "It does, and it doesn't."

Dale studied me for a long moment, then nodded. "I suppose so." He stood up and moved toward the door. As he put a hand on the doorknob, he turned back. "You know, jail is a pretty dangerous place for someone like Sebastian."

True that. All it'd take was a few well-chosen remarks to some of my former clients who were still in custody, and Sebastian's days would be numbered—in single digits. That's why child molesters are housed in maximum security, separate from the general population. The nice thing was, in this case, the folks who ran Twin Towers and the Men's Central Jail on Bauchet Street didn't know Sebastian was a pedophile.

So he'd be in gen pop—which would make it a lot easier for someone to get to him.

I raised an eyebrow. "Funny, I was thinking the same thing."

Dale gave me a little smile and left. What he didn't know was that I'd already started going through my old client files, trying to figure out who I could trust to get the job done. This was one situation I was better equipped to handle than he was—and he knew it.

After a raucously celebratory lunch with Alex and Michy, I spent the rest of the day catching up with my caseload—and searching through my client lists for the best candidate. It had to be someone who had the skill set to kill Sebastian without getting caught but also someone who needed a favor from me. By the end of the day, I'd narrowed my search down to two possible former clients.

But that night, as I drove to Niko's house, my cell phone pinged with a breaking-news alert. I glanced at it—and immediately pulled over. I picked up the phone, and as I read, my hands began to shake: *Sebastian Cromer, who was in custody after having recently been arrested for the murder of Tanner Handel, has been stabbed to death. Authorities have said the investigation is underway but otherwise declined to comment.*

I hadn't had the chance to do it. Dale couldn't have done it. So who . . . ? And then it came to me. Angelina.

Guess I'd heard from her after all. Cromer's death wouldn't stop Kingsford from trying to figure out whether he'd killed Bryan. But with two very viable suspects—Tanner and Cromer—in play, I at least knew Niko was out of the crosshairs. And that's all I cared about.

As I pulled into Niko's driveway, I could feel my stomach churn. For me, the news of Sebastian's death was even greater cause to celebrate. Now there was no chance he might beat the case and go free—and torture more little girls.

But Niko might feel differently. Sebastian's death might just make him feel even guiltier. Guilty enough to change his mind and confess?

No. Not at this point. My real worry was that he'd pull away and eventually leave me, resentful of the choice I'd pushed him to make. And Sebastian's death might only have sharpened that resentment.

I decided to leave the duffel bag I'd packed in the trunk. I might not need it. I headed up the front walk with feet that felt like lead weights. And as I unlocked the door—I'd finally agreed to take a copy of his house key—I braced myself for the possibility that this might be the last time I'd see Niko.

As I walked through the foyer, I saw that the living room was dark. Maybe he wasn't home? But I'd texted him that I was on my way when I'd left the office. I paused in the hallway. "Niko?"

His voice came from the bedroom. "In here."

I moved toward him with tentative steps, unsure of what I was walking into. But as I entered the bedroom, I saw that he'd lit the fire and poured us each a glass of wine.

He came over to me and gave me a warm, tight hug. "I heard about Sebastian."

I stayed in his embrace, afraid to look him in the eye. "And . . . ?"

Niko pulled back and looked down at me. "What you said about justice?" I nodded. "The more I thought about it, the more I realized you were right. I never meant to kill Tanner—though I agree, he's no loss to society. But beyond that, I couldn't stomach the thought of setting someone like Sebastian free—even if it meant letting him go down for a crime he didn't commit."

The wave of relief that washed over me was so intense, I might've fainted if he hadn't been holding me up. All I could muster was a breathy "I'm so glad."

He stared off for a moment, a puzzled expression on his face. "It's kind of perfect that he got killed in custody." He looked back at me. "Almost too perfect."

I shook my head. "I had nothing to do with it." Though I wished I had.

403

"Well, whoever did should get extra desserts for a year."

I laughed. "Those county jail pudding cups are treasures."

Niko smiled. Then he gave me a deep, lingering kiss. And then another.

And as we sank onto the bed, I thought maybe, just maybe, we were going to be okay.

ABOUT THE AUTHOR

Photo © 2016 Coral von Zumwalt

California native Marcia Clark is the author of *Blood Defense, Moral Defense*, and *Snap Judgment*, the first three books in the Samantha Brinkman series, as well as *Guilt by Association, Guilt by Degrees, Killer Ambition*, and *The Competition* in the Rachel Knight series. A practicing criminal lawyer since 1979, she joined the Los Angeles District Attorney's office in 1981, where she served as prosecutor for the trials of Robert Bardo—convicted of killing actress Rebecca Schaeffer—and, most notably, O. J. Simpson. The bestselling *Without a Doubt*, which she cowrote, chronicles her work on the Simpson trial. Clark has been a frequent commentator on a variety of shows and networks, including *Today, Good Morning America, The Oprah Winfrey Show*, CNN, and MSNBC, as well as a legal correspondent for *Entertainment Tonight*. For more about the author, visit www.marciaclarkbooks.com.